Bert & Carol,

Hope this attempt to O.T.

brings a portion of the O.T.

alive to you.

11/18/04

Now
that
Forever
has
Ended

TOM STEINBACH

TEN
PUBLISHING

Family edition, first edition.

ISBN: 0-9649219-2-8 softcover

Library of Congress Catalog Card Number: 96-90290

Published by
Times Ten Publishing
PO Box 36
White Pine, Michigan 49971

Printed by
Eerdmans Printing Company
231 Jefferson SE
Grand Rapids, MI 49503

This family edition is dedicated to three
men we greatly respect for their leadership
in institutions well known in the arena
of Christian education excellence

REX ROGERS
Cornerstone College

JOSEPH STOWELL III
Moody Bible Institute

CHUCK SWINDOLL
Dallas Theological Seminary

JoAnn and I would also like to dedicate this
family edition to those who are doing all they can
to make their marriages work in this very
trying day and age.

Let the Lord be your fear, let Him be your dread
                              -the prophet Isaiah-

PART I

HIS

FAVORITE

713 B. C.

*

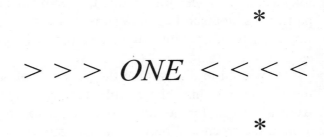

*

Hezekiah's head whirled insanely. He awakened only a few seconds before with his thoughts spilling over each other—words doubling in his thoughts in sentences which were overlapping themselves with abandonment.

When his reason returned enough, he realized he would soon lose his supper.

He rose, found that his balance was faulty, and fell back onto the bed.

Off it, in another direction, he stumbled toward the wall. Caroming from it, he scudded toward the doorway and then through a couple rooms. Though it was taking all his effort, he knew he had to get to the basin.

He was very light-headed.

Out of control, he was barely able to keep upright. His stumbling steps through the rooms were hardly cognizant of his mind's commandments, except its main goal: he collapsed by the basin and retched. The reversing action of his stomach came powerfully. His head whirled. His body chilled. He knew foremost in his rushed, panicked efforts he had to assist his stomach to empty itself of its poisonous contents.

After each retching seizure he therefore held his head up long enough to feel the involuntary movement in the lower part of his stomach begin. Against his will, he also stuck his finger far back onto his tongue to provide the movement with assured velocity.

He paused in discharging the poison to attempt to call for the assistance of his chief chamberlain. His attempts, however, were too weak for he was too enclosed on the floor curled around the basin and because he had moved too many rooms away to get the attention of his servant. His body was boiling on the surface. It was a chunk of shimmering ice beneath.

Violently shaking shimmering ice.

The inward movements began again and automatically his finger helped nature rid his wracked body of its powerful flows of food morsels and phlegm.

Extremely chilled, he tried to call Mehujael again. And again. And again. Finally, he raised up to be louder. His chief chamberlain rushed in.

"I need blankets," he shivered.

Mehujael returned immediately with many coverings and a new basin to replace the used one. Hezekiah's innards acted as if they did not notice that a new basin had been placed before him. The forced retching labored on and on.

Over an hour passed. Hardly any food solids came with the convulsive heaving of his being, but almost always more phlegm came. He kept up the voluntary emptying because he searched his mind for the cause of his body's violent seizures and decided upon food poisoning, though his mind ruled out attempted poisoning. The chills would not let up.

The moonlight on the wall in the room had moved forward significantly by the time he felt that his continued emptying was working upon an empty reservoir. However, his head still swirled and the nausea was barely below its returning point. Hardly moving and staying covered, he nevertheless hoped the worse was over and that time was on his side.

When he tried to rise, he barely got to his feet and was forced to drop back down to the basin. He retched, brought up some newly discovered fragments.

No more retching came after that, but the violent shivering continued. He therefore remained curled by the basin with the covers jumbled around him.

When he began to rise again, he found that his anticipated relief was premature. Though its source had been removed, the poison had spread throughout his being. Therefore the swirling dizziness was no less intense than when he had first awakened. He thought in morbid jest: this should happen after one turns forty; not while a man is still thirty-nine. Mehujael brought in more quilts and helped him to the couch.

Hezekiah slept, coming in and out of consciousness the rest of that night and far into the next morning. Though never awake enough to draw any major conclusions, he attempted to ponder what the significances of this assault could be.

Was it to show him that he did have the will to fight death if it finally met him face-to-face this warring season? That he did have the will if he had to face death in the form of the empire's crown prince and his marauding army which had been devastating his towns and lands—instead of facing it in the overwhelming dizziness and stomach cramps he had encountered throughout the night?

Feeling no strength within his being, he truly wondered if

11

he had learned that he had that great of a will. The roaming Assyrian army was at that moment making their way toward his capital. He arose, looked out his window toward the rising sun, and weakly wondered aloud to the opened window lattice: *"Will I ever really be able to face death if that uncircumcised heathen comes within our gates?"*

*

> > > * < < <

*

"Number forty-five is ours, Sir."

"So soon?"

"Their gates have opened, their surrender flag waves over the wall, and five men are walking our way."

"Well, well."

"Coming?"

"Yes."

"I thought you would."

"You know I would, my Tartan."

"Hezekiah?"

"Hezekiah will not have any extra men here, but he will fear greatly when he hears of this swift surrender. Now only three more cities stand between us and him."

The empire's Crown Prince Sennacherib would not waste any time with the menial duties which had to be done with this trifling village. The five frightened messengers were therefore brought to a halt in their humbled trek halfway to him.

On most surrendering days the humbled ones were forced to go all the way into his mammoth tent to be abased before they were escorted back into their cities to communicate his demands to their peoples: with the marks of their abasement readily evident. But not this morning. His words to the leaders and soldiers upon the wall had to be made quickly and clearly.

"You!"

The five turned to one of the officers, to one who spoke fiercely in clear Hebrew.

"Remove your outer cloaks!"

The five began slowly, hesitantly, to remove—

Five guards bolted from their ranks and yanked the clothes off the surprised men and tossed them as despicable rags high into the air behind their backs.

"Down on all fours!"

The five looked startled, though not nearly as bewildered as when the soldiers struck them from behind at the shoulders: collapsing them to the ground!

"No more hesitation, peasant pigs!" the Hebrew-speaking officer shouted.

"Crawl!"

The five instantly went to their hands and knees.

"Crawl to Prince Sennacherib! Crawl to the only prince of princes! Crawl to the perfect one! Crawl to the flawless one. Crawl to the world's next king of kings!"

As one, the men from the village had begun moving as the first angry word was bellowed.

"Heads low!"

Their heads and upper torsos begged lower toward the ground as they sped toward the crown prince. If any lower, their noses would have left five parallel trails in the dust.

Prince Sennacherib, his personal servants and threescore guardsmen waited for the men. He sat upon a straight-back throne which had been brought out for him. The palatial chair had an elaborately-stitched footrest projecting out in front: it was perfect for the duty which was at hand. He sat tall in his ceremonial headdress of priceless splendor, in his regal robe with his long ornamental cape hanging majestically over the back of the chair. He gripped an arrow as his scepter in his right hand. Even at this extreme end of the empire, far away from his administrative capital, magnificent regality was going to be, as always, at its intimidating best.

Forty-eight of the menacing, battle-ready, spear-carrying, mail-clad sentries stood six abreast as the envoys crawled between their rows toward the prince who was surrounded by his servants and the remaining dozen soldiers on both sides of him and standing behind.

One of Sennacherib's knee-high-tied sandals had been removed by the time the men had wormed their course to his feet, their heads still inches from the ground.

Immediately, as the order was given, each of the quintet obediently kissed his bare foot as it rested on the footstool before them...and, in turn, returned bowed low...and did not speak, nor move, nor rise, nor breathe until they were ordered by the dark overbearing officer to next kiss the crown prince's right hand and the large opulent ring he wore on that hand. They immediately obeyed, then returned to their humbled, face-to-the-ground state: looking only at the sandaled feet of the servants who were standing on either side of the makeshift throne, cooling the prince with feather fans.

"Unlike too many of your other self-willed, mulish cities, in surrendering you have acted wisely. And, in coming out here in lowly obedience to our mighty Crown Prince Sennacherib, you have saved your lives. Because you have come, we will not rip the skin off your backs nor off the bodies of any of your people. We will not behead you, nor any of your people. We will not burn your city nor any surrounding homes. We will not put any mark upon you. We will not even enter within your gates."

He paused. But not because he was through.

"Yours is the forty-fifth city we have conquered here near the far end of our kingdom, in the land that you call Judah.

Only one more city! Once we bring one more terrified village to obedience, we will attack your fortress towns of Lachish and Libnah in the foothills. Soon those two frightened cities will also bow in obedience to us! Then we will charge into the backbone mountains of your nation and your capital we will conquer! Then Hezekiah, rebellious Hezekiah, we will bring to a towering humiliation! To an sobering humiliation! If your peasant ruler does not readily surrender to us then as you have done, we will destroy all that is within your mountain capital! We will spoil it of all its riches and burn it with great fires!"

This pause was shorter. "Return into your village. You have until our great guiding and protecting disk, Shamash, is risen another ten degrees to send out to us five hundred young fighting men and three hundred of your lovely young maidens. Your very choicest young men and maidens."

The five cringed within.

"Take a dozen of our empty wagons into your village with you to your granary. While your leaders are gathering together the muscular men and the beautiful maidens, your people are to heap the wagons full."

Within *five* degrees of the sun's movement all was accomplished and the loud, exuberant, laughing, ruthless army was marching with their added abundance toward their last planned stop before Libnah and Lachish. Toward number forty-six. Only that city and its surrounding towns, then those fortress towns were to be brought to their humbled knees.

*

\> \> \> * < < <

*

"Such overwhelming beauty."

"Hannah certainly is more beautiful than any of the others

who have been brought to us to be prepared for him."

"And so modest about it."

"Again Sarai has been right. Long ago she said Hannah would become Hezekiah's favorite," the quietest and last-to-speak of the three maidservants offered after they had excused the latest young maiden under their care back to her room.

"I simply like to be with her."

"Me too!"

"And me. I *like* to be with Hannah."

The end of the time of her preparation was near. Within a few days she would be presented to Hezekiah, and all agreed she would conquer his heart like none other had.

"She always causes me to feel that just being here with us has been such a wonderful time for her."

"That is true!"

"She is so unlike all the previous ones who have paraded in here thinking—"

"—that they are our nation's *premier gift* to our king!"

They all laughed.

"Last warring season I showed Father that I was ready for this extended campaign to bring this end of our territory into complete obedience once again," the crown prince boasted to himself, to his officers, and to all else within hearing range as his splendiferous chariot carried him, his driver, and his bowman along. "This year I traveled as soon as weather made it possible, so I could destroy their northern cities and lands," he continued. "I have conquered and devastated the resistance of all the inhabitants of every city and surrounding village all the way to the Great Western Sea. From there I have led my disciplined armies southward. I have devoured heaps of grain and fruit and much booty along that route bordering the Great Sea. I have left a path of destruction and alarm all the way to the borders of Egypt!"

"Sir, will we—"

"Now, returning back toward their central mountains and peasant capital, I have destroyed number forty-five."

"Sir, will—"

"Tomorrow I will force forty-six to that same fate," he continued, becoming furious at the interrupting officer. "Then, in Asher's might, we will begin our ascent up to Hezekiah. Up into that peasant seditious ruler's capital! It is his to know and understand and learn that it is most unwise to deny me and my fighting troops under my leadership the resources and tributes we demand each year!"

"Sir, will we have enough time?" the officer asked in full, as the crown prince finally took a natural pause. The boldness of the question greatly infuriated the crown prince even more. This one, this former lowly aide whom he should never have raised to a place of honor, had inquired all too often and all too loudly these last months about the large number of towns he had ordered destroyed in this land so far away from their home this warring season. In his rising anger, Sennacherib thought with defiance: one of my officers, this undeserving nothing, is telling me, his lord and master, that I have not been prudent in conquering their towns and entire territory instead of making our way up to that vile peasant ruler more quickly. This lowly one is telling me that I should not have conquered their cities all the way to the Western Sea. That I should not have forced my troops to destroy their land all the way down to the borders of Egypt. That I should have done nothing but go up straight into that peasant's—I have been wise!" he shouted out. "I have been expedient! Expedient in utterly devastating every major city and town in this peasant's wretched realm! I have been perfect in my planning! Even as I have been most perfect in my plotting to soon replace my father as the ruling monarch of the greatest empire this world will or has ever seen!"

The moment would not be lost.

"Of course we have time enough! We will conquer forty-six by tomorrow evening! We will then move to Lachish the morning after! We will put that peasant fortress under siege. From there I will send my elite forward unit up to that despicable one who is without judgment and I will demand much more than he has ever been forced to pay! I will show him he was wrong to stand up in revolt against my father and me! I will show Hezekiah that we will never tolerate any rebellion, wickedness, or any changes in our commands from this end of our territory again! In the names of Shamash and Assur and Marduk, in their exalted names, I will humiliate that peasant pig! *Off with this one's head!"* he shouted, with spittle flying in all directions and his forefinger pointing in violent rage at the offending officer.

All knew the order was forthcoming. All had seen their young prince in his uncontrolled fury often before. Therefore the swish of the broadsword came the very moment the second word of the command left his mouth.

*

\> \> \> * \< \< \<

*

"Hezekiah is going to love Hannah," the first maidservant said with delight.

"That he is."

"If our master ever beckons for her," the third said, becoming very original with the statement.

"He will."

"Not if that Assyrian army continues to come any closer to our capital," the third added.

"She might be right."

"I agree. Hannah's presentation to our master could be delayed for a long time."

"That would be a shame."

"A real shame."

"A terrible shame."

Their capital they knew was safe within its high defensive walls, but the Assyrians' destroying presence had been in their land all summer and now its destructive troops had moved away from the southern areas along the Great Sea and was making its final journey toward what all knew was the ultimate goal of its planned merciless campaign, back toward their capital and their king, Hezekiah.

"I pray to our Lord God that those Assyrians leave soon. They scare me."

"Me too."

"They really scare me," the quieter one said from her place in the room.

*

> > > * < < <

*

That night after his units had completed their siege of number forty-six, Sennacherib plotted aloud how he would make this year's home-coming declaration to his citizens concerning this successful season's warring campaign so far: "Forty-six of their walled cities and their surrounding villages I captured! I destroyed! I devastated! I burned with fire!" I did not do all those things, he mused in his tent. However, that is what my people and my father will hear—and that is what I may someday put upon my own annual announcement plaques when I become the sovereign leader of our greatest of all of the kingdoms which have ever ruled the world! When I return and enter our capital's mammoth gates with all these captives and spoils, it will be grander than even last year's triumphal entrance after our highly successful season in those northern mountains of Urartu, and that was the greatest up to now! "Enough time? That fool! I am Sennacherib! Son of Sargon II! I will demand I have enough time! I will demand that the splendor of my majesty will overcome every monarch who does not submit to my yoke!

"How I hate that peasant ruler! How I hate that one hidden in those mountains who is without judgment! How I hate that ruling thief who has caused his people not to pay to my father and me all that we have coming to us as guardians of the entire world and has caused his peoples to revolt against us! He and all of them will accept servitude once again! Much greater servitude! I will humiliate him! I will humiliate his peoples! I will put great fires to that peasant thief's dwellings and leave their large timbers in flames! In the anger of my heart I will demand that he humbly prostrate himself before me!"

Adrenaline flowed so hard through him he would not sleep most of the night. In his anger he got up and paced furiously in his tent. Had he not captured nearly all of that vile one's cities and his territory? Still, because of the slain officer's senseless goads of having enough time, he was full of unbounded fury to get up into the hill country without any more delay and cause that factious one to wring his hands in great fear! He hungered to see Hezekiah cringe. He longed to hear that peasant pig cry out in long, fearful pleadings for mercy! Enough time?

Why did that officer keep asking that?

The warring season, of course, was moving closer to its end, and, of course, he might not have the needed time to force the vile one up in the mountains who was forever overstepping his bounds to surrender his city and make obedience for his sin and to bend the knee and crawl before him on all fours.

Time was always against his plans. But, he would easily have time to demand and carry off all the booty he had come to get, and that was what he loved, that was the reason he was way over here at this humble end of their kingdom in the first place: simply to gather the staggering, priceless spoils these campaigns allowed them to bring back to Assur and Calah, all of the burdened camels and heaped-up wagonloads of booty with which he always triumphantly marched into his capital and his royal residence. He was set.

As soon as his men had that fortress Lachish under siege, he would send his elite vanguard up to the rebellious thief demanding instant payment of his tribute. Then, it would not matter how long that fortress city held them outside their walls. His advance troops and chariots and camels and wagons would have plenty of time to gather the tribute from Hezekiah.

That decided upon, he had but one goal as he continued to pace back and forth in his tent: they had to get to Lachish without any more delay. He had to get this present city to bend immediately in the forepart of the coming morning! He had to! This city had to immediately bend! Therefore his assemblers of their siege-towers would have to work through the night— *by moon and by torchlight!*

*

> > > * < < <

*

The breach in the defensive walls came fast. It occurred long before noon after his men, swinging their large battling ram within the legs of their swiftly assembled, huge siege tower, smashed those timbers of the main gate of city number forty-six as if into twisted shards of pottery. The immense, powerful ram equally smashed all hope the inhabitants of the city might have had of holding off the empire's movement toward their capital for awhile.

Watching the glorious violence of that moving log entering into the previously impenetrable opening of the city's defense, he thought of himself: proud and invincible and confident, he would *always* achieve everything he went after. He watched as the fear of the inhabitants surged out of that pitiful town and as his own being exploded with renewed energy surging through him which would not be quenched until vast multitudes in that captured place were exceedingly humiliated in their fear. Until they were drastically cut down to the role of slave: to that of the lowest beast of burden.

He would teach them not to open their gates to him! They should never have resisted his officer's call of surrender and never have forced him to order his men to assemble the siege tower and ram! He bristled with a demand to reach out in power, to strike out in overwhelming anger, to strike out and raise himself head and shoulders above all the troublesome, rebellious peasants of that defenseless city! If only he had the time, he would diminish every one of them to their lowest, to their most despicable, humiliation! Time, his utter lack of it, was their only salvation.

"Where's my cupbearer?" he yelled, his face as red as the most brilliant setting sun. He raged, knowing full well where the chief officer was, and realizing full well that the sun would move another degree or two, possibly three, before his faithful Hebrew-speaking aide would come into his presence.

But he was livid! He was overflowing with ripened fury! And his was the need to always let every one under him know that what he wanted and demanded...he would get! This venting of his fast-rising anger had always worked for him in would work for him for the next thirty or forty years! As the soon-to-be monarch of the greatest kingdom the world would ever know, he would always rule in fury! All would always know that he would tolerate no slothfulness under his rule! He was Sennacherib! Prince Sennacherib! Son of King Sargon II! At the exalted command of Nabu and Marduk, at the precious nod of Shamash, the daytime warrior, with the might of Assur, he would make the noises of his army resound and he would always enter and destroy every city and its surrounding towns in his way and thus no enemy, small or great, in any end of the empire would ever know that he was anything less than the absolute monarch of the meanness, the most opulent, the most ruthless, and, the most intolerable kingdom the world has ever seen! "Did I not call for my cupbearer?" he cried.

"But, Sir, he is—"

"Off with his head!" he roared, thinking in blind fury: 'But, Sir!'—nobody *'but sirs'* me!

"Hezekiah, I hate the very mention of your name!" he wailed in the middle of the night when he awoke in a delirious sweat. "I so hate you that I will hang your severed head on a pole which I will tie across the mighty shoulders of the horses which pull my magnificent chariot! Your lifeless skull, will lead me and my army back through your land. Your skull will lead us back through your defeated land and on our way home with all your spoils!" He laughed hard and long into the night.

*

> > > * < < <

*

Hezekiah received the first report by runners soon after the rising of the sun on the third morning after: *'A vanguard left our fortress early this morning. The approaching unit consists of a large chariot corps, of sixty empty wagons, and nearly an equal number of camels and riders.'*

Throughout that day he was kept informed by a series of reports. The final message was blunt. *'The unit's movement is relentless. Left unhindered, they will arrive at En rogel shortly before nightfall.'*

En rogel, easily within sight from Jerusalem's southern walls, was their capital's lower spring-fed reservoir and its surrounding oasis. Hezekiah therefore knew long before he sat down to eat his dinner and long before the final morsels of food left his mouth to settle in his stomach that the Assyrian's elite forward unit would be rested—and would be at his main gate by the morrow's rising of the sun.

An hour later a large group of his nation's elders came to the palace to discuss the day's last message. He was extremely pleased with the unflinching fortitude he displayed while they were there. After he explained to them the dire situation, he inquired, "Their elite vanguard will be outside our gate in the morning, what shall we agree to?"

"What choices do we have now?" Cononiah, a leading Levite, was the first to ask in return.

"We now have no choices, except to give to them all that their crown prince demands of us through them," he answered. Then added, "Of course, men, we will get them to lower most of their requested amounts."

"Has our spokesman for the Lord been advised?" another Levite, Kore, the son of Imnah, asked.

"I have sent word to him, but I have not seen him nor received any form of response."

"I suggest we agree with Hezekiah unless a contrary word comes to us through our prophet Isaiah," Azariah, the ruler of the house of God, offered.

"I agree to that, as long as you earnestly attempt to make the empire reasonable in their demands," Kore added, first speaking to Azariah and then to Hezekiah.

After that meeting Hezekiah went into his bedchamber. Feeling unrest with every action he started to do, he crossed to a window and watched the setting sun's final rays brighten the olive trees over on the hills beyond the valley with their special lighting from the opposite horizon.

Until that distinctive brightness left the trees' uppermost clusters, he found that he could not make any move. When the brilliant lighting left, he called for his chamberlain. Having decided, he ordered him to begin preparing the room for the new maiden's presentation.

*

> > > *TWO* < < < <

*

Once prepared, Mehujael moved in behind him, and took hold of his robe at the shoulders.

It being a nightly ritual, the robe's removal was easily

executed in a singular deft movement.

Mehujael then led him into the bedchamber where he hung the robe up with precise care. He pulled back the multi-linen curtains which hung down from the cornice of the mammoth bed and hooked them in place. He turned the bedspreads and linen sheets down. He fluffed the pillows up and offered his hand to help his monarch into bed.

Hezekiah watched his chamberlain as he extinguished the flames in the three much larger brass lamps standing in their ornate lampstands and as he lit the two smallest olive oil lamps in the room. The upwardly rising trails of smoke from the newly darkened wicks of the brass lamps and the much reduced lighting of the twin small scented lamps casting their soft glow upon the walls caused the feeling and mood of the room to change, as it did in nearly every other evening in this bedchamber, to one of romantic intimacy. He shut his eyes and took a deep breath of the smell of the room.

Near the head of the bed one dim lamp spread a faint glow in a small arc around Hezekiah. Across the room where the maidens stood when they entered was another lamp which cast a similar dim glow upon that area. On the wall near that lamp hung a woven wall hanging. Its beauty concealed a scented door which opened directly to the palace's attached house of women from his bedchamber.

Mehujael pulled the large ornate tapestry back and hooked it securely in place. He glanced around the room to be certain that everything else was also ready for the presentation of the elegant young maiden. When he was assured, he bowed to his master, opened the fragrant door, took one last look, and left through it.

Hezekiah, while he was lying on his bed waiting, tightened his stomach muscles many times. He watched the valley form and reform between his hips and his chest.

He breathed in, filling his chest cavity to its greatest

capacity and tightening his stomach muscles as tight as possible, and smiled as he watched the firm valley slope deeper and deeper into a rock-hard ravine.

Once again he was assured. The new young maiden would be very pleased. Even at thirty-nine, he still looked majestic; was certain he would for another decade or two; was certain his bronze body still resembled a mighty cedar when he tightened his arms and knotted his stomach. He raised his arms and stretched long on his bed.

With his arms over his head, he clasped his hands together and brought them down behind his head. He flexed his biceps, and felt the various hardening muscles ripple against each other across his back and shoulders. Glimpsing again at his expanded chest and the rock-hard ravine of his stomach, his chest appeared even larger to him. The new young maiden would indeed be pleased. Very pleased! That might be true, he thought. Nevertheless, as he lay there, the dreadful turmoil of the morrow's uncertainties and of the vanguard's possible actions relentlessly churned throughout his being underneath those rippling muscles and his seemingly calm composure.

Soon came the three quick raps on the heavy cedar door over on the far wall. He looked at the door, looked back down at himself, breathed in one last inhale, smiled, unclasped his hands, pulled a linen sheet and cover over himself, and then ordered those waiting to enter.

Three maidservants escorted the new maiden into his room. All four bowed low and long. Very long. When they arose, the smiling trio removed the striking maiden's outer garment. Two of them then began their fussing gestures over her. Meanwhile, the third moved over to the sitting portion of the room where she carefully folded the outer robe and draped it over an ivory-inlaid, high-back chair which had an identical mate and a matching reclining couch on that opposite wall. All three pieces of the furniture were highlighted in rich blues and reds and majestic purples, and with thin strands of gold, and, had been created back in the days of his father as a gift by the renown craftsmen of Phoenicia.

The beaming maidservants, prolonging their final fussing about and around the maiden as long as Hezekiah thought they thought was possible, finally stepped back from her: back from their exceptionally beautiful one, and inspected her one last time. She was standing tall.

She looked every inch a goddess.

The three turned and smiled to him, and then turned to one another with grand approval. Communicating that approval to their young friend through their eyes, they turned again toward Hezekiah and bowed deeply to him lying upon his magnificent bed...again the bow seemed to last as long as he thought they felt they could make it last. Then they left quietly: noiselessly opening and closing the heavy door behind them.

She stood poised for a long time in the soft mellow glow of the nearby olive oil lamp. She was as picturesque as any woman he had ever seen. Pleased, taken back by her extreme beauty, he said to her, "You *are* a very lovely one. Come."

Slowly, she began moving toward him. She was truly magnificent: gracefully slender and exceedingly beautiful. Her luxurious hair was long and black. She wore it straight and flowing. Her unadorned, pure, white tunic, her only piece of clothing, was of the finest linen and was perfect for her.

He had been reigning over Judah for fourteen years, he thought while he watched her glide effortlessly closer, why had this young lovely one come this evening?

Why this evening? Why had she not come in any of all the previous evenings? Why had she come to him on this most threatening night of his rule? Why had she come to him on the one night in his reign in which he had already covenanted with his Lord that he would not lie with any woman? Why? Look at her face. Just look at her.

Mehujael had told him earlier that evening that the new maiden prepared to be presented was young...fourteen when she had entered her training...and, that though now just fifteen, was a very mature maiden. A very beautiful, mature, young maiden. She stopped near his bed.

Hezekiah did some quick perceiving of his own as she stood so close before him. He noted that she seemed not to be vain. Nor had she presented an aura of conceit in her short time in his chamber. Nor had she seemed overly proud of her obvious beauty as she moved toward him.

She looked nineteen to him. A very lovely nineteen, he agreed with himself. He also agreed that this newest member of his house of women had even carried herself as much older than that. Exquisitely calm was the words his mind had given him as he had watched her movement across the room. It was indeed that. It had been astonishingly stunning.

Her being and her movement had so pleased him that his throat and mouth became very dry. And natural breathing became difficult for him. Very difficult. His whole being had filled with a quiet warmth which pulsated within him with much stronger waves than the warmths that normally inundated him. Fighting surreptitiously for his breath and for some moisture to wet his parched mouth, he shut his eyes, and thought of two pleasant comparisons. The first similitude had to do with Abishag: young, beautiful, passionate Abishag. She was their young Shunammite maiden who had been sought out and was brought to their nation's aging King David to minister unto him and to lay upon him to bring warmth back into his ailing, wasted body. To find such a stunning, beautiful maiden was the last resort in the minds of King David's elders. Having searched their nation over, they found beautiful Abishag. If she failed to warm their beloved monarch, he would die.

She failed. He died.

The chief thought clambering for recognition within Hezekiah's heart concerning Abishag was: if the exquisite one standing before him at that moment would have been brought to David instead of the beautiful young Abishag the famous dying monarch would have warmed up immediately and would have wholly revived. There was no doubt about it in Hezekiah's mind. None. David would have recovered!

The other resemblance fighting for immediate recognition within his mind as the maiden stood so nearby, so beautifully nearby, dealt with Solomon's 'fairest among women' about whom he wrote their nation's moving love song. The thought: even that obviously, exceedingly fairest-among-women would have stood back and enviously starred at this statuesque daughter of Judah who was poised before him.

The maiden wet her lips with the tip of her tongue.

As he watched her he thought: our people and towns do not make statues or other alike graven images to represent various gods and goddesses as do the nations around us. I am fully agreed with our practice, but, if we did smith such items, this elegant one before me would be every artisan's favorite choice to have stand and pose for them. Why then, did she wait until this night to be brought to me?

Before she had come in, the more he had thought on the idea of having any new maiden come into his room on this troubling night, the more he had chided himself that he had allowed Mehujael to prepare his room for a new maiden. No new maiden would help him forget the dreaded uncertainties of the terrifying, coming morning with the Assyrians.

He smiled at her, and thought how very, very wrong he had been concerning her. She had only been in his room for minutes and she had already made him forget that he had lain there in bed for some time regretting this moment.

In answer to his, she returned an absolutely splendid smile of her own and moved a half-step closer. Standing very close to him, she inhaled a deep breath. Stood tall. And stretched to her full height as she extended her arms and hands confidently high up over her head. Again he struggled for his breath.

Again his mouth and throat went totally dry.

Again his mind went thoughtless to everything else in their universe: their Lord God had indeed given her a perfectly flawless body. Attempting to moisten his mouth's dry roof and its inner surfaces and his slightly opened lips, he moved the very tip of his dry tongue over them.

The maiden watched as the slow, barely-visible movement of the tip of his tongue moved slowly across the minutest opening between his lips. She grinned. Her look then shifted to his eyes. She saw that his eyes had been watching hers. Her grin became another buoyant smile.

King Solomon! he exploded within. *What a phenomenal song you would have written if you had experienced being with this one*! O My Lord God, how I thank You for bringing this one into my house of women! How I delight with the thought of being able to be in her presence! Still, Lord, I wish You would have brought her in unto me any other evening.

Any other evening.

Her hands met and held each other as she reached higher toward the chamber's high ceiling.

Any other evening, Lord.

Any other.

My dear young magnificent one, our mother Eve must have looked altogether like you when she was brought to Adam...altogether like you there in the garden of Eden! You would have easily brought warmth and renewed health back into King David's wasted being!

Smiling freely, she moved quietly onto his bed. Where, kneeling beside him, she gently removed the spread and the light linen covering from off his leg nearest to her.

With skillfully strong fingers, she began massaging his

31

thigh. She powerfully worked her fingers in and around his muscles; working her fingers slowly down onto his calf and working deeply into that knotted muscle. She moved next to his ankle and foot: always massaging as if she could sense a turmoil within him. Her fingers worked long on his ankle, and lingered even longer on his foot, spreading his toes outward as she amiably kneaded the top, ball, and arch of it. She selflessly continued. Incredibly, though so young, she probed his foot as if she felt and knew every stress within him.

She brushed his nearest limb with her body as she reached to uncover his other leg. At the bodily contact, she glanced up at him and, seeing that he had felt it also, smiled.

He looked at her smile, at her mischievous, wonderful smile, then down at her flawlessly smooth, linen-clad body, and then back again at her radiant face. Still looking up at his face, her hands began massaging his other foot.

He stared into her soft eyes until he finally shut his. Her skillful fingers seemed to work even more intensely: stretching and rubbing the large knotted calf muscle of his other leg. Then they moved up to that thigh, uncovering him as they went. Clearly, she was not going to cease probing until she had succeeded in abetting her troublesome monarch and lover to attain releasement from all his deep, knotting anxieties.

The unknotting finally came.

When it did, they both sensed it simultaneously. It caused them to pause...pleased with each other in reaching the goal. They smiled at each other: feeling united in the euphoria of their unspoken closeness. "Thank you," he said tenderly.

"Please, my monarch, tonight my desire is only to bring pleasure and release to you."

"You have. Oh, how much you have! For that I thank you. But beyond that you have brought so much more," he said what he knew she had already felt his body express.

"Thank you, my lord, my love," she said in response, and

added a short, "That is my duty."

The euphoria lasted for quite awhile. In his presence was the most exquisite woman that he had ever seen, the most lovely maiden that had ever been introduced into his house of women, the most in-touch lover that had ever come into his room: the most caring, the most giving, the most thoroughly trained maiden to lovingly exhume stress from deep within his muscles that he had ever had. Here was the woman whom he would rather be with more than any maiden he had ever had.

Duty. *Duty!*

If any of his other young maidens or wives had ever understood what this one has understood of pleasing another!—he thought. She speaks of duty, and yet everything she does springs forth not from duty but from somewhere deep within her! From somewhere down very deep within her mature fifteen year old being...she intrinsically understands the spirit of performing willingly and spontaneously. Giving, giving, giving...and never, never, never taking. Finally, he said to her at one point, "I have had a multitude of maidens in here who have tried to do in duty what you are doing so naturally. They hopelessly failed. Utterly, hopelessly failed...because they all had come out of obedience to the duty of pleasing their ruling monarch." He paused, then finished, "No, my extremely pretty one, you have not come in here only because it was your duty." The others: yes. You: no.

"My uniquely lovely one," he added as he looked into her eyes, into her tender loving eyes, "something...somehow... even though you are so young, somehow you understand the true spirit of giving to another and of loving another."That, my exquisite one, is why I am so enchanted by you. That is why my total thoughts are upon you right now. And because I see that: "I graciously thank you."

"Please, my lord, I thank you."

"You need not worry; I accept. I wholly accept, even as I

also desire that you know deeply that I am truly sorry that I have been so wound up."

"You have been wound up. I could feel it."

"I knew you could, but how?" How could you?—you are so young, he asked within, but he knew. It was simply that caring, natural, spontaneous loving spirit of hers which walks far beyond obedience in everything she did.

"That is my training, my lord. Sarai teaches as no other under whom I have learned."

Yes, it is partly because of Sarai's training...it is so much, much more, however. I saw that you were indeed different when you first entered: as you stood in the soft light over by the door. I could easily sense it. Even as I sensed that your maidservants had also perceived it long before they had ever brought you into here. Sarai surely had seen it long before them or any other...and, even if she is our most qualified teacher of my women—

"If you have learned it from Sarai," he said, lifting one hand and placing it up on her shoulder, "then you have learned from her far more than any of my other maidens and wives have ever learned. What you have conveyed goes way beyond Sarai. It also goes beyond duty. What you have done tonight has touched me as none other has ever touched me."

There was a fairly long pause after that statement, then, "For that, I thank you."

"You are everything our nation's song describes, my lord. I am sorry, I should not have looked so sad before."

"Looked so sad! No, your forlorn feelings were natural. I am the one who was wrong to hang on as long as I have to the thoughts battling for tonight's dominance within my mind. Be gone with them I say! I have you with me tonight. I am sorry that I have been so wound up."

"Still I should not hav—"

"You came here to love and cherish me as no one has ever

come in here. You came here to help me through the roughest evening I have ever gone through—though when you entered you did not know that was working devastation within me. When I did not respond after so long, your visible disappointment was natural...beautiful."

"Thank you," she said quietly.

"You are welcomed. It is my pleasure that everything about you is so beautiful."

She blushed.

"I saw disappointment in your forlorn smiles, though I did not see anger. I did not see a rebuke, nor any sign of selfish concern on your part. I only saw in your eyes a love which was hurting for my sake, not for your own sake. My present peace of mind has come only because of you. I am indebted to you being able to convey to me what your fingers have so clearly perceived within me. You can be assured, my exquisite friend, what you have already done has surpassed anything any of my other maidens have ever attempted in the past."

"Thank you," she responded again, naturally adding, "it is my du—"

When she stopped, they both smiled. Looking deeply into each others eyes, they lay still for quite some time.

She then began quoting from their nation's lovesong she had been taught in her months of training for this first encounter with her nation's monarch. Many other maidens had quoted from that renown poem to him in this similar situation before. None, however, had moved him with so much natural outflowing love as this one had in the short time they had been together. It was as though she had created the gracious words especially for the affectionate moment they were experiencing: "My beloved is handsome, well-favored, and the choicest of ten thousand," she said, looking him straight into his eyes.

Though she was quoting the exact words many had spoken to him in the past, he responded to her with a smile which made it apparent that he had totally forgotten about the Assyrians and the fearful uncertainties of the coming day.

Lowering his voice to its lowest range, tightening his stomach and arm muscles, and expanding his chest, he asked a main question from the poem, "O thou fairest among women, what is your beloved more than another beloved?"

"His legs are as pillars of marble, set upon sockets from fine gold: his countenance is as Lebanon, excellent as the cedars," she responded with sincerity, with admiration, with pride as she moved her hands up and down his solid thighs with approval. She then moved on to the next phrase in the song as she slowly moved her hands toward the broad valley of his drawn-in, rock-hard stomach. Her fingers kneaded its solidness, "He is as excellent as a mighty cedar. My beloved is like a gazelle leaping upon the mountains, like a young deer bounding over the hills." He listened enamored, not surprised that she had also perfectly learned that portion of the song in her time of training. "Behold, he stands by our wall, showing himself through the lattice. There he speaks and says to me."

"Wake up, my love. Arise, my fair one: come away with me," he cut in, saying his part. "For the winter is past, the rain is gone. The flowers are springing up, the time of the singing of birds is come. The voice of the turtledove is heard, the fig tree puts forth her green figs. The vines with the tender grapes a pleasant smell. Arise, my love, my fair one, come away."

She worked one of her hands upward: agile fingers playing upon his rib cage, upon his hairy taut skin. He breathed in and expanded his chest again to its greatest expanse. Then, closing his eyes, he slowly, silently, effortlessly let his captured breath escape out his mouth. She moved her head slightly closer to his and looked at his handsome, relaxed face. Their eyes met.

He smiled. She returned a brilliant one. He felt his body become very warm. He looked at her eyes, then at her flawless body and again back to her eyes: he thought, however, no matter how much I want you; I cannot have you tonight.

The thought snapped his serenity. Not knowing what was wrong...but not getting the response that her deft movements should have received; she raised her head up, and lowered it back down upon his chest with her face away from his.

She began again with the poem, with the maiden's portion of their nation's song of songs, "By night on my bed I sought him whom my soul loves. I sought him, but I found him not. I will rise now, and will go about the city into the streets. In the broad ways I will seek him whom my soul loves.

"The watchmen that go about the city found me seeking.

"To them: 'Have you seen him whom my soul loves?'

"It was but a little that I passed from them, when I found him whom my soul loves. I held him and would not let him go." Her hands moved around his chest, and she squeezed him harder to her. She turned her porcelain-smooth face toward his and looked back into his eyes. Trusting that she was bringing relief and peace to him again, she added with confidence, "I am the rose of Sharon and the lily of the valleys."

He replied with a smile and a low, deep voice. With the words he knew she wanted to hear, he said, "As the lily among thorns, so is my love among the daughters."

More brightly, and obviously happy to see his smile again, she voiced the words of the lovesong which makes the comparison of her monarch to all the rest of the men in the land, "As the apple tree among the trees of the wood so is my beloved among the sons."

He applied additional pressure to his hands on her. She moved her head closer to his. They smiled.

"I sat down under his shadow with great delight, and his fruit was sweet to my taste," she resumed, smiling, and raising her head even closer to his face. Not realizing that the time together was almost over, indeed, believing that it was back on course, she added this with deep meaning, "He brought me to his banqueting house and his banner over me was love."

She moved closer. She was like none before. He received satisfaction from everything about her. Her looks. Her light carriage. Her loving personality. Her determination to please him in every move she made. They were smiling face to face. His hands holding her head. He asked her name.

"Hannah," she replied.

"Hannah, what a beautiful name."

"Thank you," she answered, and turned her head enough to place a light kiss upon one of his hands which was holding her face inches away from his own. She then marched her fingers through his hair's dark mane as she returned to the lovesong, "His head is the finest gold. His locks are wavy. As black as the raven." She lowered her fingers to softly caress his brows and cheekbones. She added, "His eyes are mourning doves sitting beside the rivers of water. Bathed with milk and fitly set. His cheeks are a bed of spices, a pillow of sweet flowers."

She placed a kiss upon his cheek.

Their eyes locked together: saying that neither wanted this moment to end. Trusting, she moved her hand slowly toward his mouth where her finger lightly fondled his lips: tenderly touching them back and forth, up and down, corner to corner. She looked at his, wetted her own with the tip of her tongue, and said, "His lips are lilies. His breath is liquid myrrh. My beloved's spiced mouth is most sweet." Her fingers moved to the nape of his neck and massaged the back of his head.

Her lips were barely away from his, she waited for him to pull her face down upon his and kiss her with urgent kisses of his full mouth. His muscular hands did not move her closer. She finished the words, "Let him kiss me with the kisses of his mouth." His hands still did not pull her toward him.

She appeared undaunted, smiling a stupendous smile with dancing eyes and cheery cheeks and animated lips. She looked into his eyes with a look of pure, unhurt love, and moved on with the song, "His love is better than wine. He is altogether lovely. You, my lord, you are altogether lovely. You are my beloved, and you are my friend."

"Being with you, Hannah, has given me much solace and pleasure this troubling night," he shared, the barest space still separating their faces. "I truly thank you for coming this night to minister unto me."

"You, my monarch, are the one who has brought your maidservant much pleasure."

"You have been good for me, Hannah. Your complete openness in your offering to me your beauty, all of your love—and all of your selfless giving of yourself—has truly been an honoring gift to me from our Lord."

With one hand he began caressing her back.

Though appearing encouraged by that act, she did not try to move her head any closer to his face. She simply accepted both his hands loving movements: one caressing her back with tender feeling and the other weaving its fingers up through her hair. Her cheery bright smile faded, however, when he added, "Tomorrow I will call for you early. But, tonight we will go no further, my lovely one."

"No further? Why, my lord?" she asked. Clearly surprised and forlornly disappointed after that extremely touching time with his asking her name and of her so clearly requesting the kisses of his mouth, she waited for the answer.

"I have received a forboding message which forbids me to enjoy any greater pleasure with you this evening."

"But I desir...but I was told that I was to stay here with you all night, my lord."

Oh, and I desire, my desire must be stronger than your desire, my astonishingly lovely one.

"You need me—" she stopped. Though the evening had proved her right, she changed her words in mid-sentence, and quickly repeated a line from the poem. "You are my beloved

and my friend, my lord. You are so strong," she gripped his shoulders. "And so muscular," she ran her hands down his arms and across his chest and his tight stomach. "And so tender," she said hoping to change his statement into a 'yes' as she kissed the wrist of his hand which was playing with her hair. "My King Hezekiah, you are so very tender to me, my lord, my love, and my friend."

"And you are so very tender with me. Nevertheless, we cannot remain together much longer tonight. However, I promise you with all my heart that I will call for your presence very early on the morrow's evening."

All he saw was big, beautiful, forlorn eyes with tears forming throughout. "I promise I will call for you. I will call very early in the evening tomorrow. I promise: you will stay with me until the next morning—until the next three or four or five mornings," he added, smiling, hoping to cause her light gaiety to return and lighten up both of their faces.

However, she did not permit any light gaiety to come to her moist cheeks. Still, he waited before speaking again.

"Nevertheless, for now I simply desire that you stay where you are for a little longer."

"I will gladly stay here looking into your eyes as long as you permit, my love," she responded. "And if I must leave," she continued after a moment of perfect quietness, "I will long for nothing tomorrow except the soon arrival of your chief servant informing my maidservants that the time has arrived for our gathering together again tomorrow evening."

They remained in the same position of staring into each others eyes for another long period.

Sweet smelling daughter of Judah, long ago you banished out of my mind every thought of the coming army. My thoughts are only of you: of you staying here with me tonight. Forever. I want you—no other do I want. I simply want you.

"Hannah, I trust you truly know that I want you tonight.

40

But, my love, I cannot have you. Long ago I determined what I could do and what I could not do if I was ever faced with a major crisis. In the morning, my love, there is going to be one colossal crisis. One which I am sure will cause me to have to enter into our temple before the veiled personal presence of our Lord God Almighty. When that possibility of entering into the temple becomes strong along with having to fall prostrate before the presence of the Lord God, then I have chosen to ask myself the question that Ahimelech asked our anointed David when he and his men were fleeing from King Saul for their lives. That former priest in our nation's history asked David this one pointed question: 'Have your men kept themselves at least from women?' Hannah, obviously I have not kept myself completely away from a woman this evening, but I have not aggressively touched you, and though I greatly desire you and want you right now with me through the night, I believe I have truly kept away from you in the sense that Ahimelech meant."

"One night I slept, but my heart awakened," she quietly quoted from their song of songs, cutting into his explanation. "It is the voice of my true beloved saying, 'Open to me, my darling, my love, my undefiled dove. For my head is covered with dew, and my locks with the drops of night.'

"'I have disrobed, shall I dress again?' I answered him. 'I have washed my feet, shall I get them soiled again?'

"My beloved put his hand to the door and tried to unlatch it. I was then moved for him! I then rose up to open to my beloved! My hands dripped with myrrh, my fingers with sweet smelling myrrh, as they tried to release the latch!

"Finally I opened to my beloved!—but my beloved had withdrawn himself and was gone. My beloved had withdrawn himself, and was gone," she repeated sorrily, letting him know her hurt. Tears glistened on her cheek as she turned her head and let it drop softly upon his chest.

Tenderly he responded, "She soon found her lover again in

the story. And tomorrow evening, Hannah, we will find each other. We will renew our time together. We will fully love each other. And we will stay together forever. I promise it, my love, I promise it: we will stay together forever."

When she later raised to leave, she paused motionless as their eyes took in the beauty of each other's perfect form, then she gently kissed his warm moist lips. "Thank you, my lovely one," he said, looking up into her eyes, his own very wet.

"Thank you, my lord," she replied, lingering with large, still hopeful, still pleading eyes.

He raised his head and kissed her. With the encouraging response, she asked in hope, "Could not I greatly help you through this night? My desire is to please you ever so much."

He knew that she could.

He knew that he wanted her to.

For the moment, he hated his tenacious refusal to let go of his previously formed decision: the decision he had made before she came into his bedchamber. But he had to hang onto it. He had to continue to cling to it. She could not remain with him if he had to go before their Lord God in the morning. He needed to go before Him as a man who had *some* strength.

She smiled a plaintive smile at him. The finality of her sad, pitiful smile almost caused him to throw his precautions away and ask her to stay with him for the rest of the night.

Nevertheless, he had always lived with strong convictions and long ago he had decided on this particular commitment: he would always answer with a yes if Ahimelech's question was ever required to be answered to. He only hoped in the coming morning when the Assyrian vanguard became boisterous and demanding...that his citizens would be as unreservedly willing to accept him as Hannah had been.

"I will think about you all night," he told her. "I promise I will think about you all night, Hannah. I promise I will call for you very early tomorrow evening."

"All my thoughts will only be of that coming time with you, my lord," she said.

She then lightly blew him a kiss as she left him to retrieve her outer garment lying on the chair.Directly facing him as she pulled the heavier linen on, she did not hide her pain. Blowing another kiss, she opened the highly-scented, heavy, wooden door. And left noiselessly through it.

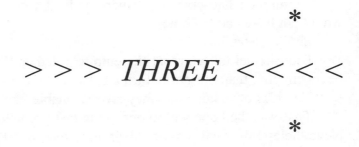

*

> > > *THREE* < < < <

*

Early the next morning he passed by the other royal bedchambers on his way to breakfast.

The twitching shadows of the clay, olive oil lamps sitting in their little niches in the long hall beckoned eerie feelings within his being.

Weird feelings which added to the many-headed, troubling thoughts swarming over each other already in his mind. He was relieved when he entered into the more brightly lit dining room. However,he was stopped suddenly in his steps.

"Mother!"

"Good morning, Son."

"What are you doing here at this early hour?"

"Shimei stopped by my room last evening. He told me about the report."

"He was to tell no one."

"Son, he felt that I might be the only one who could offer you comfort this morning."

"He is probably right." That is, he thought in remorse, since I cannot see Hannah until this evening.

"I could not sleep."

"Neither could I, Mother."

"So I came sometime ago."

"I thought I had come over here early. I truly wish you would not have had to come."

"So do I, Son."

"Did Shemei tell you that the empire's demands will now be much more than our normal tribute."

"He did. Let us hope that they are reasonable."

"That was the hope within our group last evening, Mother. Nevertheless, they will not be. Their army has conquered forty -six of our walled cities and all their neighboring villages. I have been reviewing the empire's other campaigns under King Sargon, Prince Sennacherib's father. They will now demand much more than we will ever want to give. Much more, I dare say, than we may have enough of to give. I only hope that we do have enough to give them and that they will offer to return our conquered cities back to us after they leave."

"What will we do if we do not?"

"Which? Have enough or get our cities back?"

"Either."

"I truly do not know. If the Lord would only come to our aid. He did quite often in our nation's past. But so far He has not, and if He continues to remain silent, our hope is that the Assyrian forces will not have time in this warring season to defeat Lachish and still come up here against us."

"What would happen then?"

"If that holds true, and they do not have enough time or at least if they believe that they will not have enough time, I believe that then they will accept less than they truly want: just so they can return to their capital with the booty before the real cold season sets in."

"That would be wonderful, Son."

"That is what we are counting on. I am afraid, however, their demands will be much more than we can pay at this stage if they do actually make it up here to our capital. It might by far more than we have any ability to pay."

"I understand, Son. Nevertheless, if we pay what they demand, whatever the amount, you believe they will return to their capital and will leave from besieging Lachish?"

"I do. They will, I am certain."

"It will be good to have them gone."

"Would it not?"

"More than wonderful."

"However, I cannot raise any revenue from the forty-six cities and from the other neighboring villages which they have conquered. Without those normally available resources I do not see how I will be able to raise the tribute demands the vanguard is bringing here this morning. We have very little gold in our various treasuries. With silver we are sitting fairly comfortable if their demands are not too high. But we have very little gold, Mother. There has been almost no trading done this year because of their army in our land—no trading whatsoever from the north. All our monies that would have normally come in just from those cities the empire's army has already plundered."

"Tell them that."

"Mother."

"Then maybe the Lord will still come to our aid."

"He might, it would be the answer. However, He has not helped us any all summer. That I still do not understand."

"Even so, I read a few of King David's Psalms last night."

"Do not we all in troubling times like this? I also read quite a few last night after midnight. I did not spend the entire night engulfed only in Sargon's reports."

"In what?"

"In King Sargon's reports."

"I should hope not."

"We need to know our adversary."

"Son, we need to deepen our faith in the Lord."

"I understand, and I agree with you, Mother. I am hoping that we will experience one of those supernatural deliverances falling out of the heavens that Moses, David, Elijah, and many of our other leaders seemed to have happen so often."

"Would not that be wonderful. I was certain that you would be reading some of King David's writings last night."

"But what good is reading them if the Lord is not willing to come to our side for some reason?"

"Let us pray that He will, Son. I am praying that He will send hundreds and thousands of His avenging angels to protect us in any way He sees fit."

"I would like to see it happen, Mother. However, I have tried to obey the Lord for the last fourteen years, and during that time I have not had any kind of supernatural assistance within my realm anywhere. Not one time! I wandered through those years in my mind all last night as I lay fretfully awake and I could not recall one instance. To be truthful, and I do not want you or Him to get mad at me, but even though I read this morning about a few of His many recorded deliverances, I really do not expect—"

"Hezekiah, do not say that! No visible supernatural aid has

come, Son, but I am thoroughly convinced that you have had a great amount of help, heavenly help, which neither you nor I nor any of our people know anything about."

"Possibly."

"Perhaps a mighty visible one will come this time."

"How could it? I have cried out to our Lord all summer and He has not helped any of the forty-six walled cities or their villages. No, Mother, I thank you for trying to encourage me, but I really do not expect our Lord to help us in any supernatural way at all. Not this time."

"Son—"

"Instead, I am hoping that He will work a smaller work: say in the vanguard leader's heart."

He sensed that she understood correctly that his words at that point, though perhaps sounding pretty good, were also merely empty statements. For some unbeknownst reason, their Lord God would not help them at all.

"Possibly those forty-six cities really needed a good whipping from the Lord, Hezekiah."

"All forty-six of them? What is He going to do to us if we do also?"

"I do not know, Son."

"I thought I had turned our nation back to a place—I tried to get our people back to a place of obedience to Him. To a place of pleasing our Lord, Mother. But, even with all that effort, none of my prayers for supernatural help have been answered this summer by Him. It is as though He is sleeping."

"Your grandfa—"

"He has answered none of them. Not one prayer."

"Your grandfather always proclaimed that, as a nation, we were not even close to living as dependently upon the Lord as we should have been. I wish he were here now."

"Me also. He could help us. I always liked the way he lived with such a strong belief that we should all hope to the

47

very end. When I was younger he had me believing right along with him. He so trusted in the power of our Lord, I was right along there with him in that trust, and that has stayed with me upon the throne. With you I do wish he were here now. Possibly then, even though our God has not helped us as yet, I would be able to once again believe in His supernatural power producing some kind of action coming to our aid in our facing the vanguard this morning."

Grandfather Zechariah was one of those Hebrews like Samuel and Elijah who were able to understand visions and revelations of God, he thought. Thus, in my paternal great grandfather Uzziah's reign, Zechariah was much like Isaiah, our present prophet, and even more like Joseph: being able to understand the dreams of those Egyptian cellmates down in the prison. As long as grandfather Zechariah was living, King Uzziah continued to seek the Lord. It was only after he died that King Uzziah seemingly in pride attempted his wrongful act of actually entering within the temple with the express purpose of performing an act which was wholly the duty, the exclusive duty, of a priest by burning incense upon the holy altar and he was punished by becoming irreversibly leprous.

"I do wish that my father were here, Son, but the Lord God has given you another Zechariah, Isaiah, to listen to."

"Thus far, dealing with your father would have been much better for me than trying to deal with our prophet. Isaiah and I do not get along very well. But whatever, I sent an urgent message to him last evening requesting a word from the Lord. As I told my elders, I have not heard any word from him."

"That is what Shimei said."

"I guess I really expected no response. Like I said, for some reason he and our Lord God have chosen to remain silent whenever I have needed them throughout my reign."

"Silent?"

"Oh, Isaiah and other spokesmen have been plenty vocal

enough in the street and in the palace, it is just that, whether you want to agree or not, the Lord, or they, or whoever have never produced any visible sign or any supernatural help in my reign—when I have asked for it."

There was another long pause. During it he glanced up and noticed by her expression that she was deep into considering if she should speak forth on another one of her concerns at the moment or not. Apparently her desire to won out.

"What about your wife?" she asked.

"Which one?"

"The only one I accept—Hephzibah."

"I have not seen Hephzibah to speak to for more than a week or two now."

"Why that long? Why did you not talk to her last night? It had to have been a very trying one for you."

"Hephzibah has been in one of her melancholy, depressed, miserable periods again and during those times she has very little good to say about me, or anyone else, and during those times I can do nothing right, absolutely nothing right, in her eyes. The most recent report would have only proved to her that her opinion of me is correct: that the Assyrians are coming because I am not capable of ruling over our nation."

"What happened between you two?"

"Mother, it happened over the years, and we do not have enough time this morning to discuss Hephzibah and her reoccurring periods of moody depression."

"Son, I too am a woman. Let me offer you some advice."

"What is it?—I do not have much time."

"You need to place less interest in your house of women. Spend more time with your wife."

"That is not new advice at all, Mother."

The times you have harped upon the evils of my having a house, he thought within, is without number. With Hephzibah being as she is, I *need* that house. Take lovely Hannah, if

Mother only knew how extremely helpful that newest young maiden was last evening before I sent her away.

"Son, you should not have your house of women."

"David had many more wives and concubines than I have had and the official statement of our Lord God concerning him was that he was truly a man after His own heart."

"Yes, Son, he was a man who claimed to be after our Lord God's heart even as a hart pants after the water brooks."

"The Lord Himself said to Saul that He had chosen Him another, that He had sought a man after His own heart."

"That was when he was young. I will also acknowledge that later his many wives and maidens did not turn his heart to go lusting after other false deities. But, even though that is true, David should never have multiplied wives and maidens unto himself in the first place."

Although he had not felt that this distressful morning was the appropriate time to get into this discussion, since she had raised it to him many times in the last fourteen years, he was primed and ready to answer this argument.

"It was in his jealousy that Saul caused David to have to find a second wife. When he had David's first wife, Michal, married to another, to Phaltiel, the son of Laish—that is when David took his second wife."

"Hiding out there in the rough wilderness, how did David even know of the giving away of his wife? But, even if he did, he did not have to go unto another woman."

"I disagree, Mother. He had to!"

"He had to?"

She looked at him, waiting.

"You know the story of Abigail. Working in her husband's field day after day, young David saw what an attentive, truly wonderful woman she was. And, I am certain, that word had come to him through his blood-brother Jonathon about Saul having wedded his wife Michal to another."

"Abigail was truly wonderful: yes. And married to a louse who was better off dead: yes. But one to whom David should have given his marriage vow: no!"

"Mother, she proved that she deserved him."

"Son, she proved that she deserved someone a lot more faithful than that one to whom she was married, I agree. So when his heart gave way and he died, possibly one of David's chief officers could have and should have received her as his wife. But the command is clear: our rulers are not to multiply wives unto themselves as the heathen monarchs do all around us. Therefore David should not have even touched her."

"But he was not our king."

"David knew at the time that the Lord God had promised all our kingdom's rulership unto him."

"Granted."

"He also had already been anointed by Samuel to be our king as soon as Saul died."

"I also agree with that."

"Hezekiah, look what David did shortly after taking Abigail as his second wife."

"Yes?"

"He then took Ahinoam, some beautiful maiden from Jezreel, for his third."

Mother is right there.

"That is always the pattern, Son: a ruler takes one additional wife, and then soon another, and then soon another, and so on, and on and on."

Mother's argument is good this morning. But after spending the evening with Hannah, with lovely Hannah, and already longing with all my heart and being for this evening's time again with that exceptionally, exceedingly, lovely one to begin, I need to return this back to my strongest argument.

"David's numerous wives and concubines never stole his heart away from following after our Lord, Mother. And my many wives and maidens have never turned my heart away either. Certainly you have observed that he and I have been extremely faithful in worshipping the Lord exclusively."

"Yes, I have seen that and I am grateful that those maidens have not turned you away. Nevertheless, if your grandfather was here now, you know he would tell you that you will never be able to get our people to turn totally back to a complete willingness to obey and follow our Lord unless you as their leader also make a complete turn."

He did not want to hear that, not after last evening. She was right, David's main problem was that he could never get his people to truly serve and trust in the Lord. Add to that, that King David even had ordered one of his most valiant officers killed in battle because, in a moment's lust from watching that officer's extremely beautiful wife bathing herself upon her rooftop, he had called for her—for that very faithful warrior's wife—and had caused her to become with child.

"Also how about Bathsheba, Solomon's mother?"

"Bathsheba?—what about her, Mother?" Have you been looking into my mind?

"Solomon's mother, Bathsheba, entered David's palace after she had committed adultery with him here in the palace and after David had ordered her very faithful military husband Uriah killed out in battle. Neither one of those acts were acts of one following after our Lord God, Son. Did not Nathan, the prophet, say that our Lord God Almighty would have to gravely punish him and our nation for those two acts?"

"Yes, Mother, for those two vile acts. But not for taking her here into the palace to be his wife! He never punished King David for his marrying Bathsheba. The Lord even chose *her* second son as our nation's *next king*!"

"You do not need to get excited with me, Son. But do tell me, what happened to our vastly growing nation when his son became our next king."

She is right. I did become too excited, but that was an excellent point I made. Still, her argument is also very strong. But, if she could only see and understand my loving Hannah through my eyes. I cannot, I will not, give up the opportunity I have with being with Hannah tonight and for as long as I reign here upon our nation's throne. My wife Hephzibah has no trust in me. She has no intimate love for me. Since our second one was born, she has had time only for our daughters. But, sweet Hannah—exquisite, magnificent Hannah—none of my wives and maidens have ever treated me so wonderfully. She could be, *she will be*, the lovely one who will re-create in me the confidence I need to once again lead our nation in strength.

"Son, I asked you what happened to our nation when David's son became our king."

"Solomon's many foreign wives and concubines turned his heart away from the Lord, and, as a result, the Lord punished us by dividing our kingdom."

"Exactly."

"But David's women did not!"

She gave him the look again, before she said:

"David's adulterous wife bore him a son who tragically pointed our nation unto other gods and goddesses."

Come on, Mother. His adulterous wi—

"What other tragedy happened in our nation's past because that tempting woman came into David's palace after adultery and her own husband's murder had been committed?"

Was grandfather this persuasive with great grandfather Uzziah? Is that why he so faithfully followed our Lord as long as mother's father was alive?

"What else happened, Son?"

"As I said earlier, our Lord divided our nation."

"Our Lord stripped almost everything but this, His chosen city and its surrounding land, out of Solomon's hands."

"I am afraid you are right there, Mother. It is sad, but that is exactly what happened." I would be ruling over a very wealthy, united kingdom if he had not sinned so greatly. I could have kept Hannah with me last night if it were not for him. "Believe me, Mother, even last night I was agonizing over what happened back then."

"That is why you are a good ruler and a faithful king for our people, my son."

Obviously, she does not know why I was agonizing over Solomon, and his wrong choices, last night.

"But, Hezekiah, you have never faced up to what you need to do concerning our Lord's command for our kings in not multiplying wives and maidens unto themselves. After my father died, you know that Uzziah turned from true obedience unto our Lord. Even though he had faithfully served for a great number of years, later in his reign he became exceedingly proud for Judah had become very strong and prosperous under his long reign." That was true. "So he entered into the temple as any heathen monarch enters into his false temple. I was there. I saw him go in to burn incense just like any old heathen monarch. I was there. I saw Uzziah come out of the temple with the telling result of that rash act."

Yes, he knew she had been there.

She had told him often how their Lord had struck his great grandfather's forehead with instant leprosy when he would not obey his high priest's orders to immediately stop his plan of executing an act which was exclusively for only the priests of Judah. For all intents and purposes his great grandfather Uzziah had been instantly eliminated from being the ruling monarch of their people—though he was not slain outright.

"He had to immediately move out of this palace," she continued as if she had been waiting years to talk to him about this so vile act of his great grandfather on his father's, her husband's, side, "and was forced to live in a specially built house separated from the throne and the people. Fortunately for us, his son moved into the palace's chief chambers and Jotham was a good king like Uzziah had been before his prideful entrance into the temple. Of course, every time the younger Jotham received some communication from his displaced father in Uzziah's separated house across the way he had another perfect visual reminder to remain faithful."

"But even King Jotham still continued having and filling our house of women."

"And what was his reward?"

"His reward?"

"His hideous son Ahaz, your father, my husband, was one of the most vile, prideful and adulterous rulers our nation has ever had. Ahaz was horrible, Son. He treated me exactly as you are treating your wife Hephzibah."

"You have also told me that concerning Father before, and I am afraid that living in the palace as I grew up I agree with you about his cruelty. But, Mother, how can you say that regarding Hephzibah I am like him? She is not like you and I have turned our nation back to the true worship of the Lord."

"But what will your son be like if you also do not forsake all those maidens and concubines in your house of women, and if you do not rekindle your love for Hephzibah?"

"My son! Hephzibah cannot give me a son!"

"One day she will."

"Daughters are all she can give me. My prince will have to come from a second, third or fourth wife." Hopefully one day I will receive a son from Hannah, he thought within his mind.

"I pray to our Lord that your crown prince will come from your own true wife Hephzibah, but my question to you is: Hezekiah, what kind of king will he be if you do not follow our Lord God in every commandment?"

"You know that when I get a son I will raise him to follow the Lord perfectly."

"But you are not even doing that."

He silently acknowledged her all-morning-long excellent line of argument. During the pause two sentries requested permission to enter. Upon approval, one of the two quickly stated: "Excuse me, King Hezekiah, but our watcher at the southeastern gate has come with a most urgent message."

"Permit him in."

He knew the dreaded moment of the morning's terrifying uncertainties had arrived.

*

> > > *FOUR* < < < <

*

"Gracious king," Kore said, after he had bowed to both him and his mother. *"The Assyrian vanguard's troops have ceased watering their animals in our lower reservoir and are on the road coming around the bend this side of the oasis."*

After they left his mother chose that moment to emphasize her last piece of advice: "Son, you still have time to decide to cease having women in your house."

"Mother."

"If your grandfather had—"

"The troops are almost here."

"If your grandfather had been around to see all that you have done here in Jerusalem and Judah to show obedience unto the Lord, I know he would have strongly counseled you in the name of righteousness to rid your palace of that house."

"Mother, the—"

"Hezekiah, I fear that without a correct decision on your part our city is going to suffer much grief."

*

>>> * <<<

*

Black pitch.

A camel's skin painted within and without with pitch, was the thought the Rabshakeh's mind furnished him when he first faced the early morning sky after having thrown back the flaps of his tent. The jetty blackness on the sky's canopy remained during the entire breaking of camp. The charred sky stretched far when he ordered his vanguard to move deliberately away from the oasis. His men's movement on the dusty road was retarded, but not halted. He was pleased they had encamped so near to the peasant ruler's capital.

A faintest pink tinctured the awakening horizon to his right when his troops approached on the road paralleling the base of the ridge on which Jerusalem's eastern walls stood. The barely visible light tier on the horizon became broader, and deepened to crimson, by the time he deployed his troops into position.

The attack began when a soft orange washed most of the eastern sky, silhouetting the olive-tree covered hills across the valley to his back. Their assault was fierce, loud, and cruel.

It was with words though, not spears.

Hezekiah heard the choleric shouting from his favorite window in his chambers. Though distant and dim, the arrogant words were clear. In very good Hebrew the voice demanded an audience with the peasant ruler of this puny mountaintop capital. Of course he would not honor that. Fear shuddered through him, nevertheless, as he thought about the impending need of the sending out of his five envoys.

He rubbed his fatigued eyes. The long, tiring night had crawled slowly. It had not been simply last night, he reminded himself as he listened to more to the brazen insolence; he had not slept well for the last four months:not well at all for the entire dry season—during which the Assyrians as a pack of hungry lions had moved at will throughout his nation.

Soon his men were ready to go out.

They came hesitantly into his presence.

"This is the first time in my reign that the empire has oppressed us with duress this harsh," he began. "I do not therefore have anymore grasp than you what will happen here today. I know that we must present ourselves to the Assyrian's vanguard this morning to receive their conditions of peace."

"Why do we not invite their leader within our gates to receive those conditions?" one asked, one frightened about going beyond the safety of Jerusalem's defensive walls after hearing the hate-filled shoutings of the morning.

"It is up to us whether we go out or they come in. My opinion is that we have more control if they do not have any idea what our city is like within these walls. I am therefore ordering you to go out, to be adamant in getting a reasonable set of demands, and, as soon as you have received all their demands, to return immediately into the safety of our city."

After a little more instruction, they left. Though he feared that an imminent nightmare might be lying on the other side of the walls, the time of briefing them had been one of growing renewed hope. During the talking, his confidence increased that in receiving and dealing with the Assyrian's demands he would finally be able to bring the summer woes to an end.

He yawned. Stretched. Shut his eyes.

Yes, yes, all was going better than he had ever hoped. The longer the men were gone, the longer the still morning air was not filled with any new shouting in clear Hebrew, the more his confidence and hope grew. Indeed, the more he became certain that he would be able to lower all of the demands.

Then came the scream.

It ripped the still, pregnant air! It was a high, screaming sound of an animal in extreme anguish and terror! It froze him motionless! He knew that it was not that of a wounded animal! The shrill was that of a man! One of his envoys! It completely negated his growing hope.

A second howl had him on his feet running! At the nearest window his eyes swept the top of the wall knowing exactly for what they were looking: to his right!—a sentry, running like a spurred camel, was fast barreling toward a wall tower straight out from his palace! He gathered his robes in one swoop, raced across the room and, shouldering his way, crashed through his bedchamber's far doors, running headlong out on his private roof garden: the end of which would furnish him with the palace's closest hearing vantage to the swift-running soldier.

The shrieks became non-stop.

"They have stripped one of our envoys naked! They are flaying his flesh in one huge strip off his back!" the messenger cried when he was close enough to be heard over the din.

"My God, my Lord God, help him!" Hezekiah exclaimed, his heart pounding wildly. Knowing for the first time the fullest meaning of terror, he groaned another petition as he fell immobilized near the edge of the roof. Am I just a peasant ruler in Your sight as this haughty Assyrian has been shouting all morning. Has my rule been so puny that You are going to allow it to be driven off the face of the earth? Have all my

Tom Steinbach

righteous reformings been of no earthly—

Another long scream, the first from another envoy, came over a wall! He cringed: he *felt* that envoy's flesh being ripped at. He longed to cry, longed to remain on the floor of the roof, longed to regain the sleep he had lost all night. He jumped to his feet, however, and raced back across the roof faster than he had come, faster than he had ever run in his life! As he ran he began shouting to the runner, shouting to the Assyrians, and shouting to the sky:

"I am coming!

"Harm them no more!

"I AM COMING!"

Bursting through his myriad of rooms, he raced down the stairway, exploded out the front of the palace, and ran without dignity across the stone courtyard.

He was confronted midway in his race to the gate by a group of his city's elders who had heard the screams and his own shoutings. He attempted to evade them by skirting around them. That failed when he was grabbed by his robes, was held unto by his arms, was turned back and forth and round and round by various younger and older men trying to force him to slow down long enough to hear them out!

Dragging them along as he was being spun, he explained to them that their envoys did not have time for any meetings! Nor for any delays! Nor for any dialogue!

"You cannot go out there!" they screamed at him.

"Someone has to! And I am the only one that heathen wants!" he shouted back.

"Then let us send our army out," came a terrified cry from the back of the group.

"And force them to haul the rest of theirs up here to do to us what they are doing to our men out there? No! I will risk that our Lord God will come to my and our envoys' aid—*if you will let me get out there!*"

"But you are the king! What if—"

"*What if?* They have already conquered forty-six of our cities and neighboring villages! They have already conquered most of our land! They are known to be extremely ruthless! Have you not heard the screaming? Do you not have a heart which pleads for our men out there? Have you not heard the shouter's arrogant boasting all morning? I am going out and promising to them everything they have come up here after!"

"You cannot do that!"

"I have to do that!"

"You can tell them that from in here!"

"Not anymore—*let me go!*" At his command he was released, and nearly fell on his face.

Was it my command that convinced them or was it that sickening cry of a third envoy which came in over the wall at that same instant? he asked himself as he stumbled and tripped and scrambled forward on all fours until he was fully upright.

Whichever. It did not matter.

He was free and running and his men in charge of the gates had better see that he was coming!

They had seen him and had the restraining bars removed even as he approached. He, before he fully comprehended it, bolted through the gap of the opening doors, and was out beyond the protection of the city's walls!

"I am King Hezekiah!" he shouted, running a dozen paces beyond the gate. "I am the king of Judah!" he shouted, when he stopped to catch his breath near the first dip in the road.

As he stood there focusing, he saw scores of chariots in front of him on the road parallel to the city's walls all the way to the eastern gate in front of Solomon's Temple. From before him and on to the south, he saw dozens of camels and their riders and as many empty wagons stretching far beyond in that direction. However, the sight which caused him the greatest horror, and the one which made him realize why the screams were so savage was the horrifying view of three of his envoys tied tightly against the broadsides of their empty wagons. They had been stripped. Their hands and feet had been stretched and tied. What he saw of the backs of two of them was nothing but scarlet red—as if their backs had been lowered into one of the city's caldrons of daily caught blood from the sacrifice of slaughtered bullocks. The third envoy had red gashes from his shoulders to his waist. A dagger in one of the Assyrians hands was moving to the top of his back to make a horizontal cut.

"Stop!" Hezekiah yelled. "I am King Hezekiah! I have come out as you have ordered!" The loudness of the third envoy's screaming was too much for the monstrous Assyrians to be able to hear Hezekiah's yelling. The horizontal cutting was made: increased screamings and twistings of that terrified envoy overwhelmed his attempts to shout even louder.

Hezekiah began running again—searching for the only one who would be able to understand his words. He remembered he had seen one leader turn toward the city when he had first come out. That one was now looking toward him once again. Soon, two others looked toward him from their battle chariots. Encouraged, he began slowing down, intending to stop. Then he saw the glistening dagger dig into the man's lower back! The beaming officers looking back toward the scene.

"I am King Hezekiah! I hav—"

There was no justice. The screams of the one he was trying to save were vastly overpowering his own shouts. Not being a trained soldier, and fear being greater having witnessed what had been done to the first two envoys, the third screamed continuously: in pain, and also in preparing himself.

Please, Lord, he prayed as he neared the nightmarish scene. "I am King Hezekiah! Do him no more harm!"

The officers looked his direction, nodded to each other and beamed brightly at the running, shouting, robe-drawn-up peasant ruler. Laughing at one another, the three then shouted the long awaited words in their own language.

Thank You, Lord, he prayed as he slowed his pace.

They had stopped the torturing, therefore, he decided he would not cover the final short distance to them: he needed them to make some concessions also for the sake of getting them to back down on their tribute demands. He soon stopped, but it was they who stood in their immaculate chariots as if they were the rulers in this mountain nation—as if they were the *only* rulers in this puny mountaintop capital!

He stood still. After a long, tense waiting the Assyrian leaders' chariots began moving.

I have showed them by coming out here unarmed that I will bend a little...now they are also showing me that they also are willing to bend a little, he thought to himself; feeling better with his decision to come out to the aid of his envoys. If we can keep this mutual bending going: my continuing to be willing and their willingnes—

All-out-to-the-bone panic swept across him as they came closer in their large battle chariots. The panic forced him to reconsider if he had been wrong with his elders, and lacking in wisdom in his leaving the walled security of the capital. Even as he wondered if he should forget his plan altogether and run for it!—ordering his army to send a barrage of arrows and spears and large rocks toward every chariot and archer which followed him back toward the gates: he decided he really had no choice, he therefore stood and waited. They came very close before they reined their horses to an abrupt stop.

Feeling totally dwarfed, encircled and overwhelmed by them, he looked straight up at them, knowing that any wrong move would cost him his life, and waited for the clear Hebrew to begin spewing out of one of them.

The tall dark officer he had first noticed stepped down out of his still vibrating chariot and walked up close to him. The lofty Assyrian turned and grinned an arrogant grin to the other two. It was a hideous grin that said: *this* is the lowly one to whom I have to talk? To Hezekiah he sneered, "So, *you* are the peasant ruler of this puny kingdom which is standing up against the almighty Assyrian Empire."

Hezekiah's mind surprised him, he felt remarkably at ease once the leader had dismounted from his chariot. He said nothing. The Assyrian introduced himself as the Rabshakeh, the chief cupbearer of Crown Prince Sennacherib, and the vanguard's chief officer and spokesman.

"King Hezekiah, peasant ruler of this lowly mountaintop city!" he shouted close to his face, spittle spraying freely. "You think you can defy the mighty Assyrian Empire by not paying our demanded tribute! It is your nauseating action!— your rebellious hostility!—your utter disobedience!—your con -nived thievery that has forced these men of yours to suffer so! If you continue to refuse to invite us into your city, and to refuse to pay us our tribute as the representatives of the world's greatest kingdom, you will cause much greater suffering to come to yourself, and to your men out here, and, to all your men and women inside those walls! Do you not feel the heat of the rising hot sun?"

"I am here," Hezekiah replied. "I came to you as you demanded. Now you will commence to untie them."

The Rabshakeh stared at him, then at the two officers.

"I have come as you have demanded!" Hezekiah repeated. "I have come against all the advice of my elders. I will do no more until you first untie my envoys and allow my men to carry them back into the city."

The Rabshakeh turned sharply; demons stared deeply into his eyes. Hezekiah did not flinch. The Rabshakeh reddened, started to say something; but stopped. He turned back toward the wagons, and shouted in his own language: "Cut the peasant paupers free!"

Hezekiah breathed a silent relief and a silent thank You. His weary mind pleaded with him to shut his eyes, to relax, to lie out flat: to sleep. He continued to stand ramrod straight nevertheless and to stare into the dark evil eyes which were once again staring deeply into his own.

"Puny peasant ruler, you are to understand one thing! It is we!—the renown Assyrian Empire!—who are in charge here! You will no longer tell us what we can or cannot do! We!—the mightiest empire in the world!—we are in charge here! We are not here to talk with you or your emissaries! We are not here to stand out here in this hot sun! We are not here to do anything but gather tribute payment which you owe us! It is ours! We will not take any arguments from you or your elders or any of your people! Do you understand?"

Hezekiah did not answer.

"Do you understand!"

The red-faced, red-necked commanding officer of the elite unit shouted the last harsh words directly into Hezekiah's face, spraying it freely again.

"I understand," he answered, realizing he had nothing to gain by refusing.

"Good!"

The single word was a word of smug victory. It was not at all a word of reconciliation between the two of them. And to prove the truth of that, the Rabshakeh began laying down the rules for their meeting. "When our empire's mighty army comes to your city, you are not to make us stand out here as if we are some measly beggars waiting for permission to enter! You are not to send some lowly messengers to converse with us outside the walls of your city...as if we are some rotting, infected group of lepers! We are the mightiest empire in the world!—the lustiest and the greatest!—and we are prepared to show every peasant ruler that we will not be treated as you have treated us! *Do you understand, Hezekiah!*" He appeared as if he wished that Hezekiah would not appease his wrath.

"I understand."

"Good!" Again the single word of ultimate triumph. A triumph which would not be short-lived if the monstrous Rabshakeh had anything to do with it.

"Then we are ready to enter into your city!"

Hezekiah did not move.

"Right now!"

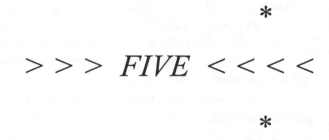

"Open the gates and send men out to help our envoys!" Hezekiah shouted.

"No!"

"No?"

"My men will bring them," the Rabshakeh ordered at point-blank range.

"But my—"

"My men will take them!"

Hezekiah looked at him and wished the venomous demon

back into its lair. He then turned and shouted to those on the wall, "Send no men out to help them!"

He began walking toward the opening gates knowing that he was, indeed, a mountaintop peasant ruler in that man's eyes and, before he left, the angry shouter would do everything to force his people to thoroughly understand that.

The Rabshakeh's decorated chariot swerved in directly in front of him before he had gone ten paces. So he is going to lead me as a defeated captive into my own city. What does it matter? Here goes our city's awesome defensive position.

The two other decorated chariots followed the Rabshakeh and Hezekiah. In one of the chariots, one also with a canopy over it, was the *Tartan*, the Rabshakeh explained as they moved on. The Tartan was the commander-in-chief of the vanguard. Riding next to him in a third chariot, a duplicate of the Rabshakeh's even to the coloring of the pair of horses which drew it, was Crown Prince Sennacherib's chief eunuch, the *Rabsaris*. He was, he explained, third in command.

The Rabshakeh then reemphasized that he was the crown prince's chief cupbearer, and it was for his extremely faithful service—and even more obviously because of his very clear and fluent Hebrew, Hezekiah thought to himself—that he had been commissioned to be the chief officer of this highly important tribute gathering. So that is why he is coming on so strong, he also conjectured. He wants me to see him as chief officer of this special vanguard—but, in reality, he is really number two to the Tartan, and, maybe even number three after the Rabsaris. In this tribute gathering up to the Hebrew peasant ruler's capital, however, he is the vanguard's leader, the chief officer: with the canopied Tartan naturally right behind! After those two chariots came the elite chariot corps, probably three score of them: with a driver, shieldsman, and archer in each chariot. Since they could not be anywhere as effective up here in the mountains as they were down in the open terrain, he considered that they had come simply as a show of might. They were tailed by the sixty empty wagons, and the wagons, by at least five dozen camels and their riders.

They have traveled up here prepared with all their wagons and camels to exceedingly rape us of all our wealth and all our treasures, he thought, and felt all the more the utter despair overwhelming him because of his having allowed these heathens into his capital so easily. Full of despair and fear, he also wondered how many more new things he was going to have to learn about fear. He hoped it would not be too much.

The Rabshakeh led as the conquering monarch. He rode, however, into absolute silence. He therefore took satisfaction, in observing the quivering peasants cowering backwards, to the point of tripping over each other in many cases, from that demonstrative power emanating from him and his troops as they moved confidently along the narrow road.

Hezekiah followed the Rabshakeh with his head held high, though he felt like walking with it low. He had saved his envoys, it was true, but even as he walked behind, he wondered if they were being cared for.

The magnificent splendor of Jerusalem's temple and the complex of royal, palatial structures were to their right as they entered; still, the Rabshakeh, the officers, and their men had no intention of going straight that way.

First, they were going to go on a little plunder hunt of their own. Thus the chariot corps turned southward away from the temple toward an avenue which smelled as if it housed the city's greatest number of vendor carts and selling stalls. Food was their goal and they found themselves in the midst of the city's open bazaar. The Rabshakeh gave total freedom to his men who looted food and gifts, and did lots of destruction to the selling stalls and their canvas tops.

During the humiliating time, Hezekiah worried about his envoys and simply stood watching. Then he allowed his mind to return to the previous night, thought only momentarily of Hannah and then of the annals through which he had slaved throughout the entire night—these were the yearly collections of readings which were of King Sargon's empirical boastings. He had been certain, if the vanguard had not been already down at En rogel, that those overly long and overly boring reports would have quickly put him to sleep. Jamil, the Arabian desert traveler, and seller of anything and everything he could get his hands on, accumulated that vast number of annuals for him through the years. At a cost, of course.

At one point not too far into his sleepless night, he had read one short one he knew he would not forget: *'The splendor of Ashur, my lord, overwhelmed Ursa, and with his own iron dagger he stabbed himself through the heart like a pig and ended his life.'* Hezekiah decided then and there that he would not carry an iron dagger with him in the morning—deciding that it would not be good for a ruler of Judah to strike himself through the heart like a pig!

Another sobering report stated:*'Iaubidi of Hamath, caused the cities: Arpad, Simarra, Damascus, and Samaria to revolt against me. He made them of one mouth and prepared them for battle. I mustered the masses of Asher's troops and at Karkar, his favorite city, and I besieged and captured him together with his warriors. I torched Karkar with fire. Him I flayed. I killed the rebels in the midst of those cities.*

'The cities of the Manneans...I captured and carried off their spoils. I flayed Bagdatti. Daiaukku, with his family, I deported and settled in the land of Hamath. Ullusunu, heard of the deeds I was performing, and came flying like a bird, and seized my feet. I forgave his innumerable transgressions, I forgot his crimes, I had mercy upon him, and had him placed once more on the throne of his kingdom. Twenty-two fortresses, altogether with two of his strong cities which I had taken from the hands of Ursa and Mitatti, I gave back to him

and repaired the damage his land had suffered. I made an image of my royal self. The might of Ashur, my lord, I inscribed thereon in Izirtu, his royal city.'

Watching the Rabshakeh and his men, Hezekiah knew that he would certainly not go running to him nor to Sennacherib or any of the other officers and seize and kiss their feet. Nor would he allow any ruler to build an image of himself or his god in this his Lord God's chosen city. But, he liked the part about Sargon's forgiving the king's transgressions and his forgetting his crimes, and the part of his having mercy upon him and his giving back the cities which he had taken and his repairing of the damage his land had suffered.

The caravan next traveled through a rich, residential area which was protected from their soldiers by a tall stone and clay wall along the street. When the troops came up to a well-guarded gate the Rabshakeh looked back toward Hezekiah.

He explained that it was called the king's gate for it was the entrance of primary use leading from the populated portion of the city into the huge courtyard which surrounded the royal buildings of the capital. He commanded the guards to allow them to pass into the court, which command the sentries appeared greatly relieved to receive.

"In front of us to our left is our beloved house of the forest of Lebanon," he explained, as they stopped before a cedar-pillared building. "The trees used in all these royal buildings before you came from the mountains of Lebanon through Hiram, the king of Tyre during the time our King Solomon had these buildings built. Thus, Solomon named this building, of which we are very proud, in praise of those mighty cedars."

Mighty cedars—what a difference a day makes, he thought wryly to himself, as he thought about what Hannah had happily said about his own muscled trunk the evening before.

We have got to get through this day.
I need and want her right now.

The Rabshakeh, the Tartan and the Rabsaris dismounted from the chariots and led him into the house of the forest of Lebanon. Its walls were covered with valuable artifacts. He feared the building would be emptied of its treasures before they left—and, if it was ransacked, that this would not be the first time in its history it had been, nor would these Assyrians be getting the best of all the spoils gleaned from within its doors. For, back when it was first built, Solomon had heavily stocked all its walls with five hundred golden shields of two sizes. Also at that time, every vessel in it was of pure gold only. For Solomon had made it very clear that not even silver vessels were to be used in this structure which he had built to honor the home of those huge trees.

When he was through explaining and showing the house, Hezekiah went with the Assyrian leaders toward the northern doorway to take them out onto the portion of the courtyard which would lead toward his throne room. The Rabshakeh stopped him and directed him back through the eastern doors, back to their standing chariots. He and they were not going to go to his public throne on equal footing, he reminded himself.

On their chariots once again, and he on his feet, they began a slow ride and walk around the house of the forest of Lebanon. The sun was hot. He wondered if his envoys had been taken anywhere for help—*dear God, they could not still be lying unprotected in those wagons in this heat.*

With the hot full sunlight shining from a high angle to their right, they rounded the corner of the house and stopped and stared at the brilliance of the glorious temple up on its mount. It was a few buildings over but clearly was the main edifice in the public area. Being built on a higher level than the others and its tall porch, its extremely tall entry porch, caused it to easily command attention from every vantage point in the city and this spot was one of the best. "Solomon's Temple," he said, wishing he knew more about his envoys.

71

Tom Steinbach

Next came a large porch of pillars, the portico which led into his public throne room. Slightly larger than half the size of the house of the forest of Lebanon, this porch was a raised, pillared, open-air platform with a massive roof. Walking across the spacious porch they entered into the capital's hall of judgment. It was paneled in cedar from floor to ceiling. The high-beamed hall was the home of his public throne.

The Rabshakeh swaggered up the steps and seated himself on the throne which was constructed solely of ivory, and overlaid in pure gold. He jested something in Aramaic to his companions and looked as if he was planning on staying seated there for awhile. Hezekiah decided to use the time to meander again through Sargon's writings—through those annual reports of the empire's present king which had been his companions through his long, mostly sleepless, night.

Especially, did he think of one who had attempted to flee from before King Sargon. *'Mutallum, a wicked Hittite, put his trust in the king of Urartu and stopped the yearly payment of their tribute and tax, and withheld their gifts.*

'In the anger of my heart, with my battle chariots and cavalry who never leave my side, I took the road against him. When he saw the approach of my expedition, he left his city and was seen no more.' Hezekiah knew he had had that alternative. But why do so, when his land had already been overrun with Assyrians and his capital's walls were his best defense against any enemy. Why run thus, when his elders had already agreed with him that he should stall for as long as he could and then he should offer to pay the vanguard most of what was demanded.

One very long report concerned King Sargon's previous summer's campaign. That ruler wrote it as a correspondence addressed to the father of the Assyrian gods: *'Ashur, father of the gods, the great master, who dwells in Eharsaggalkurkurra, your great temple, hail, all hail! Ye gods of destiny, ye* goddesses, who dwell together in Eharsaggalkurkurra, your great temple, hail, all hail! To the city and its people, greetings! To the palace in its midst, greetings! To King Sargon, the holy priest, the servant, who fears your great godhead, and to his camp, peace, abundant peace!'

"Enough of that!" Hezekiah remembered shouting out loud the previous night. Even now he smiled at the remembering.

'With the strong support of Ashur, Nabu and Marduk, I directed the line of march into the mountains. That land of the powerful Medes heard of the approach of my expedition, my devastation of their lands in a former year was still in their ears, and terror fell upon them. They brought their heavy tribute out of the lands and submitted to me in Parsuash. Ullusunu heaped up supplies of flour and wine for the feeding of my troops. He delivered to me his oldest son with a peace offering. Large draft horses, cattle, and sheep I received from him as tribute. Before me he prostrated himself: he and his nobles, the rulers of his land, directed prayer to me, crawling on all fours like dogs.' Praying to him! Crawling upon all fours like dogs! He certainly would not go to any extreme that harsh to appease the Assyrians!

The Rabshakeh came off the throne displaying a pompous loftiness. The Tartan strutted up the stairs to take his place on the regal seat. Hezekiah worried even more about his envoys as he continued to think about his previous night's thoughts:

'I destroyed the walls of twelve strong walled cities together with eighty-four villages of their neighborhood.' Sargon continued, 'I set fire to their houses inside, I destroyed them like a flood, I battered them into heaps of ruins. One who was without judgment, whose speech was evil, who was forever overstepping his bounds, to the gods I lifted my hands, imploring that I might bring about his defeat in battle and turn his insolent words against himself and make him bear his sin. Ashur, my lord, heard my words of righteous anger and he *sent at my side his terrible weapons.*

'The exhausted armies of Ashur, who had come this long road and were weary, who had crossed innumerable mighty mountains whose ascent and descent were most difficult and their appearance became changed. I could not relieve their fatigue, give them water to quench their thirst, nor pitch my tent, nor strengthen the wall of the camp; I could not send my warriors ahead nor gather together my equipment or army.

'I was never afraid of his masses of troops. I did not cast a glance at the multitude of his mail-clad warriors. With my single chariot and the horsemen who go at my side, who never leave me in a hostile or friendly region. I plunged into his midst like a spear—like a javelin. I turned back his advance. I killed large numbers of his troops. His warriors I cut down like millet, filling the valleys with them. I made blood run like a river dyeing countrysides and dyeing highlands red like a royal robe. His warriors I slaughtered about his feet like lambs. I cut off their heads. To save his life, he abandoned his chariot, mounted a mare, and fled.'

What boasting! The crown prince and these officers will use similar boasts to exalt what they have done here in my capital and in my land and in my many cities, Hezekiah thought with anguish as the Tartan descended from the throne.

'I, Sargon, guardian of justice, the humble worshipper of Nabu and Marduk, I stood victorious. Over their mountains I poured out terror. Their powerful fortifications I smashed like pots. Their great wall whose foundation platform was founded upon the very bed rock of the mountain, whose thickness measured eight cubits, I began with its upper wall, destroyed it completely. I brought it to the ground. The dwellings within it I set on fire and left their large timbers in flames. Their filled-up granaries opened, my army devour the unmeasured grain, and, like swarming locusts, I turned my beasts into its meadows, and they tore up the vegetation on which the city

depended, they devastated the plain.

'From Ushkaia I drew near Tarui and Tarmakisa. Strong walled cities, whose outer walls were well built, and whose moats were very deep and completely surrounded them, in the midst of which are stabled the horses reserved for his royal army. Their people who live in that district saw the actions of my royal valor which I accomplished against their cities, and they fled into arid regions, places of thirst.'

Raw, fierce intimidation, Hezekiah thought, the monarchs of the empire want all of us to the very ends of their kingdoms to blatantly fear the least rebellion against their rule. All these insinuations—it was with deepening tremors he watched the Rabsaris next make his heady ascent to the throne.

'My warriors made the noise of iron axes to resound. No quaking heart escaped from that fight! Before the onslaught of my attack which they could not meet, terror poured over them and they became as dead men. They left their mighty fortresses and trod the slopes of their mountains. As with the dense cloud of the night, I covered that province and all of their great cities like an attack of a swarm of locusts. Their great heaps of barley and wheat which during many days they had heaped up in their granaries, I had my whole army load on our horses, mules, camels and asses, and heaped up in the midst of my encampment like mounds: ample provision of supplies for the return march to Assyria they made in gladness.

'Argishtiuna and Kallania, their foundation walls being visible to the height of two hundred and forty cubits. They had seen the overthrow of the neighboring province and their legs trembled. They abandoned their cities and fled like birds. On my return march Urzana failed to come bringing his ample gifts nor did he kiss my feet. He withheld his tribute, tax, and gifts, and not once did he send his messenger to greet me. In the fury of my heart I made all of my chariots, and my many horses, and all of my camp, take the road.

Tom Steinbach

'At the exalted command of Nabu and Marduk who had taken their course in a station of the stars portending the advance of my arms and, as a favorable sign for gaining power, the moon God, lord of the disk, came to rest at the watch portending the overthrowing of Gutium; and, at the most precious nod of the sun God, Shamash, the warrior, who wrote upon the entrails of my sacrificial animals the favorable omens which indicated that he would go at my side. With a single battle chariot and one thousand of my fierce horsemen, my bearers of bows, my shield and lance, my brave warriors for battle trained, I set out and took the road to Musasir, a difficult road and brought my army up Mount Arsiu, a mighty mountain whose ascent is like the climbing of a peak.'

We, here in Jerusalem, claim to be safely placed on the backbone of a range of decent mountains, Hezekiah thought, but our mountains are truly nothing when compared to those extremely high ones over beyond the eastern deserts. Even my reading about their exploits up in those ranges causes me to fear greatly when I think of these men in the empire's army.

'In the Upper Zab, Elamunia, I crossed among high mountains, lofty ridges, steep mountains peaks which defy description, through which there is no trail for the passage of foot soldiers and among which mighty waterfalls tear their way. The noises of whose falls resound like Adad and are full of terrors for the one attacking their passes; wilderness land where no king has ever passed, whose passages no prince who went before me had ever seen; their great wild tree trunks I tore down and cut through the steep peaks with bronze axes.

'A narrow strait road where my soldiers passed sideways, I made for the passage of my army between those. My battle chariot came up with ropes, which with several mounts of horses, I took the lead of my army. My warriors and their horses, who go at my side, narrowed down to single file and made the wearisome way. Over that city I made the loud noise

76

of my army resound and the inhabitants went up on the roofs of their houses and wept aloud bitterly. To save themselves they crawled on all fours before me wringing their hands. Into Musasir I entered in might. In the palace I took up my abode.

'I broke open the seals of their treasure: thirty four talents of gold, one hundred and sixty seven talents of silver, carnelian, white bronze, lead, lapis lazuli, and many other precious stones in great quantities. Ivory, maple, baskets for vegetables of ivory and boxwood, whose inlay was of gold and silver, vases, lots of drinking vessels and golden daggers. These things together with his great wealth which was without calculation I carried off. Ursa sank down to the ground.'

He would never be made to sink down to the ground before these Assyrian warriors, he had promised himself aloud during those late hours of the night as he thought of the horrible terror the empire brings into every province they enter. He would not kiss any feet! He would not crawl upon all fours! He would not bow to the ground. He would not do anything that would show to the Assyrians that the gods and goddesses of their nation was above his God. And he would not pray to any man. The Rabsaris descended.

The three officers moved back out onto the large open porch. Hezekiah followed and thought about Sargon's son, Crown Prince Sennacherib. Leading under his father's banner, Sennacherib also completed his successful role of leadership the previous year in the northern mountains of Urartu. This year, of course, he has come farther westward and has already conquered forty-six fortified cities and their neighboring cities. Forty-six walled cities! Unbelievable!

He could see in his mind's inner eye the prince returned to the empire's capital. Gesturing with flailing arms and loudly proclaiming with great sounding words, he would shout with pompous, regal pride: "Forty-six of the Hebrew walled cities I captured! "I destroyed! "I devastated! "I burned with fire!"

He was thankful that the crown prince had not devastated nor torched any of his cities. However, he did truly wonder which reports the peoples of Assyria would hear in the public speeches—and read on their stone monuments.

My Lord, he also wondered with rising anger, has not mine been a righteous reign? How could You have allowed so much loss of land to happen in my reign? Why was it during mine and not during my father's wicked reign that You dragged the empire's army over here against our nation so drastically? I would have thought, and believed, and relished the idea that if You did allow these heathen Assyrians to come against us during my reign, that You would have also made one colossal sacrifice out of them here in our land. But You have not. You have not hindered them at all. You have done nothing. Why?

He watched the Rabshakeh signal his troops to move in. As the chariots began to fill the courtyard in front, and on either side, of the porch, he thought of his father. Ahaz had gone out of his way to court favor with these Assyrians back in his reign when they were ruled over by Tiglath-pileser. He sent to Urijah, his high priest, the pattern of the altar which Tiglath-pileser offered sacrifices on in Damascus. He ordered Urijah to fashion one identical to it for the inner courtyard of Solomon's Temple. Soon after,when he returned to Jerusalem, he entered at once through the king's gate, went straight by their house of Lebanon, straight by this judgment hall, straight by his palace and, beaming with pride, approached the new altar. There he offered a burnt offering, a drink offering and a meat offering. He ordered the brazen altar, which had been placed before the temple at the command of the Lord, to be moved over to the north of the newly constructed one. Once there, Ahaz ordered the new one to be reserved strictly for his own use: that by it he alone would make inquiry from his many gods and goddesses.

When Tiglath-pileser came to present himself, father also

had the brass workmanship cut off from every vessel in the temple's courtyard. The brass bases and the wheels of the ten cleansing lavors were thus cut off and given to the haughty Assyrian monarch. The enormous cleansing lavor, ten cubits in diameter and five cubits deep, was removed from off its twelve-oxen base and placed to sit on just a stone base. All of its brasswork, three oxen in each set standing together facing one of the four directions of the winds of the heavens and all twelve standing looking outward, were cut off and given to him. To what advantage was his disobedient behavior toward these Assyrians? he questioned as he viewed the last of the chariot corps filling the appointed place before the porch. In his attempt to make an alliance with the Assyrians, one which never worked for us, he gave up too many treasures.

What am I going to be forced to give up this day? Now that I have allowed them into our capital. Now that they are the ones in control. Still, I had to go out there. I had to protect my men. I had to. *O Lord, I pray for their safely!*

Behind the chariot corps, fanned out in a semi-circle, came in the fifty or so camels.

Before these Assyrians entered our city I was certain, he thought as he continued to watch the planned official assault by the elite vanguard to his right to rule in his capital this day, I would have been certain that I could have been able to get them to lower their demands. Now what? What can I now do? I cannot do anything.

Moving behind the camels and around either side were the empty wagons. While these last-to-arrive were coming in, he watched his bravest—that is, at least, his most curious—men and women occupy the vacant spaces everywhere available back toward the rear of the courtyard. Mostly they were close together along the walls.

Then, to his utterly painful shock, came the wagons carrying his envoys! They were being driven up close on either side of the front of the porch. He looked at his suffering men, shook his head in total disbelief, felt himself going faint, and prayed that he would soon be able to get them the physical attention they needed. They had not been administered to at all! Nor had they been protected from the fully risen sun.

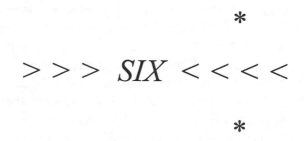

*

> > > *SIX* < < < <

*

"King Hezekiah," the Rabshakeh shouted.

"Peasant ruler of this lowly city which has chosen to defy the mighty Assyrian Empire, to you and to your rebellious peasant people.

"I present your envoys!"

That spoken, the two who had been flayed outside the gates were raised upright upon the wagon beds, one on each of the wagons.

As soon as the audible wave of gasps by the women began to die down, two huge soldiers impaled the envoys on massive spears and lifted them high for all to see. A surge of dread and anguish racked Hezekiah and raced through every man and woman in the crowd. The charge was greatly intensified when the third envoy was quickly forced at spear point to stand up facing them.

Twisting him violently around, two other soldiers grabbed the loose corners of his sliced skin and before any Israelites realized what was happening, ripped the rectangle downward in one well-practiced yank!

The envoy's loud shriek could hardly be heard over the screams and wails of the Hebrew women in attendance.

"Stop!" Hezekiah yelled at that moment, and though none off the porch had been able to hear him, his chest instantly received the butt end of the Rabshakeh's mighty spear.

Two Israelites were dead, impaled on spears before the people. Two other Israelites were also before the people, both in excruciating pain. But both alive. One, another envoy, was shrieking in burning pain with absolutely no idea as to what to do or how long he would stand there before more flesh would be ripped and torn off his body; the other, the nation's ruling monarch, was gasping in panic for breath as he lay doubled up before all to see on the porch's pavement.

The utterly frightened Israelites pushed backwards against one another, trying to hide behind each other, being instantly united in their belief that those ruthless, inhuman tortures were going to spread in their direction at any moment.

The Rabshakeh jabbed fiercely again at Hezekiah with the blunt end of his spear. He then kicked him out of his way as he moved to the very front of the platform. His massive violent presence accomplished what he was after: he appeared like a mighty siege tower all by himself!

He waited to speak with anger radiating from his vicious eyes, and from his tightly drawn cheekbones and mouth, but there was too much commotion in the crowd and too much screaming being done by the envoy. He therefore gave a barely visible nod. Immediately a spear was raised up through the envoy: forcibly raising him high off the wagon bed. Simultaneously, every archer in the fifty chariots turned toward the crowd with their arrows drawn taut.

Instantly—Completely—The gasps and mourning ceased.

Instantly! Completely! The city became deathly silent.

The Rabshakeh shouted in clear Hebrew, "Your peasant ruler did not welcome our vanguard into your capital! No, no! Instead, he sent men out to us to inform us that we were not going to be invited inside! No city! No monarch! No people treat the mighty Assyrian Empire in that manner! *Do you understand!*" There was no response. They understood.

But needing some action and response and needing to explode toward someone, he violently kicked Hezekiah again! —causing him to grasp harder for breath as he lay huddled in very great pain. Hezekiah, in turn, pleaded silently with his Lord God to strike the murderous heathen down immediately without any show of mercy. That too received no response.

In violence, the heated Rabshakeh shouted aloud, "We came this morning to this despicably puny city as the official delegation on official duty to collect your unpaid tribute, sent by Crown Prince Sennacherib himself, sent by the chosen successor to King Sargon: the reigning sovereign of the almighty Assyrian Empire!" He looked straight ahead toward those pushed back against the courtyard wall as hard as they could press. "As such, we were naturally expecting a royal escort into your city!—and a royal welcome by your elders and all your other officials!—and a royal banquet in your palace! Your peasant king offered nothing! Such offensive treatment demands punishment!"

Two huge soldiers instantly ascended the steps to the platform and powerfully kicked Hezekiah twice each: once to his head, once to his stomach and twice more to his chest. At the moment of the last kick, other soldiers forced the remaining two twisting and turning and squirming envoys to stand up. Once they had them upright, one in each wagon, the four stripped their tunics off them.

"We were abominably disregarded out there! Abominably! Your gates would not open to us!" the Rabshakeh shrieked in rage. "You forced us to shout to make our presence known! And, then, after a contemptible length of time, your gates finally began to open! But not to let us in! Oh, no. No! They only opened to let these five *peasants* make their way out to us! Then your gates closed again promptly! You do not treat the Assyrian empire like that! This entire city should be put to the sword!" Immediately a visibly-shakened group of one half dozen of the most frightened Israelites, running scared, broke for the safety of the king's gate. At the same instant, a half dozen arrows flew, one arrow striking each runner fatally before they had gone five paces.

Where are you, Isaiah?—we need the intervention of our Lord God Almighty *now*, Hezekiah wondered and hoped and pleaded and prayed as he looked from his prostrated position on the porch's pavement. Lord, why did You allow this day to begin? he wondered in extreme pain and helplessness. Lord, why did You allow these Assyrians to come into our city? You know how Prince Sennacherib's father entered into cities and countries, and raped them of—*My Lord God, help me somehow to get a message to my chief chamberlain!*—he desperately pleaded within as a sudden, even greater, gripping, overpowering terror entered full-blown into his mind!

"Peasant ruler!" The Rabshakeh waited. Then shouted even louder, *"Peasant ruler!"*

Hezekiah looked up from that pavement, shook his head and mind to bring himself back to the beast before him, and began trying to double up onto his knees. He finally succeeded after great effort. But he was forced by internal pain to rest a moment. He swallowed a swallow of air. When he did not receive another jab from the Rabshakeh's spear, he forced himself up enough to rest on one foot and one knee. After a pause in that position, he pushed down a dizzy nauseating wave, then determined himself to rise to nearly full stature.

Finally attaining his goal, after another longer pause he felt vaguely certain that he had his balance. Then, only then, he moved forward, slightly weaving and definitely scuffing...but obediently forward. He slowly shuffled as far as he could to the front of the porch to where the confident Rabshakeh stood. The two soldiers who had already manhandled him moved in close on either side. The Rabshakeh stared at him, waited, and then demanded: "Order parchment, a reed, and lampblack to be brought up here this moment!"

When the writing materials had been brought, he ordered him to write his surrender. I have no choice, Hezekiah thought. Any hope I had early this morning of forcing some agreements with these savage creatures has dissolved before my eyes.

He wrote slowly: 'I have offended. Return from me and my land. That which you put upon me, will I bear.'

"My men and I are hungry," the Rabshakeh demanded, when he saw the reed being laid down and the heated clay being brought to seal that statement. "The sun is overhead. We will have dinner over there in your house of the forest. Our horses and camels are thirsty. We want them watered now."

With those orders he produced a sealed scroll containing the long list of demands which he had brought up to Jerusalem from Sennacherib and gave it to Hezekiah.

Using those commands as his means to get free from the crazed-madman for a space, Hezekiah forced enough air into his convulsive lungs to order his men to fill earthen jars and vessels with water for the horses and camels: so that the leader of these monstrously trained Assyrians would be satisfied that 'this peasant ruler' was indeed carrying out his biddings.

With the natural break he then, with an even greater

sacrifice of comfort, moved his bruised hurting body into and through his throne room and out its back door. From there, he stiffly lowered himself down the steps to the pavement of the courtyard and worked his way across to his palace. It took him much longer than usual. When he entered the front gate of the palace, many of his servants met him at the door.

It was with great effort he issued orders to everyone in sight as fast as his slow methodical breathing would allow him to speak. Fearful that he might sound like that callous Assyrian himself, he gave orders to each servant in his turn; but especially he ordered for Mehujael to hurry to him as soon as possible. He then called his own family into his presence and gave stark orders to them not to make themselves visible at all until those insane Assyrians had positively left.

When his servants returned, he repeated his orders to them emphasizing for them to continue to remain inside the palace until the Assyrians had left the city, and until he himself had returned to assure them that all danger of capture, or of being impaled, or of being skinned alive or raped had positively ceased to exist. He then entered his business chamber, where he sat down before a very long table and, foregoing his body's demand for sleep, broke the scroll's seal.

Impossible! he thought. And again, impossible. And again. That time he shut his eyes in complete fear and bewilderment. But then the images of the bodies of the five envoys and of the six fleeing citizens began weaving in and out of his mind. No, there was no way those demands could be impossible—that madman will order our women stripped and flayed next!

One by one, the members of his inner circle nervously gathered into the somber palatial room. The foreboding long list was passed among them.

"We cannot raise these amounts."

"We must."

85

"Yes, he is correct. We have to!"

"We have heard of many reports throughout this summer from our fellow brethren in their towns in the north and down in the plains that these Assyrians were extremely ruthless; but to see it before our very eyes, I cannot believe that humans could do such detestable things to other humans."

"That is because our God and our Hebrew religion place a value which is extremely high upon life itself."

"And these Assyrians only place high value on absolute domination of all the other kingdoms of the earth."

"Especially of the *peasant* kingdoms."

"Please, men," Hezekiah cut in wearily, "that is all true, but we have very little time. Under no circumstances do we want these murdering soldiers staying within our protecting walls overnight." It was not only because of his desire to be with Hannah that he was saying that.

Still, the room was not quieting down.

"Men, these spear and arrow-slinging savages would like nothing more than to have an excuse to stay overnight here in our capital and remind us again all day long tomorrow how ruthlessly mighty they are." Silence finally fell.

He began with the first item on the list. When discussing the amount of the fifth item, two wagonloads of sandlewood, Mehujael entered their room. Noticeably relieved, Hezekiah drew out of his robe a note he had written when he first entered the room and handed it to his chief chamberlain.

After dinner, he had been ordered by the Rabshakeh to send his musicians and dancers to the house of Lebanon where the officers had decided to remain for awhile to be entertained after eating. Before the entertainers began performing, the Rabshakeh also commanded Hezekiah to order four high back pure ivory chairs to be brought and placed near the front of the porch of pillars. On his own initiative while the Assyrians had been eating earlier, he had ordered his flayed emissaries taken from the wagons and the felled citizens carried away to be properly prepared for burial. He also had the various pools of blood washed from the stone pavement.

When the Assyrians left the house of the forest of Lebanon for the porch of pillars they found that the high back chairs had been placed for them, and that many of their items had already been brought and placed near the porch. Seated with his Tartan and the Rabsaris, and extremely pleased to see that his reign of terror was working, the Rabshakeh ordered the loading the tusks of ivory, the house chairs and couches of ivory, the stacks of elephant hides into wagons. The maple, sandlewood, and large sandu-stones were next placed into five other wagons. Then valuable gems, jewels, antimony, and other treasures—which had already been very carefully wrapped with either coarse or fine linen, and were also in crates for safe traveling—were loaded into another pair of wagons. All was moving along smoothly. Even the three hundred demanded talents of silver began arriving.

Fifty talents were brought and loaded. Then one hundred. One hundred thirty. One hundred fifty. One hundred seventy-five. Two hundred. Two hundred twenty-five. Two hundred forty-five. Two hundred and forty-five talents of silver were brought, and loaded unto the wagons.

The Rabshakeh grabbed his list! Looked down at the total demanded and angrily asked, "What did Sennacherib order?"

"Three hundred talents."

"Then three hundred is what I take!"

You do not need to scream at me. "What we brought is all that we have in our treasuries."

The Rabshakeh impetuously raised his arm! And arrows from two directions instantly felled the servant which had brought the last talents of silver. Hezekiah saw the two archers immediately refill their bows.

"Lower your arm!" he yelled at the Rabshakeh.

The next to the last carrying servant let out a loud gasp, and fell face first onto the pavement.

"Please."

"You are never to shout at me, peasant ruler!" with a beet red face the furious Rabshakeh yelled, "Never!" Five more servants cried out, and fell with arrows sticking through their backs. The Rabshakeh lowered his arm.

Greatly distressed that more servants were unnecessarily slain, Hezekiah requested permission to be able to call one of his priests. That granted, he called for Shemei to come down from the temple. When that temple servant of the Lord arrived at the porch of pillars, Hezekiah went down and talked very softly to him as he pointed back toward the shining temple.

As he watched him leave, the Rabshakeh nodded to his Tartan. The two of them left the Rabsaris in charge to watch things. And they followed the priest. *This one time*, Hezekiah hoped within himself, *this one time, may two not from the tribe of Levi enter the temple of our Lord God with Shemei.*

The Rabshakeh and Tartan followed the priest, however, only up to the top steps of the gate of the upper courtyard of the temple. From there they viewed the temple, and its golden pillars, and its doors, and its bronze altar. Mentioning its fine craftsmanship to one another, they stated their astonishment of the small size of the temple proper compared to the massive temples back in their homeland. Magnificent structures built so enormous that thousands could gather together within them to participate in their numerous rites and practices. This temple before them could never start to hold the vast numbers their temples could hold. They incredulously concluded that this building was constructed first and foremost as a dwelling place only for the peasant Hebrews' gods and goddesses; and that the poor peasants could not have many of them unless the various deities all resided in the extremely tall front entryway.

While they waited for sign of the added silver coming out of the temple, they looked over toward Hezekiah's palace. From the advantage of the high location, his house of women could be easily seen as an edifice of many rooms added to the back of the palace. They smiled at one another.The talents of silver were soon brought forth, and they returned with the carrying servant back to the huge porch of pillars.

What am I going to do? Hezekiah asked himself while the Rabshakeh and Tartan were returning. We have no resources anywhere to come up with the demanded gold. I could quickly raise it if I was still in leadership over the forty-six defeated cities. Still, even then there would be no way that I could bring it here as promptly as this hideous murderer demands.

He looked toward his elders. They still looked as ashen as when the flying arrows viciously cut down their seven servants, they were still white in shock. But their countenance became more disturbed, more agitated, as soon as they noticed the two Assyrian leaders returning and his looking in their direction. Their appearance was as if they promptly coveted that he would cease looking their way. Understanding their fright, he stopped gazing at them and turned to watch the Rabsaris walk by and inspect a few of the wagons.

Lord, he prayed, please do not allow any more violence here in Your chosen city. Nevertheless, because of the gold he knew there would be. The last of the silver finally came.

With it came the Rabshakeh and the Tartan and another priest. Leaving the priest at the edge of the crowd, the Assyrians stalked over to the loaded wagons of silver. They surveyed each one, they picked up and handled some of the precious metal, they acted proud indeed. Very proud.

"Three hundred talents of silver was the prince's demand, and three hundred talents of silver is what is packed and ready to be delivered! That is what I call a task well done. He knew I could be counted on!" His Hebrew was extremely good. "And, now, we will have the thirty talents of gold brought," he said after he had gone back up to the porch's platform, and after he had sat down once again in his high back chair.

Hezekiah paused, and then stated, "Rabshakeh, officer of the mighty Assyrian Empire's elite vanguard, I am truly sorry, but all the gold we have in the city is twelve talents." Then he added immediately, "It will do no good to kill any more of my people. We have searched everywhere and we honesty do not have any more gold. I have ordered my servants to bring the twelve talents; but please do not fault the servants who bring it for our not having any more gold in the city. Your armies have conquered many of my cities and towns from—"

"You!" The Rabshakeh pointed at the priest who walked back with them. "Come up here!" Raving mad! His demonic eyes staring, searching, scrutinizing Hezekiah to detect another clue that he was not telling the whole truth as with the silver.

"Honest!"

"Come here!" he yelled at the priest.

"We do not have—"

"Order your priest up here!"

Neither Hezekiah nor the priest moved.

Two huge soldiers bucked from their place near that priest and dragged him up the stairs.

"Strip him!"

"No, I will not—"

A long spear, thrown over thirty paces from behind him, struck him at arms level, and came out a sword's length through his heart in front. The servant of the Lord barely coughed for breath as he instantly crumbled at their feet.

O God! He was one of Your priests! Why did You allow him to die? When are You going to put an end to all this? Why have You not sent Isaiah out here to us to bring down Your wrath upon these vile heathens?

"Ruthless, uncivilized, blood-hungry murderers! Strike me

down next!" he shouted, rising out of his chair and rushing toward the Rabshakeh, who also immediately stood up, pulled out a dagger, and prepared to use it across Hezekiah's neck.

"Go ahead, you filthy, murdering butcher! Cut my throat! Cut my hands and feet off! I told you we have absolutely no more gold! Further killings will not be able to produce the gold you and your Tartan want!"

"Not what we want, peasant king!" His arm impetuously swung and caught Hezekiah across the face. The blow sent him sprawling over the slain priest and across the platform: his robe being sliced by the sharp end of the spear.

"Sennacherib has demanded that we gather thirty talents of gold!—and we do not leave here without those, peasant king!"

Hezekiah's hand went to his smarting face. His other held his stomach which contorted in reactivated pain from that sudden twist and the jerking fall. Rising, as soon as he could, he knelt on one knee and waited for the arrows, the spears, the sword, the dagger, the whatever which would end his life and his reign without having a male heir to take his place.

He waited. All waited. Soon the Rabshakeh spoke.

"You have more gold. A lot more!"

Hezekiah looked up at him and shook his head: knowing the action would precipitate another violent outburst or even a series of such actions. He was wrong. The Rabshakeh simply stated, "If you do not have the thirty talents of gold in your public and personal treasuries, then I demand that you order that it be stripped right now from the great pillars and huge doors of your temple!"

"From those? I just had—"

"You heard me! My orders are to return with thirty talents of gold!" The dagger was still in the throwing hand of the demented, dark demigod.

Hezekiah gave the orders. Then he thought about how badly the temple looked when he had ordered the extensive

91

repairs to be done to it in the beginning of his reign. The gold overlay on the doors and the twin pillars was near to the last, and was by far the most striking, task his workers had performed. Oh, Lord...oh well, the thirty talents of gold is the last major item on the prince's list for us to gather. If we are still alive when the vanguard leaves, then we will somehow begin again—that is, if my people still want me to lead them. *Hannah, I could use your soothing probing fingers and hands on me right now. I am in so much pain, my lovely one—my magnificently lovely one, I could use the unconditional love and exceptional admiration that your devotion produced toward me last night.*

The Rabshakeh had been shouting something to him and was very, very angry!

Come on, mind, concentrate on this beast! or you will not see Hannah tonight or ever again.

"Peasant ruler, do you hear me?"

"Yes, yes, I hear you. I was...just...trying to figure out how many talents of gold we overlaid—"

"I ordered you to take the Tartan, and the Rabsaris and myself into your palace."

"Into my palace, my palace, my...yes, yes, I will do that," he replied, trying to think through all the potential problems such a visit could hatch.

"Now! We want to go there *now!*"

"Yes, yes, I was only...please come."

"No. You get up and come over here. You will ride with me in my chariot."

"That is all right, I will—"

The dagger struck him in the chest over the heart. He let out a wail of anguish and tumbled back upon the pavement, certain that death had also finally come to him. He was dying, he knew it. The fierce, excruciating pain where the knife had dealt its death blow, could not have been any closer to his heart. He clutched his hands to the spot and instinctively felt for the knife, for the blood: but discovered that there was neither. He discovered the blade had never touched him, that the handle had never turned in the flight, not even once, and that the knife struck him butt first. The pain was terrifyingly real: but not fatal, not final, probably not even disabling.

"Surprised, peasant ruler?"

He only looked at the Rabshakeh.

"Every warrior and leader in our elite forces has had a dagger in his hands since he could walk and talk! If you do not want the next one blade first! Then you will cease disobeying me at my every demand! And you will do everything as I command it!"

$$*$$
$$>>> \quad * \quad <<<$$
$$*$$

In the luxurious throne room in the palace, the Rabshakeh, the Rabsaris and the Tartan took turns sitting up on Hezekiah's golden covered ivory throne. When the Tartan ceremoniously ascended and seated himself upon it, the Rabshakeh ordered Hezekiah to bow in obedience before him.

Dumbstruck for a instant—*'you will do everything as I command it!'*—he then argued against it, hoping now that they were alone in his palace away from his unit that the Rabshakeh would not need to act so blatantly almighty.

He quickly stated that even though the Tartan was the official commander-in-chief of the vanguard, he would only be forced to bow before a conquering sovereign. The refusal hung pregnantly in the air. And then passed, because the Assyrians' lusts were on a much different priority at the moment.

"While we were looking over your temple we noticed your

house of rooms which has been built on directly to this palace. You are to have us taken to that house immediately."

Hezekiah hesitated.

"Do not forget that our chariot corps know where we are."

He still hesitated.

Gripping the hilt of his sword tightly, the Rabshakeh shouted, "Would you prefer, peasant king, that we bring our entire vanguard into that house!"

"Come this way."

Mehujael, I pray that you have done more than I requested in that note.

On their way, one of Hezekiah's daughters, Maachah, not knowing that they were in the palace, came out of her room as they were going down the hall. The Assyrians looked straight at her and could hear that there were others also in the room. Agonizing, Hezekiah rushed the trio toward the house of rooms, wondering what more could go wrong?

Hours later, when the gold had been stripped from the doors of the temple and from Jackin and Boaz, the brass pillars which stood on either side of the entrance, and when it had been placed in the wagons, and when the three Assyrians had returned from the house of women, the arrogant Rabshakeh made it emphatic that the empire and its army would never, ever again tolerate such a reneging attitude from Hezekiah and his peasant people.

"Now before we leave," he said, pausing and smiling his fierce arrogant smile, "I have taken notice that you and your citizens are too calm and are taking our last moments here in the 'capital of the Hebrews' too much in stride. I therefore have two more unfinished details to accomplish."

Too calm. Too much in stride. Two unfinished details to accomplish! My people cannot breathe without a dozen of your murderers whipping out an arrow, or a spear, or a dagger!

"First, peasant ruler, order your women out here."

"Out here?"

He involuntarily flinched...as he expected the Rabshakeh's arm to swing up again at his retort. It did not. The different kind of lust was still domineering the Assyrian.

"You will send your women with us to add to the tribute."

"To add to the tribute! But Sennacherib did not—"

"To remind you never again to treat us so wrongfully!" he said as his eyes became piercingly demonic once again. "And for arguing with my demands on every count, order your male and female dancers and musicians to come out here!"

"The list did not—"

"And your daughters, peasant ruler!"

Staring at him, hating him, and wishing God's immediate damnation upon him; he did not question the Rabshakeh again, nor did he move to obey him.

The Rabshakeh, shaking with hatred, stared hard into his eyes, and then violently ordered his Rabsaris to take the entire chariot corps and raid the palace of Hezekiah's daughters, and of his many women, and of all his musicians and dancers, and, of whomever else they could find!

My Lord God, how evil do You judge I have I been? How dreadfully wicked have I been? How could You allow all this to happen to me, and to my people? Do we not mean anything to You? Does not this city mean anything to You anymore? I thought I was doing much to bring this city, my priests, and all my people back to the true worship of You.

Protect my daughters, my Lord. Why did You allow them to make themselves known at that wrong moment? Surely You could have kept Maachah and the others silent in their room. Protect my mother. Protect Hephzibah and all my other wives. Protect Hannah—*Hannah! Oh, help Mehujael hide her!*

Maddening screams and wailings could be heard coming from within the palace. The Rabshakeh and Tartan laughed.

Hezekiah detested them, but knew that the prince and his father would highly honor them for the overly abundant tribute with which they would be victoriously returning once this was all over. His women and young maidens were dragged and pushed out of the palace: some shoved into various wagons but most onto the pavement for immediate gratification. Back on the porch, the Rabshakeh was directing his troops to pick out hundreds of Hezekiah's finest men for their army.

Lord, why will You not come to our aid? Why will You not? I have read of many times when You came to help our peoples at times like this. When You blinded the enemy, or rained down upon them with hailstones and loud thunder, or when You split the earth open and completely swallow them. Lord, in those and in many other supernatural ways You delivered the enemy into our forefathers' hands. Why will You not come to our aid now when we so desperately need Your help? Please, Lord God, we need You now. Now, Lord.

The women and musicians, packed into a half dozen wagons, were brought down from the palace area.

His eyes searched through the wagons. Not one of his daughters was missing. If he had any sons, he was convinced that they would have also been taken. '*In my fourth year I raised my hand and I overthrew,*' King Sargon had bragged in those writings of his, '*...his wife, his sons, his daughters, all the people from his palace, together with much property. All of them and all of it I took and reckoned as booty.*'

He could not find his mother and wife. Mehujael must have hid his mother and Hephzibah: they were not in any of the wagons.

He kept searching.

She was not among them either!

*

\> \> \>   *   < < <

*

The Rabshakeh had also been earnestly watching.

Watching him.

Watching only Hezekiah.

He had watched him find what he had thought was every one of his daughters. When that search was done, he had watched him search through the rest of the wagons and seemingly be satisfied.

But then....then...he started searching again with another intensity. It grew as an even greater one. One which seemed not to have been fulfilled when he had looked through to the last wagon. Interesting! Very interesting.

There must be someone very close to him that he could not find in the wagons. Who could that be? Who would that be?

That would have to be more deeply investigated. He would continue to watch the peasant ruler.

*

\> \> \>   *   < < <

*

Hezekiah next began to scan the crowds.

First he searched among the wave of his people closest to the wagons. Then farther back along the courtyard's wall he stopped at each face. One by one, he searched.

Apparently puzzled, but obviously not finding what he was looking for, he ceased his looking.

*
> > > * < < <
*

The Rabshakeh, however, did not...and would not.
He continued to watch Hezekiah's eyes.
Just Hezekiah's eyes.

*
> > > * < < <
*

Soon Hezekiah was looking through the front edge of the crowd again. Searching. Ever searching. Obviously searching for someone he had not been able to find anywhere else.

Searching, stopping and squinting; searching, stopping and squinting some more. Retracing here and there. Going back along the wall. Moving through the middle of the crowd.

Coming back up near the front and stopping at every face: one by one eliminating each person.

*
> > > * < < <
*

There! Hezekiah's eyes have caught someone. Do not look into that portion of the crowd yet, he told himself, keep staring at his eyes. Let them direct you to his...his...*his favorite!*

$$*$$
$$>>> * <<<$$
$$*$$

Hezekiah squinted. The hooded material draped over her caused her to appear much smaller. If she would only look directly at him—*and smile*—then he would know for certain.

Not able to get her attention, he looked away. Soon his eyes were at her again. Staring intently at her.

$$*$$
$$>>> * <<<$$
$$*$$

The Rabshakeh stole a look into the crowd. Seeing no one in that area who looked like she would be the peasant ruler's favorite consort, he quickly returned to the task of allowing Hezekiah to reveal her.

His eyes returned to Hezekiah's.

He was enjoying this game.

$$*$$
$$>>> * <<<$$
$$*$$

Hezekiah's eyes were still not fully satisfied.

They had left that area of the crowd and began scanning along the courtyard wall again.

Not finding there what they were looking for, his look came back forward to the original spot.

*

> > > * < < <

*

THERE! Recognition complete! Where exactly did it come from? Where is this majestic beauty he is looking at?

The Rabshakeh glanced again in the direction the peasant ruler had been gazing. I believe I have it, he thought to himself great with satisfaction. But how can that be? It must be the little woman in the dark hooded throw over. He looked back at Hezekiah. Yes! She has to be the one! He does not appear as anxious as before.

Looking back at the little hooded one, he thought: either I am mistaken and she is not his favorite...and she is therefore his wife, or mother, or priestess...or the little hooded one is not as she appears to be. I choose the latter!

She has to be his favorite, he thought. And patted himself on the back: for this further proof of Prince Sennacherib's wisdom in choosing him to lead in this tribute gathering.

He made a mental note.

*

> > > * < < <

*

At the moment of the Rabshakeh's back-patting, Hezekiah turned toward him, and, seeing him looking into that portion of the crowd near Hannah, chastised himself for his extremely unwise, momentary weakness. He prayed: My Lord, please ...please do not let that heathen beast understand who she is.

*

\> \> \> * < < <

*

Preparing himself for his next move, the Rabshakeh said, "Now that your daughters, your women, your musicians, and your dancers are here my first demand is complete. My second is directed toward your stubborn, rebellious people. The time has come for them to witness the brutal, awesome, terrifying strength of the mightiest kingdom in the world!"

He descended full tilt down from the porch, mounted his battle chariot behind his driver and deft archer, and shouted a command as he raised his arm over his head, swung it around, and ordered his driver to lead the entire chariot corps without delay! Instantly, that chariot and the others began their rushed movement out of the courtyard!

Standing tall, next to his chief shield bearer, he was livid—immediately alive with the overwhelming desire to force every last frightened Israelite in the peasant capital to always remember his hardened intolerance, his arrogant confidence, his ruthless power, his forceful leadership, and his extreme hatred for each and every one of them!

Raising gigantic clouds of dust, his chariot, with the rest of the chariots following directly behind in extremely close formation, shot recklessly out through the king's gate, heading straight toward the most heavily populated section of the city! Triumphal in their glee and in their loud shouting, they urged their bolting steeds to pull them even faster! Rounding many tight bends, they raced full gallop down long straight-aways! Rushing to outdo each other whenever the straight-aways

101

became available, they trampled many panicked aged men, terrified mothers and screaming youngsters under accelerating hoof and wheels in the narrow passageways! Spearing every vendor cart and stall awning as they sped next through the bazaar sections of the city, they drove their hastening chariots with abandonment throughout the labyrinth of the city streets! Goats, and chickens, and dogs, and young bullocks were tossed up within the clouds of dust created by their chariots and were battered around in midair until the last chariots crushed over them, and left them without form! After an abominable length of crazed, horrendous circlings of the city's streets and avenues, they re-entered the courtyard through the king's gate and halted to a dust-filled stop directly in front of Hezekiah and the horrified crowd!

The Rabshakeh, satisfied that all future resistance had been castrated—totally, finally castrated—out of the peasant ruler's mind; and also thoroughly satisfied that his demonic anger and his innate cruelty had been deeply, indelibly inscribed within the terrified minds of every Israelite who was peeking from behind banner staffs, wagon wheels, large clay water pots, vendor carts, watering troughs, barely opened doors, heaped piles of drying flax upon their house rooftops; and, also thoroughly satisfied that his harsh, sarcastic, unforgiving grin had been deeply burned into the memories of all who braved moving out of the corners and shadows, huddling together in small groups close enough to intimately view the ruthless proceedings in their city's courtyard...with his back ramrod straight, his face granite hard...he, the Rabshakeh, looked Hezekiah straight in the eye and said with a sneer, "Peasant ruler of this most puny capital, your aged men, slow to move mothers and panicked youngsters do not respect us any more than you do! We do not accept that with any capital under our sovereignty! Perhaps after today they will!"

He then glanced over into the crowd to make certain that

their little hooded one was still there. Seeing her, he faced Hezekiah, and waited until the latter looked him straight in the eye. Sneering, he spoke, "Peasant ruler of this most puny city, I have one more demand. Just one more, and then we will return to Prince Sennacherib with all these gracious, wonderful gifts you have provided for him and for us."

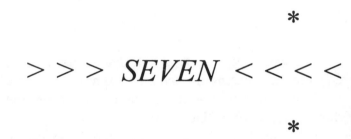

*

> > > *SEVEN* < < < <

*

Hezekiah stared back—not believing his ears.
One more demand!
One more!
You are a liar as well as a murderer.

You said you had two demands, and we have endured those two. What more is there that you could want?

You have taken everything as it is. You have demonstrated yours and your empire's monstrous vileness in every hideous way conceivable.

There is nothing more you could want! I cannot wait until you get out of our city! One more demand! One more! What

Tom Steinbach

could that be?

```
                              *
        > > >  *  < < <
                              *
```

"I want your favorite."

```
                              *
        > > >  *  < < <
                              *
```

The words were soft, so soft that at first Hezekiah did not connect the meaning immediately. When he did the blood left his face as instantly as if a floodgate had been opened in his throat. My Favorite? No! NO!

He began to look her way, but stopped himself lest he give her location away. My favorite? The Rabshakeh was looking her way earlier when I had found her after searching through the crowd. Could he know? Lord God, do not let him know.

My favorite? I have only been with her one evening. I have not even known her—though I will tonight if this foreign Goliath ever leaves. Or will I?

My favorite? I have not even called her my favorite, but he is right, of course. She is my favorite.

In fact Hannah is my most *favorite* favorite. My heart told me that the very first instant I ever set my eyes upon her. Truly, my mind confirmed that with every action, with every movement, with every devoted word she so said to me last evening. Of course, she is my favorite. Why else would I give Mehujael the note ordering him to remove only her out of my

104

house of women, and to hide only her where they could not find her? Why else was I so devastated when the entire host of Assyrians went charging into my palace and into my house of women? I was certain that she could not have evaded an entire searching party. Why else did my heart jump in renewed hope when I could not find her in any of the miserable wagons?

But...but....how did he know?

Lord, help me! Come now in Your power! Split apart the heavens and sweep mightily down upon us! *Now, Lord!* Please come and split apart the ground, and swallow this beast and all his heathen uncircumcised companions alive! Please come and split apart their eyes with blindness! Come and do whatever You do, but please come, and help us...and do it now!

NOW, LORD! Please, God. *Please.*

*

> > > * < < <

*

"Peasant ruler, order your favorite to come over here to me." Hezekiah just looked at him. "Now. Order your favorite to come to me. I want your favorite to come *now*."

*

> > > * < < <

*

My heart, my heart, must have somehow told him that Hannah was not included among the others in the wagonloads as they passed by. He has been too ingenious, too cunning, too certain of himself. A brother and a son of Lucifer, he must be.

My trembling heart cries out to You, my Lord. Please, You have to come and help me protect my lovely Hannah from this son of Lucifer! Come quickly, my God, please come quickly!

He must have known all the time. He must have watched me search through the crowd. No! *No! NO! HE CANNOT KNOW WHERE SHE IS! HE CANNOT!*

Why the grin?—Why that blasted grin?—The one which formed on his lips when he first asked me for my favorite, why is that still there? Why is it getting broader? You realize, that is it, you uncircumcised son of Lucifer, you realize that I myself have realized what you know! You are laughing! Have you been reading my every thought?

Lord God, do not let him know that my eyes could have directed him to her. Please, my God, I have lost too much already. I have lost too much already! There is no way I could bear her being taken away also. Lord, please do not let him, or the crown prince, or any Assyrian touch her. Please, Lord.

I so clearly remember her entrance into my bedchamber: she stood poised in the soft mellow glow of the nearby olive oil lamp. She was so picturesque. Taken back by her extreme beauty, I said to her, "You are very lovely. Come." She began moving toward me. She was truly magnificent: gracefully slender, and exceedingly beautiful. Her hair: long, and black, and flowing. Her unadorned pure white tunic was of the finest linen...and was absolutely perfect for her.

I have been reigning over Judah for fourteen years, I remember thinking as I watched her glide effortlessly closer. Why has this most lovely one come this evening? Why has she come on the most worrisome threatening night of my rule?

She stopped near my bed. She stood tall and smiled as she stretched to her full height and confidently extended her arms high over her head. I remember that I was breathless. When she saw that my eyes had been watching hers, she grinned a buoyant smile. I looked into her eyes, I thought, no matter how much I wanted her I cannot have her tonight. I placed a hand on her back and my other upon her long, sweet-smelling hair. She was like none before. Her fingers moved to the nape of my neck and massaged the back of my head. Her lips barely away from mine...she waited for me to pull her lovely face down upon mine and to kiss her with the kisses of my mouth.

$$*$$
$$> > > \ * \ < < <$$
$$*$$

The Rabshakeh had all proof he needed. He ordered his archer to draw his bow to its full strength. He directed him to begin to pivot. Slowly. Surely. His aim left the platform and moved to his right. Slowly.Surely.

His pivoting finally stopped when his stretched bow was aimed toward the one in the hooded garment.

$$*$$
$$> > > \ * \ < < <$$
$$*$$

Hezekiah's heart stopped.

$$*$$
$$> > > \ * \ < < <$$
$$*$$

"Peasant ruler of this puny mountain city, if you will not give me your favorite," the Rabshakeh said, as he paused with

Tom Steinbach

arrogance, paused with the greatest of confidence, paused with
the most vile look of blatant mockery, "then, I now demand
my archer to take the life of that hooded—"

"NO!" Hezekiah demanded.

The Rabshakeh's grin broadened.

"No?"

"Why does there have to be any more killing? We have
given to you every—"

"You have not provided me with your favorite!"

"With—"

"I demand that you order the one in the hooded garment to
come this moment to me!"

"I will not."

"You will not?"

"I would die first."

"So, peasant one, you would die first."

"Yes, I would."

"I believe you would die first. Everyone has one for whom
he would die. And I knew if we searched long enough that we
would find the one who will cause you to always remember
your hideous disobedience to our all-controlling Empire! And
to the vanguard and me! Never again will you refuse to pay to
us your tribute! Never again!—by taking your favorite we will
break your rebellious heart, peasant ruler of this puny city!"

"She is not on the list."

"Nor were the others."

"You have taken and done enough already in our capital so
that I will never forget your visit." He paused, wondering what
he could now do. "If you take the hooded one, or harm her in
any way, I vow to you that one day I will once again defy you
and your murderous empire."

Do not let him, dear God. Do not let him!

Please, Lord. Help us.

Help us now, Lord.

Please, Lord.

The Rabshakeh snickered broadly, *wallow in the mud that I have made for you, peasant ruler, wallow in the mud!*

He then turned toward the girl, and with his hand motioned for her to come to him. "You, come here!" he demanded when she did not begin moving in his direction.

Apparently willing rather to die by arrow shot than to go with him, she did not move. Accepting that willingness, he ordered his archer to swing his bow away from her and back to the platform and straight toward Hezekiah's heart. Slowly. So slowly. Surely. So surely. The steady arrow honed to its mark.

"Exceedingly pretty maiden that you must be, come here or I will have your beloved monarch shot through the heart before your eyes!"

Squirm, peasant ruler up on your peasant platform! I have my jagged dagger deep within you now and I will twist it and twist it and twist it for all it is worth! Your favorite is coming with me, peasant one! You have led her to me and there is nothing you can do now!

"Worthless mountain peasant ruler, if you ever defy me and our empire again, you will be the first to fall within these walls! I swear it! And you, maiden, is it your pleasure that I first order my men to strip your master, then that I command them to rip every inch of his skin off his body...and hang it along with his severed head on his palace gates? Is it? And then, if you still will not come, then I will order my men to come after you and do the same to you. I vow to you that your master and you will never get away from me and my men. My chariots, my arrows, my spears will come after both of you, and run you down before you go twenty paces!"

She glanced up at Hezekiah.

"Now, pretty little maiden, are you coming? Or should I order my men to make their way toward your beloved peasant ruler? Up this platform toward your beloved monarch?"

She began moving toward him. Slowly.

But she began moving.

*

> > > * < < <

*

No, no, do not go, Hannah. She neared the edge of the crowd. The people opened the way for her. *Please, Lord.* She broke into the open space. *Come now!* She slowly walked in the direction of the Rabshakeh. *Please come in Your power!*

*

> > > * < < <

*

When she had moved close enough, the Rabshakeh leaned over and with his mighty arm swooped down and yanked her up into his steady chariot with him. Pulling her hood back, he saw her great beauty, kissed her mouth hard, and turned her towards the crowd to display her awesome beauty.

Then his hands forced her face back to his mouth...back to his dark bearded face, where he again kissed her much harder, and much longer. Much longer.

The archer, with bow still poised, waited for Hezekiah to

make one false move. Or just one signal to his soldiers.

Hezekiah made no move.

He would not make any move.

His Lord God had utterly...miserably...completely...failed him—and without His Lord God's help he knew his soldiers were helpless. Sadly. Shamefully. Helpless.

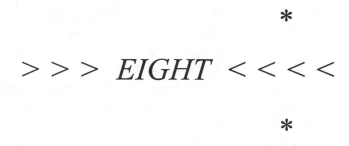

*

> > > *EIGHT* < < < <

*

Blackness reigned supreme.

Heavy clouds blanketed the heavens' canopy. They painted the canvas of the sky with pitch—as if in a very deep mourning.

Not a star, nor the moon, could be seen. Blackness ruled. It also reigned supreme in Hezekiah's life. And had reigned supreme since the day the Assyrians left. Blackness, absolute blackness and a death wish, reigned supreme in him.

The meticulously-woven tapestry which hung majestically in his bedchamber faithfully hiding the door to his house of women had not heard a voice in the room since the day after

111

the vanguard left. The layers of regal linen curtains could testify to the same as they hung obediently: unhooked and straight down from his bed's cornice without any hint of Mehujael's movement to pull them back. The brass lamps and the clay lamps stood sentry-like in their positions. Neither set was flooding the bedchamber with its special mood. They had not for over two months. That bedchamber was empty. Cold. Had been for nine weeks.

The very next day after the vanguard left, Hezekiah moved into his winter house for good. Therefore he moved at least two months earlier than normal into that house which had been constructed for their nation's kings to stand the rigors of the few colder months. The edifice, like the palace, was build of the finest of materials but was much smaller and was much less in the-thick-of-things than the palace. That latter reason was the motive why he chose to move so quickly.

In the winter house there was no scented, wooden door in his bedchamber hidden behind some elaborate wall hanging. If there had been one he would not have had a use for it. His house of women was empty. It would be for some time.

The immense square house had an entryway which led to the left into his private quarters, and led to the right into the capital's public chambers and meeting rooms. Straight ahead, the hall led to an open-roofed central courtyard around which the house itself was built. The house was divided down the center into two equal sections. The public half, off to the right, included a huge meeting room, a formal business room, and, a large, regal dining room on the first level. All the rooms in the winter house were comparable to their respective rooms in the palace. None of those rooms were heated.

The rooms in the house being heated were his bedchamber on the second level of the private side and the kitchen on the main floor also on the private side. To this day he had eaten very little...and he had never left his room. In the weeks since the vanguard left, no elders, no advisors, no spokesmen for the Lord, no foreign emissaries, and no Arabian traders had been invited to come into any of the public rooms. Many had come desiring to use one of the rooms with him but none had been invited in. No posts had been sent inviting any to come and be entertained with him. Nobody except his servants had been allowed into the house. Regardless of their rank, every friend and visitor had been simply and politely informed that Hezekiah had no intention whatsoever of doing any entertaining with anyone for any reason for weeks to come.

Totally defeated, he had immediately stalked toward his palace after the Assyrian vanguard left the city. The arrogant, boastful, confident laughter of the Rabshakeh would always linger within the haunting memories of all his people, he had known it would. But he was certain that not one of them would remember the debasing visit anymore than he.

In the parting scene, the haughty Rabshakeh, grinning broadly and triumphantly—and completely assured that he had destroyed all of Hezekiah's heart and will—had, with a patting-of-his-own-back-gesture, vauntingly thanked him for the great anticipated pleasure that his daughters, and his palace women, and his dancers, and his musicians and, especially, his favorite would bring to him and his men and to their crown prince, and all their soldiers left down at Lachish. Bursting forth with a cruel, menacing, very high-pitched laugh, he then ordered his trusty archer to release the tension on the bow which was still aimed at Hezekiah.

The leader of the mission next, with an overconfident gesture, had motioned to his men to begin leading the many burdened wagons, the scores of heavy-ladened camels, and the multiplied hundreds of walking captive men toward the capital's loudly-creaking, swiftly-opening gates. With Hannah still at his side, he then ordered his driver to speed him up to the front of the caravan. The scene was too predictable for the

Tom Steinbach

hurting Hebrew monarch to handle: the conquering hero leading his troops with the bountiful plunder and the beautiful heroine. Hezekiah watched in his almost numb state. He himself, as the ruler who had to save whatever face he might still have left, remained upon the porch until the last of the Assyrians had left and was out of sight. Then, and only then, did he began walking back toward the palace.

At one point in his solemn journey, he had glanced over to the wall and had watched his soldiers as they, in turn, were watching the leaving vanguard. Thinking, he speculated that the Rabshakeh's cruel, boastful, haughty laugh would also remain especially within their minds:within their tortured minds for many of them had stood along the top of the wall hoping that a signal would come from him directing them to fling their spears and arrows and large rocks at the hateful beast and at his monstrous chariot corps. Many times he had wanted to give such a signal; but that would have only brought the empire's entire marauding army up to his city with the express purpose of: *Conquering it! Defeating it! Devastating it! And burning it with fire!* Whether it was right or wrong, his purpose had been to save it from that fate.

As he neared the palace, he had looked up toward the sun-washed southern side of the temple, and, still numbly thinking of the intense humiliation the Assyrian chief officer had forced him to go through, he thought a great evil against that most sacred dwelling place and against the One who supposedly dwelt within its walls.

If You indeed are real and are dwelling there, my Lord, I will never understand why You did not help us in any way or at any time during this whole, terrifying massacre...he had complained in his stupefied mind. His chafing thoughts multiplied with ease: I will never understand why You did not come to our aid. If You truly are real, and if You truly dwell in this city, I have to wonder what trying to obey You and Your

114

many commandments for these fourteen years has merited me in Your eyes! It cannot be much! Not much at all! How could You allow such an evil force to invade our capital in my reign. You never allowed any destruction anywhere as bad in my father's violently wicked reign. Why?

Lord, my father did not even allow You to dwell in Your earthly dwelling place in the temple. Look at that place now! I still cannot believe what we have had to endure this day! Never in my imagination could I have come up with all that has gone from bad to worse this day! My father had Your brazen altar moved from its chosen place for his own corrupt use—and You never did to him and to our country back then what You have allowed to happen to me in just this one day!

During my reign I have had the many linen veils replaced. And I have had all the occultic statues removed. I have had the entire temple repaired and cleansed. And, most importantly, right in the very beginning of my reign, I invited You to once again enter into its most holy place once again. My God, I even invited all, including our northern brothers who forsook this city long ago, to come back here, so they could correctly worship You. What have I received in return? The terrifying, unmentionable, incredible events of this day!

Tears had filled his smarting eyes.

Anger had filled his doubled-up fists and his heart.

Breathing heavily through his nose as he walked alone, he shut his eyes and asked, How will I ever be able to reign over these my people again? How will I ever be able to face them again? How many more times will You allow that murdering army into our land again? How many times will You allow that savage, uncircumcised boaster into our city again and...not do one thing to aid us or to stop him? They will come back. It is certain they will. You and I both know they will. They will have to return. For one day I will again stop sending their extravagant tribute: with which they build more temples unto their gods and goddesses, and with which they further arm themselves to greatly expand their heathen territory and with which they will feed the hundreds and thousands of their male and female slaves which they have lead captive from here.

You know what that Assyrian King Sargon is doing right at this instant back in his land. He is creating a completely new capital to move into with all the spoils his crown prince is bringing back to him from this Your supposedly chosen capital and nation. A capital in which he will build a multitude of brand new elaborate temples for his gods and goddesses!

Hezekiah had never lost anything until these summer months had begun. He had never been stood up to like he had been all summer. He had never had to plead so pitifully to the Lord before. In one summer, and, even more so, in one day, his whole life had become a humiliating failure.

Total humiliation. Total rejection. Total helplessness.

He grieved: how could he even think of continuing to be Judah's reigning monarch? His life, his reign, had become a failure in all those areas in one day. And he dreaded: for he knew that the same Rabshakeh would indeed come again someday...and that his Lord God, upon Whom he would have to once again trust for help, he knew that He and Isaiah would probably remain hidden and silent to his pleas as they have this time. And that would be intolerable. Implausible to even think about! For without the supernatural intervention of his Lord God Himself he would still not have any recourse but that of humbling himself before the uncircumcised heathen.

Which action he would never do again! Never!

A feeling close to hatred, but deeper, had filled his being as he had headed up toward the entrance of his palace. Though he was close to entering his own building, *in his mind* he had long before passed by the entrance and was climbing the stairs up to the temple's courtyard. *In his mind* he was stalking up toward the denuded doors and pillars of the temple. In his mind he was entering the temple. In his mind, though deeply angered and bitter, he did not know what he would do next.

He would probably start out yelling or waving his fists or, at least, speaking forth with great contempt. He would probably then end up in a weeping heap on the golden floor of the temple, crying his heart out to their Lord God before the heavy veil...before the curtains behind which the Presence of the Lord supposedly dwelt.

In actuality, he had entered his own palace and barricaded himself in his own private chambers. And, in the safety of his own palace, had raved contemptuously for some time toward the Lord for not helping him and his people in the least. Then he had ended up weeping his heart out upon his bed.

*

>>> * <<<

*

Later when Hephzibah requested permission to be with him, he had word sent to her that he really needed time alone to himself. However, a couple hours after sunset she would be permitted to come for awhile.

Even at that hour, he had not wanted to see her. He had wanted to see no one. His concept of living securely in peace under the watchful eye of his Lord God Almighty had been completely devastated. He needed time to deal with it.

How could his Lord remain silent for so long of a period? The ebbing of his belief of an always protecting, ever present, ever watchful, ever almighty Lord God was by far the hardest dilemma for which he had no ready answer. The vile Assyrians had been the almighty and domineering ones, and now without some specific, observable knowledge of a real and powerful presence of the Lord in his reign he knew of no place where he could start in remaking his kingdom.

They had been the almighty ones. He therefore decided he would do nothing. Absolutely nothing until a complete plan of action came to him from their Lord God. Until then, he would see nobody. He would not see his elders. He would not see his priests. He would not buy reports from Jamil. He would not see Isaiah. He would not see his mother.

And after a little while that night, he would not see his wife again until some complete plan had come.

*

\> \> \> * \< \< \<

*

Between the public half of the winter home and his own private living quarters was a large, central courtyard with the open air roof. Often in his reign, and in the reigns of many of the former rulers of Judah, that courtyard had been the place of many festive occasions in the late autumn and early winter.

Nevertheless, no celebration nor entertainment had sounded its mirth and jubilation within that central courtyard during the last nine weeks. No cooking had been done in the large, open-fire pit, nor in the nearby stone oven, and none had since it was last done at the end of the previous winter season.

He had no appetite. He had eaten very little in the nine weeks. What few meals he did eat were cooked on a small metal brazier and brought on it to his room. He lay sick this evening upon his bed. Though it had not yet been confirmed, he was near death. His sickness was caused by an aggressive, highly infectious boil, not by his fast in anyway.

This evening was the last evening of the ninth week. It was a cold evening. Outside, that is.

The fire blazed in the fireplace in his bedchamber, and he

was comfortably warm in the room. He was thankful for the warmth, but it really did not matter. Nothing had seemed to really matter for the last nine weeks since the Assyrians had invaded his city...and had taken Hannah.

He lay there thinking about it. He had seen his wife once. Exactly nine weeks before, late on the same evening that the empire's vanguard had left. Besides her, he had remained true to his objective of not seeing his mother nor his elders nor any underlords. Also since he had moved he had not entertained a single caller. And his present plan, if he survived the excruciating pain of that growing boil, was to remain steadfast in seeing no one for months to come.

Thinking upon his painful illness as an extension of all those miseries he suffered under the Rabshakeh and his murdering gang of uncaring thieves, he was brought face to face again with the angry obsession which had captivated his mind for those last nine weeks: why had his Lord God Almighty not work on his behalf during any of that day's terrifying events? As with his fight with the large, pus-filled boil, not once in all his calling out to his Lord did the Creator of the heavens and the earth respond on his behalf. Not once. He could not handle it.

Therefore he earnestly hoped that the painful boil would bring his death this night while he was asleep.

*

\>\>\> * <<<

*

Of course, long before he would be able to sleep, he would again lay feasting upon the melancholy rantings of another righteous man who cried out in despair when *his body* was also overrun with boils and when he *also* could not get their

Tom Steinbach

Lord God to respond to any of his requests.

Dear old Job—evening after evening, Job was there in the room with him as he pulled out the old parchment scrolls— 'The earth is given into the hands of the wicked,' Job miserably moaned in their nation's most famous sacred writings dealing with pain and unjust, unright, unfathomable happenings in one's life. 'The earth is given into the hands of the wicked.' Indeed, Hezekiah had discovered the full extent of that grave truth: the powers over the earth *had been* given into the hands of the wicked.

Also from Job's collections: 'The Lord covers the faces of the judges. If not, where and who is He?' He had been forced to agree...and ask right along with Job. Even as he completely agreed with the ailing patriarch when he complained: 'The Lord God is not a man as I am, that I should talk with Him and that we should come together in judgment. Neither is there any daysman between us that might lay his hand upon us both.'

Hezekiah thoroughly agreed with his reading partner-in-pain: that it would be wonderful to know of someone who could lay his hand upon his weary shoulder, and could also lay his hand upon their Lord's shoulder. Somebody who could talk to both of them as intimate friends. He knew he needed that someone. Then, possibly he could know for certain if their Lord God was really real. And, if He was, then he would know for sure that the Lord indeed did dwell in their sacred temple behind the many veils which hung in there. If he had that daysman who could commune with both him and the Lord, then he could also ask that one to petition their Lord as to why He treated his nation as He did when the vile Assyrians came into his land and into his city. And, why the Lord never answered any of his pleas.

He thought of Zachariah, his grandfather, his mother's father. He certainly was the closest he could think of who could have been a kind of daysman for him. One who could stand between him and the Lord. But he was dead: had been for some time. Now Isaiah, Judah's resident spokesman for their Lord, was the closest he had to Job's concept of a daysman. However, that prophet had never laid a hand on his shoulder...and he was certain that he had never laid a hand upon their Lord God's shoulder either. No matter how in touch with their Lord Isaiah was, Hezekiah was certain that he never had that intimate relationship with the Lord that Job must have had in mind when he pleaded for a daysman.

He leaned over and grabbed the well-worn scroll which was next to his bed. Rolling through it, he found what he wanted. He read of Job's groans as if the words were his own: 'My soul is weary of my life. Therefore I will say unto my God, do not condemn me; show me whereof You contend with me.' "Job, my friend in much pain, I have prayed those exact words of yours hundreds of times in the last nine weeks." he said aloud as he lay there in greater pain this night. "Show me, Lord, whereof You contend with me. My Lord, show me whereof You contend with me. Sho—" Wringing, wrenching weeping overcame him down deep within his being.

Lying there in his galling pain, weeping openly because of the unjustness of his sufferings, both public and private, he knew all too well that it was as a righteous being that his partner in pain had called out his afflicted heart's pleas to their Lord. Equally so, at least, he believed it was equally so, it was certainly as a righteous ruler that he wanted to know why the Lord was contending so fiercely against him and his reign.

'You know that I am not wicked; and yet none can deliver me out of Your hand,' Job had pleaded in the scroll. 'Your hands have made me and have fashioned me round about; and yet You are destroying me.' Why, Lord? Why did You treat Job in that manner? Why are You treating me in that manner?

Tears, far beyond the counting of the stars, which had freely fallen down his cheeks the last nine weeks, were once again freely falling down upon his chest. Falling as they had done nearly every day and night during his long soul-searching hours since the awful vanguard left.

'Remember, I beseech You, O Lord, that You have made me as the clay; and, that You are bringing me to the dust again,' were Job's next words—words which forced Hezekiah to turn and crush his face into his pillow.

"Why did You not remember that I too am made of clay? I know I am the king," he cried. "I know that I am the leader of these Your chosen people, but I hurt, Lord. I hurt deeply. Do You not understand that? And, like Job, I cannot handle all the galling, ripping pain You are continually bringing my way. I cannot handle being brought to the dust again."

His body quivered with inner convulsions:with blows delivered as crushing wave after crushing wave of grieving sorrows cried out within his being.

"I cannot, Lord," he cried aloud. "I simply cannot."

Dedicated, beautiful, exquisite, ever-giving, never-taking, noble, superb Hannah would not have thought much of my masculinity tonight, he thought as he clung his arms tightly around the pillow that lay the closest to him, and wished with all his might that somehow it could be her.

He pulled its substance as close as he could, and hugged it as hard as he could. He smothered it with kisses. With kisses which that beautiful, magnificent one had begged from him that wonderful night nine weeks before.

Overcome with a deep passion for the pillow—for the one which that pillow was the substitution for—he wished with all his might that somehow he could bring Hannah back. In his melancholy misery and his introspection, he hungered with all his heart that somehow the flaming, enlarged, hurting boil would immediately go away. Or that it would immediately take his life. As with so many in that woeful mood, he wondered for what purpose did he have to live?

After sleeping for awhile, he awoke and found his arms still wrapped tightly around the pillow. He also knew that it was in the middle of the night. At least, that it was sometime in the darkest part of the night.

He called his chief chamberlain.

Mehujael came immediately and relighted the oil lamp near his bed. He then fetched him something warm to drink. Next, Mehujael called some maidservants to remove the sodden dressing from Hezekiah's abscessed boil. They washed the corrupted area with hot towels, being extremely careful not to burst the boil and send its poisons throughout his body. They then dried the area and dressed it once again.

When they were done, Mehujael brought something more to drink. Strong drink would probably have been the choice of most rulers in Hezekiah's painful condition, but his ruler had never drunk strong drink and Mehujael was certain that his ruler would not begin in the state he was in. Even if it was being strongly prescribed for him. He then helped Hezekiah lean forward, so that he could puff up his pillows for him.

Afterwards he had placed the scrolls and the pouch on the bed close to him once again. Looking around, he then made ready to leave. At which point Hezekiah asked him to look in on him in the next watch again since the boil was extremely painful, the worse it had ever been.

Soon after Mehujael left, Hezekiah had the well-worn parchment opened once again and was reading words directed toward the Lord which touched him as potently as could any strong drink:'You hunt me as a fierce lion. You increase Your indignation upon me. Why then have You brought me forth out of the womb? Oh, that I had given up the ghost, and no eye had seen me! I should have been as though I had not been. I should have been carried from the womb to the grave.'

This says it all! You have increased Your indignation upon me; why then, have You brought me forth out of the womb?

Why then? I could not have stated my plight any clearer. For years I had felt I had been used by You to turn our nation around. Then...when You had the grand opportunity to present Yourself in all Your might and punish the wicked Assyrians... what did You do? What did you do? You did nothing. You stayed hidden safely away with Isaiah behind his closed door!

Or You hid safely behind the linen veils in Your temple with the golden cherubim upon the mercy seat!

Or You hid safely up there in Your Heavens with Your living cherubims all around worshipping You! Wherever and with whomever You remained hidden and silent, and offered none of Your help to me and my city whatever! Thus, my wish is Job's weeping wish: 'I should have been carried from the womb straight to the grave.' That is the cry of my heart!

Humiliation, helplessness, rejection and failure are all You have dealt toward my people and me since this summer's warring season began. In Job's case, Your enemy, Satan, came before You requesting permission to destroy your righteous servant. With me, Satan came right through our main gate in the person of one of the most wicked, arrogant and conceited murderers that we have ever met. Surely You could have said no to that evil one that time.

But, instead, once again You sat back and did not come to Your righteous servant's aid. He shook his head in disbelief and heavy grief. When he looked back down at the scroll, staring him in the face was the sorrowful cry of his heart: *'Oh that my grief were thoroughly weighed and my calamity laid in the balances together. It would be heavier than the sands of the sea. Your arrows are within me. Your terrors are set in array against me. Oh, that I might have my request, and that You would grant me the thing that I desperately long for! Even that it would please You to destroy me, that You would let loose Your hand and cut me off!'*

"Lord, You completely turned Your back on Job's requests

and especially upon that last request; and You have been silent to all my requests this whole summer. In the dead of this night I ask You to grant me that same request. I ask that You destroy me. That You loose Your hand from me. That You cut me off from the living before I wake again. Please, do it tonight."

*

\>>> * <<<

*

It was with great disappointment that he opened his eyes again before morning light. His sleep had been very fitful. He was still alive and the inflamed boil seemed more than twice as large and as painful as ever. Having hoped to cease existing during the night, when he awoke he was crushed.

Why could he not just be cut off with no further pain? Why did he have to suffer through another day?

Clearly his Lord knew that he did not want to live without Hannah and that he did not want to die a death that was long and drawn out. Why did he seem destined to live neither in pleasure nor in glory, nor to die in just plain peace.

"You have not answered my other pleadings all summer, nor this one...but...from the way I feel this morning, this one You have at least considered," he complained aloud in his misery. "Surely You know that I am in excruciating pain, and, You must realize that my illness is twice as close to ending me as it was yesterday. I need to ask of You: Why then did You not answer my request in my sleep? Am I that wrong in Your sight? Am I *that* vile?"

Later, having called for Mehujael, he requested something warm to drink, and for him to regather his scrolls which had fallen off the bed and were lying scattered on the floor. When the drink had been brought and the leather pouch of scrolls placed once again so that he could reach it, he unrolled a different lengthily parchment of Job.

Running his fingers across the very familiar words, he stopped when his eyes alighted upon the portion that had always especially angered him: Bildad's jarring accusation against the righteousness of Job. Bildad and his friends had originally come to counsel Job as companions and friends of this godly man when they had heard of all the sorrows he had encountered. Therefore, they arrived ready to console and uplift him. But when they saw the horrible state of the pilferage, deaths and destruction plus the sorry state Job was in himself physically, they were not even able to say one word for seven days.

Unbelievably, they then turned an about face from their planned goal of comforting and consoling, and unmercifully scandalized him as the most despicable sinful hypocrite in the country. His great losses, and his present exceedingly painful condition, proving his grave sinfulness absolutely to them...they further denigrated him, because he remained adamant in his claims that he had retained his righteousness and in that he had done nothing wrong to precipitate all the judgments which had befallen him. Eliphaz, one of the friends, was first to undertake their task of getting him to confess to them of his great transgressions, and of his secret iniquities, believing that if he confessed to having actually participated in wrong living: forgiveness and restoration could then be given to him. 'Behold, you have instructed many and you have strengthened the weak hands. Your words have upheld them that were falling and you have strengthened the feeble knees. But now trouble is come upon you and you are fainting. It is touching you, and you are troubled. Remember, Job, who ever perished being innocent? Or where were the righteous ever cut off? The righteous and the innocent never were. Even as you and I have seen, they that plow iniquity and sow wickedness reap the same. By the silent blast of God they perish and by the breath of His nostrils they are ever consumed.'

It certainly did not take much creativeness, Hezekiah thought, for that friend, beholding Job's consumed, slumped frame, to come up with his last two phrases. His arguments sounded so right to him, but he was firmly rebuked by Job as one who was bringing the false accusations of one who did not know the correct situation. 'Teach me, and, cause me to understand, wherein I have done any iniquity. How forceful are right words, I agree! But what does your arguing reprove? Look at me. It should be evident if I lie unto you! I have not sinned. That is my confession! I have not done any iniquity.'

Bildad, following Eliphaz when he was finished, did not accept Job's statement either, for he also agreed that their time-honored principle demanded: that massive judgment and destruction from the Lord meant massive iniquity had been done by the one receiving the excessive judgment.

Hezekiah broke his reading, thinking: I have also always lived by that rule before this summer. If I wanted to be blessed by the Lord, I always agreed that I had better live righteously unto Him. Now that I have suffered through that vanguard's bloodshedding and devastating visitation into my nation and into my own reign and my own life, I am now no longer able to make the principle so cut and dry. How can I? Like Job, *righteous* Job, I now have to look at massive judgments much differently...for, I have tried to live righteously before Him, *and*, I certainly have received massive destruction from our Lord God. He turned back to his reading.

'Job,' Bildad spoke, 'if you were pure and upright, surely our Lord God would now awaken for you and would make the habitation of your righteousness prosperous. And though your beginning was small yet your latter end should greatly increase.' *Though your beginning was small!*—does their

127

friend Bildad not know how great Job's possessions had been! *Though your beginning was small!*—that is the trouble with cut and dried ideas! Our scrolls tell us that in the beginning Job was the greatest of all the men of the east in wealth.

'Can rush grow without mire?' continued Bildad. 'Can the flag grow without water? While it is yet in its greenness and not cut down, it will wither before any herb. So are the paths of all that forget God.'

The words made Hezekiah more angry. Job was not like that. Surely they did not know of the first portion of the story and of the Lord's evaluation of Job, which He had candidly offered to His chief enemy, to Satan, when He had said, 'Have you considered My servant Job, that there is no one like him in the earth, a perfect and an upright man, one that fears Me and eschews evil.' Lord, Why did You allow these to continue to strike him without mercy with their harsh, cutting words?

I read Job's words to them, words obviously spoken by one crushed by grief: 'How long will you vex my soul and break me in pieces with words? I cry out of wrong by you, but I am not heard. I cry aloud, but there is no judgment. He has fenced up my way that I cannot pass and He has set darkness in my paths. He has stripped me of all my glory and He has taken the crown from my head.'

Laying the scroll in his lap, he noted the fierce increase of intense pain associated with the added swelling of the boil and of the enlarged tender area around it, and repeated the last lines as being exactly what the Lord had done to him. 'He has set darkness in my paths. He has stripped me of all my glory and He has taken the crown from my head.'

Why have You crushed Job and me so? The question still had no answer. He looked toward the window and still could not see any hint outside that morning was ready to dawn. Blackness still reigned supreme. Nevertheless, he decided, then and there, what he would do the moment the sun had risen high enough to be seen over the hills to the east.

*

> > > * < < <

*

Still feeling content with that idea an hour or two later, he opened the scroll again and read Job's next complaint: 'The Lord has kindled His wrath against me and He counts me as one of His enemies.' Lord, I feel exactly like that. That it is I, and not the treacherous Assyrians, who is Your enemy. Why have You counted me as such? 'Have pity upon me, have pity upon me, O ye my friends.' Job, I understand exactly! If I felt I had one who would understand what our Lord has done to me this summer, I would quickly have him brought into my presence. Tears formed anew when he thought that Hannah could have, and should have, been that sympathizing friend.

'Have pity upon me, have pity upon me, O ye my friends, for the hand of God has touched my flesh.' Job, why did He strike both of us first with major widespread destruction, and then with a coming against our bodies with boils? Why would He do that to us? Why Job?

In a couple hours he awoke again. The pus-filled swelling was much larger. The pain, exceedingly great. The sunlight, apparent everywhere, had conquered the reigning blackness. The sun itself would soon rise over the hill to the east.

Though he had long ago decided that he would never call anyone again into this winter house, his new decision was to ask Mehujael to go into the city and tell Isaiah, their spokesman for the Lord, of his greatly lessening condition and ask him to come immediately to the winter house.

With the exciting anticipation of seeing another person

129

again, came the thought of his last night in the palace, to the last time he had any visitor...to the night his wife Hephzibah came into his bedchamber.

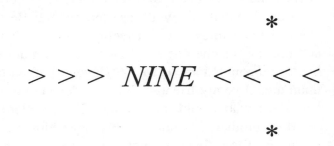

*

\> \> \> *NINE* \< \< \< \<

*

He had already decided to see no one for a long time; however, because her daughters had been stolen from her, he had given Hephzibah his permission to come and see him.

Exactly two hours after sunset she had come into his room.

Possibly because both she and he had been hurting so, being together had been an extremely wonderful time for each of them—a rare experience for them in the last few years.

As they had lain nestled together afterwards and all the other small talk was exhausted, she asked of the new maiden. "You had a special relationship with the maiden, my lord?"

"Yes, a very special one. But unfortunately also a very

130

short one," he had answered honestly, keeping her cradled in his arm be- side him. "I never knew her, I had only met her last evening, but she was the maiden who helped me through those extremely troubling hours of the evening."

"I wish I would have been the one you had called."

"Hephzibah, I needed someone who could relax me and accept me as I am."

"And a new maiden could do that?"

"How could I have known? I had not planned on seeing anybody. But Mehujael came into my room and said a new maiden was ready to be presented to me."

"I would have come."

"Hephzibah, very seldom has being with you been a relaxed time for us."

"But—"

"Last night especially you would never have accepted—"

"How can you say that?" she had said, hurt. "I have come unto you tonight."

"I am glad that you came."

"My lord, you are the only one who can help me make it through this troubling night."

He thought again of their daughters being taken and said, "If I can, I will, though I am very drained myself."

"You can. You have already. I only wish you had called for me last evening." When he said nothing, she cuddled closer and said, "I wish we spent more nights together."

"We could, Hephzibah. I would treasure having compatible times with you. However, you have had your daughters to take your time and I have had all my other—"

"What was her name?"

"The maiden's?"

"Yes."

"Hannah."

"You would have known her soon?"

"Tonight."

"Tonight?"

"Hephzibah, she is gone. If you had been the one who meant so much to me last evening, the Assyrian would have sought you out and would have found you and you would be gone tonight."

"And you would have had your Hannah tonight," she said sulkingly—her way of implying he really did not want to be with her.

Disregarding her words, he said, "She was a lovely virgin who was extremely well trained in pleasing her monarch. It grieves me greatly that such a lovely and understanding one could be carried away to a far land to experience the torture of that Goliath and the rest of those uncircumcised heathen."

"You will miss her?"

"She was very special. Very special."

"I still do not understand, my lord. 'Woman' was made for man, not 'women'. How can you justify—"

"You do understand that David and most of our forefathers had more than one wife and that they often had a number of maidens or concubines?"

"Yes, they did, my lord; but I do not understand how you could continue the practice of multiplying wives yourself?"

"Hephzibah, the practice of our kings multiplying wives and maidens began long before I knew you. Let us just be thankful that I still have you."

She did not rebuke him further at that moment but he felt her body stiffen next to him. That, and her silence, letting him know that she had not believed that he had meant what he had just said. He said no more.

When he did speak again, he spoke on the subject that he truly wanted to share with her:

"I would not even have you now if Mother had not torn you away from the children as they were about to be taken and hid you away with her. Honestly, Hephzibah, I am very thankful that it was you that Mother saved."

Her tenseness did not abate.

"I have heard about that look you gave the young girl from the platform," she complained, when she finally spoke. "Have you ever given me one like that?"

"As I said earlier, she has been the most special maiden to ever come into my bedchamber. She treated me more graciously than any woman I have ever been with. I never knew her, but, she would have easily become my favorite."

"How can you tell me that?"

"Hephzibah, I am hurting too."

She turned away from him, though staying next to him.

"I am truly grieving, Hephzibah. I did not want to see anyone tonight. If you had not lost your daughters—"

"Why do you keep saying *your* daughters?"

"Hephzibah, this is what you have always done with me. You do not allow me to share my heart and my needs with you. You are so, so jealous, so self-possessed. I am grieving over our daughters. I just was emphasizing why I knew you would be hurting: cause they are your daughters. You are the one who carried them You are the one who gave birth to them. You are the one who nursed them. And you are the one who has raised them. I am grieving over them. I am also grieving over the loss of all my women, and of all my dancers and musicians, but my grieving over the maiden is much deeper. No one has ever cared for me like she did."

"No one? How can you—"

"No one, Hephzibah. If you had been taken I would be grieving—deeply grieving—also over you. I would have been. I am grieving down deep, please understand that and allow me the right to answer your questions truthfully out of my heart."

"What did you say her name was?"

"Hannah."

133

"Hannah," she repeated slowly.

"Hannah. I will name our next daughter after her."

"Our nex—"

"I told you, I never knew her!"

"But our—"

"Hephzibah, in one evening with her, she represented to me the greatest ideal relationship that our Israelite peoples should have with their king."

"I venture she did!"

"I told you, I never knew her."

"But you would have!"

"Oh, most assuredly I would have. Tonight. And I have no doubt but that she would have been supreme."

"Supreme!" she mimicked.

"Nevertheless," he continued, not allowing her jealousy to get into his time of truth-telling, "I did not know her last evening—and our evening was still supreme."

"More supreme than any with me?"

"Tonight with you was very wonderful, but look at you now. You are simply too full of jealousy or something to maintain a supreme time with me for the entire evening."

He felt her body literally cooling. He probably should have quit, but the only way he felt he knew as to how to work through the problem with her was to keep talking about it.

"My time with her was supreme. It was far beyond description, and the time with her will remain stronger in my memory because we never knew each other." He paused.

He earnestly hoped that he had stated his feelings toward Hannah in a way that she would understand. He also was hoping Hephzibah would say something. When she did not, he added with a heartfelt finality, "Hannah will always be a very wonderful, very beautiful, very obedient daughter to me."

"Daughter!—she came in unto you, my lord!"

"Yes, in willing obedience," he said softly.

"In...willing...obedience!" she mimicked, her hatred overwhelming her. Sitting up, and not caring if her rising jealousy showed or not, she spat out, "How can you claim she was so perfect? You only saw her one evening! You never had the opportunity to see her when her monthly depressions hit!"

"I do not believe they would ever hit her."

He had answered her quietly, he had remained calm. He had not meant to, seriously he had not meant to, however, he realized that he had made her twice as angry.

"You never had a chance to see her during her hard time of her month! You only saw her when she was...was—"

"I have had many, many maidens in my house and I know that not every woman has those depressing lows as extremely low down as you do, Hephzibah."

Continuing her thought as if she had not heard him at all, she screamed, "—when she was...was...was riding high! Yes! When she was riding high and happy! Any woman can be excited and charm you when she is riding hig—"

He slapped her hard across her cheek with the back of his hand and commanded her that any more such talk and shouting would force him to order her from his room!

"I am sorry!—but you make me so angry when you start rattling about all these young girls who you see for the first time and you think that they are angels sent from Heaven."

"I have never thought that all of them were angels given to me from Heaven."

"Not *all* of them!" she again mimicked. She was burning with hurt and hatred.

"Hephzibah, remember that this has been an extremely trying day for both of us. Either calm down or leave."

It was several minutes before either of them spoke again. She settled down onto his arm, though coldly and without any affection. Thinking back upon it, he remembered that as the total silence continued between them that there did arrive the semblance of peace, that it had once again entered the room.

He remembered that her voice was tender and reserved when she began speaking again. Tender and reserved...still, he knew she was going to try to prove her right to be jealous and to prove her right to allow their time together to drift into any kind of fight or discussion—good or bad, quiet or vicious— rather than allow it to flow into a really enjoyable time for the two of them: a time relegated to love and tenderness only.

"Back to your many wives, my lord," she began tenderly, though he knew that she was really forging ahead with her argument. "Now that all your young maidens have been taken, are you going to fill that house of women again?"

"That is no subject to talk about tonight, Hephzibah. All the maidens in that house are trained that evenings are the time to please one's monarch, not the time to get into discussions and fights with their monarch. Either you, as my wife, also learn that or we will return to what we had before when I would not ask you to come into my presence in the evening."

"It needs to be talke—"

"I thought you were concerned about losing our daughters and wanting me near to comfort you."

"I am and I do. I have been grieving all day. And I did and do want to be here so you can comfort me, my lord. But, with pain, I have accepted that we will never see them again. That will not be possible. So, if we never see them again, I want to have you alone just for me, my lord. I ask you, I entreat you, keep that horrible house behind our palace empty."

"That is up to—"

"No, my lord, it is up to you! It is a decision that you alone can make."

"Our nation has always had—"

"But our nation and its leaders have done lots of things which you have stopped following as a national practice now that you are our leader and now that you have put into action many of your wise reforms."

She has thought this through, I only wish she would have spent as much time and energy in thinking through how to love and treat me as a husband, he remembered wearily thinking that evening nine weeks before.

"You must have spent the first portion of this evening talking with my mother," he said, feeling extremely famished.

"I have spent a goodly portion of many evenings speaking about a number of topics with your mother. They have been good evenings. But even more so, I have had many nights alone to think it through, my lord."

"Yes, I suppose you have," he agreed, and then thought that he had wished his mother would have talked at great lengths with her on her truly becoming a loving wife.

"In that second complete giving of the law, Moses was directed to lay down a very specific commandment concerning our kings," she said, overriding his thought.

"I know the command."

"Since you are not obeying it, I think I should at least state it to you. Before, when everything was going well and you had all your women, you probably would not have listened."

"That is not true."

Arguments can go on forever, he had thought. If only you were willing to forego your pestering arguments, Hephzibah, and if only you were willing to learn, as that maiden had, the art of becoming a truly loving person.

"You can say that it is not true now, I still truly believe it is," she had pushed on lying next to him, and not realizing at all that she was nailing the doors between them shut with long spikes, and that it would remain closed for at least nine weeks. "And you may not want to listen to me now, but it is for your own walk with the Lord that I bring that horrible house up."

"For my own walk—"

"Yes, for your own walk with the Lord. Now that all your

women have been taken, obviously I hope that you and I can live as husband and wife like any other family in our nation."

"You know nothing of being a wife, Hephzibah."

"Nothing?"

"You know what I mean. Your training has taught you how to be a mother; *my mother*, I am afraid. Your amorous feeling for me has never lasted long. It never has, you know that. And as soon as you are carrying our next child, you would not—"

"I would not cuddle next to you?"

"Oh, you would cuddle next to me, but not the way I would like you to. And surely not the way you would if you were yet hoping to become with child."

"That is not fair."

"But it is true. And what is true, should be fair. Once I gave you your first daughter, Hephzibah, you did not go a month without screaming your head off at me. There has to be another Hannah out there who will not rush into screaming whenever depressions engulf her mind and body. There simply must be another."

"You are unfair!"

"There you go screaming again, Hephzibah. You will not let me talk to you. You will not."

"You fill that house again, and the Lord will bring back those murderers!"

"There you go, screaming and changing the subjec—"

"It is wrong! Evil! Totally wrong for you to commit adultery with every young virgin your servants strip away from her home and parents!"

"It is not adul—"

"It most certainly is!"

"Not when my wife will not—"

"There *you* go! Blaming me again for your lustful—"

"It is not lust! It is—"

"It is what?"

"It is one of the nicest activities that can pass between a man and his w—"

"His what? His wife or his women?"

"I suppose the greatest would be with one's wife, but you have never—"

"There you go again! Blaming me for your lack of control! Now that the Lord has taken away your hou—"

"The Lord did absolutely *nothing* today! The Rabshakeh took my maidens away!"

The raging anger, surging through his body, had become greater than that within her...and she apparently realized it. Surprising even herself, she said more tenderly, "I hate him also. But could not our Lord God have desired your maidens gone so that you could, before your own people, start again: by showing them that you will obey all of the commandments of our Lord. Especially, those which are exclusively directed to our nation's rulers?"

If that was true that he should get rid of his house of women, he had thought back then in his anger, why did his Lord have a heavenly angel brought into his bedchamber—on the very last night before He was going to force him to obey that command? Why the most beautiful maiden he had ever set his eyes upon? Why the most giving he had ever encountered? Why the very lovely one named Hannah?

"Is it good for you kings to attempt to get our people to only change *their* disobedience into obedience?" she continued tenderly, but also with a sound that seemed to attempt to rule over him with some kind of motherly control again.

"Must you not also chang—"

"Hephzibah, your arguments may be good but you are not talking to your daughters. One of our main problems is that you have never learned to be a wife, my wife. What is it that you are now trying to insinuate? That I, as king, only want others under me to change their styles of living? How can you imply that...when, of all men in our nation, I have sought— almost single-handedly, I might add—to bring about a multitude of reforms and even as I have sought to bring this country of ours back to a true worship of the Lord?"

That time it was he who pulled his arm out from under her head and who turned away from her.

He remembered thinking then that at that moment she had almost treated him as a wife: when she moved tenderly toward him after he had turned from her. Nevertheless, the tone of the beginning of her next statement had a much different quality written all over it as he interpreted it, causing her loving actions and her words not to mesh in the least.

"My lord, I am extremely thankful for all the major nationwide reforms you have enforced upon our people and I stand fully behind those refor—"

He had wanted no more of her presence that night!

Throwing the sheets back, storming out of the bed, crossing the room, he yelled at her, "Yes, I also am thankful that I have done all those 'major nationwide' reforms!"— emphasizing her voice's sarcastic tone, and the insinuation that they were not really that big and major, even if she might have accepted that those reforms were nationwide. "I have instituted them, and I am very proud of each one! Very, very, proud of them, Hephzibah! When are you ever going to look at the reforms and see all that I have done through those reforms in righting the multitude of wrongs in this place?"

"I ha—"

"No, you have not! All you ever look at is one little command which not one single one of our monarchs has ever obeyed! You are not willing to trust me! You do not treat me as a wife! You want to treat me solely as my mother! And, you want me to look only at that one commandment!"

"I do not feel that I treat you as a moth—"

"You have always treated me as my mother!"

"That is not true."

"Then why are you continually bringing up...get out!—Get out! I do not want to see you again!"

"But, my lord—"

"GET OUT!"

At that moment he had not given her any more chance to explain herself as he had burst through the double doors out onto his roof garden. Once on the far side of the garden, he determined that he would not enter his bedchamber again until he was certain that she was indeed gone. Absolutely certain. When he had gone back in, she had indeed gone.

He had not seen her nor any other visitor since in either that palace or in the winter house, he thought, as he wondered how long Isaiah would take before he came to tell him if the Lord was going to bring a healing to the enlarged boil or not.

He had not seen Hephzibah since then...but he had thought long and hard on what she had said that night. Long and hard and often. And as he had just proven again, he still could act out the entire dreadful scene by heart. He was certain that she had not, but, he only wished that his wife had also been thinking long and hard and often upon what he had said.

In the end though...he thought as he dozed off again... neither of them would probably ever cause either partner to change from his or her set ways.

When he came to again the pain from the boil was so great that Job's words also came clearly into his mind, 'What is my strength, that I should hope? And what is mine end, that I should prolong my life?'

A thought also came clearly to his mind that Hephzibah had not been the last one he had seen and conversed with before he came to the winter house. Lying there in exceedingly great misery, waiting ironically for some encouraging word

141

from Isaiah, he thought about the other one he had seen the morning he had moved from the palace to the winter house.

*

> > > *TEN* < < < <

*

Nine weeks before and long before early light on that far away morning, their city's resident spokesman for the Lord had come out of his house.

It was the first time the sixty-two year old prophet had gone through the city since the word had come that the empire's vanguard had initiated their move toward Jerusalem from down in the foothills.

Isaiah had been very solemn as he walked through the ravished bazaar area of the city. Even at that early hour many of their merchants had already risen to begin repairing and cleaning up their wrecked and torn stalls: hoping to have at least some of them ready for life as usual once again, now that the enemy was gone. A large number of the badly broken stalls and carts, and nearly all of their cloth awnings, appeared damaged beyond repair.

As Isaiah traversed the capital, he remembered how certain his ears had been the long day before that the vanguard's chariots and horses were going to burst right into and through his house. Thus he walked slowly, taking it all in.

When he reached the temple area and began ascending the stairs leading into the large inner court which surrounded the temple, he could not yet see the morning sun which was still behind the olive-tree-covered hills to the east, but its rays were shining upon the high upper porch of the sacred building.

By design, the exceedingly tall porch of their temple received the day's very first rays into the city every morning. He paused, and gazed upon the brilliance of those precious stones embedded in the white limestone and upon the brilliance of the white limestone itself—the limestone that eighty thousand hewers in the mountains made ready in Solomon's day so that neither hammer nor axe nor any tool of iron would be heard in the construction of the house or in its foundation or in the various courtyards. In the brightness of that morning sunlight he allowed himself to be reminded once again that within their one building in all the earth dwelt the Glory of the Lord God, the Creator of Heaven and Earth.

The gold-stripped twin pillars and doors surprised him greatly though and looked naked, humbled, without their gold overlay. That did not lessen his esteem for the building any, of course. Instead he thought, as he had often in the past and as he knew it had been his purpose in coming that morning, back to the vision he had seen of their Lord in the year that Uzziah died and in the day Uzziah's son, Jotham, ascended up onto the throne of Judah. Back then he had also been standing in the same courtyard, yet much closer to the magnificent temple.

He walked toward that place where he had stood that incredible morning forty-odd years before. On the way there he thought, I saw our Lord God sitting high above the temple upon a throne encircled within a brilliant rainbow. Earlier I had watched Him descend out of the high heavens above on that fiery throne which looked like a great cloud of dazzling fire infolding itself. It was bright! It was living! It was pulsating! My first wonder back then, when the flaming, self-existing sphere had still been a small speck far off in the distant sky, was if it just could have been a fiery chariot like that one upon which our prophet Elijah had been taken up from the earth. The larger the fiery ball loomed as it grew closer, if it was indeed a flaming, heavenly chariot, I wondered for whom was the chariot coming? Instead of it being a fiery chariot, however, I discovered that it was the magnificent, cherubim-carried, celestial throne bringing our Lord down to this His chosen dwelling place of all the earth. Being brought back because the leprous-judgment of Uzziah had finally come to its end with his death and Jothan, his son, was that day assuming the throne...though he had been the ruling leader of our nation since the leper incident.

As he walked, he smiled about how wrongfully he had thought at the time that everyone in the packed capital was also watching the heavenly spectacle right along with him.

He stopped midway to the brazen altar and continued to reminisce...the fire-infolding cloud stopped above the colossal porch of the temple so that it was high above the temple's main structure, 'high and lifted up' was how he liked to refer to it whenever he talked about it. It had remained stationary in the air. Hovering right up there, he thought, right there in midair—it was not resting upon the temple at all. It was much larger than a fiery chariot would have been.

It was very large. The Lord Himself was upon its throne as the appearance of a man sitting. The color of His being was the color of amber...as the appearance of the fire round about within it. The throne and the Lord's being had the appearance of fire and that brightness round about the throne had the appearance of a bow on the day of a rain. Seraphims attending the Lord flew around the throne in midair. An innumerable host of angels filled the panorama above and around the throne and were continually singing praises unto the Lord. The scene within the cloud just continued to increase unbelievably and such singing! Such glorious singing! It was more than singing. It was the most solemn warning to all who would listen:

Holy! Holy! Holy! This place is now holy for the Lord of hosts, He Who is holiness itself, is present!

Isaiah's eyes had been wide open that first day, taking in all that they could, but on that morning after the Assyrians had left, he had allowed his eyes to shut as he was looking up so he could more clearly recall the entire moving scene.

Also, on that latter morning, he had tilted his head up as if he was still looking up and actually seeing his God's glorious being and the ever-radiating throne again. His eyes still shut, his mind re-created the singing in his memory: 'Holy! Holy! Holy! Holy is the Lord of hosts'

Swaying with the melody in his long-flowing white robe, he let the celestial, supernatural singing of that glorious morning surge through his mind again, and again, and again:

'Holy! Holy! Holy! Holy is the Lord of hosts. The whole earth is full of His glory.'

*

> > > * < < <

*

He had also left his bedchambers at the breaking of that day's morning, Hezekiah thought...as he tried to put together the events that had brought him and Isaiah together before the temple on that morning. He had gone out onto his roof garden feeling badly about his time with Hephzibah. Very bad, and, very remorseful. Misery, frustration and helplessness had him swamped, and he had felt more than ever that only Hannah could ever help him. He was still very angry with the Lord. He was trying to keep his anger peaceful. It was useless. The night had not produced the desired rest...and the pressing problems of the former day were no less pressing.

All too soon in his morning stroll through the garden he had to admit that his attempt to remain at peace with his Lord God was purely hypocrisy. His Almighty One had not come to his aid and it would probably always anger him. While he miserably attempted to be thankful, those words spoken so exceedingly, and so wonderfully, by Hannah two nights before came drifting into his mind: 'I rose up to open to my beloved...my hands were dripping with myrrh, my fingers with the sweetest smelling myrrh. I opened to my beloved. But my beloved had withdrawn himself...and was gone.'

He paused to think how beautiful Hannah had been when she had stopped with: 'my beloved was gone.' He remembered immediately telling her that the maiden in the story soon had found her beloved again; and, that in the next evening she and he would also be together again. That is what he promised her.

My beloved had withdrawn himself. My beloved was gone. Those had been her words. *He was soon found again.* Had been his. He kicked a bench when he thought how utterly miserably wrong he had been. He had known absolutely that he would not go back on his word to be with her. Nevertheless, he had been miserably wrong because he had not even thought that Hannah herself could have been the one who would be gone.

His anger deepened greatly as he thought that the Lord had not kept her from being stolen away. With tears in his eyes and anger in his heart, he walked. First over to look down at the walled garden his father had built in the southwest corner of the palace. That walk did nothing to lessen any of the fury which had been ignited within him, so he crossed to where he could see the side of the house of rooms attached to the back of his palace which had housed Hannah and his other wives and maidens. Staring at the darkened house in the faintly dawning light, he prayed for her safety. The utter darkness emanating from the house caused him to greatly bemoan his own stupidity in making her known to that pagan. He felt so faint that he had to sit down on one of the solid ivory benches.

Was it possible? Was their glorious forever together gone? Had their forever ended? Soon he was crying aloud: "*Hannah in your hooded garment, if I ever get you back, I will request night after night that you enter my room wearing that wonderful hooded garment.*"

After some more moping, he walked over toward the northeastern edge of the roof and squinted at the temple. Because of the rising sun and because of his angle of viewing, he could hardly tell that the gold overlay was missing from the capital's most famous building's pillars and doors; however, he knew it had not been a dream.

Until enough gold could be gathered for it to be repaired, that would be the most visible reminder that the Rabshakeh would always take *all* of every demand that was required of them. Hezekiah determined he would have to somehow correct the pillars and doors quickly. Even as he would have to fill his house of women again soon, even as his people would have to repair all the damage the horses and chariots did to everything in the streets of the city in their mad dash throughout it. Even as he would have to recruit more musicians. Even as he would have to get more dancers.

It was at that moment, at that very moment, that still looking toward the temple, he had asked himself, '*It must be—* does that not look like our prophet Isaiah over there on the stairs of the altar in the courtyard?' Determining that it was, and that...what better time to meet with him than before the city woke up. He decided to head right over and to talk to him

147

in the temple's courtyard. *Our spokesman for the Lord*, he thought as he rushed back into his chambers and got ready to go out, *you better still be there when I arrive!*

Holy, holy, holy!
Holy is the Lord of hosts
The whole earth is full of His glory'
"Holy, Holy, Holy—"

After singing and swaying to its melody, Isaiah lowered his head, and opened his eyes. The sun's rays had covered more of the face of the temple's porch and had become even more brilliant on it. He interpreted the added brilliance as a smile from his God directed to him. Thanking Him for it, he then looked over toward the brazen altar and toward its ever-burning coals. How could he ever forget?

For it was from those live coals of that altar that one of the attending seraphims on that first morning had picked out a red-hot coal with golden tongs and had flown over to him to touch his lips with that chunk of burning coal.

He shut his eyes again as he thought about that amazing event: he had been so thrilled, and spellbound, with the spectacle of the magnificent throne and then of that archangel flying down so close that when the archangel had gathered the live burning coal and had come toward him to touch his lips with it, before he realized what the heavenly one was going to do it had all happened so quickly he had not had the time to stop it, if he had wanted to. Once he knew it was he himself that the archangel was flying toward, and once he was certain what that angel was going to do with the red-hot coal, he remembered that he had been really certain that it was going to be horribly painful. After all, the heavenly archangel was using a golden tongs—presumably to protect *his* hands!

His lips never felt anything! That was the greatest, the most awesome, the most unusual, remarkable happening he had ever experienced! The searing-hot coal had not burned him at all! Physically, that is. Inwardly, it was another matter. Even before the heavenly one he had felt clean. He had the pure, cleansing knowledge that every sin of his had been purged away...that all his iniquities had been burned away.

He then thought about that great coronation day. Uzziah's son, Jotham, had filled in for many years for his father when the latter had been stricken with leprosy on his forehead near the end of his extremely long reign. Whether their Lord had left the temple when Uzziah sinned, he did not know. But he knew without doubt that at the time of the heavenly visitation: that the Lord and His train once again filled the temple.

"No doubt about it," he said aloud. "That was the only reason for His trip down here to the earth."

He remembered how exceedingly grieved he was when he found out that not another person had seen that remarkable visitation. None had seen the celestial throne. None had heard the heavenly singing of praises. None had even heard him respond aloud when their Lord had asked, 'Whom shall I send? Who will go for Us?' No one had heard him!

He had not shouted his answer out, he had not felt that he had needed to, but certainly...he had thought those present would have responded along with him. Or that, at least, many would have seen the angle fly toward him and have heard him answer aloud. But after he had watched the seraphim return up to the throne, and after he had watched the fiery sphere rise away up into the heavens, he sadly found out that the awesome scene and in particular his own part in it was strictly for his own eyes and ears alone.

Tom Steinbach

How could his nation have missed the sight? How could those in the courtyard that day have missed his reply? 'Here am I! Send me!' But none had heard him. None of that vast multitude who had been there in the city for Jotham's official ascension and for all the festivities which went with it had seen or heard his unique heavenly calling.

If they would have only seen what he had watched. If they had only seen their Lord God in all His amber splendor and would have rehearsed to one another each one's various details of that vision at the many yearly feasts for which they had gathered for the past forty years, he was beyond certain that the lives and attitudes of his people would have been what one would expect of those claiming to be the children of God. He was also certain that no wicked Ahaz would have come and have been able to sit upon their throne for so long, and that they would have remembered Uzziah's sin and leprosy and fall from his place of ruling, and that his peoples would have continually encouraged each other daily to remain faithful to such an all-glorious, all-jealous One. If only they had seen their Lord 'high and lifted up' as he had seen Him...the tragedies of the day before would have never happened.

How could they have?

Standing there, he knew that others had the big 'why' question in their lives, but he still knew that the big one in his own life had to deal with not understanding why his vision of commissioning had been for his eyes and ears only. He still could not understand why that had not been also for the rest of the nation to have seen: everything about the vision had been above any human experience he had ever heard about! Why had not one single other human seen it? It was all too obvious that they had not. All he had to do was look at the shallow and evil lives that his own people were living even after all his preaching and after the vast destruction visited upon them during the summer months. Why? He did not know.

But he knew for himself, that even if no one else had seen the Lord upon the celestial throne, nor had watched the fire infolding within itself, nor had seen the radiating rainbow or the multitude of angels, nor had heard the host of seraphim and cherubim—he had all the proof he needed.

'Go, and tell this people,' had been the Lord's command to him in response to his offering of himself. Go. Go and tell them. Once the thrill of it all had congealed into a destined reality within him, he had been extremely itching to go and tell. He had felt so clean and desirous to go and extremely certain that all his people would be overwhelmingly glad to hear their Lord God's latest words to their nation.

Repent, would be his cry throughout the land, and repent would be what his people would gladly do. He had been so confident that the Lord's command to 'go and tell' would be the easiest, the most enjoyable, the most rewarding task that he would ever be asked to accomplish in his entire life. After all, had he not witnessed the most astonishing sight of his life? He had been so wrong. Even in God's chosen dwelling place, His people did not desire to hear such a vibrant word from Him.

He had ascended the stairs of the huge alter to where he could see its glowing coals. Standing there, staring into the deep red, glowing brilliance of those ever-blazing coals, he reminded himself that subsequent to being touched on the lips with the coal he had asked the archangel about the length of his calling. His question had been a simple: How long, Lord?

How Long? So simple. No, no. Standing there, it seemed so foolish to even think that he had inquired about it. The length of his calling had already been over forty years...and he was certain that if he preached daily against the sins of the people, they would never turn completely away from their greed and lusts. "No wonder," he mused, aloud, "that the archangel had answered my naive question, 'Until the cities be wasted without inhabitant, and the houses without man and the land be utterly destroyed.'"

He would never forget that description. Even the summer's experience had fallen far short of that extremely terrible description. That heavenly utterance had told him that his calling would last a very long time—probably until he died.

When Hezekiah arrived, Isaiah was off the steps and back down upon the pavement of the temple's courtyard. They talked for some time about the destruction the capital had received the day before which Isaiah had surveyed and which Hezekiah had not had the heart nor the interest nor the time to go out and observe. With surging anger pulsating within him, Hezekiah explained to his prophet that he had many times earnestly asked for deliverance, or at least for some sign from their Lord God, on that previous day during all the horrifying, deadly demonstrations. Isaiah's reply to him made him more angry. He said that the Lord had specifically ordered him to not leave his house when the Assyrians were in the city and that their Lord had also ordered him not to pray for the city.

When Isaiah saw his ruler's increased anger, he said— possibly with the goal of appeasing him, though that was not his normal way of dealing with his rulers—"Hezekiah, your father was your opposite. In his days, when my son was still living at home with us, I was sent to give unto your father the message: 'Ask Me for a sign, Ahaz, to prove that I will crush your enemies as I have promised.'"

Having never heard of it before, Hezekiah waited to hear what his non-God-fearing father did with that offer.

"Unlike you, your father would not ask for any sign. He said he would not tempt the Lord."

"Why did you not come out when I sent for you two evenings ago or even yesterday and offer that same offer to me," Hezekiah asked Isaiah, his anger spilling out profusely with his words. "Why were you not allowed to come out?

Why did the Lord refuse to rescue us? He could have easily crushed our enemies!"

"I was ordered to give the sign to your father anyway," Isaiah told him without giving any indication that he would answer any of his monarch's questions. "The sign was that a child would soon be born, and that, before he was old enough to refuse evil and choose good, Rezin of Syria and Pekah of Israel, both avid adversaries of your father's...they would no longer be a threat to him nor to the nation."

Seething, Hezekiah asked, "Why did He not have you bring a similar word to us yesterday?" Isaiah did not reply. Hezekiah calmed a little, and added, "I remember Father saying something about that."

"You should have. It came about exactly as the Lord had spoken it to me. Syria's Rezin and Israel's Pekah were both dead within a couple years."

"Yes, I do remember that. I also remember that Father said that you had better not come gloating over the prediction."

"That was your father for you."

"He was serious."

"Did I go back?"

"No, you did not."

"Hezekiah, now there is something even more important for you. For I had another word for your father at that time. It was this: 'The Lord shall bring upon Judah days that have not come since the day that the kingdom was divided into two. It will come to pass in those days that the Lord will shave Judah as with a razor that was hired by them which are beyond the Euphrates River.'"

"Beyond the Euphrates?"

"Yes."

"By the king of Assyria?"

"By the king of Assyria. Then I added that the army of Assyria would come in large hordes spreading across the land, even into desolate valleys, and caves and thorny places. And that, when they were finally through plundering, if our farmers had a cow and a pair of sheep left...they would be fortunate."

"That few?"

"I also said that it would come to pass in that day that where there were a thousand vines flourishing before there would only be briers and thorns growing after they left."

"This summer's devastation of our cities, and the great losses we suffered yesterday within our city, was the carrying out of that dreadful prophecy you uttered back then in my father's reign," Hezekiah acknowledged.

Isaiah nodded. "I was also impressed to tell him that the soldiers would come with bows and with arrows."

"Bows and arrows."

"Deeply impressed to say that to him."

"Let me do what my father would never do. I acknowledge to you that not only was the devastations you foretold extremely accurate in every detail—though I do not understand why those devastations occurred during my reign instead of during his—but, but, even the specific matter of the bow and arrows had a dreadful significance yesterday."

"More than their just coming with them?"

"Oh, yes, it was much more than that. You should have been out to watch them put on their hideous demonstrations."

"Then perhaps now you will be more anxious to hear the rest of the prophecy."

"There was more?"

He was obviously curious to hear the rest...however, the thought of his spokesman for the Lord having already said that his calling would not end until the more complete destruction had come to Judah...that thought smothered the response, the affirmative response, he was ready to give him. Not believing that he could handle any more dooming prophecies at the moment, he immediately changed the subject.

On his way over to the courtyard that morning, he had teetered back and forth in his desire to mention his women to Isaiah or not—the biggest fear: if he said close the house of women down there might still be another Hannah out there somewhere in their country ready to be found and brought unto him. Nevertheless, he needed to move quickly to a new subject. Therefore he asked, "Now that the house of women has been emptied by the Assyrians—"

"Oh, I had not heard."

"Yes, it was."

Isaiah said nothing else: he would apparently wait for Hezekiah to finish his question. And he, not being certain that he really wanted to go on with that question now that the subject had been changed, he simply added: "Yesterday."

Isaiah still said nothing nor asked anything.

Angry that his prophet waited. Angry that he was being forced to plunge forward with his question, he asked, "Will you seek from the Lord if I should refill the house again as all our rulers have done, or if I should keep it empty and remain only with Hephzibah, my first wife?"

"That is one of the many differences between our present ruler and your father," Isaiah replied. "Ahaz would never have asked the question and you would. Nevertheless, do we need to seek our God's preferences on a matter that He has already made His will so known, so clearly known, to us in His law?"

He remembered exactly what he had thought about Isaiah at that moment: that is precisely what I do not favor about prophets. They speak with such assurance that they are right and their words are to be accepted as absolute finality!

"I can tell you, Hezekiah, your people—our people—will never turn to the Lord, and you will never reach the height of rulership you desire, until you clear your palace of your multitude of young maidens."

"Of my maidens?"

"Yes." Again he did not like the authoritative answer. He argued, "Then why did our God choose Bathsheba's son as the one to follow David? He had scores and scores of offsprings who could have followed him to the throne besides Solomon. And, surely his mother's entrance into the palace was among the most notorious ones that any queen of our nation has had."

"I cannot tell you why, Hezekiah. However, I can tell you that if the Assyrians have rid your house of its women, that it was the Lord Himself who emptied your house."

That was what Hephzibah had said. He thought of Hannah.

What if his servants had not taken her, and not brought her to the palace? Certainly she would still be there at her home at this moment. Or would she be? The Assyrians would have seen her beauty when they took all of his cities. They might have caught her right there in her own hometown. Might have. *Might have!*—what I know for sure is that because my men stole Hannah away from her home and brought her here, she has been taken—not just 'might have' been.

After they had parted company in the temple courtyard that faraway morning, he had stalked up to the front of the temple and inspected the damage done to the doors and pillars.

"Sorry, Boaz," he had said, touching the appropriate pillar on its newly bared surface, "but do not blame me. Blame your resident Lord God. It was He who would not come to your, or to our, aid. Do not ask me why."

When he had opened the large doors, the morning sun, still low off to the east, shined brightly, directly into the front entrance of the temple. The bursting of its light into the room caused the temple's interior to gleam as a highly polished jewel, as hundreds of such gleaming gems! And, even more so, when he opened the inner doors: the vessels, the lamps, the lampstands, the tongs, the palm trees and open flowers, the table for the sacred bread, the carved figures of cherubim in many positions, the snuffers, the utensils, the basins, the censers, the ceiling, walls and floor, their nails and door fittings: everything inside—*everything*—except the veils on the far western wall was made of the finest gold, and everything glistened spectacularly!

At that moment, Hezekiah perceived more clearly than ever that the temple was indeed the personal, opulent, dwelling house of their God alone. In the awe of that sight, he trembled and wished he had not had been so sarcastic with Boaz. The temple was for their Lord God alone. It was His place of residency. His only place of living down here in His entire earthly creation. That truth, however, did not lessen the burning anger which again had begun churning within him toward the One who supposedly dwelt within and toward Isaiah: that One's merciless spokesman. His footsteps did make slow progress, nevertheless, as he proceeded into their Lord God's magnificent, golden home.

Once he had entered into the temple proper and was still alive, he closed the doors behind him and waited for his eyes to adjust to the soft glow of the seven golden lamps. While he was waiting, the overpowering thought of standing in the midst of all that gold caused him to think of that extreme wealth which Solomon once commanded in their land—the vast amounts of gold and riches which mostly went down into Egypt after the division of the kingdom—all the wealth which should have remained within their capital. Because Solomon had sinned so gravely in bringing foreign idol worship into the Lord's chosen land and capital, Pharoah Shishak, a later king of Egypt, had been able to easily march his armies up into the weakened southern nation of Judah after the Lord had ripped the northern ten tribes from their territory. A year after that victory Shishak died and his son, the new Pharoah, recorded the largest giving of riches to the gods and goddesses of Egypt in their history. The gifts included more gold and silver than any of the other Pharoahs ever recorded. Hezekiah had always been certain that most of the gold and silver and wealth the new Pharoah had given to his gods had came from Shishak's plunderings of Solomon's, and of Judah's, vast treasuries.

The weight of gold that came to Solomon in just one year alone in his reign was six hundred and sixty six talents! Indeed our God was true to His promise to King David's famous son. For the house of the forest of Lebanon he had made two hundred targets of beaten gold: six hundred shekels of gold went into each target. For that same house he had made three hundred other shields of beaten gold: three hundred shekels of gold went into each of those shields. His throne of ivory was overlaid with pure gold, as was its footstool. All of Solomon's drinking vessels were of gold. His ships went to Tarshish and returned every third year ladened down with much gold and silver, ivory, apes and peacocks. All the kings of the earth, to seek a presence with him to hear his impressive wisdom, brought large quantities of gold and silver vessels, raiments, spices, horses and mules as presents. He had four thousand stalls for horses and chariots in strategic cities as well as here in Jerusalem. He had twelve thousand horsemen. His territory included all lands northward up to the Euphrates River and southward to the border of Egypt. Over to the west, his united kingdom of Israel covered the coastland of the Mediterranean excluding the divided narrow strips of the Philistines.

Six hundred and sixty-six talents of gold in one year!—he was livid!—for he had to strip Boaz and Jachin and the entrance doors to be able to gather together just thirty talents!

When his eyes had completely adjusted and he had moved forward toward the base of the elaborate curtains, he wondered how near he should stand and, how he should hold his hands as he talked to the Lord's presence behind the veil. Finally, he simply stood there on the golden floor and spoke. "I am not here to ask a word from You, my Lord. I am here because I need to know why You left my city and me completely helpless yesterday. I understand what Isaiah told me out there, but what about my righteousness? What about my removing all the high places set up by my father and all our other kings to worship other gods and goddesses? What about my destroying all the public idols so that they could never be used again by another bad king who might rule in our nation? What about my cutting down the so-called sacred groves where the demented spirits were habitually conjured up? What about that brazen serpent which Moses had graven to heal our stricken people in the wilderness? I even ordered that most sacred object of our people's history to be smashed in pieces because our people had made it an idolatrous object of worship! Do those actions not count for anything?

"Why did You not stop those hideous ones from doing so much damage for my goodness alone? Why has my righteous reign received such treatment? Even my evil father never went through the kind of torture we endured yesterday—and have endured all summer. I have lost everything. Everything! This building of Yours has lost most of its exterior gold. That has happened after all I have done to bring Your people back to a much greater and to a more correct worship of You! Why did You allow those Assyrians to strip the gold off Your dwelling place? Where is the justice in what we have experienced all summer and in what we experienced yesterday? How can we ever recover from such a lost? Look at this temple!"

In the quiet solitude of that room, he knew his mounting anger was out of place, but he could not help it. He continued, "In the very first years of my reign I brought this earthly dwelling place of Yours back to its former condition as well as I could with what we had. Of course I obviously did not have all the gold and silver lying around that You provided for Solomon through his father King David and many others. *And now look at it!* Isaiah says that life with You is an inward thing. What does that mean? This temple is Your dwelling place. Could You not even protect Your own dwelling place from the vile Assyrian?

"Your spokesman also said that the Assyrians would most likely come back one day, and that I had better find out how to receive a good response from You!" He paused, seething with anger. "You had the chance to act on our behalf yesterday. I do not know if You would do anything differently if they returned again! What about Hannah? How could You bring me such a giving beauty and then allow those heathen to cart her off!"

Before Isaiah and he parted, he had asked him most of the same questions. "Perhaps the Lord did not want to protect you, the maiden, and the capital," had been Isaiah's answer.

"Perhaps He did not want to!" Hezekiah had shouted back. "I do not accept that! What kind of God is He if—"

"I have been ordered to leave," Isaiah cut in. "You have much to learn of Him, Hezekiah." With that, he had turned and walked away toward the courtyard steps. Hezekiah watched his long white robes swaying majestically behind him.

"I have not dismissed you!" Hezekiah shouted.

"No, but the Lord has!"

Isaiah turned to face him. With words loud and strong, as stern as he had ever seen him, he said, "Righteousness is not just outward actions. I have been preaching against the sins of our people for over forty years and I believe that our Lord was justified in inflicting this slight chastising upon our selfish—"

"Slight chastising!"

"Did we suffer the fate of our northern brothers? Did we suffer the destruction which is going to come some day? We were only spanked! Chastised so that we might return more fully to our Lord God as a nation."

"What about all the righteous reforms I have instituted?"

"Those are outward acts, Hezekiah. You know our people are not fully behind them with the right motives. You know that our people are still far from being obedient unto the spirit of your reforms. We have talked about that before."

"Granted!" he yelled in return. Taking three steps toward him, he shouted. "I am telling you that it was me that the Lord punished yesterday! It was me who lost all my silver and gold and precious gems! It was me!—who lost all my precious treasures!—and all my works of ivory! It was my work of beautifying this house that was stripped and hauled away! It was my daughters that were taken! And my musicians! And my women!—who are probably right now being forced to sin gravely against our Lord by we do not know how many!"

"Then simply accept that it was truly you that our Lord wanted to chastise," Isaiah said purposely as he began moving back closer to him.

"Me? Why me? I am the one who has brought our people so much closer to Him."

"That is what you need to seek Him for the answer. He is there waiting within His dwelling place."

"Is He?"

Isaiah looked at him in disbelief. Still, from his perspective the reality of the challenge had to be stated.

"Need I say?"

Hezekiah had wished he would have. But instead, fearing to go up into the sanctuary as his prophet had suggested, he asked, "But can I go in—"

"—in your anger and bitterness?"

"Yes, will He not strike me dead in there?"

"Hezekiah, do you not understand our Lord at all? He has taken everything away from you so that you will be forced to go in there and spend some time with Him. He needs your righteous reforms, He needs your desire to serve Him...but now, even more, He needs you to know that He loves you."

"He showed me yesterday how much He loves me!"

"Let Him show you how the reforms you have instituted now have to become a part of—"

161

Tom Steinbach

"Two nights ago He brought an angel unto me. Now apparently He has brought you! Yesterday, in doing nothing for us, He took that lovely angel away! When is He going to take you away?"

"Hezekiah, you are bitter."

"You are right, I am bitter! I have every right—"

"You do not have any right to be bitter! You are treading upon very dangerous ground."

"Dangerous ground! What more can He do to us? To me? He has taken everything away!"

"You still have your nation."

"What nation! I have nothing! Get out of here! *I still have my nation!* I do not believe such a statement! I *still have* what is left of this puny mountaintop capital!"

"Is that all you think of this chosen city?"

"It is all that He thinks of it! Look at my treasuries! Look at the stripped pillars and doors!"

"Go inside. You will find that no gold was sacked from within there where He dwells."

"What human being would ever attempt such a dangerous plundering?"

"From what you say, those Assyrians would have."

"They would have!"

"But they did not. Go in and—"

"Their demanded amount of gold did not require it."

"Certainly you know that our Lord would never have allowed one of their men to step—"

"Of course not! Those heathen would have made *our* men, *our* priests, go inside and do the cuttings, even as it was our men who had to strip the pillars and doors!"

"Hezekiah, my experience and age tell me that you need to back off and rest awhile."

"I am not ready to back off! I am not ready to accept all our losses! I expected justice! All I received was getting kicked in the teeth! I expected our Lord's deliverance and all I got was my breath literally smashed out of me! Two or three times! Holy help, supernatural, holy help was what I expected from our Lord, and all I got was my heart ripped in two!"

"Hezekiah—"

"I ask you, what good have any of the many righteous acts been that you and my mother have pushed me to carry out? What good are all the reforms I have performed because I wanted to perform them out of my own heart? What good are any of all those righteousnesses I have done!"

"Many of your servants can hear you."

"I want them to hear me! I am mad! I am angry! I feel that our Lord has treacherously treated me!"

"You are wrong, Hezekiah."

"Get out!"

"You are tak—"

"GET OUT OF HERE!"

Back in the temple he was still complaining, "Lord, if You are in there You know I feel that I have been treacherously treated by You. You know that I feel that Isaiah should have been brought out to us yesterday. You know that I cannot see where it has been any good to do all my righteousnesses before You. You must know that I am angry! Angry and ready to fight! Angry at all that has happened against our nation this summer! And extremely angry at You!"

Before he stalked from the temple he had also expressed what he expected for the Lord to do if the Assyrians ever returned again. When he left he felt discouraged, but calmed. By letting it all go he had hoped that his anger and bitterness had been removed from his being even though he had not made any confessions nor had he forgiven anything. But, he had decided upon a projected plan of action for the coming weeks and months. Hoping he would be able to carry through on the plan without showing forth much anger, he had failed drastically within an hour.

"Son, I need to see you. Mehujael says that I cannot."

Effectively being blocked from entering into his chambers by Mehujael who was stopping any further movement by her into the opening of the double doors, his mother was pleading into his chambers. She had come as soon as she had heard that he had said that was leaving the palace and he had ordered all his servants to move him at once to his winter house.

"I have not granted Mehujael permission to let anyone see me!" he had shouted back and slammed some clothing down.

"But, Son—"

"Mehujael, I have not granted to you permission to let even my mother to see me! SHUT THE DOORS!"

*

> > > *ELEVEN* < < <

*

One month later, Abijah beckoned Mehujael aside in the winter house to ask him how her son was.
"He is still in a state of extreme mourning."

"When he ordered me to leave that first day without seeing him before he left the palace, it hurt deeply. It grieved me to not be able to help him in that despairing time. Then I finally thought that maybe it was a good idea for him to get away and have his time of secluded mourning after losing so much."

"He needed the time."

"Mehujael, it has been a month, are there any signs?"

"He grieves constantly. Much of it over losing the maiden. And over losing his daughters. Surely some is over his loss of much of his wealth. But I believe he grieves mostly because he believes our Lord God let him and our nation down."

"Oh, my heart cries within me. I do wish that he would let me see him."

"I also do. That would greatly help. He desperately needs your counsel now."

She then asked about the cities which had been conquered and taken by the Assyrians. Knowing the details of that one, Mehujael was glad to be able to share something tangible with her. "The crown prince of Assyria took the plunder he wanted when he went eastward and gave all the conquered cities to the kings of Ashdod, Ekron and Gaza."

She then talked about how sad it was that their country's very important seventh sacred month had been a period of total national silence. Hezekiah had ordered posts to be sent demanding that for obvious reasons none of the many feasts or holy convocations would be observed.

"Hephzibah?" she questioned.

"No, he has not asked for her."

"Never?"

"Never."

"She must come."

"She does. So far though he has not offered her any permission to enter into his presence."

Abijah already knew that answer. She thought by bringing

it up knowing that he could do nothing except give her an unsatisfactory answer, it would cause him to be more desirous of trying to help her more completely with her next question—and she really wanted an answer to her next question.

"The house of women?"

"Six maidens have been chosen so far."

"Six already?"

"Three will arrive this week."

"Young?"

"Beauty is youth, is it not? All six are the age of the taken maiden: fourteen or fifteen years old."

"No, beauty is not just youth."

"Not just, Abijah, I agree, but youth almost always qualifies. Whereas any other—"

"I understand. But he still has his Hephzibah. I just cannot believe fourteen and fifteen year olds. I also cannot believe that he is going to refill that house, Mehujael."

"Why not, Abijah? He wants another maiden like the one I took into his bedchamber that evening the Assyrians had come and camped down by En rogel."

"Because of the law, Mehujael."

"The law?"

"In the giving of the law, Moses forbids our kings to multiply wives unto themselves."

"But all our—"

"He will not have any of them brought in...before their time?" she asked cutting in quickly, hoping to keep the answers coming by keeping him off guard.

"No, he will not. Each of the young maidens is required to go through many months of training and beautification."

"Mehujael, precisely what do you know of what these maidens go through?"

"Most everything. I am his chief chamberlain. I oversee nearly everything that touches his personal life."

"It will be months before any maiden is presented to him?"

"Very definitely."

"My son has one whom he, or you, ah, consider to be a favorite instructor, teacher—"

"Yes, of course, there is a favorite of us both. Sarai is our favorite instructor. She was the one most responsible for the last maiden's training. I have already told you that your son was very pleased with her."

Abijah did not respond immediately.

Mehujael therefore underscored his appraisal by adding another firmer:

"Very pleased."

"I understand, Mehujael, I am not questioning that. And I have heard and have grieved about the pain that heathen Assyrian leader forced him to go through concerning her."

"It was bad, I had her hidden among the crowd. I thought I had completely fooled the Assyrians, I thought she was hidden so well—your son has never reprimanded me for it."

"I am certain you had her well hidden."

"I certainly had thought so. Still, of all our people standing there watching—*of all of them!*—that vile one picked her out, and even identified her as our master's favorite."

"It must have been eerie."

"It was uncanny. It scared me."

"Sarai will immediately begin instructing those maidens coming this week?"

"Yes, most definitely."

"Can you arrange for her to come to my chamber this afternoon, Mehujael?"

"I am certain I can."

Noticing the pleasant look he gave her, she smiled her thanks. However, almost coinciding with her smile, his pleased look turned to one of worry. He expressed his concern, "You will not attempt to turn her away from bringing another exquisite maiden into your son to resemble the former one?"

"No, Mehujael. No, not anything like that."

Just the opposite, my good friend.

Just the opposite.

*

> > > *TWELVE* < < <

*

Hezekiah stood, staring out the window. The shutters had been opened wide and he was overlooking all that was within view. There was not any trace of darkness left outside.

He was brooding.

He still had not seen anyone but the few necessary servants.

Looking out southward from his high elevation, he looked over the city, and over the wall: seeing quite far as he had often done in the past. However, he was not dreaming of great plans as he had so often done in those past watchings.

He was solemn instead: he had always thought that he was

going to be the Lord's king to lead his nation forward in regaining much of the land and wealth that his people had lost at the division of the kingdom. Some in his realm had even suggested that he was the coming Messiah foretold about back in his father's reign. The one promised by Isaiah back then who would come and set up a righteous kingdom in Israel. That king upon whose shoulders the everlasting government to rule the entire world would be placed. Those dreams, all those dreams, had left his hopes exactly nine weeks ago.

Thus, as he stared at the tinted horizon, he wondered if there was a Lord at all. And, if so, if that Hiding One would ever lend His zeal to perform the bringing about of the eternal kingdom upon his behalf. His lending His aid was beyond fathoming, He certainly had not offered any form of helpful zeal during the Assyrian siege nine weeks before.

"That is the great problem of Your being invisible and removed from us," he said aloud. Watching his breath mistify in the cold, morning air, he continued, "We have pouches full of old parchments declaring all Your powerful past deeds here in Your chosen land of Judah and Israel. But we do not have one instant I can personally point to to reassure my own mind that You actually exist and that You truly desire to show Yourself powerful on my behalf."

Moving over to another window, he watched a priest go up those distant stairs to prepare to sacrifice another bullock on the huge bronze altar. He needed to know—if the Lord was not truly there, he did not want his priests playing games over there on the stairs and within the temple.

"Why did You not make Yourself known to us this past summer, I ask? What good has my being the king of Judah been if You are not able or willing or interested enough to come down, or to come out, or to do whatever You do, and rush to our aid? You have caused fear to become my constant companion. It has become my many-headed enemy: with a new head popping up whenever I have been able to get rid of any of the previous ones. Before this year had begun, I had been an extremely confident monarch. Before this summer, I was ruling over a very forward-looking kingdom. You know all that has changed now—if so much devastation could strike within my nation and here within my city with such ease, what other terrifying horrors lay in wait for the rest of my reign? I still can hear those Assyrians laughing and celebrating to this day!" He glanced as far as he could see toward the east. "Has that uncircumcised heathen already discarded Hannah? I do not believe what You did to me. You allowed that beast to mock me with a multitude of unchallenged words. You let him blaspheme You. Indeed, You let him do whatever his heart desired and all You did was remain absolutely, totally, buried in Your temple as he did each vile deed after vile deed!"

He clutched his eyes shut til a savage pain within the boil subsided. "I cannot understand it. I do not understand it. I will not understand it. Whatever happened to the prosperity and blessings You promised to all who sought to obey You? Whatever happened to?—'Be strong and be of a good courage; be not afraid, neither be dismayed: for the Lord your God is with you —with you—whithersoever you go.' Whatever happened to?—'He that sits in the heavens shall laugh, the Lord shall have them in derision...then shall He speak unto them in His wrath, and vex them in His sore displeasure.'

"Or how about, 'Ask of Me and I shall give you the heathen for your inheritance and the uttermost parts of the earth for your own possession. You shall break them with a rod of iron; and you shall dash them in pieces like a potter's vessel.' Whatever happened to those promises!

"Whatever happened to this one: 'If you will walk before Me as David your father walked, in the integrity of heart and in uprightness, to do according to all that I have commanded you and if you will keep My statues and My judgments: then I *will establish the throne of your kingdom upon Israel forever.'*

"Whatever happened to that promise! I do not care what manner of help You would have come to aid us with: a mighty whirlwind, an unleashing of Your angels upon them, a fearful, violent earthquake to swallow them up, some silent mysterious blast, whatever! I just can not believe that You, and Isaiah, remained completely, utterly silent! Utterly, utterly silent!"

He went over to his personal pouch of scrolls.

Picking out the soiled one which was near the front, he cried, "Lord, I have read and reread portions of this story of Job nearly everyday since that vile day!" He pouted, waving it back and forth in the air, and felt the pain of the boil greatly heightening with his flared up actions. "I have read it every miserable day! I have not allowed my wife entrance into my presence lest she also demand of me as Job's wife demanded of him: to curse You to Your face! I have not asked any to come into my chamber lest they counsel me as corruptly as Job's 'friends' advised him in their attempt to place unfounded guilt upon him and his alleged wickedness!

"I have not permitted those to happen but Job's sage arguments against You and Your seeming willingness to let wrong overtake him have become ever more strongly my own contentions against You! Oh, I am exceedingly thankful and awfully jealous of all the blessings You gave him in the sunset of his life; still, I do not understand why You let him suffer so before that! *He was righteous!*—even You said so!

"If You caused him to go through all those miseries to show us what You will do for us afterwards if we truly make it to the end, why have you forced me to go so far as to also argue with You even as he did? Do each one of us righteous ones abandoned by You have to confront You face to face as righteous Job did? And if so—Why! I now know that until I see You actually intervene somewhere in my own life or in the life of my nation that I have no desire to live or reign any

171

longer." He moved to the ivory-inlaid couch and sat down with an effort showing a great pain.

"Until the Assyrians came I could always justify my wonderings with some ethereal hope that of course You would come to our aid: that You had just never done so because we never had a real enough need for You to come. That was before they came and devastated our place! Now what do I do? I wish I knew! Fear has entered my being and has become extremely exaggerated within me, my thoughts and my goals of life have become paralyzed. I wish You knew what it is like to live each day in a vague, nameless dread. A foreboding dread in which you are always reminded that when the time of real urgent help came—Your promised protection did not!"

He walked over and returned the scroll in the pouch and pulled out a different one. Through a strange set of circumstances Moses achieved a place of high authority in the court of Egypt. One day he killed an Egyptian in an attempt to protect a fellow Hebrew. It was a rash move and the next day he found that the deed was known. He therefore fled, in fear of the throne, into the wilderness east of Egypt. Looking out toward the awakening sky, Hezekiah thought, I know exactly how you felt, Moses. This winter house is my place of escape, my place of solitude, my wilderness east of Egypt. And, like you, Moses, I do not know if my people will ever desire me to reign over them again either.

Moving back to the couch, he wasted no time reading through Moses' forty year stay in the wilderness...for he knew where he wanted to get. He was not sure that his own people were murmuring yet but he was certain that, if they were not, they soon would be. He paused in his search at the mighty plagues and the splitting apart of the Red Sea. At the emotional: 'and Moses stretched out his hand over the sea; and their Lord caused the sea to go back by a strong east wind all that night, He made the sea dry land, and the waters were divided,' he reminded the Lord that this was precisely why he had been fasting and had been in isolation for so long: he also needed to receive a similar mighty sign from Him.

"Lord, if only You would have done a like mighty deed when the Rabshakeh was standing upon the porch doing his big, indestructible Goliath act then our people could have responded as our people did when David slew the first giant. They could have fallen in behind me and encouraged me to greatly expand Your kingdom here. Now, if You bring the Assyrians again without presenting to me any sign of Your power, my people are going to respond to my leadership exactly as our people reacted back when they were first freed from the Egyptians and then saw that those Egyptians were charging once again after them."

He returned to his bed and backed up in the scroll:

'The Pharoah drew nigh, the children of Israel lifted up their eyes and were afraid. They cried out unto the Lord. Then they said unto Moses, Because there were no graves in Egypt, is that why you have you taken us away to die in this wilderness? Is not this the word that we told you in Egypt, saying, Leave us alone that we may serve the Egyptians. Then Moses said, Fear not, stand still, and see the salvation of our Lord God which He will show to you today: for the Egyptians whom you see today, you shall see them again no more. The Lord shall fight for you, and you shall hold your peace.'

"Lord, how I would like to be able to speak the same thing the next time the Assyrians come. When they come again I will have to be able to speak the same thing. I will have to act in that manner: I will have to perform some miraculous act even as he lifted up Your rod, and stretched it out over the sea, and divided the sea so that the people could pass over on dry ground to escape the Pharoah and the Egyptians."

He lay back, shut his eyes, prayed that the pain would lessen, and soon dozed. When he came to, he wondered how long Isaiah was going to take, and then he read on in the story. Three days later as they journeyed into that wilderness, they could find no water good for drinking. Soon the people were murmuring against Moses saying, 'What shall we drink?'

When he had purified a body of water so that they could safely drink and when they had journeyed from there for another month and a half, the entire congregation of the children of Israel murmured bitterly against Moses and Aaron again: 'Would to God that we had died by the hand of our Lord God Himself in the land of Egypt when we sat by those flesh pots, and when we did eat bread to the full; for you have brought us forth into this wilderness to kill us with hunger.'

Again he read: 'And the people thirsted in Rephidim for water, and murmured against Moses saying, Wherefore is this that you have brought us up out of Egypt to kill us and our children and all our cattle with thirst? And Moses cried unto the Lord, What shall I do unto this people? They are almost ready to stone me. The Lord said unto Moses, Go on before the people, and take with you your elders of Israel...and the rod with which you smote the river: take it in your hand, and go. Behold, I will stand before you there upon the rock in Horeb; and you shall smite that rock, and there shall come water out of it, that the people may drink.

'And Moses did thus in the sight of the elders of Israel. And he called the name of the place Massah and Meribah, because of all the chiding of the children of Israel and because they tempted the Lord, saying, Is the Lord among us or not?'

An excruciating pain forced him to stop his reading and to bemoan the fact that his resident spokesman for the Lord had not yet arrived. *Where was Isaiah?* He lay back and shut his eyes tightly and made only a slight movement of trying to save the scroll as it slipped off his lap and fell to the floor.

'Is the Lord among us or not?' He thought as the pain subsided. "Your people are always going to ask that question,

Lord. If I am ever going to get them to trust You to be our Almighty God then we, they and me, are going to have to know that You are here among us. I am convinced that after the visitation by the Assyrians that our people right now are in the same trust as our people were back there in Rephidim— *and they were ready to stone Moses!"*

He slept again for awhile shortly after that.

When he awoke, Mehujael brought word that Isaiah still had not yet come. He also brought him something to drink. He also gave him another scroll, and replaced the fallen one in the pouch. Hezekiah opened the new scroll, and found that it was indeed the one he had requested: the fourth book of Moses— the writings which chronicled thirty-eight of the Israelites' forty years in the wilderness. He read of the spies going into Canaan to spy out the land. Only two of them felt they should immediately go up and take it. Ten of the spies said, 'All the citizens that we saw in the land are men of a great stature. In it we saw giants. And we were in our own sight as grasshoppers. One of the two good spies said, The land which we passed through is an exceeding good land...a land which flows with milk and honey. Only rebel not against our Lord, neither fear the people nor the giants of that land; for they are bread for us: their defense is departed from them, and the Lord is with us. But all their congregation shouted and bade stone those two with stones. Then the Lord's glory appeared in the tabernacle of the congregation before all the children of Israel!'

Word came then to Hezekiah that the prophet Isaiah had finally been seen leaving his house.

His interest piqued again, and his heart warmed from the words of Moses that he was reading, and knowing that more murmurings had to arise, he continued further: 'Korah, and his friends, rose up before Moses with two hundred and fifty men of renown. The challenge had to be spoken. They came

Tom Steinbach

that Moses had too much authority and that they wanted more say in the nation, especially in the area of Aaron's priesthood. Moses told them they could come into his presence the next day, and that they should all bring a censer and incense with them to lay before the Lord. On that next day they all put fire in their censers and laid their incense thereon before the dwelling place of their Lord God. Then Korah stepped forward and gathered all the congregation against Moses and Aaron.'

Mehujael entered and said Isaiah was nearing. Wanting the blessing he knew would flood within his soul, he commanded him to have the coming spokesman for the Lord to wait within the middle courtyard until he was called.

'Moses cried to everyone, By this shall you know that our Lord God has sent me to do all these works; for I have not done them of mine own mind. If these men before you die the common death of all men then the Lord has not sent me. But if our Lord God makes a new thing, and the earth opens her mouth and swallows them up with all that pertains to them and they go down quickly into the pit; then...you shall understand that these men have provoked our Lord God to wrath.

'It came to pass as Moses ended his speaking, that the ground clave, and the earth opened her mouth, and swallowed them up and their houses, and all the men that pertained unto Korah and all their goods. All of them and all that pertained to them went down alive into the pithole and the earth closed upon them and they perished. And all Israel that were round about them fled at the cry of them. There came out fire from the Lord and consumed the two hundred and fifty men that offered incense with Korah and his friends.'

Rolling up the scroll, he settled back, and breathed out a long exhale. Ready to hear the healing verdict from his Lord, he called Mehujael to order their spokesman for the Lord up to his room. Assured that finally, even as he had just read, he would be vindicated by their Lord God as Moses had been.

*

> > > *THIRTEEN* < < <

*

Isaiah had entered the winter house, and was waiting where and as he had been directed. The cold, barren, middle courtyard of the house made him think of the death sentence he had come to deliver.

Having been given that opportunity to stroll in that desolate yard for a time, he realized that the reclusive Hezekiah must have already accepted his message nine weeks before.

He must have left the palace early to come over here to die. The entire place reeked of impending death. When he was ordered to go up to the second floor and to enter Hezekiah's room, however, he found the opposite: warmth and very adequate lighting. He saw a monarch lying upon his deathbed. But he did not see a man who was ready to die. Nor did he see the man who had forcefully shouted him out of the temple's

177

courtyard a couple months before. Instead he looked into the hopeful, pleading eyes of a ruler who did not want to die. A monarch who wanted his representative from their God to pronounce renewed life to him. A monarch who realized that if he died that David's dynasty would be finished. Nevertheless, Isaiah had the Lord's message to deliver and his manner was not to move cautiously. Timidity could never be, and not this day especially, a trait of one selected for his position.

"Hezekiah, I have received the message that you have asked for me to seek."

"Is He going to give me a sign?"

"Hezekiah, thus says the Lord: 'Set your house in order. For you shall die, and not live.'"

Set my house in order. I shall die and not live.

God will not cast away a perfect man, neither will He help the evildoer, Bildad had told Job. Set my house in order—I do not even have a house. I do not have a male heir. The Lord knows that. Why did You give me so much time today while I waited for this word from Isaiah? Why so much time to read of how You miraculously helped Moses in his chosen task? Why so much time to thrill to the real deliverances You brought to him in his troubled leading of those murmuring children of Yours? What did Job answer Bildad: 'I know it is so of a truth; but how should a man be just with God?' Have all my reigning years been wasted years?

"Isaiah, I cannot accept—"

"Hezekiah, it is final! It is the word of the Lord!"

"But I—"

"You are to set your house in order! You will not recover from this sickness! Good day, Sir!" Isaiah swung around and left, his white robe swinging majestically.

He has remembered our last meeting in that courtyard, he thought. Isaiah may have expected some outrage from him but he was too much in shock to have offered anything. He simply lay there and watched the swaying white robe disappear.

Before his prophet had taken a step beyond his chamber door the shock turned to a monumental fear. One that was shattering in its towering finality. A fear that completely destroyed his sense of an orderly world in which attempted righteous deeds yield added blessings to the doer. For nine weeks he had tried to work through all the manifestations of his many-headed fears and then in one deadly sentence, all that he had begun to hope for was torn away from him. The fear turned into extreme panic and bitterness. Panic and bitterness which instantly crystallized into overt anger:

"GET OUT!

"GET OUT OF MY ROOM!" he shouted at his servants.

He swung over unto his side in his roaring anger, causing pain to shoot in spasms through his body from the boil! Then buried his head into the wall. Wailing, he prayed, "Lord, You listened in his hopeless times to Your servant Moses. I beg. I plead. I cry out to You—do You not remember how I have walked before You? I have reigned in truth and with a perfect heart! I have always done that which is upright in Your sight!

"O Lord, my pain is unbearable. I am at the gates of the grave. Why are You cutting off my days? Why am I deprived of the residue of my years?"

Long high-pitched wailings with loud weeping and a rambling of invocations mixed in continued to burst forth from between his two trembling lips. Soon he was wailing and chattering like a maniacal swallow as an uncontrollable, confused anxiousness swept over him. "Shall I not see You, even You my Lord God, once again in the land of the living," he cried. "Shall I behold man no more with the inhabitants of the world? Mine age is departed, and blown away from me like a shepherd's tent in a gale! My life: it is cut off like a weaver stopping at his loom with his patterns only half completed! You are cutting me off with pining sickness! You are making an end of me from day even to night.

"All night I have been moaning! This illness has already been like being torn apart by a lion! I am oppressed! Undertake for me! Do not be as the lion that would break all my bones in bringing me to my end! O Lord, I am in trouble! Help me! But what am I saying, are You not the One who has brought on this sickness?"

He placed his hands around the outer edges of the very painful boil, as he took a deep breath...and waited for an extremely harsh hurting to subside. "If I have to die then," he began again much quieter, "can You not let me go more softly and not in this intense bitterness of my soul? But—but—No, I cannot accept that! I cannot accept the death sentence pronounced upon me through Isaiah. Have You not created us to live! TO LIVE! O Lord, heal me! O Lord, make me live!

"O Lord, touch me just this one time!" His tears were flooding down his cheeks. "O Lord, I have done much speaking in the bitterness of my old soul: do not condemn me. Do not shackle me. Show me why You are so harshly contending with me. Show me why I have to mourn unto You constantly like a dove. Show me why my eyes have to grow so very weary with a continual looking up toward—"

*

>>> * <<<

*

As Isaiah reached the lower level door leading out to the courtyard, he sensed that his Lord God had another mission for him. He paused at the door, listened intently...and the word came crystal clear.

Incredible.

But clear as crystal.

*

> > > *FOURTEEN* < < <

*

Isaiah stood by the fire pit warming himself. Earlier, he had ordered it filled with small kindling and lighted. At this time he could not see any trace of the kindling pieces as the heavier wood which had been added to the pit on top of them was fast ablaze.

He was waiting—even for him it had been an extremely strange day—he had been waiting for some time, waiting for Hezekiah's servants to carry their monarch out of his room.

It had been a strange day indeed.

When he had been sure that he was to return back to Hezekiah's room, he ordered some servants to kindle a blaze in their fire pit in that central courtyard of the house. As the first large flames shot upward and he had not yet gone back up to Hezekiah's room, he had thought: If life is going to be

181

given back to that dead man up there, then life should also be given once again to this dead fire pit here in the courtyard.

When Hezekiah smelled the smoke and heat of the fire rising up outside his window, he shouted for the meaning of it. Upon finding out that Isaiah had ordered its life and was still on the grounds, he wondered if he should curse his prophet's audacious act...or if he should accept his continuing presence in the house as a hopeful sign. As a very hopeful sign.

In faith he chose the latter and decided to act as if the Lord was truly going to heal him and give to him a glorious, victorious end. Staking upon that decision and upon Job's prosperous end, he more politely asked all his servants, who had come in at his call, to leave his room. Next, he ceased his wailing, and mellowed his anger enough, to ask the Lord to forgive him for being so harsh toward Isaiah. For Job, his partner in pain and through the winter evenings also, had been told that he had to pray for his oppressors in the end of his story before the Lord could bless him—he acknowledged the rightness of his Lord God to do whatever He wanted to do. Job did it, so Hezekiah decided to also. And, in further obedience to the demands which the Lord had placed upon Job in the end of his book, he next asked for forgiveness for having so sharply ordered Isaiah out of the temple's courtyard those nine weeks before. Soon after he finished with all his different repentances, Isaiah strolled in with his new orders to relate to Hezekiah and with his white robes swaying majestically.

"Hezekiah, our Lord God has told me that renewed life and heat will permeate this winter house of yours and your palace from this day forward, even as life and health will permeate your being from your head to your toes."

"Thank You, Lord!"

Isaiah said nothing more.

"Justice is still alive in our nation, Job!"

Isaiah stood there.

"Is there no more?"

Isaiah stood there.

"It is only half of what I have been pleading for."

Isaiah stared at him in disbelief.

"I have been pl—"

"You do not need a sign."

"I will not be able to reign if I do not know for certain that the Lord dwells here in our city."

"Your healing will be your—"

"No, that is not sufficient."

"You have me to pass our Lord's messages on to you and to your people."

"I do not mean messages. I need to have a sign from Him. You yourself said our Lord offered to give one to my father, to my very wicked father. Why will He not give me one?"

He was extremely close to crying: first the excitement of the promised healing, and now the embarrassment of having to so plead. Why was Isaiah making him plead.

"Your healing will be sign enough."

"No, it will not. Do you not understand? Job finally saw the Lord. Moses had his righteous leadership vindicated by many signs from the Lord."

"Your healing will—"

"Even you, Isaiah, have had a wonderful vision of our Lord God in all His supernatural glory. I have hardly eaten, or drunk, anything for nine weeks. I have seen nobody but my servants for nine weeks. I have read and reread and reread and reread our sacred parchments for the last nine weeks. All for only one reason: I need to know!"

"That He is real."

"Yes, that He is real! I need to know that after what we have gone through with the Assyrians. I have reigned for fourteen years here in Judah telling my people that He is real. I have forced one reform after another upon them: leading them to believe that He is real and should be rightly worshipped. I have beautified His house and reinstituted the correct priestly functions to get our people to worship and serve Him as an all-powerful Being worthy of all of our praise and devotion. Then nine weeks ago He failed all of us, by remaining hidden. You and He never showed yourselves." He raised a hand to quiet the protest which he knew Isaiah was about to produce. Isaiah started to anyway but then allowed him to finish.

"Whether He failed us, or used that army to gravely punish us, I am not going to argue. But, Isaiah, He did nothing to let those Assyrians, or us, know that He is indeed in this city. And because He did not, I cannot now rule in His stead and demand that all our people continue to do all the reforms that I have been demanding. Unless He is now willing to show me and our nation a definite sign of His living presence with us, He might as well not heal me from this boil."

Isaiah stood quietly, reluctant to offer that assurance that a sign would be forthcoming. "Certainly you understand. I have ceased living for nine weeks to get Him to show Himself." Isaiah still said nothing. "If He will not show me Himself through some sign," Hezekiah said nearly in tears, "I will order the fire down there to be snuffed out immediately and I will continue to wait in here for nine more weeks or nine more months or nine more years—if He still allows me to live."

"You will not have to do either. He will give you a sign."

"When?"

"Today," Isaiah answered without hesitation.

"Today?"

"Here is the message He gave to me in your doorway. I received it before I even had gone out into your courtyard: 'Go and say to Hezekiah, thus says the Lord, the God of David your father. I have heard your prayer. I have seen your tears. I will heal you. On the third day you shall go up unto the house of the Lord, and I will add unto your days fifteen years.'"

"Fifteen years!"

"Fifteen years. 'And...I will deliver you and this city out of the hand of the king of Assyria. I have heard your prayer, behold, I will defend this city.'"

"I knew they would be returning."

"But our Lord God Almighty has promised that this time He will defend the city Himself: for His own sake and for the sake of His servant David."

"That is all that I have ever been asking Him to do."

"'And this shall be a sign unto you from the Lord—'"

"He said that also!"

"He did. He is going to give unto you a sign so that you will know that He will do the things which He has promised."

"He had already given you the promise of the sign?"

"He had."

"Then why did you not tell me?"

"Hezekiah, you still have too much pride."

"Pride! Who gives you the right to decide what you tell me and what you do not tell me of the word of the Lord?"

"You are a very prideful monarch, Hezekiah. One whose pride is going to lead you into some more unwise decisions."

"Some more?"

"Yes, Sir, some more. And giving you a sign in your pride will not be good for our nation."

Frustrated, Hezekiah shook his head. He started to speak, then quit. Finally in control, he answered. "I have been fasting for over two months for this one thing, for a sign that He is real and is indeed residing within our city...and, you say that giving it to me will not be good!"

"It will not be."

"Why?"

"You say that you have been studying Job and Moses."

"I have been."

"Hezekiah, you have not come anywhere near to that place where Moses arrived out in the backside of that wilderness, nor have you come anywhere near to that final place where Job achieved his full restitution with the Lord"

"But I have just—"

"I am the Lord's spokesman, let me finish my message."

"What shall be the sign that the Lord will heal me, and that I shall go up into the house of the Lord the third day?"

"Here's how the message ends: 'The sign that these things will come to pass is that the Lord will move the shadow on the sun dial ten degrees.'"

"*Ten degrees!* Our Lord will control the sun even as He did in Moses' day?"

"Ten degrees. The choice is up to you if you want that shadow to go forward or backward."

It would be a light thing for the shadow to move forward those ten degrees, he thought—no, that would not be sign enough. "Let the shadow return *backwards* the ten degrees."

"Hezekiah, our Lord's exact words to you were: 'Behold, I will bring the shadow of the sun, which has gone forward on Ahaz' dial, ten degrees backward.'"

"He had already told you He would bring it backwards!"

"He had, He knew your heart. I have to go out now and cry unto Him with all my being that the sign come forth."

"But I have to see the sign."

"Then have your servants carry you there—if you go over there soon, you will have time."

Quickly his servants brought long sheeting and two poles, and also made speedy mention that it was very cold outside. Surely too cold for him in his condition. "Truly, it will be the death of him," one agreeing servant whispered to another.

"Maybe he wants to die," the other one retorted.

Disregarding them, he directed his servants to carefully lay him upon the makeshift burden bearer, though there was no good way for them to place him on the quickly covered poles so that his painful boil could be trouble free. He then ordered them to carry him down to the courtyard. He wanted to see Isaiah and the fire before they carried him to his palace.

From the fire pit Isaiah watched Hezekiah look first at it's blaze and then at him. They then both looked up and watched the rising smoke and the many sparks rising even more quickly into the clear sky. Nodding to each other, Hezekiah made a comment of how good the fire smelt and then immediately directed his bearers to get them on their way.

"Before you go," Isaiah said, making his way over to him and his bearers. "Do you remember that I said I had received another prophecy in the days of your father's reign?"

"Yes I do," he replied, still not wanting to hear its contents and also not wanting to put the sign off but realizing that he was really too uncomfortable and too weak to object.

"I had said that the Lord sent the Assyrians to punish, not to utterly destroy, our nation. And that the small herds of a cow and a pair of sheep were His promise that He still desired this nation to be a witness to the world for Him."

"Yes, I remember those words."

"The Lord told me next to tell your father that when that time of trouble happened, that it would come to pass that those animals would give milk abundantly. So much milk that everyone throughout our country would have plenty of milk and honey to eat and drink." He paused to show concern. "Nevertheless, where the vineyards grew plentifully before... those same places would be full of briers and thorns."

"Yes, yes, I understand."

"Those places, however, will bring forth all the wildlife your peoples' hunting will ever want. And those same lands will also be good for grazing of your farmers and shepherds' cattle, sheep, and goats."

"In other words, His promise to us is that we will slowly, but certainly, recover from this invasion. Even if it is not doing the same work as we did previously."

"It is also true that our people will be able someday soon to move back into being productive again in their former ways:that is of course if our people have learned from this chastisement and now desire to serve Him."

"Thank you for sharing it with me. When I meet with the elders I will tell them and then we will post it throughout whatever land we have left."

On their shivering way across to the palace, they saw a small gathering of Beduion traders standing, talking, and laughing over by the wall of the public courtyard: passing the time and, at the moment, watching them.

When he noticed them, Hezekiah instructed his men to carry him over near to them. Once he was close to them, and though it took a great effort to project his voice out there in the frigid cold, he said, "Friends, you are going to see a miracle today that you will not believe. Just remember that I have told of it...then you will always believe that the Most High God of the heavens and the earth dwells here in our capital with us."

"Take me up to my chambers," he ordered the servants when they arrived at the palace.

"But, Sir, it will be very cold in your rooms. They have been shut up for—"

"—yes, Sir, we will take you up," another servant cut in.

"No, do not take the time to light the lamps," he said as they entered his chambers and one of his servants moved directly toward a brass lamp. "I am not staying in these rooms. Take me over there out upon my roof garden."

Once they were out there, he directed them to lay him near

the southwestern edge of the roof overlooking the lovely flower garden his father had built. The sun dial was in full light and could be seen extremely well from that location.

Looking down, he noted on the dial that it was the ninth hour of the day. He was there, he wondered how long he would have to wait.

*

> > > *FIFTEEN* < < <

*

A new maiden stood in the soft mellow glow of the clay lamp by the distant wall. Named Machal, she was the sixteenth young maiden to have come through the time of training and beautification since the Assyrians had taken his favorite.

Standing there where Hannah had stood nearly a year earlier: she looked very beautiful, very, very beautiful.

Her maidservants, looking extremely proud and awfully comfortable with their task of finally presenting this new maiden, removed her outer garment and laid it carefully upon the back of the crafted, ivory-inlaid, high-back chair that the same three had done with Hannah's linen outer garment.

Machal reminded him of her. Her long, flowing, luxurious black hair; her graceful, ready stance; her soft, stunning eyes; and her bronzed, trim slenderness...more than any of the other fifteen who had preceded her...she reminded him of Hannah. Convinced that the one before him was the quest for whom he had been long seeking, he made certain that she and her maidservants clearly saw his shining approval in his eyes.

The maidservants let him know they had. Smiling happily, very, very brightly, the three of them bowed more deeply and much longer than they had since Hannah had been taken. During their bow before him, two accomplished musicians—a male lute player and a female harpist—entered the room through the heavy, wooden door and seated themselves to the left of the maiden. They quickly prepared their instruments. They would start playing as soon as the maidservants left.

Enjoying once again the overt satisfaction which their monarch persisted to show them, the maidservants stayed their movements as long as they felt they could. They finally looked at Machal a last time, winked their approval, turned to him, bowed one last bow, and left: closing the door behind them, leaving Machal standing as confident as Hannah had stood.

When all became perfectly still and her musicians nodded their sign of being ready, she looked down and relaxed her posed stance. Her feet stood apart. Her legs bent forward even as her shoulders rounded forward. Her arms hung straight down, and her chin rested lightly upon her chest—causing her long, raven-black hair to fall straight down in front of her.

The harpist began to weave her fingers softly and Machal began to weave up and down on the balls of her feet. With the first note ensuing from the strings of the male player's lute, she drew her feet back tight together and weaved upward higher until her entire body straightened to an erect, melodious form. One hand with locked fingers capped the movement by pointing straight upward toward the ceiling. Her other slender arm, bent at the elbow, was drawn up tight to her lower ribs.

With a sudden sharp hop, Machal twirled around, jumped another cute little jump, and moved across the floor toward him in perfect time with the music. Near him, she stopped abruptly with her back arched and with one leg bent at the knee and partially raised, her foot pointing straight forward.

Another quick jump on the other foot followed as she spiraled around and quickly high-stepped back across the room. Machal ended the movement with a cartwheel and leg splits, settling softly upon the floor with her legs artistically stretched out effortlessly in front and behind her. The combination dance step had been executed beautifully, more beautifully than Hezekiah had ever watched even his regular dancers perform the step.

She held the pose, lying there in the splits, her arms resting upon the floor on either side of her and her head resting upon the knee of her forward leg. Again her long hair, spreading out naturally in a spray, accented the pose. Her smooth back rose and lowered evenly with her breath. He was astonished at her beautiful form and seemed confidently assured that his previous judgment of her had indeed been correct.

Finally his new favorite had been found. Finally his new favorite had been brought to him. Finally his new favorite had been trained and beautified. Finally he would have one with whom he would proudly share the leadership of the kingdom.

Rising with the music, like Hannah, she was magnificent: gracefully slender, exceedingly beautiful. Her raven-black hair was long and luxurious. She wore it straight and flowing. Her pure white tunic of the very finest linen was her only piece of clothing. It was perfect for her. She looked a goddess. She rose to her full stature, twisted sharply in a circle, took a couple quick steps, turned another cartwheel, and ended near him, standing: facing him with her legs slightly spread apart.

After a moment of perfect stillness, swaying rhythmically, her back and arms began leaning slowly backwards in an arching motion. She continued that ever-so-slow arching until both of her extended hands were resting solidly upon the floor behind her. For this dance, her maidservants had designed a sheer tunic of the finest linen which was split at the thighs and gathered at the ankles. In the moderate lighting of the two tiny olive oil lamps, her form was exceedingly lovely.

Strikingly lovely. He was pleased. So pleased, that, natural breathing became difficult for him. His throat became dry....

From the arched backbend she slowly raised one leg, toes pointing straight forward, until it was high enough to spring the other one up to it, and continued the swift movement until she had formed a motionless headstand. It was perfectly performed, as was her coming down out of it.

Having remained motionless with her feet pointing straight upward even as the instruments continued to play with a spirited, though also quiet, manner which kept them in the background, she came down out of that headstand with a single, fluid movement which ended with an upward thrust, a lively bounce, a circled prancing, and another headstand which did not end in its zenith as the former one did, but instead with a startling forward flip. Landing as smoothly as a feather upon a sleeping kitty cat, her position again was only a foot or two from him when she paused to breathe deeply.

Their eyes met. He smiled. As she!—though she quickly changed her marvelous smile into a coquetting one, and, began a slow, soft, rhythmical backing away from him, keeping her eyes locked with his. Swaying as she moved, she stopped within the soft glow of the small flame near the door. There, producing no movement which would detract his apt attention from the playing of the instruments, she stood posed — waiting for the change of tempo in the music.

On the first note she bounced a little bounce, spryly advanced with a cartwheel and a forward flip, and ended the dance step with a splits similar to the first one except that she did not pause in that position; but quickly bounced up out of it, twisted around in a tight circle and landed in another splits with her legs extended outward to either side. With her body and outstretched hands upon the floor resting in front of her, she was breathing heavily. Her back rose and lowered in beat with her breathing. He was breathless.

Remaining in the splits, she straightened her back, and raised her hands from the floor. Rolling them to the rhythm of the music, she leaned to her right and stretched her arms out, and patted the floor on that side of her. Then she lowered her head to that knee. There she paused perfectly stretched out.

She then raised her upper body and, with a swaying of her arms and shoulders, she did another roll with her hands out in front of her; swayed some more; and, still in the splits, turned and leaned far to her left and patted the floor on that side to the time of the music with her hands:climaxing the delightful movement with another lowering of her head to that knee.

Often at that point in the dance a companion, a strong male dancer, would come to the maiden and gracefully enter into the swaying of the music and, with nary an effort, help her up in a single deft move even as he would continue the rest of the dance together with her: the two appearing as one.

But not this time. She was alone. She wanted to be alone. Wanted no other male in the room...except the one lying in his bed before her. She was not there to simply entertain. She had come prepared to become his new favorite and her dance was her special voluntary offering of herself to him. She knew it, he knew it. She, therefore, came up off the floor effortlessly without help and continued her flawless dance movements with an ever increasing concentration and intensity.

Indeed, lying there in complete satisfaction, her master

could not find one movement, one series of steps, one angle of her form which was out of place; which was poorly executed; which did not emanate infallibly out of the fashioning of her body which she had composed the instant before it.

When she finished, and was still lying collapsed in a heap before him, he became anxious to climb off the bed and join her there down upon the floor and to tell her that he had just seen the single greatest dancing performance that he had ever witnessed in his entire life. Instead, he acknowledged to her musicians his appreciation for the part they had provided in the entertainment, and, with a nod of thanks, dismissed them. They, induced by the beauty of her movements, rose, gathered their instruments, and left as naturally, and graciously, and effortlessly as if they were dancers themselves.

Machal rose and approached him.

He thanked her for the highly entertaining, beautiful evening. He especially complemented her on her perfect form. At that same instant he decided to wait to share with her his many thoughts concerning his multiplied plans for his and hers joined future: which telling would obviously disclose the truth that everything about her from his very first glimpse of her as she entered through the passageway door, to her final collapse upon the floor immediately before him, everything about her proved that she would indeed become his new favorite.

Therefore, since he had decided to wait to say anything, after he thanked her, he simply lay there and waited for Machal to kneel upon his bed. Which she soon readily did. Even then, as she began kneading his leg with her strong fingers, he was exceedingly aware of his anxiousness to share with her that everything he saw in her awesome ability to entertain and please him had brought to him the memory of Hannah, how it had caused him to once again believe that there was indeed someone out there who was now with him, who could truly bring into his bedchambers the love and pleasure that Hannah would have brought.

As she massaged his thigh, however, she quickly proved to him that she would not become his next favorite. It was too evident. In that extremely crucial area of truly being able to please him and to make him feel that he was all she genuinely cared about, she was not another Hannah. It was incredible! Heart-rending. Crushing. He could not believe it. Her fingers upon him were as deft as her dancing form. But the ability to totally give of herself to him in complete sacrifice was not the natural emanation of her being as was her dedicated ability to execute her dance steps, and as was her obvious willingness to sit by the hour to receive her beauty and other treatments.

He had to acknowledge that instead of becoming another Hannah, Machal was an extremely extraordinary dancer who, along with those previous fifteen maidens who also had come into his chambers after Hannah to attempt to be the one who would replace her, was failing to convince him that he was indeed her chief reason for being here in his presence.

Perhaps Hannah was only one of a kind.

Perhaps Solomon would never have found other maidens like her if he had searched solely in Judah.

Her fingers worked upon his muscles: probing, kneading, pinching, pressing; nevertheless, he could sense that it has not being performed in and with unbounded internal enthusiasm. Discouraged, he acknowledged to himself that her movements were being performed out of this maiden's required 'duty' to her monarch—why could these lovely maidens not understand that pleasure given without measure would be reciprocated to them in an equal or greater amounts by him?

If you had only understood it, he thought as he lay there, you could be standing next to me in the morning. You could be next to me in possibly the greatest morning of my reign. Until you or some other understands it as Hannah understood it, there is no way your fingers can do their task as expertly, as genuinely, as caringly, as wonderfully as my favorite's deft fingers had moved upon my being. He shut his eyes.

Machal had raised such a hope in his being as she had made her entrance; she had raised even greater hope in him with her awesome devotion to her expertise in pleasing him with her dance. No doubt, she would enter his dancing troupe and would become the palace's preeminent performer. No doubt, she would greatly please multitudes wherever she put on her performances. No doubt, heads would turn whenever she walked by. No doubt about it. Nonetheless, she failed to do what she had come to do. She had failed to become his new favorite. She had failed to become Hannah.

Much more would have to come from within her. It could not be trained. He had tried with many in the past. None had been able to receive such instruction nor would this one be able to. It had to come from within her. Magnificent, beautiful Machal thus would become one more maiden whom he would never call into his chamber again. Never except as a dancer.

Turning over, accepting her massage for what it was, he lay there long and reminded himself that otherwise he was exceedingly joyful with all that was happening within Judah since the miraculous stopping and backing up of the sun.

Seven months had passed.

Seven marvelous months!

Seven months of astonishing accomplishments within his nation. Once the staggering news that the tumultuous sign accompanying his healing was spread, those reports, coupling the two, brought forth a fearsome trembling throughout his land and throughout all who traveled in his territory. The most significant, internal result was his being able to quickly gather together a large number of men, willing and ready, to form a standing army of Judah. In that he had them fully ready to fight for him as soon as the rainy season came to its end gave him even greater hope. When they practiced, they went like a rambling bank of clouds, proving to him that they would be able to quickly move out across their former territory.

Following the ever-widening, sweeping knowledge of the mighty, earth-shattering, awesome, powerful act of their Lord, they easily won back all forty-six of their lost cities...and they reaped huge spoils from the kings of Ashdod, Ekron, and Gaza—immense heaps of silver and gold, hundreds of wagons of supplies and food which the rulers had brought in to replenish the cities given to them by the Assyrian prince.

Though Hezekiah had cried desperately the need of getting some miraculous act from his God after the Assyrian disaster, the dynamism of the particular sign which was sent by Him accomplished far greater advantages for his reign, than even he ever envisioned a supernatural act could offer.

The arrival of the troupe of Babylonian emissaries in the morning, was a direct result of the miraculous sign. The soon arriving envoys from Babylon were King Merodach-baladan's personal emissaries. All scouting reports agreed that they were coming with a long train of camels laden down with many, many valuables. And, as such, their coming promised of being an important investigative attempt of an highly real possibility of their two nations joining together into an alliance to fight against the empire in both ends of its territory.

Wealth brings many friends! *Shades of King Solomon!* he thought with pride...still lying face-down upon the bed as he reflected upon the months and barely noticed Machal's hands upon his back. Reigning in Jerusalem had become eminently better, much richer, and much more fun since the miraculous happening of the sun and since his own much-talked-about miraculous healing. Indeed, a good seven months, he thought, as Machal's working fingers drew again his attention as they moved down onto his thighs. In his renewed cognizance of Machal, he slid his hand down along the bed where he lightly rubbed her bare upper thigh—and thought, even Eliakim had worked out better than he had ever expected.

Shortly after his miraculous healing, Mehujael approached him with the desire to be released from his duties over his household, naming age as his primary reason. Upon accepting his resignation, Hezekiah chose Eliakim, another exceedingly trustworthy servant of his, to replace him.

Earlier in this evening before Machal had come to his chambers, Eliakim had been over for a formal dinner and the informal time of talking afterwards. It had been a joyful relaxing time for both of them. In the course of the evening, Hezekiah had informed him that a favorable meeting with the approaching Babylonian emissaries was extremely important for the further expansion of his kingdom.

In their discussion, he also shared with his new chief officer over his household that a welcoming party had already met together with the foreigners earlier that afternoon beyond Hebron down near the southern tip of the Great Salt Sea and that the group had been instructed to initiate the preparations for his meeting with those coming couriers. He informed him that he was sending two other envoys, Shebna his scribe and Joah his recorder, along with him to travel before dawn in the morning down to meet the coming band. Once they met with them, their duties were to officially escort the entire traveling party up to the city, and as they neared Jerusalem they were to offer the watering and resting privileges of En rogel to refresh themselves and to water all their animals.

Naturally, the traders would know all about En rogel, he had told him; but he still felt it was more fitting for his men to officially offer the use of their spring's plentiful water to them and to their animals, as well as to the visiting Babylonians.

After a cool drink was brought for them, he told him all he knew concerning this clandestine coming of these foreigners: in the end, he stated, their coming to us, and the purpose why they are coming to meet with us, will be the very first truly significant action extending beyond Judah's borders to occur after his healing, and that they were to look upon it as the first of what he had hoped would be many such visits.

Shades of Solomon! Wealth does bring many friends! He wallowed in the thrill of it! Because of his extreme elation concerning the coming day, he had been more unreserved with Eliakim than any meeting with him before...and was very pleased with the additional informal insights he had observed concerning Eliakim. His pleasure came especially as regarding his person. One key aspect which he felt he would cherish was Eliakim's and his ability to joke together.

"Do you remember when I nearly died with that boil and of many of the details concerning how ill I had become and how everybody here in the capital and throughout the land had given up any hope of my ever recovering?" he had asked.

"Sure do," Eliakim had answered. "How could any of our people forget it?"

"You should have seen Isaiah at the time," he had said, having desired for a long time to find someone with whom he could share a few humorous stories regarding their city's resident spokesman for the Lord.

"The word I had heard, was that you were not even allowing him to come and see you."

"You had heard correctly."

"Even he cou—"

"Not him. Not anyone. After the vanguard left I had denied everyone permission to see me. Everyone, that is, until the boil had become extremely enlarged and painful. Then, not being able to procure any relief, and certain that I was about to die, I finally acquiesced and sent a message asking him to seek from the Lord if He would give me a word concerning the pain. Our prophet, true to his pattern, was in no hurry in rushing over with the answer. When he finally came over there to my winter house, he rushed in determined to put me—another monarch in whom he was not entirely pleased—in my place. He was so ready to tell me that my time to live in this world had come to an end, that he entered into my room with his white majestic robes just a-flowing out back of him!"

Eliakim joined in laughing with him at that description of the prophet's robes a-flowing out in back of him. Then, feeling light and comfortable with the bantering, he jocosely asked, "He was that harsh even with you?"

"Many times! Being exceedingly friendly with the throne has never been the mark of a true servant of the Lord here."

"Yes, I see where that might hinder one from pronouncing the exact, uncompromising word of the Lord. Especially in an ungodly reign."

"You are right! And he had some extremely good practice on my father! He spoke many strikingly harsh words to him: words which I often heard here in this room, words which my father never heeded."

"That was unfortunate."

"I agree, Eliakim. Well, that day with me he was in top form—probably from being isolated from me for those nine weeks. He just stood squarely before me, hands on his hips, his eyes staring deeply into mine, and proclaimed, in a tone which definitely meant: *Thus says the Lord*, 'King Hezekiah, set your house in order; for you shall die, and not live.'"

"He did not!"

"Oh, yes, he did. He certainly did."

He laughed softly and then he became very solemn.

"Isaiah said it so concisely, so succinctly, so rock-hard

sure of its finality, I turned toward the wall in the deepest despair I had ever felt in my life and I wept bitterly. Eliakim, if you had been in my bedchamber that day, you might have prayed for leniency from our Lord God when I asked you to take over the headship of my household."

Keeping the jesting, which Hezekiah apparently wanted that evening, going, Eliakim retorted lightheartedly, "How does one say no to his ruling monarch?"

Hezekiah caught it and smiled fully.

He then entered into a serious mood, and, seemingly, wanted to stay in it until he had finished telling the account. "The surety of Isaiah's pronouncement against me caused me to cry loudly in my sorrow. Mourning like a dove, cackling like a laying hen, I wailed on and on, pleading with the Lord to heal me in His mercy in honor of my goodness."

Needing to be serious or not, his descriptions caused Eliakim, glowing with great enjoyment, to cut in, "Mourning like a dove and cackling like a laying hen! *That is good!*"

Hezekiah could no longer stay in his solemn demeanor. He cherished Eliakim's response to his words, and added with a shrug of his shoulders: "What can I say? That is what I did!"

They laughed together.

Then Eliakim seriously: "And you did not die."

"No I did not, even though he spun immediately around and left my room after he had pronounced my death sentence."

"With robes a-flying?"

"With robes flying straight out!"

Hezekiah laughed with Eliakim. And then said seriously, "As soon as he had gone I cried and wailed unto the Lord without ceasing. For well over an hour I bellowed away. And, I could not believe it!—Isaiah returned to my room!"

"He did not!"

"He most assuredly did! He said that he received another word from the Lord before he had even left my house!"

Tom Steinbach

"Before he left your house? You said more than a hour later he came back up here to your chambers."

"Right."

"Why did he take so long?"

"Our prophet has a strong constitution...we both have a strong constitution, Eliakim—I got mine from my father—and, I am not so sure that our resident spokesman for the Lord was pleased with the changed forecast."

"How can that be? You have always been a more righteous ruler over our nation than your father or almost all of our other rulers ever were."

"But not as righteous as Isaiah would have liked me to have been. Also, he knew I did not have a son: perhaps he felt the Lord would have made him the prophet and ruler over our nation as Samuel had once been. I do not know. Anyway he came back into my room and told me the words that I wanted to hear: 'The Lord has changed His decree.'"

"You must have been beyond joy."

"Be...yond!"

They laughed.

"He said the Lord's amended judgment upon me was: I have heard King Hezekiah's prayers, I have seen his tears, behold, I will add fifteen years unto his days."

"Fif...teen!—now it is my turn to embellish. I had not heard that before."

"Fifteen years, Eliakim. Isaiah told me that we would recover quite well during the rest of that year from the devastations that the Assyrians had ravaged throughout our land, and, that this year our harvest would be even better, and, that next year's harvesting will be an exceedingly great one."

"He told you that?"

"Yes, seven months ago: while I was still lying upon my bed of sorrow."

"Well, Sir, he has certainly been right about your healing

and about this year's growing season. I would never have believed that we could have recovered out there in our fields as speedily and as well as we have."

"We have bounced back remarkably well, have we not."

There followed a natural pause. During which they did not even attempt to hide the pride they felt.

"I am curious, the second time when Isaiah came back into your room, were his white majestic robes still a-flowing?" The laughter and overall happy time which followed that was as natural as the pause had been prior to it. "I am also curious—though more serious. You said that you had had some dreadful thoughts before he came back up here with the new word?"

"Yes, I did. Very troubling thoughts."

"What were some of those?"

Liking Eliakim more and more, Hezekiah took a swallow of juice and answered, "One thing I remember wailing was, 'I am deprived of the residue of my years!'"

"I would think that would be one of the first things any of us would fear and say. Nobody wants to die before his time—at least what he believes is his time."

"It certainly was one of my first. Even now...I am only forty year old—my great grandfather *reigned* fifty-two !"

"That is a long time!"

"Oh, I would love to reign that long." He paused, thinking about that. He then added, "Another thought, was, 'I shall behold man no more with the inhabitants of the world.'"

They both nodded in agreement.

"And, I also remember this thought being strong within me as that time of mourning drew longer and longer: 'He has chosen to cut me off from the living with pining sickness. From day even to night will He make an end of me.'"

"Your opinion of Him was not too high at that moment?"

"No, Eliakim, I had truly thought He had previously let me and our nation down when those Assyrians came into our land.

Tom Steinbach

When they came into our city He should have come to our aid at that time and defended us. Then, after Isaiah brought his harsh, condemning word concerning the massive boil, I had to think that the Lord was once again letting me down. I could not understand it: I had attempted to bring our peoples back to a correct worship of Him, and here He was allowing me— *causing me!*—to pine away with that horrible boil...with that unbearable sickness."

"It must have been hard."

"It was excruciating."

"I am so thankful that our Lord God changed His decree against you. In my eyes you have been such a good king, and now, now you are such a good master to work under."

"Thank you, Eliakim."

"Thank you for being what you are. And, thank you for sharing your thoughts with me."

"I had Shebna write down all my thoughts at the time, possibly he can remember some other pleas to share with you and Joah as you three travel together in the morning. If not, remind me again some day and I will show that scroll to you. On that same scroll I also had him record my good thoughts."

Eliakim's eyes betrayed him once again.

"Oh, yes, Eliakim, I even had some of those! But only after Isaiah had come back into my room, you understand!"

"I understand," Eliakim said. They laughed.

"After I recovered from my sickness, one very pleasant thought I remember exclaiming to the Lord was: 'You have delivered my soul from the pit of corruption, for You, my Lord God, have cast all my sins behind my back.'"

"You felt your sins were the—"

"No, not really. In fact, my cry to the Lord after I heard of my impending death was that I had been righteous before Him. But, we all sin...and any healing is a tribute that the Lord is willing to look beyond those sins."

"The way you state it, it sounds like something David would or could have prayed in his psalms."

"It probably is certainly close to something he said, I know I was definitely reading a lot from the scrolls of his psalms as the pain got worse and worse! Eliakim, I really thank you for spending this evening with me. This time with you has been very good for my spirits."

"Me too, Sir, thank you."

"Thank you, Eliakim."

Not desiring the time with his new chief steward to end, he added, even though he had the new maiden coming into his chambers, possibly another Hannah, "Back to my dreadings, I remember another pleading which I earnestly cried out to our God in my fear: 'The grave cannot praise You! Death cannot celebrate You! The living—not the dead nor the grave—it is the living! It is only the living that can praise You!'"

Eliakim agreed with that one, "I really like that argument. I will remember that one the next time I get exceedingly sick! 'The living! The living!'" They chuckled aloud.

When the time finally came for Eliakim to leave, Hezekiah said to him, "There are many bright spots among the mire of our peoples' continual unbelief and lack of interest in obeying only the Lord as their God. You, Eliakim, are one of those bright spots. I am truly glad and thankful that I have had this opportunity to discuss these many things with you."

"Thank you, Sir."

"Long ago, Eliakim, I heard of your strong belief in our Lord. So through the years I and my men have observed your life when the occasions arose. When Mehujael came and said that he wanted to be relieved of his responsibilities, I was surprised, but I watched you even more. You understand I wanted only the right man to be my chief chamberlain. Guardedly, but with a definite eye, I watched your life and mannerisms. I had different menservants and friends ask you planted questions. Many times. On every occasion I was told of your faithfully expressed belief in our Lord God. I needed no other determinant, Eliakim—though through their counsel I also picked up many other reasons I wanted you. It was therefore with an unanxious heart that I chose you for this position. After all that I had heard, and had observed, I truly wanted you near me and over my household."

"Thank you again, Sir. I never knew."

"I know you did not." There was a tender pause. "Eliakim, I am pleased to tell you that Mehujael was highly delighted when he heard whom I was thinking to replace him with."

Eliakim lost his composure and lowered his head. When he spoke, his throat was croaky, and his head was down. "I only hope that I am able to do the multitude of duties as well as Mehujael did—and as well as you are hoping I will."

"You have, and you will."

He raised his head. They faced each other. Their eyes were both wet. Though neither brought forth tears.

Hezekiah raised his hand from Machal's leg, and moved it up to his face. The tears did not come earlier when Eliakim was with him back then, but now he had some to brush away.

Beautiful one beside me, if only you would have worked out as well as my chief steward has. If only you had become my new favorite. The three of us, *the three of us,* could have made such a team for our Lord God. Such a team.

The dawn broke bright and sunny. It would be a perfect day for meeting with, and entertaining, the visiting emissaries. Hezekiah was in one of his favorite places in all the palace: standing by his bedchamber window which looked out toward the eastern hills. His mother would soon come to eat together in the royal dining room for a quiet breakfast. The early morning sunrise was perfect. He wished that they had not arranged the meeting: she had her ways of sabotaging a bright, expectant day. Waiting, he moved over to another window which gave him a view of the entire temple complex.

He had worked extremely hard to make certain that the visitors from Babylonia would see his capital as it should be seen: lively, wealthy, glistening! Never again would the emissaries of a foreign kingdom look upon his city as a peasant's mountaintop capital. The temple had been completely repaired and looked magnificent in the morning's bright sunlight. The priests were in the best and newest of clothing and were in full numbers as they moved upon and around the brazen altar, the molten sea, the courtyards and the multitude of various lavers and basins and stairways.

Especially standing out in their bright clothing, and in their specially chosen locations-to-be-seen-for-their-faithfulness, were the priests who had stood behind his policies for the last fifteen years—those who were not continuing to push for the return of the years of his father.

Those priests included: Mahath the son of Amasai, Joel the son of Azariah, Kish the son of Abdi, Azariah the son of Jehalelel, of the sons of the Kohathites, the sons of Merari, the sons of Shimri and Jeriel, Joah the son of Zimmah, Eden the son of Joah, the sons of Elizaphan, Zechariah and Mattaniah, the sons of Heman, Shemaiah and Uzziel, the sons of Jeduthun, Asaph, Jehiel, and Shimei. They were the priests who entered into the inner parts of the temple in his first year; who cleansed it and brought out the uncleanness of his father's reign from within its hallowed confines. The same priests who took down and smashed the brazen serpent which had become one of the heathen, idolatrous symbols of occultic, mystifying powers in use during many of those rites in his father's reign.

It will be a great day for them, he thought.

He ordered many colorfully dressed Levites to be playing before their house of the Lord and near the king's gate upon their cymbals, psalteries and harps: these were the instruments of David made famous throughout the world. Many others were to sound forth with their various trumpets loud and clear. Along with them, their temple's singers and dancers were to sing and dance with joy and gladness their spirited praises unto the Lord the words of David and Asaph.

Each and every torn awning on the stalls throughout the bazaar parts of the city had been newly made and hung during the previous week. An edict had been posted throughout the city citing that all streets and avenues within their city were to be swept daily and that there should be no playing in them by their children from the day before the emissaries arrived until the evening after the party had returned to their land.

The Babylonians themselves, with the bands of Bedouin traders, had come across the desert on the deep southern route which passed through Tema. The traders suggested that route because of its distance away from the Assyrian's territory: the Easterner couriers were bringing too many precious gifts not to raise the suspicions. It was better to travel this faraway southern route. The Babylonians were also ready to pay the tax due outside the city gates required of the Bedouin traders for their being able to bring their goods into the city to trade and sell. That was their reciprocal offer to the Bedouins for bringing them secretly across the Arabian Desert. It was also further payment for the startling information that other Bedouin traders had passed on to their King Merodach-baladan concerning where the wonders originated which had occurred throughout the world seven months earlier.

Three months after the renown worldwide happenings the traders had been escorted into Merodach-baladan's presence, alleging that they had convincing evidence that the Hebrew monarch Hezekiah and his God had been the ones responsible for all the terrifying wonders which had occurred across the world's landscape and its various kingdoms. Looking for assistance from the western end of the empire's territory, the

Babylonian monarch had accepted their offer of information hoping that they really did have the goods they firmly claimed.

Once before him, they told him of the stories and strange happenings: many, many of them which they had heard in the different camps on their journey. They related that Hezekiah, the king of Judah, had appeared to them sick unto death on a stretcher borne by six bearers when they had first seen him. For some reason he had been carried out of his winter house...though it had been a very cold day, they told the Babylonian king. They then recounted how, on his way over to his palace, that the ailing Hebrew monarch had commanded his bearers to carry him over to them. And then, how he had said very weakly, but very confidently, "My foreign trading friends, today look up, and watch that sky, and especially its sun closely. For, in this day, you will see an event so startling, no man living in our generations has ever seen one like it."

They explained how at first they had laughed the utterance off as the dazed mumbling of a delirious old king returning to his official palace to die. Indeed, they had actually laughed among themselves even before he was in his palace but out of their hearing range. And it was not merely that...they had begun sharing among themselves how they were going to pass the humorous sayings on to all their desert-traveling co-journeyers in their various and sundry encampments.

Definitely inclined to put no significance to the words of the dying Hebrew king, they *were* surprised to find themselves catching each other glancing up into the sky as the moments passed. Having nothing else important to do, they finally agreed to obey him, and to remain where they could see the sky and its sun if anything did per chance happen.

Within two hours!...*within two hours!*...the earth beneath them shook violently! They were bolted them from the wall on which they were leaning! The sun, when they had the presence of mind to look at it, had reversed its position from being a degree or two passed a banner pole to the southwest of them, to being at least eight or nine degrees back on the eastern side of the pole! It was terrifying! They began calling out to every god and goddess!—and to every stick and stone!—they had ever heard of! It was incredible! It was frightening!

They then related how that when the shaking stopped and how they wanted to immediately race back into the merchant's section of the Hebrew's capital and to share with the citizens of that city about the dreadful happenings and share how their ruler had told them to watch for it...and then they explained that they decided that they should at least wait for the Hebrew king to come out of his palace to return again to his winter house...since they were very certain that he had not returned to the palace to remain the night—though they had wondered earlier among themselves why he had gone over to his cold summer residence in the first place. For certainly, they had agreed among themselves, he could have watched the sun and its shadows' various movements from some window in his winter house in much greater comfort.

King Merodach-baladan was on the very edge of that throne when they told him next of how the Hebrew king had come out through the palace gates once again, and had directed his bearers to carry him over to them. They related that Hezekiah was still as white as one of their desert tents; in fact, that he might have looked even more ready to leave this world than when he had first appeared to them. He was as white and peaked as a newly sheared lamb. In his eyes and in his words, however, had been the bubbling, life-promising assurance that in only days he would be off his bed of death. "What did I tell you!" he had cried out to them as best as he could cry out in his still near-death state. "My bearers and I almost fell right off my palace roof garden! Did I not tell you to watch the sky and its sun?

"But that spectacular happening is not the end of it," he

then further confided to them. "Come here." They had already been really close to him—him being a monarch and all—but he wanted them to come closer to him still...a mighty peculiar request from that dying, unprotected monarch of a foreign nation, they had thought. Nevertheless, having lived through that earth-shattering scene they were all believers that he was one who was not afraid of anything or anybody at that moment. Therefore he invited them over, and they obeyed.

They approached closer, he had a servant remove a couple of the heavier animal skins which were over him and then he had another servant remove the linen cloths which had been carefully placed around the largest boil they had ever seen upon a human being. They had seen huge boils like that on dying beasts of burden along trade routes on their treks; but, never had they seen one so enormous upon a human being.

"Three days from now," he said to them—forcing each one of his words because of the extreme cold chill on his flesh, "come to the visitors' courtyard of Solomon's temple."

It had not been an order. He had said it 'friend to friend'— they felt that he knew they would not have missed anything else he suggested to them! They confirmed that judgment by him by telling King Merodach-baladan that, at the moment, they would have climbed the twin pillars of the Jewish temple or would have even gone down to the muddy River Jordan and washed themselves seven times, if he had so ordered them.

"On..the..third..day..the..next..miraculous..sight..you..will.. see..will..not..be..so..earth..shak..ing," he had croaked and had poorly attempted a grin in that cold air, "but..you..will..see..me see..me..raised..up..off..this..stretcher..and..walking..around..as a..well..man..with..this..boil..entirely..gone..from..my..body."

They looked at the massive boil again, then at themselves, and again at the discolored, infectious flesh all around the boil and silently agreed that these words would never happen: no matter how miraculous the 'celestial' event had been that they

211

had witnessed, the hopeful monarch in front of them probably would be dead before he got comfortably placed back in his bed in his winter house. It would have to take an extremely mighty act of his Lord God Jehovah for that boil to be even slightly smaller in three days, let alone his being able to rise up, and walk, with the boil totally removed from his body.

But, since he had been so right on his first statement about the sky and though they had wanted to get moving to tell the outside world about the origin of the backward movement of the sun, they told Merodach-baladan, they had felt fated to remain in Jerusalem, the capital of Judah, another three days. After all, being travelers all their lives they had seen many strange sights, and had encountered extremely weird events on their many travels; nevertheless, even for them, it had never happened before that one single, so astounding miracle was told to them *prior* to the actual thing happening.

Three days later they were therefore obediently waiting in the courtyard of the heathen—that is what all non-Hebrews are called in that capital, they had explained to the king—but they had not gone there alone. They had been able to convince four more bands of desert traders to go there with them. They had tried to convince many more who had come into the city telling all manner of shocking stories of strange, violent upheavals occurring in every place where they had traveled, as well as, in every place where other traveling nomads had been who had shared with them all their similar unaccountable happenings in their different camps in their journeys.

The sun's strange movements and the wonders associated with it had dominated every conversation and opportunity of story-telling in which they had been a part...therefore in the ensuing days, they felt that everyone they would share with would have scrambled to be with them on that third day. When it was almost noon, however, they had only the four other bands with them—and, they had begun to feel that the dying

Hebrew ruler had just been fortunate in his first guess. For there was no sign of him, nor was there any sign of a large, official gathering being called for that day.

The others, having not been involved in the first marvelous happening, were getting very bored and very anxious to get back to their bartering in the streets...when...when...when they all saw a small circle of people coming out from the direction of Hezekiah's winter house! It was with unimaginable excitement, therefore, that they all squinted their eyes and looked earnestly at that company! The king must not have spread the word to his own people, they had surmised as they waited for that party to come toward the temple—for the citizens of that city did not seem the least interested in that formed party. That is, those citizens which were afar off like they were. The citizens much closer to the company quickly became spirited!—and instantly got noisy!—and posthaste!— the gathering of Hebrews grew very quickly! They themselves and those near them began to get more excited! And more intrigued!—for they could not see anybody being carried along on some pole stretcher! Their new friends then looked at them skeptically, and so they motioned with their hands where the boil had been on King Hezekiah and how large it had been when they had seen it.

Soon the coming company was nearly abreast of them. When King Hezekiah, the Hebrew ruler, spotted them—he had appeared as if he had been looking for them—and he had ordered that company to stop long enough for him to break from its gathering, he walked over to them as full of life and health and strength as a man could be! He was the sight of perfect health! The enlarged boil was totally gone! The pale whiteness of his face was gone! And the ever-so-near presence of death was also gone!

Merodach-baladan had looked at them with such unbelief at that moment in the telling of their story, that they had to repeat to him. "It is true, Sir! He was in perfect health!"

He appeared so healthy in fact, they had testified, that they would never have believed that he had been even a little sick, let alone so gravely ill that he was nigh unto death with a mammoth boil! Truly, though they had seen him up close before, their friends never did believe that he could have been so gravely ill even though all the Hebrews had told them the same story. King Hezekiah then said to them that the startling true events of those three days should prove to them conclusively that the Lord God of Israel was the all-powerful, the all-glorious, the Almighty Creator of the heavens and their earth. To him they had agreed. But later among themselves they said that they would never be able to trade in all the cities of the East if they, in actuality, embraced his Hebrew religion.

King Hezekiah also then told them that for some unknown reason his Lord had remained completely silent during the Assyrian's last devastating visit but that they could tell whatever Assyrians they met on their travels that they had better be extremely cautious of returning so ruthlessly to his end of their kingdom again.

It was that statement more than any other which convinced Merodach-Baladan that he should try to make their present overture toward creating an alliance with the equally rebelling Hezekiah of Judah. Having experienced the earth-shattering effects of the sun stopping in his own land also, and the total fear which it had brought within his own being...and, having heard of numerous confirmed reports of similar upheavals all through the lands where his traveling merchants went, he felt he had waited long enough to secure the services of these experienced desert traders to lead his men over to Jerusalem.

Near the conclusion of the session with him, the traders added this insight: "King Hezekiah seemed extremely pleased that we had remained in his city long enough to see his healing. But his heart seemed to expand even more greatly when he saw great multitudes of his own citizens coming up toward him from the city, King Merodach-Baladan.

"We have therefore concluded that he truly feared during his illness that his people were not behind him. If that was the case, and that certainly appeared to be, we can tell you as surely as our camels could lead us across the Arabian Desert blindfolded, King Hezekiah now has no dread whatsoever of his people attempting to remove him from their throne. Nor does he have any fear of the mighty Assyrian army if it indeed does return to his land. He has no worry whatsoever!"

*

> > > * < < <

*

Before he left his chambers to meet the emissaries, He thought about losing Hannah. Over the past seven months, his army had not been able to gather any information on her in any of the cities they had recaptured. The reports concurred in nearly every city that it was with a great fanfare that the empire's troops lead by Prince Sennacherib and his three proud officers had passed through their streets leading much plunder on camel back, on foot, and in their multitude of wagons on their way back home...but that no young, beautiful maiden of Hannah's description had come to the attention of any of them. If she had been reported sighted, he did not know of anything he could have done about it; nevertheless, he still longed to hear something, no matter how trifle, and he still longed for her. He desperately wanted her presence right that moment beside him. He knew that he felt that he always would. And therefore he would always hope for the slightest, the most remote, word that he might receive which would tell anything of her.

*

> > > *SIXTEEN* < < <

*

"How can our Lord God bless you in this?" his mother asked him not too long after they met that morning for breakfast.

"Mother, the Lord has been blessing me abundantly for the last seven months, why would He not continue to do so?"

"He has been. But our Lord cannot keep on blessing you if you initiate all these meetings entreating strange idolatrous kingdoms to join us in all manners of alliances, and if you still demand to retain your house of women."

"I am not going out and courting strange kingdoms and I do not keep the house up for the pleasures the maidens give me. Mother, I am only looking for another Hannah. I find her, and I will forsake the whole house."

"Why do you continue to attempt to fill it after all the Lord has done for you these past few months?"

"I told you. To find another Hannah."

"So my son, the righteous Hezekiah of Judah, is searching for alliances with pagan countries and is stripping young innocent maidens from their homes, and families, and bringing them into his house of women so that he can forsake them."

"Moth—"

"That is evil, Hezekiah, pure evil. Those maidens should not be forced to leav—"

"Mother!"

"Even if you do find another favorite, Son, will that not mean continuing to multiply wives unto yourself? Why can Hephzibah not be your other Hannah?"

Surprised, not being able to rid his mind of how genuine and truly wonderful it had been with Hephzibah the last two times, and how disappointing it had been with every maiden since Hannah had been taken, he said, "I would be extremely pleased if Hephzibah would be, but she will not."

"When did you last ask her to be with you?"

"I have asked her to come to me twice since the reversing of the sun."

"And?"

"She came, and she was very amorous."

"Different?"

"Yes, I would have to say different."

"Well?"

"Mother, you and I both realize that she has lost her children and that she was only interested in being certain that another son or daughter—which obviously means another daughter—was begun one of those two nights."

"You know that?"

"You and I both know that!"

"What if she has really changed?"

"I know her, Mother."

"Did she argue with you?"

"Mother, she wanted another child."

"Well, I have reason to believe that she has changed."

"If Hephzibah has changed, she can come and tell me. You women are always talking among yourselves."

"But how can she tell you if you never call for her?"He did not respond. She therefore repeated:"Son, I said I have reasons to believe that she has changed."

"Well, I do not. And...right now I am more interested in what the Babylonian envoys have brought and what they are going to relate to me from their king."

"Because you think not, you will not allow her a chance to show if she has changed or not," she continued, disregarding his interest in the foreigners. "Hezekiah, you will not give her a chance. You will, however, continue stripping innocent girls from their homes and villages and give *them* a chance to see if they are like Hannah. And then reject them if they are not! I think that maybe you are the one who has not changed."

"Not changed? Have I not had a colossal, supernatural sign and healing given to me?"

"You have. But you have not given anything in return."

"In return? What are you saying? I have greatly increased my efforts to make our kingdom large again."

"So it can be led by another monarch who will not give himself wholly to the Lord?"

"Mother, what other ruler in our history has dedicated himself to all the righteous acts which I have? Go out into the streets—everybody is shouting that I have turned to the Lord more than any monarch in our history."

"Then why not go all the way, Hezekiah. Why not obey our Lord God completely?"

Has she really changed? Could that be possible? During those two nights she certainly did love me closer to my liking than any of those others that have come unto me in the last few months. Still, what if there is another magnificent maiden out there? What if there is another Han—

"Son, I asked you a question."

"Yes, I know. The same question you ask me every time there is an important meeting or an approaching day in which I need a relaxed morning in which to pause and simply make certain that the important items have been taken care of."

"Once again you are answering:no?"

"She is with child. Our baby is due in a few months. I will talk to Hephzibah after then."

"But the decision concerning your house of women does not need to involve her."

"Mother, I am committed to finding another Hannah."

"Whether you obey—"

"Our Lord God told Solomon that his father had walked in the integrity of his heart! What does that say to your question, Mother? Excuse me, I have to leave!"

"Leave if you must, Son, but think about keeping your house of women as adultery."

"As adultery?"

"Yes, Son. Why is it that to everyone else in our nation it is adultery to have more than one wife or maiden? Why is it that our leaders have been instructed to not multiply wives unto themselves as the heathen monarchs do? While you are thinking about it, also ask yourself why is it our peoples have been commanded so strongly not to commit adultery? Ask yourself, Son. All the other countries across the world include acts of unfaithfulness in their religious rites and prac—"

"Good-bye, Mother."

"Why do you feel—"

"Good-bye, Mother!"

"Son, why do you feel that you monarchs—supposedly, our leaders in righteousness—can thrive in such acts and not consider those acts as adultery?"

He was already out the door when she had finished her question. He had heard it in its entirety though.

She had watched him go, but did not leave herself. It made him angry—her continual harping upon his house of women. However, she was certain that her father would have also brought the subject up continually. Hephzibah unquestionably needed her to do so: for she could notice the difference. She had changed: undeniably changed. She had to get her son to ask for Hephzibah's presence to see that change. For his sake. For their nation's sake.

That moment had been a poor time to attempt to approach him on the subject. The way that he had walked in...she knew she did not have a chance. Hezekiah was too full of monarchical pride with the capital appearing the best that it ever had in his reign, and with the Babylonian emissaries coming with such a large train of camels ladened down with expensive gifts. She acknowledged that her real plan of the morning had not been to talk about Hephzibah and those women but to laud the looks of the city. However, when he entered the room with that air of prideful, full importance, she had given up immediately any desire to pat him on the back.

After he left, she had just wished that he would give his wife a chance. Even half a chance. Then she could pat herself on the back!

*

\>\>\> * \<\<\<

*

"Please invite her in," she had softly told her maidservant on that afternoon nearly nine months before. She smiled to herself as she thought about it. All that early afternoon after speaking with Mehujael, she had her maidservants help her make her chamber as homey and attractive as she could. She had been convinced that the meeting had to have the best atmosphere right from the beginning.

"Please have a chair over here, Sarai," she had said, as she watched her every move

That had been the first time she had ever seen the one which Mehujael said was the most special preparer of her son's maidens in the house of women.

"Mother of our gracious King Hezekiah, it is a very wonderful, pleasant surprise to be asked to come to your home this afternoon. I humbly thank you for the honor you do me." Sarai had said every word so sweetly. So lovingly...she remembered being humored within by the quiet thought that it was she who had felt being honored by having the house of women's renowned maidservant come to offer her some help.

As the afternoon drew on, in the course of their time together Sarai continued addressing her as the, "Mother of our gracious King Hezekiah." Finally, she asked her guest if she would please refer to her as Abijah.

"Mother of our gracious King Hezekiah, I could never do that!" she had answered immediately with her first excitement in the time together with her new friend

But, seeing Abijah's countenance drop ever so slightly, she quickly changed her position.

"Why of course, Abijah. What a beautiful name."

She certainly had been pleasant and charming...not at all what she had expected coming out of that house. The rest of their time together had been spent in her attempting to figure out how her guest had learned to pass her wonderful qualities onto those incoming young maidens.

By the time she left, Abijah had been convinced that Sarai could indeed work congenially with Hephzibah, and, more importantly, that she could indeed change her son's wife into a

Tom Steinbach

loving partner.

Standing by the window in the front upper floor of his palace, Hezekiah was thinking about those last two evenings with Hephzibah. When Hephzibah gets passionate, he smiled, I have had none other come across with such strength and fervency. I do not even know if Hannah would have had such power. Trouble is, Hephzibah carries on with that same intensity when she is out to let me know everything that is wrong with me, everything that is wrong with my plans, and everything that is wrong with my reigning. Still, Mother said she believed that Hephzibah has changed. She certainly was nice to be with those two nights.

*

\> \> \> * \< \< \<

*

He and his elders were sitting at feast with the emissaries. The Bedouin traders had already gone on their way into the capital after disclosing to him the most recent and most startling stories they had heard concerning the weird phenomena connected to the ten degree reversal of the sun.

He thought of the empire's king. Sargon II, the legitimate king, he who reigned in the ruthless tradition of his father, Tiglath-pileser III. After a decade of hearing bits and pieces concerning Sargon's torrid reign, he did have to admit that their priesthoods knew what they were after when they backed

222

him as that son who was the legitimate one to come to the throne. Indeed it was because of the intimidating Sargon and his glory-seeking crown prince that he had agreed to this meeting with the representatives of the king of Babylon.

The Assyrian Empire would someday return to his land as Isaiah had stated, he was certain that they would. Until that future day he had decided to do all he could to help fight against the empire becoming any larger than it already was. They had stripped him without mercy, without flinching and with too much glee. They took far more than they should have. His goal, perhaps along with these Babylonians envoys, was to make the empire pay for what they had done in his nation. Even if the Babylonians envoys and he were not able to agree sufficiently to join into an alliance, he still would gain much with having this meeting together with them. That gain would be some much needed stature and the many precious gifts the envoys had brought with them.

As promised, that morning they had paid the Bedouins' taxes at the outer gate of the city. Once inside, the traders had shown the emissaries the way to the king's gate. When he had seen the travelers approaching the guards at the gate, he left his palace window, and began to make his way toward his throneroom. According to his plan, the envoys' train was ordered to remain in formation near and around the front of the house of the forest of Lebanon. They had then been escorted by the porch of pillars, had been shown Solomon's temple high upon its platform, had been led into his palace where they were brought before him as he sat regally on his throne with his elders on either side along with all the majestic beauty he could devise. His goal: to delay their being able to present to him their sundry gifts until after they first had the opportunity to see him in his most favorable setting. The strategy was working: they had seemed extremely impressed by what they had seen outside and with what they were presently observing, and hearing. His only regret was that Hannah, or some another favorite, was not there in all this glory to observe it with him.

"King Hezekiah, eminent king of the Hebrews, beloved king of Judah, to you, our own most honored monarch, King Merodach-baladan, king of Babylon, beloved ruler, chosen of Ea, Shamash, Marduk, and Nebu, wishes to bring you praise for your most spectacular healing and for the celestial signs and wonders which accompanied it. It is because of the dual signs that our king, the highly honored one, has sent us to seek a friendship with your reign and with your peoples."

In their high fashion they droned on and on. Finally, they got to the important part: to the hope that soon their two independent nations could work together on all political and economical levels in an combined effort to thwart the empire's advance into any more expansion of its kingdom. He let them know that they were talking of the same hopes and desires which were also his own. They shared also how their wise monarch had been able to gain the independence of Babylon and of the surrounding cities and lands from the empire nearly a decade before; and how he was attempting to turn southern Babylonia once again into a full-fledged, powerful kingdom: strong enough to resist every assault from King Sargon's marauding troops and his devastating war engines.

He smiled with the visitor's choice of words: a marauding lion eating its prey was exactly what the empire's army had been in his territory throughout their previous campaign. He had even referred to the enemy with those same words. He was very pleased with these men's interest in his kingdom and with their opening offer. It was with a congenial spirit, therefore, he led them from his throneroom over to the house of the forest of Lebanon where all the beasts of burden had been relieved of their loads and the multitude of gifts had been placed inside the building.

Entering the house, he saw many priceless items of eastern

origin!...proving, that, in less than a year, the optimism over his reign had made a complete reversal. The earth-shattering, miraculous event and 'sign' was paying off much larger than he had ever expected. Truly this day was going to the first of many such overtures from many scores of other nations wanting his assistance in helping them resist the empire.

Greatly desiring to shove the message of the new wealth of his rule into circulation, he moved into the second phase of his plan: into that phase of lavishing before these men all the treasures of his nation in the most opulent manner possible. Before the day was out, he had showed them all: all his silver, all his gold, all his spices and costly ointments, all his armor...all that was in every treasury he owned. There was not anything in his dominion that he had not shown them. That plan, and execution of that plan, seemed perfect...*little did he or any of them know that King Sargon would soon exile Merodach-baladan from Babylon for many years.*

Tom Steinbach

PART II

THE

SILENT

BLAST

227

Tom Steinbach

701 B. C.

Tom Steinbach

*

> > > *SEVENTEEN* < < <

*

Hezekiah lay next to Hephzibah. His body shadowing her curled body, his free arm resting on her side, while his hand lay on her smooth thigh. When he came fully awake, his hand moved to the tender skin of her stomach.

He enjoyed holding it there. He was, however, vastly disappointed that he had awaken so soon after they had fallen asleep together.

By the location of the moon's bright light shining on the wall in their room he knew it was still before midnight.

He was thankful, truly thankful, that she and he had finally become man and wife as much as any king and queen who had reigned over Judah. He was almost fifty-two...and he was in his twenty-sixth year on the throne. He and his wife were one, had been for nearly a decade, as one as any two married people would ever want to be.

Three years ago Sargon had been ambushed and killed and his corpse had been allowed to remain unburied as food for the birds of prey. Crown Prince Sennacherib, the one who allowed that to happen to his own father, moved onto the throne as the empire's sole monarch.

After thirteen years, *King* Sennacherib was commanding his Assyrian army again in a thorough raiding of Hezekiah's territory. They had been back in the land two months, they had subdued his largest cities in the northern portion of his nation and a few of the most strategic cities and their suburbs along their chief coastal trade route. Instead of wasting as much time subjugating all of Judah's cities and suburbs as in the last visit over a decade before, this year they rushed southward toward the capital much more swiftly. He had defied them again! And they were moving in on him as fast as they could.

Lachish was already near its end.

Another vanguard was down at En rogel. Its choice forces, horses, chariots and wagons would be rested and outside his walls before the sun's rays would hit the temple's pillars in the morning. Manasseh, his ten year old son and child number-two following the Assyrians' first visit, was against all the tenets of his rule. Manasseh, taught by tutors who longed to open trade with the empire and to return to the idolatrous days of his grandfather's reign, was insisting upon the rights of the empire to control Judah and to collect all the tribute they were coming up claiming.

The empire was back in the land. Sennacherib was back besieging Lachish. The vanguard was back at En Rogel.

Manasseh, his only son, was vocally against him.

And, once again his nation's Lord God still had not intervened in any of his nation's battles. He accepted that the Lord had only promised to defend him and his city and not all the other land and cities which had already fallen, but the of the elite returned forward unit camping down by his city's lower reservoir—forced him to take a good look at the promise and at his own faith in regards to it.

Hephzibah stretched and moved toward him so the space between her and him vanished. Applying a little pressure, he drew her back's full length close to him as he thought about Sennacherib's first few reigning years.

At the ascension of most new rulers of any empire, many of the vassal states test the fortitude of the newly coming in monarch to prove if he has the strength of his predecessor. The same was true concerning King Sennacherib's new regime. Hezekiah was not the only one who had ceased paying the yearly tribute. At the removal of Sargon, the exiled King Merodach-baladan also had returned to that throne down south of the empire in Babylonia, with an even greater resolve to consolidate all the smaller city-states in southern Mesopotamia into a threatening power with the aid of Elam.

Sennacherib began reigning in Assyria ready to deal with each rebelling portion of his kingdom. As the crown prince, his duties had been extensive, and had been to the northwest of the empire while his father had led his armies to fight in the eastern end of their empire nearer their capital. In carrying out his duties, Sennacherib often did not agree with his father. Their outspoken quarrelling became well known through the fireside conversations of the many traders which traveled from city to city—there was not much surprise when he expressed no passion to have his father's lying-in-the-open, exposed-to-the-birds body returned back to the capital after his death.

Merodach-baladan's renewed rebellion was the threat of highest priority when Sennacherib began to reign. Because of Babylon's proximity to Assyria's capital, he therefore directed his empire's armies southward in his very first campaigns. Charging against the forces of Babylonians, Aramaeans, and Elamites he defeated them and then forced Merodach-baladan back into exile out in the marshlands. As far as Hezekiah knew he was still in hiding or was dead.

In his third year, he campaigned eastward against the cities in the mountains of Elam to forestall any further attempted confederations or military thrusts from that border, from that always troublesome direction. Thus he waited until this fourth warring season to make this promised return into Syria and Judah in the opposite end of his empire. It was inevitable: as in the east, he needed to crush any attempted western coalition of Syrians, Phoenicians, Palestinians, and Egyptians.

He first entered Syria. The coastal city Sidon expelled their ruler and immediately surrendered to him. Many other Syrian cities also swiftly followed their leading. He then defeated an Egyptian army which had come up to Eltekeh. In that end of his kingdom, Hezekiah was the only vassal monarch left to fight before he moved down to subjugate and rule the ancient kingdom of Egypt. He longed to become the first Assyrian monarch to ever reign over that land.

This summer's warring season's plan was simple: Lachish collapses soon and the smaller Libnah subdued. Then they would force Hezekiah succumb—if he had not surrendered to the vanguard unit before those fortress cities fell—and the elite troops would take an extremely large tribute, would dispose of that twice rebellious ruler by putting his eyes out, then flaying every inch of skin off his body, and finally severing his head from the rest of his body. He would keep the latter as a prize.

Jamil shared with Hezekiah that, as the then crown prince, Sennacherib had extremely enjoyed his return to Kalakh with the abundance from this land of the Hebrews thirteen years before; nevertheless, that victory entrance had been nothing compared to the more recent glories at the end of the last two season's campaigns: the glories of marching triumphantly into *his* own chosen capital city of Ashur as the victorious *ruler* of the empire with the bountiful treasures of Babylon and of the eastern mountain cities.

He had learned in his early military days as a crown prince of all the glory and wealth that awaited the ruthless, merciless ones who ruled their territories with adept aggressiveness. He, therefore, lusted to reign in the tradition of his grandfather Tiglath-pileser III and of his father Sargon II. Intimidation and threats would be the only acceptable goal accompanying his presence in any of his realm.

The scouting reports delivered to Hezekiah describing the returned vanguard was anything but hopeful. The forces were larger than the ones which had come up against him before. Larger and mightier. If his Lord remained silent and did not come to his aid in this season's siege, he was convinced that he would not be in one piece when the vanguard left. What those reports had not been able to confirm was whether the leader of the vanguard was indeed the same Rabshakeh that had come the last time or not. He really wished he knew. But what did that really matter, he thought as he lay there. If this one was not that same one, the threatening leader of this visitation would be no less vicious, no less vile.

He kissed Hephzibah's shoulder.

She yawned, turned her head toward him, smiled, and kissed him on his mouth. She then yawned again, and settled back to sleep on his arm, facing him this time. He was kidding himself, he thought as he kissed her forehead, it really did matter—and he would know if it was the same despicable Rabshakeh on the very first sound of the very first syllable of that very first word of that very first sentence he heard the coming leader shout in clear Hebrew over the wall.

He had always known that this day would eventually come. He had probably always hoped that it would never come. And now that it had come, was determined this time not to open his gates to these heathens no matter what happened. He shuttered at the thought.

Hephzibah felt it in her sleep and groaned slightly...she did not awaken. He looked at her, he was thankful that she was the one who was lying next to him, he was thankful that she, at long last—nearly ten years ago—had become his favorite, and still was. He kissed her forehead again, and kept his lips next to her as he thought about the obvious pattern of the summer so far. It had been nearly the same as the empire's previous invasion of his land and city: the army had moved without hindrance wherever their war strategy led them.

Lord, he prayed in his thoughts, You told me long ago through Isaiah that the Assyrians would come again...but You also promised through him that when they did You would defend our city. Hephzibah stirred and he gently pulled her closer to him. She hugged him, and kissed him, smiling after the kiss, and looked at him sleepily....

*

> > > * < < <

*

When he next awoke, he was disappointed. However, he accepted that he would intermittently awaken and sleep for the duration of that night. Lying there, he thought of a time he had with Eliakim earlier in the week.

In hope of convincing his chief chamberlain, and maybe even he himself, he had decided to share with Eliakim those reasons why he was certain that their Lord would give a decisive victory over the Assyrians this time around. He gave a number of good reasons, then he offered another one which occurred with Isaiah back at the time King Merodach-baladan had sent his troops of emissaries along with the lengthy caravan of camels laden down with their many expensive gifts.

"Am I correct?" Eliakim asked, "Is he still their king?"

"No, he retook the control of Babylonia when King Sargon died, but now he is hiding out in the southern Mesopotamia marshland, or he may even be dead. No one seems to know for sure. However, back at the time of his sending his emissaries and those many presents, he was ruling in Babylon as its sovereign monarch. In fact, he was the reason Sargon sent his crown prince into our land to get their tribute the first time."

"Because he did not trust being far away from his capital when Merodach-baladan was eyeing that end of his empire?"

"I am certain of it."

"You are."

"It was only a short time after Merodach-baladan sent his envoys and presents here that King Sargon felt it necessary to send his army down there and rout him out."

"Ten years ago?"

"Around then. It was shortly after the Babylonian party came here. And then shortly after Sargon's death a few years ago, Merodach-baladan returned and regained his leadership over Babylon and the surrounding provinces."

"Then, Merodach became Babylon's sole monarch on two different occasions?"

"Yes. When Sargon was king and again when Sennacherib became king. Each time he became the sole ruler of Babylon shortly after a change of kingship in the empire."

"And he may now be dead?"

"He may be. The most recent reports I have received from that direction state that he has probably died. But even those reports are not for certain."

"So we do not know?"

"We do not. What we know concerning over there is that last warring season the Assyrian forces fought in the eastern end of their empire again and they came up with no hint of his whereabouts. If he is dead, it is too bad, because his presence over there kept the empire from paying much notice to us."

"I hear what you are saying."

"Eliakim, it is very important for these new monarchs to prove their ruthless ability to control all of their vast territory. In Sennacherib's second and third year he had to crush every uprising opposition in that end of his kingdom—and that is why he has come over here this year."

"To prove that he has total control at this end of his kingdom also."

"Yes, to do precisely that."

"I am thankful that my first chance of being your envoy was to those who desired to court our friendship."

"It was good to have them interested in being on our side back then. Here is a story concerning then that you do not know. I have shared it with very few. When I saw King Merodach-baladan's letter and all the camels laden down with those expensive gifts, I became beside myself with importance ...and with the erroneous belief that our Lord was going to use our nation and the Babylonian one to squeeze the empire from both ends and defeat those heathens. In my foolish pride and desire to show them how glorious my nation was, I personally led the emissaries through our glittering capital and showed them every precious thing I could find to place before them."

"I remember that day. I know you were riding high."

"O, my chariot wheels could not have touched the ground if the temple itself had been placed on it!" They both laughed. "That is...until Isaiah came charging back with his majestical robes flying straight out! Without any introductory statements, he speared me with question after question after question. The answer to each and every one of them he already knew: I am as certain now as I was back then. 'Who were these men? Where were they from? What did they see?'"

"I can see him doing that," Eliakim expressed, nodding his head in total understanding.

"When I had answered all of his questions, he faced me

with as stern a look as I have ever seen him give and said to me: 'Behold, the days are coming, that all that is in your house and that which your fathers have laid up in store until this day shall be carried away to Babylon! Nothing shall be left!'"

"To Babylon?"

"That is what he said, Eliakim. He even added, 'And your sons which shall issue from you'—I did not have any sons at the time— 'which you shall beget, shall they take away, and shall be eunuchs in the palace of the king of Babylon.'"

"Eunuchs?—in Babylon? You just said that Merodach-baladan is wandering somewhere, and that Babylon is once again under Assyrian domination."

"It is. And there is no present fear of any usurpers taking it over again; but Isaiah expressly said Babylon."

"Not Assyria?"

"That is right. And when he says something—like when he told me that I was going to be healed—I have learned that it will most assuredly come to pass."

"Like when he said that shadow on your father's sun dial would move backwards ten degrees."

"Precisely. We may not know the exact timing, but we know for certain that whatever Isaiah has been shown, it is going to happen as he said it would happen."

Eliakim nodded again in agreement.

"I know that the word of judgment pronounced to me in that moment of pride is going to come to pass one of these days as surely as I am still alive...though I have been promised that it will not occur while I am living. Still, it grieves me that I was the king to whom such a dreadful curse was directed. At that moment, to my shame, I said something foolish like: 'Good is the word of the Lord which you have spoken. Is it not good if peace and truth be in my days until I die?' Maybe in the back of my mind at that time I had started believing that some of our zealous citizen's were right in their claims that I would never die. I do not know. Since then the Lord has dealt terrible blows to my ripened pride, and it has been my earnest prayer and hope that He would look down upon my present reign and reverse that horrid decree."

"Maybe He will," Eliakim responded, looking as if he wished he could do something to help reverse it himself.

"I would be ever so thankful if He would; but my fifteen years are getting close to the end and our prophet has never brought the topic up again in my presence."

"How many years has it been?"

"Since my healing?—twelve."

"That long already?"

"It has gone fast, has it not?

"It has."

"I mentioned that pronouncement concerning Babylon to you to place before you another reason which makes it certain to me that it is not our Lord's will that they will overtake us again this time."

"I am with you on that one, even though it does not sound good for us either way. The Babylonians could not come and wipe us out if the Assyrians had already succeeded in that task. The prospect of that Babylonian army coming someday to destroy us is nothing to rejoice over, but I agree that it does give our nation a hope that we will survive this present threat."

"Since Isaiah promised that the great judgment would not occur during my reign, perhaps we will be able to turn our nation around sufficiently for our Lord God to reverse His decree altogether. I do not know, but I certainly hope so."

"So do I," Eliakim concurred.

Hezekiah slept again. The next time he awoke, sleep did not return so graciously. Sleep did not return at all after that. What did return was fear in its most naked state. Fear. Naked fear. It came over him without the dawning sunlight beginning the coming day. It came over him without him hearing one word from the vanguard's leader—which was the moment when he had thought real fear would have hit.

Fear.

Real fear.

Ice cold terror.

He felt his body shaking. How could that be? Had he not planned on this return visitation for years: planned on it from that moment twelve years ago when his Lord stopped the sun and shoved it backward ten degrees.

The ice cold terror was not right. Whether it is the same Rabshakeh or not did not even matter for he had done everything necessary in the last few years to assure their safety within the capital for a long time...if they were required to remain locked up within their newly strengthened walls. Simply remaining secured safely was not his true goal, of course. The Lord had promised that this time He would come to the city's aid if they waited on Him. Therefore his primary task was to do nothing but to wait for His Lord to perform His awesome wrath upon the empire's army or at least upon their vanguard. His defense had to be adequate to only preserve them until his God did that and therefore, after all that he had done, that should be sufficient. Of course, they still needed the Lord to act mightily as He has promised. So why the fear?

Why the ever-growing, cold dread?

Why the icy shivering shaking throughout his being?

That had to be the why of the fear. He knew it was his Lord's purpose to act as He has promised. He knew for a certainty what his Lord God could do. Surely the fear was: *would* He act this time?

His arm, hanging over the side of the bed, searched around back and forth until it found and retrieved one of his pillows. Raising it, he stuffed it under his head as he turned onto his side as one can stuff a pillow under his head and not move the bed so that his gracious wife does not wake up from the movement. A soft moan out of her at that instant, however, let him know that even in that he had not completely succeeded.

Later he was reminded of the former Rabshakeh's arrogant shouting for all to hear, 'If you do not have the gold in your treasury then strip it from those doors and pillars up on your temple!' And his own, 'From those? I jus—' And the Rabshakeh's, 'You heard me, peasant ruler! My orders are to return with thirty talents of gold!'

That would never happen again.

He would die first before he would let another Assyrian leader come in and humiliate him and the city again. He rolled over onto his back and thought of the Temple and of the One dwelling within. Lord, how You ever remained silent within Your Temple during their last visit I do not know, but this time I plead with You to please come through with Your promise to defend our city.

Still later, to close out his active thoughts, he flopped over as unnoticeably as possible, buried his head under the pillow, and accepted too soon, in his despair, that the move dreadfully failed to block out those persistent ramblings within his head.

Surely my thoughts know that I am tired. Surely they know the extreme losses of that last time. Surely they remember the troops were sighted last evening resting just down the road. Surely they remember that I have firmly, openly declared that we will under no circumstances surrender to Sennacherib's forces as we did the last time. Come on, faith, Where are you? Why have you not grabbed unto: 'If you walk in My statutes, keep My commandments, and do them; then, I will give peace in your land and you shall lie down and none shall make you afraid: and, I will rid evil beasts out of your land, neither shall the sword move through your land.

And you shall chase your enemies and they shall fall before you by the sword. And five of you shall chase an hundred, and an hundred of you shall put ten thousand to flight: and, by the sword, your enemies shall fall before you. For I will gave respect unto you, and make you fruitful and multiply you, and establish My covenant with you. And I will walk among you and will be your God and you shall be My people.'

He knew where and why his faith was hiding. The finality of his declaration not to surrender this time—though it was spoken in a time of great hope and trust—now it was filling him with anxiety because if the Lord did not defend the city as He had promised through Isaiah and this siege by them became unbearable, he knew he no longer had any kind of option to surrender.

Much later that night he raised his head. Raised it so he could look forward into the wall. The pillow stayed on like a tent. Like an Arabian desert tent.

He blinked his dead-tired weary eyes, and pictured himself upon the top step of the palace's stairway a fortnight ago with Isaiah.The two of them standing united as he made his public announcement that surrendering to the empire this visit would not be an option.

It had been a good day. A very good day of faith and hope and victory in front of the citizens of his city. But now...how utterly foolish that decision was going to sound when it was presented to the Assyrians' leader. Especially if the Rabshakeh is the same one who came the last time.

The pillow dropped off his head.

He started to turn toward Hephzibah, but, in the midst of that turn, changed his mind and gently pulled his covers off.

Tired, he did not want to get up.

Nevertheless he could not sleep and it was beginning to bother his legs to stay in bed.

Tom Steinbach

It was the third time he had arisen in the night. Both
former times he had risen and sat in a different chair in the
dark. Each time he returned to his bed he had been sure that
sleep would soon come—but that most desired goal had
evaded him each time. Getting his limbs to stand him up again
this third time was no light task. When they did, and when he
felt fairly certain he had his balance, he directed them to pull
him over to one of his chamber's latticed windows. Scuffling
as he went, his aching eyes drooped, as did his head with each
shuffle of his feet. He felt seventy-five: not the much younger
fifty-two that he was.

Midway to the window he succumbed to the desire to
stand still...wobbling there, his eyes fell shut each time he
opened them, he considered surrendering completely to the
cries of all his various bodily parts by collapsing into a circle
on to the floor ...feeling almost certain that if he did so
collapse he would be able to fall asleep on the spot.

He did not.

For he knew he would not.

*

> > > * < < <

*

Having braced himself at the window and having stared
into the predawn darkness for some time, he turned back to
look at his wife lying in the bed...back to the only one he had
shared his bed with for the last ten years.

His mother had been right. Hephzibah had changed. Yes,
she truly coveted another child right away, soon after their first
post-Assyrian visitation daughter—Hannah—had been born,
his wife had come into his presence as if he was the sole one
with whom she wanted to be.

From that moment on, when lying next to him, she would respond as pleased with whatever gesture his hands would make. She no longer fought against those intimate movements of his massaging hands as she had done too often in the past. Now, she would often place her hand lightly upon his, saying thank you with the gesture. That had been a major change. Nevertheless, it was much more than her just letting him be as intimate as he wanted to with her—it was more—it was her willingness to be a second Eve, a true daughter of that attractively-formed mother of all mankind, that brought to him his greatest appreciation of her change toward him.

Since spending much time with Sarai, she was now willing to be naked in his presence. Eve had had no choice: the Lord had created her beautiful and since He had put no clothes upon her before He brought her to Adam,she simply went where she had been directed by her Creator to go and in the wherewithal with which He had provided her. Hephzibah, even though she had carried, and had given birth to, and, had nursed half a dozen children, was willing to be thus in his presence; and to his great pleasure was enjoying his willingness to see her so. She would stand before him in the morning after removing her nightclothes and before dressing for the day, and would stretch, lifting her arms toward their room's ceiling to help her body adjust itself to its best standing posture. Hezekiah would always let her know that her body's best standing posture was very acceptable to him.

Also, she was letting him know that she enjoyed looking at his naked body: something she had not done at all before the Assyrians had come that first time. It was as if she had finally understood that it was equally as proper for a husband and wife to enjoy each other's body as it was for a mother to thoroughly relish the unclothed forms of each of her offsprings lying unabashed in front of her as she bathed, and changed, and hugged them to her body. She had even told him that Sarai had trained her that it was foolish to desire with all heart for her children to come running to her and hug her with all their might...if she could not accept the same desire from her husband as they lay together in bed.

Why should I pour out my love upon my children, she had told him those many years ago, and not be willing to shower it upon you who wants it equally as much, though in a way a man would want my attention? He had agreed with her.

Why should a wife do that?

He continued to watch her beautiful sleeping form from over by the window. Hephzibah, he thought, thank you for being the wife to me the Lord envisioned when he formed and brought Eve to our first father. Thank you for allowing me to be something to you and with you which I am to no other human upon the face of the earth. Thank you for being the one I desperately wanted to be with last evening even as the empire's vanguard moved in to encamp down by our lower reservoir. Thank you for truly trusting that the Lord is going to use me to guide our nation through this crisis. I need your trust...for at times like this I do not always believe that I am necessarily the one that He should use to guide us through.

$$*$$
$$>>> * <<<$$
$$*$$

The cool, fresh air of the not-yet-awakened-morning on the roof garden quickened life into his troubled being. He had reigned twenty-six years upon the throne of Judah. He had waited thirteen years for the empire to return. But, this was the first time that he could ever remember being fully dressed and ready for breakfast so early.

Though he was ready in that manner, his eyes smarted, the

fresh air causing him to blink a number of times.

Finally, his eyes ceased being irritated.

He walked toward some newly placed tamarack saplings. They had been sown in large clay vessels. He thought back to the first time he had ever come into the roof garden as Judah's ruling monarch.

A young twenty-five year old back then, he had stopped to watch some other saplings bending willowy in a gusty wind. He had watched for a long time as they whipped around seemingly to their destruction, but obviously not so. He determined then and there that in any and every turbulent storm which came against Judah he would attempt to emulate the agile resiliency of those saplings.

The remembrance of that thought at this most trying time brought a flood of hot tears to his eyes. He thanked the Lord for the remembrance and the encouragement of the thought as he sat down upon one of the ivory benches. Upon its heels, however, came another thought: it reminded him that his distressful thoughts throughout the night had not been about those saplings bending victoriously...making it calamitously through the storm. His fears had been harassing him with the concern of how do older, more mature, trees—especially those individuals planted so that they had to stand alone—how do those trees persevere through the really rough storms?

Long after he had been pumped up by the memory of the saplings and then let down by the harsh realization that neither he nor his country could be compared to youngster saplings anymore, he looked off again to the east above the olive tree covered hill beyond the Kidron Valley and realized that the day which he had dreaded every waking moment of the night was officially beginning.

He rose to go that direction.

A speck of a trace of salmon pink cut one narrow line into

that otherwise dark horizon. Everywhere else the stars were still shining: overhead and to the west they were shining very brightly. He looked back at the single thread of pink.

He walked over to an ivory bench in the garden which offered a more open view of that promised coloring of the eastern hills. He wondered if the true reason he had come out onto the garden this cool early morning was to hear the first angry words of the vanguard's leader. Words which might still be an hour away.

Turning, he looked to the west *and could not believe his eyes*, a host of large dark clouds were marching upward over that horizon and seemed to be rushing without hindrance over the entire western sky! Within minutes, the churning clouds had scudded straight over him and were fast on their quest of capturing even the eastern sky, the still-yawning eastern sky.

Looking at that sky, he saw that the horizon was still clear and that the pink line was getting broader; but also that before the remaining open sky was going to come much more alive, the wind-driven clouds would have it completely covered also.

A depression gripped him with the sight.

One much deeper than he would have ever expected when he first saw the churning clouds.

The omen came as clear as the purest gold in his private treasury: the succumbing of the awakening sky to the crazed, forward-rushing clouds was a perfect picture: a perfect omen of the fear that had inundated him earlier.

The empire had swiftly conquered his land again in *its* crazed, forward-rushing charge to totally annihilate him and his land. He feared that the heavenly scene of the swiftly-galloping clouds was a horrendous, accurate representation of what the day and the ones following would bring to his city.

If the ominous sign of the dawning eastern sky being overtaken by the menacing clouds before it really had any chance to even get started meant anything at all...it meant that if the morning began peacefully, it and the coming day were going to bring a terrifying overrunning of his city. Worse, it purported that a vastly greater mass of the ruthless blood-thirsty Assyrians were going to come up this time.

In his heightened concern he acknowledged once again how truly utterly frivolous, how completely futile, how insanely doltish his announced stand was going to sound. How ridiculously embarrassing it would sound when the coming Rabshakeh and Tartan and Rabsaris of the world's largest empire heard of it in the next few hours.

He arose and walked toward the eastern edge of the roof. He stopped very close to it. Not to jump, though he thought about it. He looked again at the eastern horizon, at the lowest portion of it, it was inundated with tumultuous clouds. He was crushed. But then!—raising his sights ten, fifteen degrees, he felt an all-out hope spring forth within his being!

A yellow-white glow broke forth and instantly blossomed into a brilliant, explosive burst of dynamic brightness: creating a large break in the moving clouds! The thrill from the glow's brightness washed over his fears, and anxiety, and dissolved them. It caused his heart to cry forth within his being:

His smile is still there!

"His smile is still there!" he said aloud, his voice following his soul's intense lead. "My Lord God, Your smile has broken through the crazed, onward-rushing, conquering, wind-driven clouds! I see Your smile! I see it through the wretched battle of the sky and it is right now shining brilliantly here upon me...and here upon this Your city!"

For the first time since he heard the last report, for the first time since he had seen the on-rushing clouds overpowering the awakening sky, for the first time in a while...he began to believe again.

He began to believe that he might still be able to find that secret he had walked out on the rooftop to find: the secret that enabled older, mature trees to make it through the roughest of storms along with the young pliable saplings.

*

> > > *EIGHTEEN* < < <

*

The circle had disappeared long before he had gone back inside and his last look out before leaving his room confirmed that those galloping clouds were again in absolute control of the entire sky.

That troubled him greatly, but not nearly as hard as the troubling thought which came next into his mind.

In the dining room, he thought as he took his seat at the head of the large ornately sculptured table: that bright glow might not have represented the smile of my Lord God at all. Instead it could have represented the flaming-hot, white-yellow midsection of Moloch's iron-clad image! The raw terror of that new thought forced him to lay his head upon the table. Growing up, he often dreamed dreadful nightmares about Molech's huge imposing image. The glow could have represented the revengeful anger of Moloch breaking through within the midst of the rushing army! The foreboding clouds representing the Assyrian army and the brilliant white-yellow glow bursting forth from within their midsection was Moloch's coming back to claim him after so many years.

The hideous, bull-headed image had claimed so many of his half brothers in his youth. His vexed mind quickly, vividly, forcibly, incredibly filled in the scenes of the first offering. His father was an eleven year old crown prince of Judah when he fathered Hezekiah. He became king nine years later. Immediately, in the very beginning of his reign, he built Moloch's occultic image a home just outside of Jerusalem: in the same location Solomon had built it during his rule.

One damp morning, his father, coming to the crest of the misty valley, took his infant from his youngest wife's arms and together they began the descent. Hezekiah and his mother, Abijah, followed and descended into that hideous valley from which volumes of smoke were arising.

Moloch's aged high priests approached the huge procession when the marchers were getting close to the huge metal statue. The one who took that sacrifice from his father had a pleasant face with a wrinkled smile which was gentle, very reassuring; but his piercing eyes did not agree with his kindly smile.

His eyes were greedy.

Very greedy.

His father did not care. He willingly handed his infant son to the chosen one.

The old priest turned and faced the human-bodied idol with the fierce immense head of a bull.

The drum rolls picked up in intensity.

The flute players changed to the minor chords, and played very loudly.

251

Tom Steinbach

His father remained calm and rigid: as rigid as the cold sides of the passageway they had come down through from the cliffs. His arms were crossed over his chest, and no emotion shown on his face as the priest began his ascent up the stairway toward their idol's out-stretched hands. From his low angle, Hezekiah could see smoke billowing out from within Moloch's midsection but he could not see past the slanting arms. But from the brow of the hill he had seen, had clearly seen, the brilliant white-yellow, fiery glow in Moloch's midsection which shown brightly from the raging fire in the idol's bowels below.

The priest raised the infant, his screaming half-brother, high over his head as the drums and flutes increased their volume and as the dancers raised their hands and uncoiled their unclad bodies upward higher and higher to the fever-pitched music and as multitudes of lesser priests chaotically chanted their numerous incantations. Then the infant was lowered and laid onto the opened palms of Molech.

At that moment, his father shouted, "O Moloch, one of the many forms of Baal, highest god of all gods, to you, I offer this first son born to me after your image has been erected. This one from my being is offered for your pleasure as a willing sacrifice from his mother and me. He is also offered for you to return to us as your future leader of our nation to serve you after I die."

The tiny infant screamed red-faced.

He did not move forward nor backward.

As his father's hopes rose, the tiny firstborn began to teeter forewards and backwards. "O Moloch, highest god of all gods," his father cried out, raising his hands upward toward the immense head before him and promising, "keep my son alive and I will dedicate myself exclusively to your service!"

The infant leveled off.

Relieved, and feeling that his most desired victory was

within reach, his father made another promise to his newly created statue before him: "O Moloch, highest god of all gods, keep my son alive and I will have my citizen's worshipping Baal images under every green tree in our nation!"

The infant began to move again.

His father prostrated himself and screamed out ever louder, "O Moloch! Highest god of all gods! You and this massive altar will be highly exalted here down in this famous valley of the sons of Hinnom just outside our capital!"

The infant's body relaxed though his face continued the pursed-lipped, red-faced tantrum; during which, he squirmed and began to slide down the declining slope of the arms toward the fiery, smoke-ladened infernal within the image's bowels. Ahaz screamed as loud as he could with his praises and promises, but his son fell out of sight. He had failed to pass the test.

Sitting there in the bright dining room, Hezekiah knew that he had been taught to reject that whole esoteric ceremony. He also had been always extremely thankful that he had been born when his father was so young and he had never been forced to go through the test of fire. He destroyed Moloch's image as soon as he ascended to his father's throne.

But now, after having been on the throne for over twenty years, why did the troubling thought present itself full-bloom into his mind?

The bright glow in the clouds' midsection: did it represent Moloch's revengeful coming back within the hideous darkness of the empire's onrushing, conquering army to finally, totally, claim him for his father's part in willingly participating in those statue's occultic rituals.

Did the sign in the sky present that his throne, his kingdom, and his life, were going to be finally claimed by the fierce, bull-headed image.

How could that be?

He did not even believe in the reality of Moloch.

Bracing himself by the latticed window in his bedchamber where he had stood before breakfast, he listened to the shouts of clear, terrorizing Hebrew coming forth from the other side of their wall. He trembled.

He could not see the loud boaster.

But he *knew*.

With the very first words he had known. He leaned further and listened to the Rabshakeh's unforgettable voice. He rested his entire troubled body heavily upon the sill of the window. I have been longing for you to return, he thought. I guess I have been hoping that it would be you, but...hearing the sound of your arrogance confidence again—

Hephzibah had also known.

She came up behind him and placed her hands upon his shoulders and neck.

When he did not respond, she began rubbing his back.

It felt like the love of God to him.

After many moments of silence together—silence inside their room, that is—he asked, "How did the children sleep?"

"Apparently the girls slept well, but Manasseh slept not at all: he was too excited with all the reports of the fighting going on down in the plains and the foothills."

Manasseh, his only son—ten year old, looked thirteen and when he would be fifteen would look twenty—yes, yes, he thought, Manasseh, with the thick, raven-black hair, and the above-average mentality, yes, yes his ten year old son would understand better than his sisters the seriousness of the hour.

"If he had trouble sleeping last night because of all the fighting going on down by Lachish, what is he doing now that he can hear as well as all our people that the same Rabshakeh and his forces have returned and are outside our eastern gate at this moment?"

"His restlessness comes because he has been wrongfully told by his tutors to reject so much that you and I believe in," she said, while tenderly rubbing his back. She went on, "I have asked you before to stop allowing his instructors to place those heathen ideas within his mind. He accepts their words and they have taught him to think in a manner that battles against everything you and I have come to accept, my lord."

If Manasseh could not sleep last night because he has rejected our belief in our Lord God and has also rejected our belief in our Lord's way of righteousness, he thought as she continued the loving back rub...then why was I so horribly distraught and so wide-awake myself through the night?

Even with the all-out fear and anger which overwhelmed me this morning, I still fully believe that our Lord can, and will indeed, come to our aid and defend us this time against the empire. Why then did I not experience the overflowing calmness and peace that I desperately desired all night long.

Why do I not feel it at this moment? Is it because I always have to add: if He will?

When He will?

"Hephzibah, Manasseh is our only son. Our one and only son. Therefore, I have told you often before that I believe that our son's lack of interest in our Lord will be remedied by the time he ascends up to the throne."

"I so truly wish you would not keep saying that, my lord," she returned, kissing the back of his neck and his shoulders. "For you know that I do not believe at all that our son will ever ascend to our nation's throne. For, you know, I do not believe that you will ever die and vacate it."

"I am sorry to disagree with you, my Hephzibah, my exceedingly lovely one who loves me now as no other has ever loved me, but I am going to die. Quite soon now...my fifteen years are pretty nearly used up."

"No, my lord." She replied, pulling her body up close to

his. "Years ago our Lord miraculously saved you when I was certain that you were going to die from that boil; back then when you would not allow me, your wife, to come over there near you. Now you have so changed in the last ten years that I am as equally as certain that you will never die."

"Isaiah promised only fifteen years."

"He promised at least fifteen years."

Next, she spoke the words which had become the fountainhead of her belief concerning him since he had changed and had emptied his palace of the house.

"You have had full health all these additional years. You will not ever die. You are the promised king about whom Isaiah proclaimed in your father's reign, 'For unto us a child is born, unto us a son is given; and, the government shall be upon his shoulder, and, his name shall be called—'"

Hephzibah, you should have been with me out on our roof garden early this morning. Before then, I might have agreed with you, but once again I know myself too well: all too well. No, I will never qualify as a candidate to be that promised one foretold by Isaiah. "Hephzibah, the only resemblance I have to that word is that I was born a child."

"A male child," she corrected.

"Granted, I was born a male child, a son, even as the prophecy foretold."

"And the government—"

"Also granted, Hephzibah," he said, turning around toward her, their bodies remained close together. "The government of Judah and therefore of all Israel—that is, whatever there is left of it—is still upon my shoulders at the present moment. But there the prophetic resemblances between my reign and that coming one surely cease."

"That is precisely why you qualify so superbly, my lord," she said, hugging him tightly and resting her head upon his shoulder. "You truly believe all the many resemblances stop there. Your humble belief in your own reign is why our Lord has been with you so wonderfully these past years."

They kissed for some time. He felt her warm tears upon his face. They reminded him of all the warm, tender love he had received from her since she had truly accepted him as her lord and husband. He agreed that the Lord had been with him and their nation up to this summer; but certainly she could see that no one could continue to claim to be blessed whose reign had endured what his had over the last couple months. His mind thought back to the galloping clouds and their uncontested rule of the skies. He also thought of the radiant circle and of Moloch's bull-headed face grinning wickedly at him.

"I have no doubt about it, my lord. None at all. You truly are the coming one. One day everyone will agree with me."

"Please, Hephzibah—"

"It is true, my lord. You say the resemblances cease with you being on the throne, but the similarities do not cease there. You, like the coming one, have already established your good reign with righteous judgment and justice."

"Hephzibah, please understand that as this day unfolds that I will be remembering what you are trying to do for me now. But for the present, also understand that I can never forget how these same Assyrians' last visitation quickly degenerated into the horrifying panic and loathing and sickening grief that it became for us and our city."

"I still shiver with scary fright, my lord, whenever I reflect back upon your father's wicked reign," she continued. "For the life of me, I cannot fathom why our Lord did not strike us all dead with a plague when your father ordered that wicked replica of a foreign altar to be placed in the temple's main courtyard. Talk about wretched abominations! That had to be the worse thing anyone could have done to show our God that He was not wanted here in our capital. Your reign has been much different from his and from any of the other kings who

have ever ruled over Israel or Judah. After our Lord God
defends you and our city this time, He will honor our entire
nation and all our people by giving to you the right to sit upon
our King David's throne forever. I know it, Hezekiah, I know
it deep down within."

In the right mood—in the right time—in a time of true
peace, he would have greatly appreciated her attempt in
building up his faith by reminding him of her undaunted belief
in the alleged immortality of his rulership; but it was too late:
he had allowed too many fears, and too much anger, to harbor
in his soul during the night.

*

> > > NINETEEN < < <

*

*The arrogant Rabshakeh again had spaced his
chariot corps, his camels and their riders, and his
wagons along the dusty road which ran parallel to
Jerusalem's eastern wall.*

However, five chariots were away from the rest and
stationed closest to him and his two co-leaders. The five were
posed abreast of each other slightly to the north of the gate.

Hezekiah stared at the cloud-covered sky which blocked out the sun he so desperately desired to see. He hoped that his hemmed-in people's minds would be as efficient in blocking out the last time this Assyrian and his elite forward unit came up to their capital.

In that hope, he knew he was dreaming.

They would not.

They could not.

"Why are we resisting the empire, Mother?" Manasseh asked as soon as Hephzibah had entered her young son's room after she had left Hezekiah.

"We all want peace, do we not?" he harped on.

"Of course, we do."

"Why does Father not just give them what we owe to them?"

"Son—"

"Why do not give them what we owe them?"

"Son, your father is doing the right thing."

"How can you say that when we are not paying what we owe them, Mother, and we are going to lose our freedom if we do not?"

"Son, your father—"

"Can you not hear that angry Assyrian down by our wall who has come up to receive their tribute?"

"Of course, I hav—"

"If I were the king right now, Mother, I would open our gates as fast as—"

"Son, you are not the king. You remember that! No matter

what your tutors tell you and you also remember that your father is the best king our nation has ever had."

"But he is not acting with our people's safety and interest as his main concern."

"You may not see it that way, Manasseh."

"You are right, I do not."

"I assure you, whether your father acts in accordance with all your tutors' numerous instructions or not, our people's safety and interests are foremost in his mind. Next to obeying the Lord, our people are surely his first concern."

"How can you say that!"

"Son, keep your voice down before me! Your tutors are filling you with their sophisticated teachings which do not take into full account that we Hebrews are people dedicated to the service of our Lord God Jehovah."

Seeing his horrid expression which plainly said: *I have heard that one before,* she continued.

"Whether you or your instructors accept it, that is our peoples' heritage: we are the chosen people of the one and only true Lord God of Heaven and Earth."

"Do you really believe that?"

"Son, I have asked your father to replace your tutors a number of times."

"Replace them?"

"Yes, them."

"Their outstanding wisdom, and knowledge, so exceeds any other teachers in our nation! I do not want to be taught by the outmoded teachers of our forefathers! When I become the king of Judah, I want to set up a conciliatory reign of peace and prosperity! A reign in which all nations will feel free to come and do commerce with us and to worship any god and goddess any way they wish."

"Son, you can say the large words, and you probably understand them, but you have been taught—"

"—the right teachings!"

"The right teachings?"

"The right things, I only hope that when Father dies there is still a reigning over our people in which I can have the chance to rule!"

"Manasseh!"

"Once again you have returned." Hezekiah was muttering aloud to himself in a faint low tone, not too certain if, after the envoys came in, he desired to go over to the wall with them to see this enemy or not. "And, this time you have chosen your position on our road to the north of our main water gate so that my royal palace would more easily be within hearing range."

He paused to hear a few of his shoutings.

The Hebrew sounded even better than last time.

"I understand that there is an advantage of having been within the enemy's walls. But I have an advantage also: I have dealt with you before. And because I know you cannot be trusted and that you thrive in the glory of being a terrorizing, murdering heathen, you will never, I repeat, never, see the insides of these walls again. Never!"

He paused to take a drink of fruit juice.

"Once again I deplore your heinous, arrogant confidence. Once again I deplore the perfect Hebrew you are using as you pierce our still, pregnant air with your loathsome, repugnant threats and bad promises. But, also once again I will stand up to you with all the nerve I possess."

He said it aloud and with meaning but he could not believe how utterly frightening it was to hear that arrogant voice again after so long of a time. It made him recall how that boaster, who did everything to resemble a massive siege tower all by himself, mounted his decorated battle chariot behind his driver and his spearman and raced recklessly throughout the labyrinths of their city streets with the entire chariot corps following in close formation. Hezekiah could still hear the screams of his aged men, and of panicked mothers and youngsters as they were mercilessly trampled to death.

'The next time I am forced to return here,' the vile one had threatened, 'because you have stopped paying what you owe us, I will personally, and with extremely great pleasure, place my dagger directly between your ears!'

Even if it came hurling through the air heel first again, he thought, the force with which that angry one throws that branding knife of his would break my nose and drive it up into my head and my brain, and it would happen so very quickly that I would not be able to defend myself.

No, no. I will never allow myself to stand anywhere face to face with him again.

I will not.

I can not.

Not face to face.

*

\> \> \> * < < <

*

"Mother," Manasseh said, in his room, "you believe that Father is that prophesied seed of David which the prophet Nathan promised would proceed out of his line; and that it is Father's kingdom the Lord God will establish soon as the coming eternal one."

"That is right, Son, and you say it as well, if not better, as I can," Hephzibah answered, hoping that her son was finally coming around to accepting her really important belief in her husband's reign: even though every action and word he said indicated nothing of that nature.

"Well, I do not!"

"Son!"

"I agree with my tutors."

"Why do you always have to agree with them?"

"As I, they believe that the offspring promised to King David through the prophet Nathan to establish his throne forever was fulfilled in all actuality in his own son, King Solomon. We therefore believe that King Solomon's throne was that promised, coming one, and that is why we study all of his writings—not just the relatively few selected works of his that have been accepted, and collected, and placed into a series of scriptures by our forefathers."

"But, Manasseh, his reign was not an eternal one and it ended with our nation being divided into two."

"There will never be an eternal one."

"Isaiah said they would be."

"How can we believe anything that old man says."

"Son, please do not talk about our prophet that way."

When he said nothing else, she continued.

"You also know yourself that your father has already ordered his own scribes to choose out and copy more of King Solomon's proverbs to be included in the pouches of the accepted scrolls of our nation's writings."

Having allowed her to finish, he rattled off, "Of course his reign was not eternal, it is my and my tutors' belief that no reign will be eternal."

"Son, there will be one."

"We do not believe that. And there is no northern kingdom of our peoples any longer...therefore we are one people once again so we can forget that argument of the division of the

Tom Steinbach

kingdom. And the collecting of King Solomon's proverbs that Father has ordered is only good up to a point."

When she did not interrupt, he finished his thought.

"My teachers and I use *all* of the many hundreds and thousands of writings which were written by King Solomon—not just the ones Father's men will accept."

*

> > > * < < <

*

While he waited to brief his men, Hezekiah remembered what his thought had been concerning the tortured minds of his soldiers who had stood along the walls and before the palace: they were forever desiring that a signal would come from him directing them to fling their spears and arrows toward the hateful beast and his monstrous chariot corps.

The thought gave him an idea.

He walked back to the window and listened one last time to the Rabshakeh. That series of threats was followed with the vile one's well-known, high-pitched laugh. With the stark reality of hearing his confident voice and that dreaded laughter anew, with his whole being shaking under his robe, he truly wondered if he could carry through with the idea.

*

> > > * < < <

*

His three men—Eliakim, Shebna, and Joah—had gone up onto the wall after they had eaten their breakfast to see for themselves if the information they had been given agreed with their own gathered observation of the vanguard.

After some time there, they had entered into private briefings with their many scouts who had been observing the approaching caravan for the previous two days. They also had met with the ones who had been on the walls throughout the night to learn what else they could.

At the moment they were in a quiet mood.

They were individually deep in thought as they slowly made their way passing by the house of the forest of Lebanon on their way to the palace.

*

> > > * < < <

*

Hezekiah's entire body trembled all over when he thought about his new idea. About his incredible idea of sending his three coming envoys out to face the shouting Rabshakeh.

If anything went wrong he would have to go out.

And if he went out again, he knew that this time he could never order the gates open to the vanguard and its leader.

Would he dare go?

Would he?—knowing there was a dagger which still had a mission waiting to be accomplished.

A dagger he had already intimately met.

Painfully met.

Yet, he thought, the idea is unpalatable and unnerving only if he has to be the one who has to have the ability within himself to back the idea.

The key to the whole idea in the first place is not he himself: it is his soldiers up along the walls.

The real vital key for this stunning idea to succeed is for him to simply allow his soldiers the opportunity to express themselves in what they had been trained.

*

> > > *TWENTY* < < <

*

"*I understand the boastful Rabshakeh must have been thoroughly convinced that every future resistance from us had been forcefully torn away from our minds and hearts after all of his cruel, hideous demonstrations the last time he came,*" he began in his talk to the trio after they had been escorted into his chambers,

"*—and he was probably right.*

"But, what he did not realize, and, still does not realize, is that I am not that One who makes the crucial decisions in this city. I do not make those judgments as you know, nor are they even directly revealed to me. They are only given to those in our nation who are the acknowledged spokesmen and women for our Lord God. And, as you also know, right now that role here in our country is being lived out through our prophet Isaiah. The Rabshakeh does not know of him, he does not know that Isaiah never once stepped out of his room into the sunlight that fateful day...thirteen years ago to see or give his brash deeds a moment's worth of his time. Of course, the Rabshakeh, on the other hand, has been saying that...that—"

It surprised him, but he could not cohesively, concretely form the angry words of that boastful one within his mind to finish the sentence. Any other time he could have rattled off volumes of what the Rabshakeh had shouted. But at the moment, it was only some whimsical thought which he was able to focus within his mind. Therefore, looking at Eliakim, he said aloud, "The Rabshakeh was very fortunate, men, that our prophet chose not to show his face that day!"

Saying that jest out loud so changed his complete mood that he stood up and wheeled around toward an opened window. Knowing that the Assyrian could not hear him, he mockingly yelled: "O loud one, it was in front of our prophet Isaiah, and not before me, that you should have made your contemptible, scornful, horrible, despicable demonstrations!"

"Hezekiah, hear me!" the Rabshakeh shouted from beyond the wall at that precise instant—instantly breaking Hezekiah's lightheartedness—and causing him and the three to wonder if the Assyrian could have possibly heard him in the midst all of his own shouting. They assured themselves that he could not have but because the response came right at the precise moment, they listened hard with greatly piqued interest for the obvious tirade which they knew was forthcoming.

"Our great armies have ravished your land, burned your cities, captured your peoples; and yet, rumor has it that you are boasting to all who will hearken that you have counsel and strength for war against the mighty Assyrian Empire!"

"So, we are boasting to all who will listen, are we?" Hezekiah responded to the trio, looking back at them from the window. As he made his way back to them, he overpowered the rest of the shouting with these words: "We are not boasting, the Rabshakeh's assertion is not right. We are simply attempting to understand and obey our living, invisible Lord God Jehovah, the Creator of the heavens and of the earth."

Believing it should be added, Eliakim inserted, "We are trying to obey and understand our living, invisible, and our *'frightfully slow acting'* Lord God Jehovah."

They smiled to one another

"That is so very true, Eliakim," Hezekiah said after a thought-filled moment. "Our Lord God acted so slowly the last time these Assyrians came that He missed out on helping us. This time He has also decided to wait and wait to act on our behalf. But our trust is still in Him and will continue to remain strictly in Him. Men, we have no other hope."

"King Hezekiah, we believe right along with you that we do not need any other hope," Joah said.

He looked at Joah and the others, smiled, and said, "That word of honest confidence in our Lord is why I have chosen you three to represent us during this visitation."

"What are we going to do until our Lord God does decide to act on our behalf and defends our city?" Shebna asked.

"We were going to do exactly nothing," he answered. "We were going to wait until the Lord decided to act."

"We were going to?" Eliakim asked.

"Yes, we *were* going to."

They all looked at him.

"Now I have decided upon another plan."

The three looked at each other.

"In my present plan, I am going to send you three out there to the Rabshakeh this morning."

"Out there—"

"This mornin—"

"I thought you had said that we were going to only talk to him from the wall."

"That had been my plan for you."

"How would it ever be possible for us to go out there to those murderers and not be tortured?"

"Sir, you are not surely also planning on going out there with us as last time?"

"No, I am not planning on that."

"That is good."

"Yes, I agree. But what about us?"

"The idea is quite new to me. It came not too long ago... and I will not order you out there beyond our gates if any of you do not agree with the idea. Let me share it with you and together we will decide if it is a wise notion or not."

*

> > > *TWENTY ONE* < < <

*

"We all agree that King Solomon was very wise, Son. But he did not live his entire life in obedience to the Lord. And there were many—"

"—writings which he wrote when he was serving all the gods of the different lands."

"That is right, Son. So it is only natural to our people that we do not accept those writings as true."

"But my instructors and I do."

"How can you?"

"Mother, King Solomon was always wise. So if we accept some of his writings, we should accept all of them."

"Not quite, Son, for many of his writings reflect wisdom which does not come from our Lord God."

"But they do reflect wisdom! And wisdom is truth whether we agree with it or not!"

"That is not always true, Son. Why do you always have to raise your voice at me?"

"But it is the truth, Mother."

"Your father has told me that there are writings from all over the world and from all the religions of the world which claim to present the truth."

"And they do."

"Son, your father says they do not."

"I do not agree with that narrow thinking."

"That is because you have rejected the Lord as your only true and wise God."

"I agree with you there. I have rejected that old concept. I believe we should get our wisdom from all the wise writings of the nations and religions of the world and especially from all of King Solomon's writings."

*

> > > * < < <

*

Having completed his time with the trio, he returned to his bedchamber, threw himself face-down upon his bed and lay there for many moments. The Rabshakeh had been silent after the series of shouts and Hezekiah could not see the Assyrian leader. Since the conduit near the road was parched and was not flowing with water as it had been the last time the forward unit had come, after his last series of shouts, the Rabshakeh had turned and begun marching past his chariot corps and past the fuller's field and was determinedly stalking straight toward the city's main upper water reservoir of the Gihon Spring. Midway there, he whirled around, and shouted aloud: "Long live King Sennacherib!"

The men keeping up with him echoed in chorus:

"Long live the king of kings, King Sennacherib!"

"King Hezekiah! Hear me! We were too easy on you that last time!" the Rabshakeh yelled. "No country on the face of the earth has been able to withstand the crushing advances of our armies under the leadership of our great monarch, King Sennacherib! King Sennacherib, the king of kings and the king of the universe! When he and our armies are through with you, then we are going to continue southward and we will destroy Egypt's power! Do you all hear me? There is no kingdom strong enough to stop us! Our goal is going to come to pass! We are going to rule the entire world!"

"The entire world," Hezekiah thought aloud, still stretched out face-down upon his bed. "Yes, I suppose if any present kingdom is that greedy and that villainous: yours is the one. But you are not telling me anything I do not already know. Isaiah told us long ago that yours would be that empire which would never be satisfied with only a little gain. Instead, he said that you would need much gain. His words were: 'It is in the Assyrian's heart to destroy and cut off many nations, not just a few.' Concerning our country, he even proclaimed that your kingdom would say: 'As I have done to Samaria and her idols so shall I also do to Jerusalem and her idols.' But if you only knew: we do not trust and rely in those idols in which the northern kingdom of Israel did. For that matter we do not officially trust in any idols any more. Long ago I forbade their presence throughout our nation. Our only trust now is in the living, invisible, Lord God of Heaven and Earth."

Our trust is in the living, invisible, *frightfully slow acting* Lord God, he thought with a grin. A grin which did not last long. O Lord, why have You not halted these murdering Assyrians in their terrifying push throughout our land. I know You have forewarned us through Isaiah that these Assyrians would be Your means to scourge both us and our northern brothers: that they would be Your goad of punishment to our nations. But, have they not done enough destructive violence against us already?

"Can you hear me, King Hezekiah?" the hardly audible Rabshakeh cut in from down past the fuller's field. "These troops here with me are only a minute portion of our entire massive army! The bulk of our forces is still with our world conqueror, King Sennacherib. They will defeat that petrified fortress city and then begin their ascent up here. Unlike the last time you rebelled against us over here, we will soon have you caged in like a defenseless bird! Do not get any hopes up, they are soundly defeating that paralyzed fortress city! Its soon surrender is as certain as it is that your spring's reservoir is still full of cool, refreshing water: though until you pay us the tribute amounts you owe us, your peoples will not be able to come out to get any!"

Hezekiah's melancholy mood vanished when he realized the distant yelling and the rash words were being voiced by the brazen Assyrian on his way down toward Gihon, the city's unprotected upper reservoir. Grinning, he thought about how the Rabshakeh must be remembering about the spring's ample supply of refreshing water for his troops and their animals the last time when they came. An involuntary chuckle sounded when he thought how the remembrances of the cool water's taste was surely quickening the Rabshakeh's pace. The chuckle turned into a pleased snicker when he pictured the angry Assyrian's shocked expression when he arrived and found that the deep hole in the ground had been totally sealed.

"Mother, let me quote the prophet Nathan's exact words to King David to you: 'And when your days are fulfilled and you sleep with your fathers I will set up your seed after you which shall proceed out of your loins and I will establish his kingdom. He shall build a house for My name and I will establish the throne of his kingdom forever. I will be his Father and he shall be My son.' Those words could have referred to Solomon only and to nobody else but to Solomon."

"We do not believe that."

"I know you do not."

"We believe Solomon gave up his rightful claim to that promise as Esau gave up his rightful firstborn claims to his brother Jacob and that therefore—"

"—there is going to be a future son of David who will build a house unto the Lord."

"That is right, Son."

"Even though King Solomon became the next king and has already built the house unto the Lord God, our glorious temple out that window."

"I know where it is, Son."

"That is the building, the only 'house for His name' to which Nathan referred."

"I am not sure what to say about what you are claiming. But I truly do believe that your father is—"

"Who else believes that? Father does not."

"Many others believe that he is."

"Why? Because he had the priests do some repairs on the temple and because he rid our land and capital of all the foreign statues and altars."

"Yes, Son, that is part of it."

"Well, I do not believe it. I believe Father was very wrong in getting rid of all those important ties Grandfather established in his day with our neighboring nations. Even King Solomon wrote many things exhorting our peoples to search out the wisdom of the other cultures."

"But he wrote those things when he was not right with our Lord God. Manasseh, all of his writings are not worthy to be studied and believed."

"Mother, it is right there where we disagree and where we will always disagree!"

Arriving at the reservoir, the Rabshakeh had found that it was solidly sealed up. Being highly disciplined, however, he immediately settled himself. Though very disappointed and thirsty, he resolved that he would not reveal a least speck of his shock to his men nor to the knowing Israelites. Instead, in a flash of inspiration, he cupped his hands to his mouth and shouted down into the remaining hollow of the reservoir: "Long live King Sennacherib!"

A resounding echo caromed back from the dry emptiness deep down within the stone circular stairway and sidewalls: "Looonnnnggggg......lliiiiivvvveeeee........KKiiiiinnnngggggg ....SSSeeeeeennnnnnnaaaaaaaa....................cccchhhhhhhh ....eeeeeeeeerrrrrrrrrriiiiiiiiibbbbbbbbbbbbb."

Whirling around, as if having won a great victory and as if

no longer feeling that he had just experienced a surprisingly dreaded disappointment, he mocked and chided toward the walls of Jerusalem with a more deeply renewed disdain for its peasant inhabitants:

"King Hezekiah, witless king of Judah! What fools you and your people are!

"Should I order my men down into this worthless chamber in the ground to confirm that that source which used to feed it is no longer flowing?

"You claim to have strength to defy the almighty Assyrian Empire! Instead, you and your miserable people are right now at this very moment already near the point of thirst! Why have you decided to offer such foolish resistance toward us? Why in the name of Baal have you chosen this hideous course of action?"

The Rabshakeh's discovery of that empty upper pool came sooner than Hezekiah had expected. Nevertheless, lying there, it was with great satisfaction that he thought about their city's large, empty, upper reservoir.

Earlier this summer while his northern and coastal cities were sealing up all the waters of every reservoir which lay outside the walls of their villages and cities and while they were attempting to stall the empire's steady movement toward the capital, Hezekiah himself had renewed a vast project which he had previously stopped in a time of peace as being too costly and visionary.

Cutting mostly through solid limestone, hundreds of his workers had begun again to toil day and night in their Herculean effort to create a new pathway for their capital's closest, oldest, and most faithful source of water: the intermittently flowing waters of the Gihon Spring which was located at the foot of the eastern slope of Mount Zion down in the Kidron Valley.

Beginning at both ends of the planned pathway where the

former crews had quit years before, the new units dug furiously with their picks and shovels:hoping that they would indeed meet in the middle as his counselors had claimed they would. Making their myriad of curves in the mountainside deep under the city's eastern wall, the workers fought against the day when the empire's greedy, devouring army would ultimately make its way up into the mountains of Israel and finally up along the dirt road which ran parallel to the walls of the city.

When the subterranean crews finally met, with only a cubit's height difference, they were ecstatic! And, as soon as the incredible word of the underground- tunneling success had traveled up to the surface, the whole city resounded with euphoria! Hezekiah and the elders of the city praised the Lord and proclaimed a feast as soon as the finished twelve hundred cubit tunnel was successful in diverting all the waters of the Gihon Spring which had formerly risen upward exclusively into the upper pool down beyond the fuller's field.

The Assyrians, and this Rabshakeh, have experienced many of our sealed reservoirs as they moved westward and southward through our land this warring season, Hezekiah thought as he raised his head up off his pillow. Last evening he must have surely found out that En rogel is also tightly sealed. Nevertheless, in each of those cases no tunneling had been done to redirect the flow of the waters into the besieged city itself. He therefore has not even thought that a tunnel-conduit for the waters of the spring could have been formed down deep in the ground underneath where he is standing, and in his ignorance he is simply concluding that we in the capital have done what all our other cities have done.

He is wrongfully concluding that we have stopped up the waters of our upper and lower spring-fed reservoirs from them and from ourselves!

Turning over onto his back, he closed his eyelids in relief

and soon was hoping that his wisdom in the extraordinary tunneling and other strategic decisions he had made at that same time would give to his leadership some much needed credence from his very frightened citizens.

*

\> \> \> * < < <

*

"I am scared of that man shouting out there, Mother."

"I am too, Hannah. But Father has said that he will not let him into our city this time."

After Hephzibah had left Manasseh's room, she had gone into her daughters' room. Hannah, her oldest living daughter was sitting on an ivory-covered, low bench placed near the foot of her bed.

Hannah was eleven, she was very obedient, and she was the offspring which both Hezekiah and her mother had wished would have been their first male child and the next in line to the throne.

"If he does get in, will he take us children with him like you said he took our sisters?"

"Hannah, Father said he will not allow that to happen again. It was too hard on all of us."

"I will not go."

"Hannah, we will not let him come in."

"How can we stop him now, Mother? Manasseh says that there is no way of stopping them from coming in."

"It is not up to Manasseh to pronounce to you what is going to happen here in our capital. We are trusting our Lord to keep those vile men out of our city. My oldest child, I only ask that you also trust that He will do that."

"I will, Mother, though I am really—"

"Do not say it, Hannah."

In his palace, Hezekiah was thinking about the other decisions he had made at the time the tunnel was being burrowed down through Mount Zion. The new reservoir into which the spring waters of the new tunnel were to flow was situated outside the southwestern wall of the city at the low base of a valley which ran along that wall. Therefore, even as the tunnel was being dug from both ends through the solid limestone, and long before he would ever know if it would be successfully completed or not, he had ordered many other tens of thousand of his men to build an extensive addition to that wall to protect the new pool and the homes which had been built out beyond the then-present wall.

The new wall, built connected to the existing one, crossed the valley to the south of their proposed reservoir, and also enclosed the inhabited hill immediately to the west of the southern portion of the city. Lying there, he also thought of the further defensive building-higher of a portion of an eastern wall south of the water gate which raised it all the way up even with the towers. He then thought of the abundance of swords and shields which had been made to equip his much larger and much more strengthened army. Lastly, he thoughts went to the meeting two weeks before: when he gathered the entire city together, set captains of war over every citizen in the capital, and then proclaimed his statement of faith to them as their leader. His words of encouragement began with a firm proclamation that no matter what he would not allow the Assyrians into the city again as he had done the last time. He proclaimed that under no circumstances would he surrender to them again as he had the last time. In closing, he had shouted, "Be strong and courageous. Be not afraid nor dismayed for the king of Assyria, nor for the multitude that is with him:for there are more with us than with him!"

He allowed those words of faith to sink in.

Then he shouted loudly, "With the Assyrians is an arm of flesh but with us is the Lord our God to help us and to fight our every battle!"

Thinking of that rousing challenge and of all the construction on the city walls and of the new tunnel and of closing the water supplies off to the Assyrians...he again could feel faith and hope building within his being. That bright circle in the midst of the rushing, wind-driven clouds might have been the smile of their God after all!

*

> > > * < < <

*

After the Rabshakeh returned to the city's eastern wall, north of the water gate, he triumphantly, ignorantly, and in poor taste, loudly shouted. "Soon you will be drinking your own piss and soon you will be eating your own dung!"

Believing he had found that ultimate point of terror to strike alarm in his enemies' hearts, he used that theme often in his next series of threats.

"Go ahead, O raving one, yell all you want," Hezekiah spake in his room after he had listened for some time.

"And use any theme your vile mind cares to use. Nevertheless we are not thirsting to death, and, no, no, we are not going hungry nor will we for a very long time."

Coming round in his chamber, he added, "You will never

ever know it, but our newly enclosed reservoir, though invisible to you, has faithfully provided us with all the thirst-quenching water that we have required of it since we created it, and that we probably will ever need."

*

> > > *TWENTY TWO* < < <

*

"Mother, I do not even like the way the man speaks as he shouts his threats."

"He has never been taught manners, Hannah. He only knows fear and horror. He has been only taught to cause his enemy to quake in terror behind their besieged walls."

"Then he has learned extremely well, Mother. I am as scared and frightened as I can be. I cannot believe it could have been worse that first time they came here. Just listening to his voice makes my flesh crawl."

"I know, Hannah."

"Do not let me go with them."

"We will not let that happen."

"I would rather die here attempting to hide in my room than to have to go with him."

"I understand exactly. I would also."

"Then how did it happen that you let my older sisters be taken away by that beast?"

"It happened all too fast before. Please believe me—we had no choice."

"How about this time? Will we have any choice this time... and where will it be any different this time?"

"Oh, Hannah, let us not rush ahead of ourselves."

"I do not feel I am rushing ahead. I am terrified, Mother. I do not want to be taken away by that vile man who scares me just with his shouting."

"King Hezekiah!"

"King Hezekiah!"

The Rabshakeh was shouting with greater confidence, since he now believed that the city would soon have to surrender because he felt that it was extremely low on water.

"Are you still resisting us because you are so insane that you have put your trust in Egypt?—in that bruised reed which if a man leans on it, it will go up into his hand and pierce it. I ask you, have those Egyptians helped any of your other cities which we have already reduced to complete obedience?

"Are they assisting Lachish?

"Of course not!

"We are violently overthrowing that rebellious fortress city of yours!

"Need I remind you that Lachish is much closer, and much easier to get at, for the Egyptians' worthless chariots and horses than is this isolated, thirsting city?"

The Rabshakeh did not need to remind him, nor did that shouter need to inform him, of the awesome renewed humbling of his cities.

He had his scouts.

He had read all the reports.

He knew of all the violent evil the Assyrian policy of extreme ruthless cruelty had left in its grim tracks throughout his land. He also knew that if he continued to hold out on letting them enter, and was defeated, he knew his women would be brutally ripped apart by the starved inhuman lusts of their Assyrian army, and, that his men would suffer vulgar inhuman tortures of another sort. Many of them, including his top aides and he himself, would be blinded, and skinned alive, and beheaded as savage reminders to any left behind that they had better obey the subjugating empire's every demand.

"Where have you placed your newly found trust?" the Rabshakeh, mocking, continued shouting. "Are you so foolish to think that you can trust in your Lord God?"

Hezekiah knew the intimidator would not understand.

Not after their highly successful last visit; but...yes, he was that foolish, O wicked intimidator.

*

\>\>\> * \<\<\<

*

An hour before high noon, his three envoys were walking along with him toward the house of the forest of Lebanon.

Unquestionably concerned, the elders of the city were watching with aped interest as to what Hezekiah planned to do with envoys this time.

Fearfully aped interest.

"Our three envoys are acting as if—"

"Certainly he has no intentions of sending these three out there beyond the gates again!"

"If not that, then, what is he planning?"

He had ordered all of his captains to meet them and the elders near the house of the forest. When they arrived, the captains were there and were ready to carry out any orders he gave them.

"Men, there is no way we will allow these Assyrians within our walls again even if I am forced again to go out there unto them. I will never request for the gates to be reopened. We also have no plans to engage in battle with them; however, we are planning to present to them a strong show of force to take some of their arrogant confidence out of their leader's mouth."

He paused to let that sink in.

"We have trained our men extensively. They probably would like to show what they have learned."

The captains nodded in agreement.

The elders looked more fearful and concerned than ever.

"Since that is true, I believe that we would be wise to do our demonstration of power in the beginning of their siege. If we wait too long, our Lord God may defend us too soon in such a way that we will never be able to show them what we have been doing these past few months and years."

The captains, and the soldiers within hearing distance,

283

rooted loudly. The elders looked as if they wished that they would all quickly calm back down to silence.

"Then here is our plan, men. The captains over our archers are to bring their men over to the eastern wall. Have them remain out of sight, but stretched out all along it from one end to the other so that as soon as you order them to present themselves, every last one of them can aim his arrow at that vile one who ordered so much ruthless violence the last time they came.

"Have every one of your archers aim their arrows at the rude, blaspheming, dagger-throwing shouter. No arrow, however, is to be released unless that Rabshakeh makes an improper move. And no bow is to be relaxed until our three envoys have talked to him and are safely back inside the gates and the doors are securely shut. Any questions?"

The only question came from one of the elders, "You are really planning to send our envoys out there again?"

"Only to give to our guests our official position."

When no other objection or inquiries came forward, he sent forth the captains.

*

\> \> \> * < < <

*

When the sun reached its zenith, the main water gate began to open. Slowly, ever so slowly, those huge defensive doors creaked to life. The envoys, carrying a sign of peace, left the safety of their city when the gates were about half open.

Hezekiah, up on the wall, had found an obscured place to stand and watch the proceedings. A bow was in his hand. A skip in his heart.

The trio walked toward the Rabshakeh: who acted as if he

would simply, angrily, do exactly what he did the last time.

Hezekiah and the captains and the archers watched as their men neared the leader and the rest of the officers in the Assyrian party. The Rabshakeh looked at the three and then up toward the wall. He saw only a few soldiers standing behind the waist-high parapet.

He turned toward the Tartan and the Rabsaris.

Then!—in anger, he swung around and shouted to his closest soldiers. They drew their glistening daggers and moved forward. They stopped after only a couple paces.

Seeing that, he started to yell at them until he noticed the extreme fright in their eyes.

Turning, he looked where their eyes had been gaping.

Highly disciplined was he, hard as iron was his boast...but he was not ready to see what his eyes were beholding in stark terror! The entire visible length along the top of the wall was solid with archers—*with every arrow aimed directly at him!* He paused, as if accepting that the arrows would all come and mow him down before he made another move.

When none came, he scanned along the wall, knowing that he had to be up there somewhere.

*

> > > * < < <

*

Hezekiah stepped out into the morning sunlight and stated with the dignity due his position, "I have sent my men out to hear why your King Sennacherib has returned and sent more forces up here again."

He paused for effect.

"You spared my life that last time. When my men return safely within our walls, we will spare yours."

285

Again he paused.
"Do you understand?"
The Rabshakeh made no move.
"DO YOU UNDERSTAND!"
"I understand," came back in clear Hebrew.

The Rabshakeh walked toward the envoys, turned, and took another glimpse toward the wall and saw that every arrow was still tightly drawn and every one still specifically aimed at him.

"Speak to King Hezekiah. Thus says the great king! The king of Assyria! The king of the universe! The one who will devastate your land! What confidence is this wherein you trust? You say, 'I have counsel and strength for war,' but those are hollow words. On whom therefore do you trust that you rebel against me?"

The arrows were still aimed at him.

"Behold, do you trust on the staff of that bruised reed...even upon Egypt?—on which if a man leans, it will go into his hand and pierce it! So is Pharoah, king of Egypt, unto all that trust on him, my friends!"

He raised the volume of his Hebrew.

"But if you say unto me, 'We trust in the Lord our God.' Is not that He whose high places and whose altars King Hezekiah has taken away and has said to Judah and Jerusalem, 'You shall worship before this altar in Jerusalem?' Now therefore, I pray you, pay the tribute that my lord, the king of Assyria, demands. After that I will supply unto you two thousand horses, you are to set riders on them for us to use in our army."

Pausing, he glanced at the line of solid humanity ready to take his life with any errant move.

"My lord asks, 'Am I now come up here without the Lord against this place to destroy it?' Of course not! The Lord God of this land, your Lord God, said to my lord, 'Go up against this land and destroy it.'"

Since the envoys stayed much closer to the wall this time than they did during the former visit, Eliakim sensed that the words he was listening to was also easily reaching all his countrymen upon and behind the wall.

"Speak, I pray, to your servants in the Aramaic language, for we understand it," he therefore said, "and talk not these words with us in the ears of the people that are on the wall."

The Rabshakeh smirked and continued, "Has my master sent me to your master and to you only to speak these words? Has he not sent me also to those men that stand on the wall and to all your people which you are going to force to eat their own dung and drink their own piss!"

After a short time more he turned from the envoys, trusting in the peasant ruler's promise—and in that ruler's stupidity for not having him shot through. The envoys, realizing that their time of meeting with him was over, turned and walked back into the safety of the city.

Once within, and, once the heavy gates were drawn tightly shut and securely fastened...only then did they breathe normally...and, only then did the line of human archers back away from their place in front of the wall and return to their invisibility.

Also still upon that wall, Hezekiah breathed a sigh of relief, his men and city had gained their first deeply-needed victory.

His was a good feeling.

But, he knew that it could only get worse now that King Sennacherib would be advised that the Hebrews indeed had no

Tom Steinbach

intent of surrendering.

*

> > *TWENTY THREE* < <

*

"Hannah, I have been informed that you hardly ate anything for dinner."

"How could I eat with that man shouting out there?"

"I understand that you are upset, but—"

"Upset! Mother, I am scared!"

"Hannah, let me share something with you."

"What is it, Mother?"

"Well, I really do not know how to begin."

"Is it something to do with that evil man out there?"

"Somewhat...and about your sisters."

"Are you worried that I am going to die like they did."

"No, no, Hannah. Nothing like that. It is just, well, it has to do with...."

"Yes, Mother?"

"It has to do with, with, with why I believe your sisters were taken."

Hannah did not say anything.

"Hannah, our people used to do a lot of things which were very displeasing to the Lord. Before Father became our ruler, they used to believe and trust in many different gods and goddesses and even worshipped those creatures at many high places and altars."

"Why would they do that?"

"I guess because all the nations around us do that."

"But did they not know that there is only one God?"

"They should have, but for many reasons they apparently wanted to worship something which they could see."

"And so God—"

"Yes, Hannah...though we do not understand why He waited until your father began to make things right again. Why He waited until a few years ago to bring the Assyrians into our land and punish us so harshly."

"Like when you or Father used to take the rod to us?"

"Exactly. It was not pleasant."

"But why did the Lord take my sisters? You and Father did not worship at those altars, did you?"

"No, we did not. Nor would we ever have."

"Then why did He take our sisters?"

"That is the hard part to explain to you."

"Why?"

"Because it has to do with...with...."

Your father loving many wives and maidens. In fact, loving one maiden so much that you are named in her honor. The simple revived truth of the thought brought tears to her eyes. Wiping them back, she tried to continue, "It has to do...with...."

Why do I feel the need to bring the hurting past up to her? Am I really doing it for her sake? Or my own? Am I using this siege to get back at Hezekiah for all the pain he shoved onto me back then?

"It has to do with what, Mother?"

"It has to do with...with...what was I talking about?"

"You were saying that my sisters were taken captive because of something that Father—"

No, I do not want to hurt either Hannah nor Hezekiah with that explanation. Why did I bring it up in the first place? What can I tell her now? He has changed so. He has been so wonderful and loving.

"Hannah, there was—" She began to cry. "Hannah, there was a time when I did not treat your father as a true husband."

"As a true husband? What do you mean?"

Oh, why did I ever get into this? "Well, I had been brought up believing that a girl grew up and got married so that, that...." Why does someone not come right now and give me an excuse to stop talking. "...that a girl married so that...that... she could become a mother and...have babies to play with, and to wash, and to dress, and to rock, and to put fast to sleep."

Hannah was confused but also smiling at the thought, as though it sounded right to her: very, very right to her. When her mother did not continue with what she was going to inform her, she looked perplexed as to what was so wrong with that.

My Lord God, how do I share with an eleven year old that I did not know anything of bringing loving pleasure to my husband as the natural part of our daily activity?

*

> > >   *   < < <

*

It was after dinner before the Rabshakeh was heard from

again. At that time he looked up toward the soldiers at their posts along the top of the wall and beckoned with utter contempt, "Are you also saying, 'We trust in the Lord.'" He spat, as if at the thought. "O fools of all fools," he said, sneering at them. "Do you want me to name one by one the multitude of cities that we have already leveled to the ground which also worshipped at your country's high places and altars?"

Eliakim, Shebna, and Joah were standing upon the wall opposite the Rabshakeh and had been ever since they had returned within the safety of their gates and delivered to Hezekiah the Assyrian's sealed scroll of demands from Sennacherib.

Forced by the direct communication of the Rabshakeh with their soldiers and sentries, Eliakim again was compelled to shout down to the abusive Assyrian in his own Aramaic language.

The Rabshakeh gave him a belittling look, spat, fingered his dagger, and shouted, "Has my great king, the king of the universe, the king of all the peoples, sent me here to speak to you and your rebellious ruler? You know better! The king of kings, the ruler of the almighty Assyrian Empire, has sent me here to persuade only those who can reason wisely! The inhabitants of this ill-fated city had better come to their senses soon or they will shortly suffer grievous agonies much worse than those experienced by any of your other pitiful cities.

"I am here to tell all who can hear my voice that we will soon have you and your capital under a massive siege if your leaders do not pay us our tribute! It is you who are going to suffer all the tortures of ravenous hunger, of unquenchable thirst, of terrifying fear until you surrender and freely open your gates to us! It is for your sake that I am here. It is for your sake that I offer the chance to disregard your rebellious monarch's foolish orders and to peacefully and promptly surrender yourselves to the bountiful mercies we freely display to all who treat us with respect. Do not let your king deceive you.

"How could Hezekiah ever rescue you and this caged-in city out of my King Sennacherib's all-powerful hand? What has he told you? 'Surely the Lord will deliver us,' and 'This chosen city shall not fall into the hands of the king of Assyria.'

"How can you believe that!

"Certainly you know that our great new monarch has an ocean of blood-thirsty, women-lusting, skin-ripping, spear and sword carrying, dagger-throwing, warmongering soldiers down with him in the plains and foothills. When those trained troops defeat your last fortress city, when those lust-laden men come up here like a immense storm cloud covering these mountains and all the land and valleys around this city, you will be so outnumbered, and so overpowered, and, so thoroughly conquered; I tell you, your homes will be sacked and burned, your men will be skinned and run through with the sword, and, your women will be ripped open or raped three days strai—"

"Sir!" Eliakim cut in, trying for the third time, and wishing that he had spoken forth an instant sooner, "please, let us use the accepted means—"

"When that host come up these roads bringing all of our mighty battering rams!—and all of our huge siege towers!—and all of our solid-iron war engines!—then what hope will you have?

"NONE!

"I am warning you! When our men come up, they are not going to allow you to then come out and surrender peacefully!

"NO! NO!

"After all that, they are going to crave everything!—all your treasures!—all your women!—all your skins!—all your food!—all your children! I warn you, they will tear and rip wide-open every one of your screaming, terrified women that is big with child!"

*

> > > * < < <

*

Even Hezekiah standing by his palace window heard those series of dreadful threats. He could only periodically hear the Rabshakeh but he was afraid the Assyrian strategy was working too well. Most of his citizens had to be fearfully buckling under with all of the continuous shouting. His only hope at the moment was a negative one: that they would well remember the beast's last entrance into the city; and, then, that they would put into that remembrance the vivid description, by the Rabshakeh, of the blood-thirsty soldiers outside the walls, and, especially of those lust-filled hordes down in the plains. His only hope was that the boastful one had so frightened his citizens already that they would simply be too scared to storm the gates in surrender. He grabbed hold of a corner of a table for support, however, as a strong quiver rippled violently through his being.

Once it stopped, he prayed:

"How long, Lord? If You do not come soon. How long will my people continue to wait?"

*

> > > * < < <

*

Hephzibah was still with Hannah and she still knew not what to do. She had not been able to come up with the right words to speak forth what she wanted to say. Nevertheless, the longer she waited, she knew that she did not want to say to her daughter what she had planned on saying. When she realized what she was going to have to say, tears again had come flooding out. Not understanding, her oldest became scared and began to cry, and began to pitifully look as if she was going to rise up and run out of the room at any moment.

Hephzibah tried to reassure her by telling her that everything was going to be all right and that she wished she would wait with her until her tears stopped flowing. Then, she said, she would be able to talk more clearly.

Hannah willingly agreed.

Instead of running away, she hugged her mother close to her, they sat close together, mother and daughter comforting each other with that special sympathetic love given mostly only to the female of our species, loving each other, greatly needing each other.

When she could, Hephzibah began, wondering how long she would be able to talk before another siege of tears would poured forth, "At first, I was going to tell you that it was your father's fault that your sisters were taken. For much of my life I have held on to that belief concerning your father. But now in the last ten or fifteen minutes now I look upon it much differently."

For I am different, Hannah, she thought, feeling the hot tears coming and burning the edges of her eyelids. I am much different, my latest firstborn. It has just happened, but I now understand our daughters being taken way back then was as much my fault as his. If not more mine.

O forgive me, Lord.

"Some would say that neither your father nor I should accept any of the blame, but I disagree with that. Punishment came into our lives for some reason. Some would say that your father should accept all of the blame, and he probably does,

Hannah. I am now certain he takes all the blame upon himself."

She paused, had to pause to blink back a couple very hot tears, then she began again.

"Your father has demonstrated these past many years that he would have been willing to obey the Lord totally if I would not have forced him to do before what was displeasing to our Lord. It is hard to explain it to you, Hannah, but once I started being—oh, it is so hard to explain!—once I began...being a wife to him instead of being...only a mother to him and his children which we no longer had—once I really, truly started giving him my evenings whenever he was free to share them with me, once I sincerely tried to please him only for the sake of pleasing him"—and, Hannah, I do not know how to tell you now, and, of course, I cannot tell you now, but I have learned, I have so greatly learned, Hannah, how to gain great physical pleasure myself from him, from that action of serving him— "then we, both of us, we stopped being disobedient to the Lord in forcing him to have a house of women."

*

> > > * < < <

*

"That bad?"

Hezekiah's inquiry was quietly directed toward Eliakim and his two companions after they were ushered back into his presence with their clothes torn as the visibly accepted symbol of their feeling of utter hopelessness.

"Worse. You probably could not hear the Assyrian near the end when he softened his tone but he totally disregarded our words and began reasoning with the soldiers and sentries along the wall. My lord, he is going to do anything he can to get someone to open our gates to him."

"I feared such. And yet no matter what that Rabshakeh says, my decision is fixed: we will not open the gates nor surrender their tribute demands this time unless the word to do so comes to Isaiah directly from the Lord."

"I am afraid that the Assyrians are after much more than their tribute," Shebna said. And then asked, "Would they really skin us alive as they did the others?"

"Their pattern of terror has never changed. It is still to leave many flayed skins hanging in plain sight in all the cities which they have conquered, and we would be their top prized trophies. My severed head would go back to the capital with them. However, instead of dwelling upon those evil actions, we need to remind ourselves that we have chosen to do nothing but wait for the salvation that Isaiah has promised is going to come to us from the Lord. Our soldiers and our keepers of the gates...do they seem to be standing with us?"

"Totally, Sir."

That was the answer he wanted to hear. Was expecting to hear. Needed to hear. After further discussion concerning the rest of their strategy for the day,the trio left. He felt pleased with his uncompromising stand with them. Before Eliakim and his friends could have walked out of the front gates of the palace, nevertheless, he too had thrown off his royal robes and had ripped his linen clothing into long narrow shreds. Pleading mercy from the Lord as he went, he quickly made his way toward the room he had only visited once before.

*

> > > * < < <

*

Hannah, how can I tell you that I have still hated your

name up to this moment?

How can I let you know that during my siege of tears, that everything about your father which I still had found fault with was washed away as with a flood.

Everything. Even my blaming him for our daughters' captivity and deaths.

Hannah, it was all washed away. I truly felt the release from it. During my crying I truly saw him throughout our marriage trying to plead with me to love him more often just for the sake of our being blessed together. During my crying I also saw myself concerned, so very concerned, with my own hurts and desires that I often shut him out of my life, and even drove him to try to find others who would simply cherish him as I would not do.

How can I hate your name? He never even knew her. She just came and showed him that she wanted to be with her monarch and with no one else and that she wanted to be nowhere else.

If it were not for her, Hannah, I would never have been shown what loving is really all about.

If it had not been for her, Sarai would never have been able to teach through to me that a wife gets back a hundredfold for all the time she is willing to offer to her husband. My daughter, I would have never believed it, but for the past ten years all that she has told me has come true.

Hannah, how has it been possible that I have hated your name through all these good years?

How? I know now, more now than ever before—oh, Lord God, teach me to understand myself and my selfish wants and that I am the one whom You had to teach, the one You had to punish.

"Hannah, this may sound strange to you, but I am so very, very thankful that we named you Hannah.

"What a beautiful name you have!

Tom Steinbach

"What a beautiful girl you are!"

$$* $$
$$>>> \; * \; <<<$$
$$* $$

Once inside, Hezekiah prostrated himself before the many veils. Before the multi-lined draperies of blue, purple, crimson, and fine linen which divided the front section of their temple from the strictly-to-the-high-priest-restricted most holy place, the Holy of Holies, wherein the Presence of the Lord dwelt.

Lying there for some time, he was reminded of two things. First, of a dream concerning David he had dreamed after the Babylonian emissaries had left and also of the talk which he had had with his mother before she passed away. Those were the two events which had the most influence upon his giving up his house of women.

*

> > *TWENTY FOUR* < <

*

It seemed like a long dream as far as dreams go, though he had no way of knowing how much, or how little, of the night it took to get through it in its entirety.

He vividly remembered King David holding a magnificent banquet in the beginning of spring in the days and weeks just prior to that year's warring season. Every captain and mighty man in his army and their wives were included among his guests.

The dream began in the midst of the banquet with the entrance of Uriah and his beautiful wife.

Shining brilliance radiated from Bathsheba's presence with every step she took. David of course had noticed her exceptional beauty long before that banquet and was once again pleased to see his mighty man Uriah and his wife moving through the crowd up toward their appointed place.

The whole affair was grandiose and festive. Much like the many banquets which were held during his own reign, except that the one in the dream was on a much more lavish scale: King David's kingdom was far greater and worth so much more than his own.

During the course of the evening in that dream, David's casual glances toward Bathsheba brought back to him from her what he felt was a little more than simple mutual responses. Therefore he found himself looking her way a lot more often than he had previously in the past. Her beaming coquetry caused the feast to be a great time for him.

A fortnight later, just prior to the sending forth of the army that warring season, another mirthful banquet was held to once again honor his captains and mighty men. Along with the previous one, the second meal was to be a lavish reminder to all aspiring young, bold men of Israel what an outstanding service upon their nation's battlefields would bring to them in sumptuous rewards and honor in such gay occasions in the palace. David noticed himself watching the entrance hall whenever any new couple arrived.

Watching, and then quickly dismissing the interest as soon as he determined it was not Uriah and Bathsheba entering.

Finally, they entered, she looking more beautiful than she had ever looked to him and far more beautiful than his scores of wives and concubines. As they moved toward their appointed place, he felt his heart beat faster, wondering if she would again respond to his clandestine glances. If she did, he prayed within that she would, he would announce a plan which he had formulated full blown during the last few days before the feast.

Earlier in the week his latest wife made it clearly known that she wished that he would not hold another dinner in honor of these men and their wives. She acknowledged that those festive occasions were annual affairs, and, she also agreed that they were extremely beneficial in maintaining national morale in light of the upcoming summer warring season, but she also made it clear that she did not care for some of the wives these men of valor had married and were bringing with them. In her discourse of ill-well, she mentioned the unfaithful actions of this pretty-but-dumb wife, and of that very beautiful but much-to-young wife, and, of another who practically slept day and night with one of her male servants when her husband was off to war.

During her talking, she came to Bathsheba. David's ears perked up when she harped on how that woman was the most vain of all that came to the banquets. She harangued about how obviously she was in love with herself and with her own beauty. Bathsheba, she plodded on, was so guilty of vainglory that she had her servants carry her bath up to her roof and bathe her there in the full light of the evening sky!

"Why would you ever say something like that?" he asked, trying to show little interest.

"I have seen her a number of times," she responded as a wife who knew more about her husband's kingdom than did he.

"Bathing upon her roof?"

"Yes!—her home is not that far from here!"

"You have seen her from our—"

"Of course, from here! Where else do you think I would see her from? I have seen her bathing out there in all her vainglory when all you men have gone to fight our nation's battles."

David not did say anything, but Hezekiah knew in observing this scene in his dream, that she should never have mentioned that detail about the openness of Bathsheba, Uriah's very lovely wife.

Tom Steinbach

"And I watched her enter the banquet hall last week and I tell you, she turns my stomach inside out with her obvious vain-love of her own being!"

Hezekiah paused in that remembering, and thought: why do wives divulge to their husbands the most doltish things? When will they understand that a man may find many faults with a beautiful woman, but that the sole fault he will never find will be in that woman's willingness to do everything she can to accentuate and improve her overwhelming beauty. A man, especially one like him who naturally finds himself around beautiful women on a regular basis, thrive on these maiden's fastidious attentiveness in eternally enriching how they appear to others.

At this second banquet Uriah and Bathsheba's appointed seating had been moved much closer to David's regal setting. David was in an exceptionally good nature with everyone near his table. He was exceedingly full of praise for all within hearing range. Whenever he glanced Bathsheba's way and caught her eye, she responded in brilliance.

She was absolutely beautiful that evening.

Her smiling eyes confirmed over and over what he had wanted to know all week. Certain of his coming actions, he began taking more notice of Uriah—not more interest in the Hittite's ability as one of his mighty men—he already had all the proof he needed for that quality in this servant's life. He took strict notice of how Uriah treated Bathsheba in public. His conclusion was what he had hoped it would be: Uriah was an exceedingly proud man, proud of his size, proud of his ability on the battlefield, proud of his muscular legs and upper body, proud of his august accomplishments in this adopted kingdom of his choice, proud of having been assigned a setting much closer to the regal table, and, manifestly, loudly, proud to be seen with such a magnificently beautiful woman at his side at these functions. More importantly, in all of his watching Uriah greatly shunned his wife. He hardly spoke with her. She was his lovely showpiece, not his intimate companion and lover.

King David, in the sensitivity that he was well known for, was convinced in the night-dream that Uriah was gravely neglecting his exceptional wife. It was as if he had already won her and now was on a further quest for even higher attainments within the kingdom. On the other hand, throughout the evening, Bathsheba looked bored and ignored and forgotten, and, to David very much like a woman needing love. Loving people who needed love was a forte of David's.

It had always been. Therefore throughout the evening with his amorous glances he had loved her much. Unfortunately...that trait had caused renowned jealousies to well up in many of his different wives, but he was nevertheless constant in that characteristic: he had always thrived in his life in loving the unloved—and the very lovely.

In the dream, by the end of the feast his determination toward Bathsheba was decisive. This warring season would be the first of his reign that he would not lead his nation's army to war. His blood pumped hard whenever he thought of Bathsheba, *lovely Bathsheba*, bathing in all her beauty under the evening sky within sight of his palace.

In his concept of righteousness, if her boastful husband Uriah did not become slain in battle he would not steal her from him but he would show Bathsheba that she was capable of being very greatly loved. Extremely capable of being loved in its fullest sense. Of being utterly loved to the point that she and not just her husband would be totally, completely, wonderfully fulfilled. In the dream, it occurred just as David knew it would. And as Hezekiah, observing the dream in his sleep, also grasped it would happen.

After the armies had left without him, the first evening David arose from his sofa, his heart beating very fast, his palms moist, and he beheld her bathing in all her beauty.

His heart pumped even faster and he knew he needed to make his lie complete. He, as casually as he could, gave a trusted servant the order, "Go and inquire and find out who that woman is that is bathing herself over there upon her rooftop."

When the servant returned with the requested information David acted informed, thanked him for the information and ordered him to send a messenger and have her brought to him.

At that point in the dream, Hezekiah pulled himself out of its memory and began speaking to the One dwelling in the hallowed room behind those many veils. He explained what the dream had conveyed for him in his making some life changing decisions. First, he had seen David as a hero in bringing love to one who was being ignored by her own husband. In Judah's national annals, on the other hand, David was remembered as anything but a national hero. The prophet Nathan saw the secret affair in the opposite light. He saw the act as that of one having been done by a man who had hundreds of women already, stealing the only one of another.

Upon much thought, Hezekiah had agreed with the prophet of the Lord. David's passion to love those who showed a great need to be loved was a wonderful, gracious, giving characteristic of his—one which brought him close to being after the heart of their Lord God Himself—however, carrying that appetite over to forbidden actions of adultery was strictly prohibited in their laws and commandments given to them from that very same Lord God. Using a good and godly reason to profanely break a good and godly commandment could never be justified in the courts of righteousness. Their prophet Nathan had to come and expose the evil deed for what it was.

Second, David's love for this beautiful woman should have been manifested in bringing her husband to the place of truly being the man who would love his wife to her fullest.

She was married, that was the crucial factor, and therefore he should have worked within their spoken and written guidelines of that fact. David's sin was that he had completely thrown out their Lord God's commandments on marriage and adultery. He had thoroughly tossed them away to that supposedly higher decree of loving those who needed to be loved no matter whose they were. And he lost. Oh, how he lost.

The prophet came and pronounced the Lord's judgment, "For your great sin of adultery and murder the sword shall never depart from your house. Because you have despised Me, I will raise up noisome evil against you out of your own house. And I will take your wives before your eyes and give them unto your neighbor and he shall lie with them in the sight of the sun. Also, the child that Bathsheba has borne to you shall die."

How the entire nation lost!

David and Bathsheba's first son did die.

Their second son was Solomon...and Hezekiah could not count the number of times that he had lamented all that had occurred to their once glorious kingdom because of the jealousies, fightings and divisions caused by Solomon becoming their king. It was then that he began to see why their Lord God had allowed all of his house of women to be taken, including Hannah.

Nevertheless, even then, even after watching that dream within his mind, he had still been adamant in keeping the house of women and in his continual searching to find another Hannah. That dream made his mind fertile earth for another to plant more seed within.

That another was his mother, he realized as he lay there. His father was dead and had lived a life which would have backed every evil deed anyone ever wanted to do. His mother, nearing her death, chose an evening when just the two of them were warming themselves by the fire. Abijah had not mentioned anything about his house of women for a long time.

She said that evening:

"Son, I have been reading Solomon's song of songs day after day for months. The more I read it, the more I see Solomon's role in it in a different light. I no longer believe that he is the hero, the young maiden's beloved, in the story."

"Not the hero in his own song of songs?"

"No, I do not believe that he is the maiden's beloved."

"Mother, perhaps you had better read it again. He seems so very obviously to be the hero."

"I have read it and read it and read it and read it, Hezekiah. Let me explain."

"Please do, but I do not think that I will probably agree with you."

"I will. But first let me read to you the end of the story of Gideon."

"Gideon? What does he have—"

"He was similar to you in many ways. Too many, Son."

"Not knowing at all of what you are referring to, I guess I had better let you read of him."

"Thank you. I am reading after the great victory he brought to our land. At that time the men of Israel came to him and said unto him, 'Rule over us, both you and your son and your son's son also: for you have delivered us from the hand of Midian.' And Gideon said unto them, 'I will not rule over you, neither shall my son rule over you:the Lord shall rule over you.' So far, so good. But then we read that Gideon also said unto them: 'I would desire a request of you, that you would give me every man the earrings of his prey':for they had golden earrings because they were Ishmaelites. And his people answered, 'We will willingly give them to you.' And they spread a garment and cast therein every man the earrings of his prey. The weight of those golden earrings that he requested of them was a thousand and seven hundred shekels of gold; and beside them they gave the ornaments, the collars, and the purple raiments which were on the kings of Midian; and, beside those things, the chains that were about their camels' necks. And Gideon made an ephod of the gathered gold, and put it in his city, even in Ophrah: and we read that all Israel went there whoring after the ephod: which thing became a snare unto Gideon and to his house."

"Why would you say that reminds you of me and my reign? I would never put up an idol in the midst of our city."

"That part of the statement does not remind me of you, Son. In what I have read, it was his humble willingness to let our Lord God rule over them that reminded me of you."

When he said nothing more, she continued reading, skipping over a few sentences:

"'And Gideon had threescore and ten sons of his body begotten: for he had many wives. And his concubine that was in Shechem, she also bare him a son whose name he called Abimelech. Gideon the son of Joash died in a good old age and was buried in the sepulchre of Joash his father, in Ophrah of the Abiezites, and it came to pass, as soon as Gideon was dead, that Israel turned, and went whoring after Baalim and Baal-berith again.' Son, in our nation you reap what you sow; even if you are the Lord's leader. Listen to this: 'And Israel remembered not the Lord their God who had delivered them out of the hands of their enemies on every side; neither showed they kindness to the house of Gideon according to all the goodness which he had showed unto Israel.' I truly believe that if Gideon would have served the Lord completely by not taking unto himself all the additional wives, that then his people would have honored his children and showed kindness to them forever."

"That could have been the case, but I am not certain that I agree with you that his many wives were the problem."

"Then why would the chronicler of his life have only

mentioned that other fact about him?"

"Like I said, that could have been the case, I know I surely do not adore the fact that his people did not treat his family kindly after he died. But back to Solomon's song of songs, why is it that you feel that Solomon himself was not the hero of his most amorous and famous song?"

"As I now read it," Abijah began, "the lovely maiden has a lover who is living among the shepherds in the fields near the city. It is because the sheep are always moving from place to place to find pasture, that though she is sick in love with him, she cannot find where he has gone with his flock. She truly is in Solomon's house of women for she realizes that she is much darker than most of the maidens living there."

"Darker because she had toiled out in the sun more than any of the others."

"Yes, because of that. She seems to have been the one to keep most of her brothers and sisters' vineyards."

"I agree. Solomon lets us know that she did not even have time to keep her own."

"Then to her comes this young shepherd offering her the choice of remaining in the palace with all the light-skinned beauties, or to run away with him into the fields...and ultimately into a small village to dwell with him."

"So you think, Mother, it is not Solomon at all that the young maiden is raving about when she exclaims: 'The voice of my beloved! Behold, he runs leaping upon the mountains, he comes skipping upon the hills. My beloved is like a roe, he is like a young hart. He stands behind that wall...he looks forth at the windows...he shows himself through the lattice.'"

"I do not think that her votary is Solomon because she is soon seeking her beloved...and when she goes looking for him...she goes into the city in the streets and in the broad ways. If her beloved was Solomon she would have not had to seek for him, she would have known where he dwelt."

"Does that argument fall apart when she speaks of Solomon coming out of the wilderness like a pillar of smoke, perfumed with myrrh and frankincense, and with all the powders of the merchants? She even names him by his name."

"She talks about him, she names him by name and she talks about his bed...a bed of fear where threescore valiant men have to stand ready about it: all expert in war and all having their swords upon their thighs because of the fear of the night. Son, I do not think that she is very impressed with that situation. I believe that she wants to run off with the handsome shepherd and therefore she encourages the rest of the women to go forth unto Solomon who wears the crown wherewith his mother crowned him."

"Thinking about it, Solomon does not say anything to the young maiden in that part of the story."

"She knows exactly where he lives, but does not know where her lover lives, for her beloved pleads to her: 'Come now with me from Lebanon, with me from the top of Amana, from the top of Shenir and Hermon, from the lions' dens, from the mountains of the leopards.' His is not a stable home life, Hezekiah."

"Yes, I can see your argument. And when her lover comes again late in the night to take her away from the women and he is forced to flee before she was ready...she again seeks for him in the city streets and avenues, and not in the palace even though she would most likely be punished for going out into the passageways at that time of night. You may have something there, Mother."

"Son, she is in training to become Solomon's wife or concubine but he is not the true lover she has been seeking. That votary had come to get her but was forced to flee for his life, nevertheless, in her passionate love for him, there was no law of the city which was going to stand in her way to try to find him so that she could leave with him."

Tom Steinbach

"The idea certainly has some merit. However, I am not so sure that I can accept it yet. When the daughters of Jerusalem ask her, 'What is your beloved more than any other beloved?' Does not that maiden's descriptive answer sounds like it was surely Solomon whom she was talking about."

"Solomon, or any goodly looking man. Son, this is her beloved! Any woman in love, given such an opportunity to speak freely about her beloved, would talk with such words. The question that I have for you is this: If he is not a third person in the story, why did she never mention his name in those portions of the story when she describes her beloved?"

"She never does?"

"Never once, Son. Though, as you have already noted, she does mentions Solomon's name at other times."

"Thinking about it, I guess that you are right."

"Listen to this, Hezekiah, her beloved is speaking: 'There are threescore queens and fourscore concubines and maidens without number. My dove, my undefiled'—that is, Son, that she is still in training and has not been brought unto Solomon yet...and therefore she is still undefiled, a virgin—'is but one.'"

"Read that again without your added words."

"'There are threescore queens and fourscore concubines and maidens without number. My dove, my undefiled, is but one.'"

"Again I agree with you. I can see a young man explaining why he needed the maiden more than Solomon who was already loaded with queens, and concubines, and maidens without number."

"Does it not sound like that?"

"It seems more and more so to me."

"How about that final statement:'my dove, my undefiled, is but one.' Does it not remind you of another report in our nation's long history? The story dealing with what Solomon's father did when he stole Bathsheba from her husband Uriah."

"You are referring to Nathan's statement to David after he had taken Bathsheba into his palace. I would have to say that it does. To this day I can see him entering the palace and proclaiming that he had his hundred lambs already and that he should not have taken Uriah's one lamb."

"The beloved in Solomon's song had the same problem: 'My dove, my undefiled, is but one,' he cried in his love-torn misery. As you say, Solomon was loaded with queens and concubines and maidens, but this beloved has just this one."

"And this one has been stripped from him."

"Yes, from him. Stripped from him by the marauding servants of Solomon as they searched through their cities and villages, always on the look for young beauties to be brought into his house for him to feast his lustful eyes upon."

"You are very harsh with Solomon. And through him with me with those same thoughts. But I have to say that you sound correct in that harsh judgment of him. I also have to agree that you seem correct in your judgment of who the beloved is."

"Thank you, Son. Listen to how the lover pleads with the young maiden, 'Return, return, O Shulamite. Return, return, that we may look upon you.'"

"Return? I never noticed it says return."

"Yes, return. He repeats it four times. He is pleading with her to return to her former hometown with him."

"That certainly sounds possible."

"Son, here is how I now look upon the story. I now believe the lovelorn shepherd could very well have been betrothed to the young maiden before Solomon's servants came into their town. Spied her. And took her away."

"You certainly make us kings sound awfully wicked when we have our servants find fresh young maidens for us."

"You are evil when you do that. Very evil."

"I will agree with you that King Solomon was wicked

when he continued gathering wives and maidens after he had so many. If the maiden's beloved had already known her before she was brought to the capital."

"Known of her, not known her."

"Yes, that was what I meant. If her beloved had already known of her before she was brought here, then that may be why the lover brought his flocks to the fields of the city."

"That is my belief."

"So he could see if he could find her and recover her."

"Yes."

"Mother, it is tempting; so that could be why he was trying to locate her through her latticed window before she became Solomon's forever. I believe you are winning me over. You are also bringing very deep shame and grief to my being. If you are correct, then I have been another David and another Solomon taking beautiful young maidens from their homes and future lovers to add to my multitude of women—though on a much smaller scale of course."

Abijah noticed his silence after his confession. She felt hope with his agreeing with her. If any king of Judah would stand up to the challenge of doing the right thing, it was her son.

"What about the end of the song?" she asked, believing the timing was right.

"The end of the song?"

"It tells us that Solomon had a vineyard at Baal-hamon that he let out unto keepers. Keepers which, I add, for the fruit thereof were to bring a thousand pieces of silver. Then we read this next statement which must be proclaimed by the beloved or the maiden. I believe by her shepherd friend because the maiden had earlier said that she did not have her own vineyard: 'My vineyard which is mine is before me. You, O Solomon, have a thousand vineyards and those that keep the fruit of your vineyards two hundred.'"

"That statement is in the end of the song?"

"Yes."

"I do not recall ever reading it."

"It is there exactly as I quoted it."

"Those words seem to add more credence to your idea, Mother. It seems to unmistakably be another example of the beloved having only one vineyard and of King Solomon having his thousands."

"That is how it sounded to me."

"Mother, I do not understand how I never saw it that way. I am going to reread it."

"That is all I ask you to do, Hezekiah. Reread it...and see the tragedy of filling the house of women from the beloved's point of view and in regard of what you kings are doing in your harsh sovereignty."

"I promise I will reread it tonight."

"Thank you, Son."

"It definitely sounds like our nation's song of songs was written about a beautiful maiden who had been chosen to enter Solomon's house of women...but who is sought after by one of her own countrymen. Possibly, as you say, by her own betrothed beloved."

"Son, it ends with her pleading to her friend, 'Make haste, my beloved, and be like a young hart upon the mountain of spices.' We are not told the outcome of the story. I am afraid that the ending might just depend upon Solomon's heart. Is he going to lust after another little lamb: another one among hundreds, or is he going to allow the maiden, no matter how pretty, her freedom to return to the one her heart truly loves?"

"So even if she is a Hannah, the most desirous young maiden to come into his house, then it would confirm to you that it is not right for him, and thus not right for me, to snatch any more young maidens away from their families and bring them into the palace to be added to his, or my, flock."

Tom Steinbach

"Yes, Son, I did hope you would see it that way;especially since the song of songs is one of your strongest arguments for our kings keeping such an house."

"You have me there. The song has been one of my strongest. It is very plausible, and, possibly the best interpretation presented to me thus far. Thank you for sharing it with me, Mother. I promise I will honestly consider it. And even more than that, if I deem that you are right, and right now I tend to agree that you are right, I vow to you right now that I do clearly see the fallacy and the sin of my taking beautiful maidens away from their hometown lovers strictly because I am the ruler...and I will cease doing so."

That had been nearly ten years ago he thought as he lay on the golden floor before the veils. Soon after that he had ordered that the task of gathering of young maidens be stopped. He also ordered at that time the maidens who were already in training in his house of women to be sent back to their homes with precious gifts and an apologetic explanation ...and that all those already defiled with him be supported out of his treasuries; that he acknowledged his sin in bringing them into his palace and he would have no more marital relationship with any of them.

Face down before the heavy veils, he reminded his Lord of that decision he had made—and that he had kept—and then he pledged he would not leave the refuge of the temple until a definite order of action was given to him.

*
> > > * < < <
*

Hours later, still within the temple, the word came clearly to him. "King Hezekiah, I have always told My people that all

I look for in a man or a woman is a willingness to seek My face. You have come here unto Me when most rulers would have trusted in some other alliance. Your crying has been heard. Send men now to My prophet. He will convey to you the further additional direction that you are seeking."

*

> > > * < < <

*

He ordered Eliakim and Shebna to get the elders of the priests once he was back inside the palace again. He then moved over to an open window—and was amazed.

Standing there for some time, he was convinced that the threats in clear Hebrew had ceased.

That there was no noise to be heard anywhere.

Even within his heart.

*

> > > * < < <

*

Hephzibah, alone in her chambers, thought back to the words of the Assyrian near the end of the first siege. The evil leader back then had said thanks for the pleasure her daughters would bring to him. Pleasures that they would bring!...our youngest two were too young for that: they could not have brought any pleasure to him and his men unless he meant offering them up to his gods.

She quit thinking about them and him, for she was certain that he had offered her daughters to his gods after he and his men were done with them.

*

> > *TWENTY FIVE* < <

*

The Rabshakeh had ceased his shouting and crying out because he had used the excuse of having no fresh drinking water to make a return stopover to the main Assyrian camp which, on his way down to the foothills, he had been informed had moved over to Libnah.

Soon, covered with sackcloth, Eliakim, Shebna and the elders of the priests were on their way across the city to see their prophet of the Lord.

It seemed to them that Isaiah had served Judah forever as their Lord's chief spokesman within the capital.

Besides bringing the word of the Lord to Hezekiah, their white -bearded, near-balding prophet had also spoken fearlessly to three former kings: to Uzziah, Hezekiah's great grandfather; Jothan, his grandfather; and Ahaz, his father. Unlike many of the prophets of Judah, Isaiah had always resided in Jerusalem. They were quickly at his place.

After explaining the reason for their late-evening mission and the contents of the temple directive, they waited for the promised orders their prophet would receive from the Lord. The wait however was much longer than any of them had anticipated. And the slowness with which the foreseer seemed to savor the meeting caused Eliakim to silently fret, I cannot believe this. I know from talking with Hezekiah that there is ill contention between the two of them, but surely Isaiah sees that we are under siege and that soon battering rams and war engines and siege towers will be added to our enemy's stock of terror.

But even he remained quiet.

Mute.

Isaiah finally rose and left the room. He was gone much longer than any of them desired.

But they waited.

They had no choice.

No choice at all.

Not any.

None. They would have waited two days, three days, a week, if necessary! Their aging man of God was the only one in their doomed city capable of delivering what they were sent to get.

*

> > > * < < <

*

"As soon as we force Libnah to bend the knee, I will bring the all my forces up to that peasant fool," King Sennacherib boasted to his returned commanding officer in his new camp near Libnah. "I am exhaustively through playing-around with that stubborn one! I want that despicable ruler gone!"

"If he would have only let me get in there again this time. I would have immediately killed him myself."

"You should have seen the fall of Lachish!"the bullish monarch continued with a subject much more pleasant to his thinking. "What a sight! What a defeat! When I return to my newly rebuilt capital, I have many scenes dancing around inside my head which I will have created on glorious, sculptural reliefs depicting all my wonderful deeds against Lachish! I told that city that they had better hope that I never returned to do battle against them again! On some of the reliefs I will have moldings formed portraying those cast down captives of Lachish marching before my victorious chariot! What a marvelous sight it was! Upon other panels I will have my artisans create large scenes which will show our numerous bowmen sending an endless barrage of arrows and spears over their walls. There will be other scenes depicting...."

*

> > > * < < <

*

Within a few hours they were immersed in dining, in lewd noisy entertainment and in oft drinking. As they continued drinking into the night, the pretentious monarch began vaunting a brewing idea to his Rabshakeh.

Staring deeply into his highly held wine goblet...staring into the liquid whose sparkling clarity appeared to him to contain fire—imprisoned fires which he imagined in his oncoming languor state to be favorable spirits—he voiced forth with the solemnness of an absorbed fortune teller, "If that mountain madman does not cave in before I come there, I will herd-drive these captive Lachish swine up to his capital, pile them one upon the other and ride my battle chariot straight into his bloody face over their squirming bodies! He will learn to cross my orders! I can feel the exuberation! The thrill of it already!"

"So can I!" his Rabshakeh agreed with a laugh. "I cannot wait to see his face!"

"I will show that Jehovah-worshipper whose gods really control this world!"

The two laughed uproariously.

Soon, more semi-clad, captive, Lachish maidens were brought in and flung into their laps.

*

> > > * < < <

*

Having returned to the room after the long absence, but having not taken a seat among the men, Isaiah began slowly.

"The Lord God says, 'Be not afraid of the words which you have heard from the one outside the walls. It is with those wicked words that that servant of the Assyrian king has mocked and blasphemed Me. Behold, I will therefore send a blast upon their ruler and he shall also hear a rumor. One which will strike terror in his heart. With those two actions I will place a hook in his nose, turn him around, and with a sharply pointed goad, I will force him to speedily return to his own land.'"

Knowing that this word from their God would cause life to once again flow within these men in front of him, and ultimately within the king himself, Isaiah then moved in closer and took his seat in their circle.

There he finished his proclamation.

"Once he returns to his own capital, the Assyrian monarch will not come again to this country. Instead, for the great evil he has completed in My land and to the innocent ones of My people, I will cause him to fall by the sword within his own false temple wherein he vainly trusts."

When the drunken merriment down on the fringe of the foothills was reaching its height, a worried aide hurried in with a scouting message which interrupted their licentious affair once and for all: one of their southern missions reported that they had sighted an extremely large regiment of armed troops preparing to head towards them from that direction.

Upon receiving the report, the drunken monarch angrily slurred to his Rabshakeh, "Why did you not get...that...that... blasted booty from those...those...those....I should have gone up there ...and...and...and overseen that...that....that piddling task myself! Now what do I have?" he continued in his self-pitying stupor. "The elite portion of...of my marching army is...is...is still standing around up in those...those...those mountains and...and.... and what do I have to...to...to show for it?"

"We are up there and we will get everything you want and more, my lord," the Rabshakeh promised, recoiling himself for the verbal fight which he knew was forthcoming.

"When?"

"Who knows? But I can assure you, like last time, what we spoil from them will be worth whatever time it takes."

"Whatever time it takes! Whatever time it takes!"

Sennacherib yelled as his wrath started overcoming his stupor. "Do you not see and hear the report, you...you...you blooming barbarian? I do not have 'whatever time it takes' now! If the Elamites, the Medes, the Scythians, the Babylonians, and.... and.... who knows who else, hear that enemy troops are brave enough to come against us down here in this end of our empire; I am going to have huge uprisings all over my kingdom! Get back up there! Right now! And force those mountain peasants to know in no uncertain terms that tomorrow is their last chance!"

"But what if they—"

"What if they what? You get back there to that cursed mountain tribe of peasants and demand my overdue tribute!— and ten thousand captive soldiers! And get them by tomorrow!"

"By tomorrow?" the Rabshakeh countered, pushing a nearly naked maiden off his lap as he stood up. "I did not go up there with the idea it would only take a day or two!"

"You did not, but you are now! And I mean now!"

"Right now?"

"Get back up there and force them to know that they had better act drastically! Persuade them to think that we have all the time in the world," roared Sennacherib, his stupor completely gone, "but that we are not going to wait for any peasant folk to surrender in their own good bidding!"

"What mor—"

"Do anything! Send fire over the walls! Scare their women! Fling spears and arrows in! Anything! Everything! But make them give in!"

"What more can I do?" the Rabshakeh finally countered with the pause. He had already decided to throw the decision back upon his monarch's shoulders. "I have threatened them in their own language until the sun was going down!"

"Threatening is not enough!"

"I will need more troops, many more thousands of them."

"How many? Fifty thousand?"

"If I have to make them buckle tomorrow or the next day, I will need," he pushed ahead, gaining confidence that he was once again in charge of the argument with his ruling head, "I will need at least another hundred thousand."

"You will have *twice* that! The first units will begin arriving around noon."

For the first time since the ominous message had come, a large grin could be seen on his red face. "And as for you," he demanded, pointing his index fingers into his chief officer's chest, "I want your terrorizing threats started before the sun rises on that evil peasant capital!"

The Rabshakeh nodded and grinned.

"Make those rebellious, Israelite, mountain peasant-swine know that I will personally be following those troops with all the rest of our forces," the very red-faced monarch continued as he tightly gripped the neck of his Rabshakeh's tunic, "and with all our solid iron war engines, and with all our tall siege towers, and with all our battling rams."

*

> > *TWENTY SIX* < <

*

That evening up in the capital, faithful messengers had passed Isaiah's encouraging report to everyone within the city's besieged walls. The most common question the various messengers were asked in return was, "What kind of blast does He mean?"

"We have no idea. The only thing we know is that our Lord God has promised to send a blast upon the king of Assyria and that He will also cause some sort of rumor to be heard by that king.

"What kind of rumor? We have not the slightest notion. But our prophet Isaiah has promised that the combination of the two, will send the foreigners fleeing for their homelands without having entered into any portion of our besieged city."

"If we get out of this alive," an astonished soldier said, "we will be like them that—"

"—that dream!" another soldier cut-in. "We will be like them that dream, my friend."

"Like them that dream," the first soldier repeated. "Like them that dream...I like that."

"Me, too."

"That message from Isaiah sounds good, and, if we ever get out of this alive, I will carry the little ditty upon my arm and on my forehead right here; but for now it is all empty words," a soldier further down the wall, leaning back against a big pile of throwing stones, muttered. "For now, from where I sit, it appears that the Assyrians have us right where they want us."

"That is not quite true, my friend," another soldier farther on down the wall taunted, "those angry bloodthirsty Assyrians want us out there!"

*

> > > * < < <

*

On cue, long before the breaking of dawn, the piercing threats in clear Hebrew shattered the placid, pre-dawn darkness. By early morning it was apparent to Hezekiah that the venomous spiels were aimed at his besieged city's weakest point: at its women. By mid-morning, his advisors had reported to him that they were convinced that the strategy was working.

Concurring with them and sensing that all the faith, high hopes and expectations of the previous evening's message had dissolved, he decided he better act immediately to save whatever hope still remained.

Soon one of his servants was quickly carrying a sealed message to his three envoys stationed above the city's main gate.

"Our Lord God, the God above all gods, the only eternal One, the only One who exalts kings and dethrones monarchs, gave us a new message last night," Eliakim shouted down toward the Rabshakeh after reading the message. "That message is that He will shortly send a rumor and a blast upon your army, forcing your king to return home."

"You talk words of folly!" the Rabshakeh shouted back in great disgust though he did wonder remarkably about the rumor part. "Our mighty Assyrian army is going to utterly destroy your nation's god in the name of Ashur!"

Then, mimicking the idiocy of the words he had just heard, he shouted to those along the walls.

"Surely, you are not listening to that nonsense!

"Going to send a blast upon us! I warn you! If you do not peacefully come out this day, it is going to be irredeemably agonizing for everyone of you who remain locked up in this waterless birdcage!"

Pausing, desiring to continue with the menacing threats, but desiring even more so to move within the tightly sealed gates once again, he choose to yell loudly for all to hear:

"Do not you realize that all my king, King Sennacherib, the king of kings, the king of the universe, wants is an agreement with you and him. You agree to give us our tribute, and come out to us, and we will agree to let you live and eat of your own vines once again. You come out to us, and you will be able to drink once again from your own cisterns.

"My great king wants you to enjoy even more than I have told you. He desires that you all come someday to dwell at peace in our lands throughout the world.

"Ours is a land of wheat and wine like yours.

"Ours is a land of bread and vineyards.

"It is a land of olive oil and honey.

"I sincerely reason with you. Do not be foolish. Do not

take heed to your stubborn and disobedient master nor to these three cowardly spokesmen of his!"

"Mother, how can you say that?" Manasseh rebutted after he and she had entered into Hannah's room, and Hephzibah had told him and Hannah that their father had been informed by their prophet Isaiah that their Lord God would keep the Rabshakeh and his war-mongering forces out of the city. "The Assyrians are soon going to rule even more of the world. That is an accepted fact. And since that is so, we need to accept it as a reality, surrender and show them that we are willingly agreeable with that fact. If we showed the Assyrians a spirit of oneness with that goal of theirs of the taking over of the entire world including Egypt and those other territories which are still not under their domination,then we would not suffer so greatly from having their destroying army in our land and we would also be in an ideal location to gain from any agreement we make with them."

"Son, our prophet—"

"Your prophet, Mother! He is not my prophet! Isaiah has always rejected all of my tutors teachings and all of their wisdom! That old man has rejected all true knowledge! He has been our nation's worst plague!"

"Manasseh!"

"Mother, who listens to him anymore?"

"Your father does."

"That is the problem!"

"That is—"

"None of us would be in this terrifying position now if

father had not listened to that old man!"

"Son!"

"Mother, if Isaiah is still alive when I ascend to the throne, I will personally see to it that he is—"

"How can you talk like that? You are only ten!"

"A very old ten!"

"I told your father that he needed to spend more time with you soon. But I fear we are already too late."

In his bedchamber Hezekiah agreed that Sennacherib had planned on taking the inhabitants of his city and was indeed going to move them. But not peacefully, and not to the Assyrians' own capital. He hoped therefore that his citizens realized that deportation of all the peoples of one city of a conquered nation to a city of another defeated country had been the claimed 'successful strategy' of the Assyrians ever since King Tiglath-pileser started doing it back in his reign.

It had been Tiglath-pileser III who was the first one to break their age-old, held-on tradition of enslaving or exterminating all the rebellious peoples found within their empire's stretch. He was the first king to execute only a few of the rebellious leaders and then to send away the bulk of the population into other regions of his vast realm. All of Judah's worries with these Assyrians seemed to have begun back in the days of the military prowess of that one monarch, King Tiglath-pileser III.

Hezekiah hoped that his folk understood that such deportations were one of the vital reasons why their rulers were able to vastly increase the expanse of their territory: by mixing up the citizens of all the different conquered lands, they diminished the cohesive resistance that any potential revolting ruler might have otherwise been able to amass.

He cocked his ear again and heard the Rabshakeh ask, "Have any of the gods of the surrounding nations delivered their peoples out of my king's hands? Of course they have not!" the shouter offered and followed his own answer with more questions. "Where are the gods of Hamath? Where are the gods of Arpad? Where are the gods of Sepharvaim?"

*

\> \> \> * < < <

*

Out on the wall, in his place of watching above the main gate, Eliakim leaned over to Shebna and Joah, and told them that he just experienced a fierce craving to fling a flaming spear through that raving mouth.

Joah nodded back.

As did Shebna.

*

\> \> \> * < < <

*

"Did any of those nations' gods save them?
"Of course they did not!
"And what about Samaria?
"Did your Lord God deliver Samaria out of our hands?
"No, no, no!
"I am warning you!
"Listen to me!

"If you do not surrender to us real soon your Lord God will not be able to deliver you from our grip either. We are not going to be forced to wait you out! Last night I went down to Lachish and found that it had fallen to our great king. Did your king tell you that? I doubt if even he knows about it. I went to our new encampment at Libnah and saw that that city was about to be taken.

"I also dined with my great king. King Sennacherib told me to tell you as strongly as I could that if you do not surrender today that he would bring our entire army up here to overthrow your city and your rebellious king.

"Listen to me!

"If you do not surrender to us today! If you do not respond to us today! Our entire army will break down your gates! Our army will rip open your granaries!—take all your treasures!—burn down your houses!—rape your women!—rip all your women with child wide open!—and skin you all alive!"

*

\> \> \> * \< \< \<

*

Shortly after noon, thousands upon thousands of Assyrian soldiers on horses and on foot began being seen and heard marching up the main road toward the city!

Near-panic set in within the confined city.

*

\> \> \> * \< \< \<

*

"Sir, a multitude of divisions is ascending toward us in

329

waves like lice!" Eliakim reported as swiftly as he and his friends were escorted into Hezekiah's presence. "Their Rabshakeh must have been telling the truth. The Assyrian's main army must have defeated our remaining fortress cities and now are coming to direct their final assault on our city!"

"Have any of the empire's large battle engines or siege towers been sighted?"

"No, but they are marching enough soldiers up here to fill the great Salt Sea."

"Let us pray that Sennacherib has not conquered all our cities and that he will continue to need those battering rams and his war engines and his attack towers down in the plains. Let us also not forget the word we heard last night from the Lord. You know, and I know, that our help at this moment can only come from our Lord God Himself. Men, we would do well to accept that now, more than ever, we need that awesome sustaining faith which so often protected the greatest of all our rulers. It was in times like this—times when there was no hope anywhere in sight—that our young shepherd David and then our King David excelled in simply looking to the Lord for his desperately needed salvation."

"We do need to remember that, Sir," Eliakim agreed, wanting to also deeply believe. After a thoughtful moment, he added, "Our Lord God is our only hope of deliverance. You can be assured that we will return out to the wall and to our people and will continue to place that hopeful thought before them. Thank you for reminding us again."

"And, Sir," Shebna said, stopping midway to the door, "we will also remind them to wait for the rumor and the blast from our Lord God. Whatever He meant by that."

"Whatever He meant...He said it would be coming," Hezekiah cut in, feeling better all the time. "That promise, my friend, is what is important to us."

"That is for certain."

"Excuse me, Sir! This sealed scroll just came hurling over the wall secured around a weaver's beam of a spear!" a shaking servant cried after he had been allowed to enter into the room.

Aspiring to instill ultimate hopelessness so overwhelming that continual resistance would be considered massive suicide, the king of Assyria had so composed the clay-sealed message. Treacherous as always, Hezekiah thought, as he rerolled the scroll shut. The vile monarch of the Assyrians was too ruthless, he was too vicious, too despicable, too smart, to abandon all his monstrous terrorizing up to his Rabshakeh.

*

> > *TWENTY SEVEN* < <

*

"Look out the window for yourself!

"You can still see the panic that the empire's sealed message has had upon our citizens down in the courtyard!"

Manasseh was crying to his mother and sisters, his younger two having also entered Hannah's room.

Tom Steinbach

"No, girls, I do not feel that you should do what your brother has said," Hephzibah commanded sternly, though she was not certain that it would help any.

"At least you should come, Mother."

"No, Son, I do not need to see it."

"Why not? How long are we going to keep our eyes and ears shut and our heads and minds in the ground, and not accept how terrible this mess is that we have let ourselves to get in?"

"Son, your father is in control. You do not need to go around here making your younger sisters more frightened than they already are."

"Mother, are we going to be able to keep that loud shouter and those wicked men out of our city?" Hannah cried with tears of fear in her eyes.

"Let us pray and hope so."

"But I hear that they already have us surrounded and that more and more of the enemy keep coming up our roads."

Hephzibah looked over at Manasseh, for he was the only one who could have told her those facts.

"She needs to know what—"

"Manasseh, she does not need to know anymore than I believe it is necessary for her to know," she replied with her eyebrows drawn in, and with her stern, steady eyes staring deep into his.

"You will not let them take—"

"Hannah, I have already talked to you about that."

"But now—"

"Hannah, your younger sisters are here...you are not to ask me anything else about what we talked about before."

"I understand, Mother. I am sorry."

"How can you quit so soon?" Manasseh asked in unbelief. "Where did you learn that? I think we should know what is going on around here? We are completely surrounded! And

332

soon they will be knocking our gates in, or coming over the walls and storming into our city, and they will be killing—"

"Manasseh! I told you that I do not want you to speak anymore of that kind of talk here with your sisters."

"Then get them out of here! We need to talk!"

"Son, you are not the one who gives the orders here!"

"But we need to know what there is that we can do!" he replied in anger, in fear, and in a terrified rage.

"Son, I do not want you yelling back and there is nothing that you or Hannah or I or your younger sisters can do about anything happening out there. We have to wait and see what your father and the elders decide to do."

"That scares me, Mother!" Manasseh said trembling, shaking his head and allowing the flowing tears to sail freely off his cheeks. "That really scares me!"

"Allowing Father to put together the decision does not terrify me, Mother. But knowing that thousands and thousands more of their soldiers are coming up here to break down our gates and enter into our city has me sobbing inside. It has me trembling inside!" Hannah said, as she burst toward Hephzibah and nearly knocked her over as she leaped into her arms.

Her two younger sisters, petrified and running and with tears streaming down their faces, did knock the two of them over as they quickly followed in her steps.

*

> > > * < < <

*

"Lord God of Heaven, I agree that it is true that the kings of the empire have destroyed all those other nations and their lands, and that they have cast all their man-made gods and goddesses into the fire," Hezekiah prayed again in Solomon's Temple only moments after he had been delivered the ominous scroll.

The scroll was spread wide open on the floor before him so the evil threats would be clearly visible to the Lord. "But, my Lord, those statues were no gods, only the carved images of men's hands, merely graven stone and wooden figurines, that is all. Remind Your people that that is all the Assyrians have thrown into those fires in the various nations. Remind them by a living touch of Your hand that You are so much different from all these other conquered gods and goddesses.

"You alone are our God.

"You alone are the true God of Earth and Heaven. You alone dwell enthroned between the cherubim behind these multi-lined veils. You alone control the destiny of kings and nations. I realize that the kings of the earth assemble themselves against one another believing that the question of who will be the supreme ruler of the world is open to contest. I also understand, my Father, that they believe that some ruler can emerge dragged up strictly by his own might and determination...and by some military genius provided by his gods: by his no-gods.

"O Lord God, they do not realize that the question of ultimate rulership is not so blatantly open to contest. You alone, my God, are the One who determines the destined fate of world leaderships. Lord God our Creator and the Holy One of Israel, the vile ruler of Assyria believes that it is up to him and his god Ashur to say who is going to govern this land and nation which has been given to us by You Yourself. Oh Lord, my God, open Your eyes and see the words of Sennacherib written upon this scroll before me here which he is sending to reproach not only this Your chosen dwelling site in all the world, but also to reproach You and Your beloved name. My Lord God, I have also brought in here with me the various copies of the vile boastful words of Sennacherib which I have purchased from the Bedouin trader, Jamil. Hear these words of praise to his many gods and goddesses...and of the praise he is bestowing upon himself for his great wisdom."

With that, he opened the first of those purchased scrolls, and read with emphasis:

"'Sennacherib, the great king, the mighty king, king of Assyria, king without a rival, prayerful ruler, worshipper of the great gods; guardian of the right, lover of justice, lender of support, the ruler who comes to the aid of the needy, who turns his thoughts to pious deeds; perfect hero, mighty man, first among all princes, the flame that consumes the insubmissive, who strikes the wicked with the thunderbolt; the god Ashur, the great mountain, has entrusted to me an unrivaled kingship, and above all, those who dwell in palaces have made powerful my weapons.

"'At the beginning of my reign when I solemnly took my seat on the throne and I ruled the inhabitants of my empire with mercy and grace, Merodach-baladan, king of Babylonia, whose heart is wicked, an instigator of revolts, whose belly and mind are of rebellion, a doer of evil, whose guilt is heavy...this one, brought over to his side Shutur-Nahundu, the Elamite, and gave him gold and silver and precious stones, and so secured him as an ally.

"'To me, Sennacherib, whose heart is exalted, they reported to me these evil deeds. I raged like a lion, and gave the command to march into Babylonia against him. I set out from Ashur ahead of my army like a mighty bull; I did not wait for my army, I did not hold back. In the anger of my heart, I made an assault upon Kutha; the troops about its walls I slaughtered like lambs and took the city. The horse and bowmen I brought forth and counted as spoil. I raged like a lion. I stormed like a tempest...with my merciless warriors I set my face against Merodach-baladan, who was in Kish. And

Tom Steinbach

*that worker of iniquity saw my advance from afar; terror fell
upon him, and he immediately forsook all of his troops, and
fled to the land of Guzummanu.'*

"Lord, I do not want to flee, I will not flee; nevertheless, I
have not seen one act performed by You against this wicked
boaster of ruthlessness. Not one act! My Lord God, my
confidence is in You alone; but if You do not act soon...this
bragger's confidence will far, far outshine mine. Lord, I have
attempted to make Your temple and this Your city places
which would magnify You; however, listen to this vile
monarch extol his grand building projects back in his newly
chosen capital of Nineveh. Ninevah, the renown ancient home
of all their no-gods and no-goddesses. Listen, here is a writing
of what he believes that city is:

*"'Nineveh, the noble metropolis. The city beloved of
Ishtar— wherein are all the meeting places of gods and
goddesses; the true everlasting structure, the eternal
foundation; whose plan had been designed from of old along
with the writing of the constellations; the artistic place, the
abode of divine rule, into which have been brought every kind
of artistic workmanship, every secret and every pleasant plan
of god; where from of old the kings who went before, my
fathers, had exercised the lordship over Assyria before me: not
one among them had devoted his thoughtful attention to, nor
had his heart considered, the palace therein, the place of the
royal abode, whose habitat had become too small; nor had he
turned his ear, nor brought his liver to lay out the streets of
the city, to widen the squares, to dig a canal, to set out
plantations.*

*"'But I, Sennacherib, the king of Assyria, gave my thought
and brought my mind to achieve this labor according to the
will of the gods. The former palace, which was three hundred
and sixty cubits on the sides and one hundred and twenty
cubits on its front, which the rulers who went before, my*

*fathers, had built, whose structure they had not, however,
made artistic: that pitifully small palace I tore down in its
totality.*

*" 'In a propitious month...on a favorable day...in that
river's hidden bed, for a space of seven hundred and twenty
cubits on both sides, and four hundred and eight cubits on the
front, I bulwarked over great mountain boulders and made a
field rise up from out the water, and made it like unto the dry
land. Lest in the passing of days its platform should give way
before the floods of high water, I raised up great slabs of
limestone around its walls, and solidly strengthened its
heaping of earth; over those great slabs I filled in the terrace
to a height of one hundred and seventy tipku. On it I had them
build a palace of ivory, maple, boxwood, spruce, cedar,
cypress, mulberry and pistachio, the Palace without a Rival
for my royal abode. Beams of cedar, the product of Mount
Amanus, which they dragged with difficulty out of those
distant mountains, I had stretched across their ceilings. The
great door-leaves of cypress, whose odor is pleasant as they
are opened and closed, I bound with a band of shining copper
and set them up on their doors. A portico which they call in
the Amorite tongue a bit-hilani, that patterned after a Hittite
palace, I constructed inside those pleasant doors, for my
lordly pleasure.*

*" 'Eight lions, open at the knee, advancing, constructed out of
eleven thousand and four hundred talents of shining bronze, of
the workmanship of the god Ninagal and full of splendor,
together with two colossal pillars whose copper work came to
nearly six thousand talents, and two great cedar pillars, which
I placed fast upon the colossus, I set up as posts to support
their doors. Four mountain sheep, as protecting deities, of
great blocks of mountain stone, I fashioned cunningly, and
setting them toward the four winds, and I adorned their
entrances. Great slabs of limestone, I had the enemy tribes,*

whom my hands had conquered, drag through the gates, and I had them set up around their walls, I made them objects of mighty astonishment.

" 'A massive park, like unto Mount Amanus, wherein were set out all kinds of herbs and fruit trees, such as grow on the mountains, and in Chaldea, I planted along the palace's side. That they might plant orchards, I subdivided some land in the plain above the city into plots for the citizens of Nineveh, and gave it to them.

" 'To increase the vegetation from the border of the village of Kisiri to the plain nearing Nineveh, through mountain and lowland, with iron pickaxes, I cut and directed a canal...the waters of the Khosr, which from of old sought too low a place, I made the waters to flow through those orchards in irrigation ditches. After I had brought to an end the work on my royal palace, and had widened the squares and made bright the avenues and streets and caused them to shine like the day...I invited Ashur, the great lord, the gods and goddesses who dwell in Assyria into its midst. I offered oblations and sacrifices in great numbers and presented my gifts.' "

Hezekiah raised up on his knees as he continued, "My Lord God, this ruler loves to praise himself, and to praise all that his god Ashur has done for him and his kingdom. I am certain that when he returned from our land that last visit, that he lauded himself and his god Ashur, and that he blasphemed You and this Your city. I am absolutely certain of it. My Lord God of Heaven, my absolute trust is in You. Still...what can we do if they build a mound to come up over our walls? What if they do as I saw the rushing clouds do the other morning?— moving without hindrance up over the trees on our western horizon and within a very short time completely inundating our sky. They are already moving up around us as countless as the sands of the seas;if they begin building a mound—which obviously is what they will do, if You do not hinder them—

how then could we defend ourselves from them: and therefore from an endless invasion of the world's most ruthless warriors?"

At that point, he wiped his brow with his sleeve, and opened a different scroll. To emphasize his fear of an earthen mound being erected next to the capital's lowest wall, their northern wall, he read another account that Sennacherib had his scribes write upon a cylinder within his capital:

" 'The Tebiltu River, a raging destructive stream, which at its high water had destroyed the mausoleums inside the capital and had exposed to the sun the tiers of piled-up coffins and from the days of old had come up close to the palace and with its floods at high water had worked devastation with its foundation and destroyed its platform: that small palace I tore down in its totality. I changed the course of the Tebiltu, I repaired the damage, and directed its outflow through its covered bed. Below reeds, above mighty blocks of mountain stone, I covered with pitch, and raised up a field out of the waters and I turned it into dry land. That in days to come its platform might not be weakened by future floods at high water, I had its walls surrounded with mighty slabs of limestone and so I strengthened its structure.'

"Lord, could he not do the same thing here? Could he not move earth and boulders as adeptly here? We could never stop them from building a mound over on our northern wall. We could not, Lord.

"We desperately need You to act for us with Your help. We need to see Your strong arm in action. We have seen You act mightily. You made the shadow of the sun stop and move backward ten degrees! And You caused all that extra terrifying phenomena throughout the earth! And You healed me miraculously of that deadly boil.

"O Lord, You are not made by man, nor by our hands, nor by our puny imaginations.

"You are the living God!

"You alone are the Lord, the Creator of Heaven and Earth and everything therein! Therefore, Lord, I plead to You to deliver us out of Sennacherib's hands that all the kingdoms of the earth will know that You are the true Lord God of the heavens and of the earth:and You only...and not his god Ashur."

*

\>\>\> * \<\<\<

*

When he left the floor of the temple, the setting sun had only begun casting its evening glow upon the olive trees on the eastern hillsides across the valley from the temple's shadow-covered front entrance.

As he walked slowly back to the palace, he could hear a dull, continuous, thudding behind him—sounding like it was coming from just beyond the northern wall.

It sounded like....

*

> > *TWENTY EIGHT* < <

*

"Yes, they are, sir."

"How long have they been at it?"

"For two, three hours now. But with a new wagonload every few minutes I have to believe the Rabshakeh: By sunrise tomorrow, King Sennacherib and all his sea full of forces will be storming over the wall into our city."

"And our people, Eliakim?"

"They have lost all hope, Sir."

"All hope?"

"All hope, Sir."

"That is because they have not spent the last six hours before our Lord God. I cannot tell you what He is going to do ...I cannot give you any of the details, but I can assure you that our Lord is going to finally come through for us in a mighty way, Eliakim.

Tom Steinbach

"I can feel it!"

"Mother! Manasseh says that the Assyrian army is building a mound of rocks and stones and mud and clay and sticks on the other side of our north wall so that they can climb up over it and get into our city!" Hannah shouted the panicking thought as she and Manasseh raced each other into Hephzibah's room, running and nearly tripping each other as they sought to see who could get in first.

"That is true, Mother! I have heard many say that the soldiers are bringing large stones and much ground-fill in wagonloads after wagonloads!"

"That is enough, Manasseh!"

She stared deep into his eyes.

"I have charged you that I do not want you passing these things on to your sisters until you first tell me about them."

"But then you will not tell them about them, and it will be us that the Assyrians will take!"

"It is not that I want to conceal any of these things from you and your sisters, Manasseh. It is just that the Lord is not going to allow the Assyrians to enter into our city."

"That is not true, Mother!"

"It may not appear so to you, Son, but that is what He says to us through Isaiah."

"Through Isaiah! That old man is going to cause the Assyrians to destroy our city!"

"Isaiah is—"

"—our city's worse plague!"

"Manasseh!"

"Just because he goes and hides in some place in his house and then later comes out and tells our elders or even Father: 'the Lord has said this and that, and that He is going to do this and that,' Mother, do you not see and understand that that old man is going to get us all killed!"

"Why did you not come in here alone and talk to me about these fears of yours, Son?"

Manasseh did not answer.

"Hannah comes and talks to me, why do you have to always go to her and to your younger sisters?"

Again he said nothing. She said a silent prayer.

"Hannah, come here," Hephzibah said softly to her oldest, "you do not need to cry like that."

"She does need to cry like that!" Manasseh broke forth.

Hephzibah looked at him.

"She needs to cry and run and hide, Mother! Father is going to soon allow that man and his army to come up over our walls and get every one of us children!"

"Son."

"That man is going to come over our wall sooner than any of us realize, and we will be carried away like your other children were the last time!"

*

\> \> \> * \< \< \<

*

"Are we to begin boiling the pitch-oil, and begin readying our archers and our stone-throwers?"

"Once we begin preparing for that, Eliakim, then what? We would have an endless barrage of arrows and spears flying in, and if they have an ocean of men coming up here as you say, there is no way we could ever entirely stop them from

343

finally getting the mound built and scaling in over our walls. My friend, in ourselves we have no hope of keeping them from coming in here. We are going to refrain, therefore, from beginning to do any battle with them. Instead, we are going to do nothing more, but patiently wait for the salvation our Lord God has promised."

Eliakim nodded in agreement.

Hezekiah winked confidently.

Eliakim returned the wink.

"The promise will come."

"Yes, sir, it will come."

Looking out of the flaps of his tent in his encampment down in the plains, King Sennacherib could sense the hopeful encouragement the residents of Libnah felt by the vast depletion of his standing army. He hated the vile rumor that much more for he knew that with his whole army he could have made short work of this last fortress city before he moved his hungering men up toward the peasant ones' capital.

*

> > *TWENTY NINE* < <

*

"King Hezekiah!"
It was the Rabshakeh.
"Look around you! This is your last chance. Look here behind me on these slopes, and over on the hills covered with those olive trees.

"Look across the valleys to the south and west of you, look to the north and listen to our men laying a foundation for a mound against that most accessible wall.

"I warned you that you would be caged in like a bird! I warned you we would soon find a way to get into your rebellious city.

"By noon tomorrow the greatest monarch of the Assyrian Empire, Sennacherib, the almighty king, king of the universe, king without rival, king of kings...he will be leading the world's largest army along with all our solid-iron war engines and all our siege towers and all our massive battering rams up this worn road! By this time tomorrow, our forces will be inside your capital brutally teaching your men and women that they should not have resisted our entrance into your city!

"By this time tomorrow!—are you hearing me?—our army will be galloping into your city! And ripping every one of your women with child wide-open! By this time tomorrow!—hear me!—our forces will gushing into your city and running their spears and swords through thousands upon thousands of your men, women and children! By this time tomorrow!—I am warning you!—our forces will be storming the palace and taking all its women and children, and the flayed skins of all of your leaders will be left hanging on the gates and walls of your city!"

*

> > > * < < <

*

"Mother, that man scares me!"

O, I wish I could tell you that he scares me also, my precious lovely little one. Please, Lord, we need Your mighty hand to help us through this overwhelming terror.

"What did I tell you, Mother! We have to surrender now before it is to late!"

"Trust your father, Manasseh."

"Trust my father! He listens only to Isaiah! If he waits until tomorrow to surrender it will be too late, they will not even take the time to listen to us!"

"Son, did you know that the Lord spoke directly to your father today in the temple?"

"Manasseh! It is your father you are talking about!"

"Mother, in times like this, I often wish that he would die so that I—"

"Manasseh! We will have no more talking like that!"

"But—"

"Our Lord God has proved that He is real with those marvelous tasks He did back at the time of your father's healing. Those also show that He wants to be able to show His awesome delivering power to those of us who will truly worship Him and who will look to Him for their protection."

"Those happened before I was born, and my tutors say that they can all be explained naturally."

"Well, then you had better leave us now and go listen to them. For you have broken every commandment of our Lord God and of King Solomon's proverbs concerning your respecting, and your listening to, your father and me. Come along, Hannah. You and I are going to your sisters' room and encourage them."

"You cannot leave me, Mother!"

"Son, it is you who has left us long ago."

"But I am terrified!"

"Manasseh, your father and I are no aid to you if you will not listen to us."

"I do not want father's help! But why will you not talk to us the way I want you to talk."

"You do not want help, Son. All you really want to do is scare us into surrendering and we have already decided and declared that we will not surrender this time."

"Father has declared that?"

"And we back him totally. Now we do not want to hear any more of your bad-mouthing him...or any of our other leaders. We want to continue to build up our trust in the only One who can come to our aid now."

"If you and father would only listen to my tutors...they

Tom Steinbach

could truly help all of us."

"Son, I guess *that* is where we will have to agree to disagree. Come along, Hannah."

*

\> \> \> * < < <

*

Later that evening, the messenger from Isaiah was brought into Hezekiah's chambers.

"My master sent me here to tell you that the Lord spoke to him again tonight."

"Tonight!"

"Tonight. Isaiah said the Lord God gave him this message, 'King Hezekiah, that which you prayed to Me against the ruler of Assyria this afternoon; I have heard.'"

Reigning king or not, he was touched to his very depths: a warm flush swept across and emptied his face of its blood; a large lump, an uncomfortably large lump immediately settled in his throat; and tears, a stream of endless hot tears, flowed uncontrollably down his cheeks onto his robe. "Thank you, Lord, thank You. What other nation has such love flowing from their gods and goddesses—from their no-gods and no-goddesses—I am thankful that I have had the privilege and opportunity to know You, the one true and living God."

*

> > > *THIRTY* < < <

*

Hours later in the dim light of the night sky, messengers were again silently moving throughout the city and along the top of the walls.

"A meeting is planned tonight for all our citizens down beyond the Millo citadel," was the discreet message they were spreading to everyone.

"Arrange the large throwing stone as dummies," were the additional quietly given orders to the sentries on assignment upon the walls and in the towers.

No one remained in any post.

Once all had gathered together in that original city of David, they were ordered to spread out before the house of Gibborim. The aging sepulchre of King David's mighty men had been chosen for the awesome significancy that the city had always given it in the name of those for whom he had it built. There they were led in a solemn time of heartfelt singing.

The chosen songs for the occasion were the well-known hymns of degrees of King David, hymns of deeply felt praise. Interspersing the singing, many of David's stories of his incredible deliverances were also told.

The emphasis of the entire evening's gathering was that David's many salvations, whether as a shepherd boy or as their ruling monarch, had come forth directly from the almighty hands of their Lord.

During the inspirational praise time, Hezekiah moved into their midst with the messenger from Isaiah.

He looked upward and noticed there were not any clouds in the sky.

He glanced involuntarily over toward the western horizon and was further pleased to notice total clearness in that direction also.

The two of them waited til he felt that the spontaneous praise and its resulting tentacles of faith had spread outward far enough through the old city with ever-widening, ever-increasing, circles.

Then he introduced the prophet's messenger asking him to share the Lord's latest word to the people...not the personal word which was to him...but the rest of the message which concerned the capital's present crisis.

Moving in front of David's old stately vine-covered sepulchre, their spokesman began by first repeating the dreadful boast of the Assyrian king, "'With the multitude of my chariots, I am come up to the height of the mountains. I, King Sennacherib, the king of kings, have dried up all the rivers of besieged places. I have laid waste your fenced cities into ruinous heaps. Those cities were dismayed and confounded before Me.'

"Mind you," the messenger continued loudly, with no concern if his voice could be heard by the Assyrian soldiers outside the city walls or not, "our Lord God ordered me to repeat all these sayings of the dreadful king so you would know that He also has personally heard them. Our Lord God asks that none of you challenge the evil boaster. Instead, God chooses to answer the villainous intimidator Himself with these words:

"I know of your rage against Me, King Sennacherib. It is because of your rage against Me that I will put a hook in your nose, and a bridle in your mouth, and I will turn you back by the way that you came!"

With his words, a new living hope began flowing through the old city as spontaneous praise, which had been ignited by the evening's inspirational singing and storytelling, began to crackle and erupt into a blaze.

Propelled by that evident enthusiasm, by the expressed oneness of purpose, by the pleased look on all—but especially on the face of his ruling monarch—the messenger continued on more loudly than before with his triumphant word of the Lord:

"The boasting king of Assyria shall not come into this city!"

With the proclaiming of that straight-forward promise the city-wide giving of thanks mushroomed into a braveness, a loudness, an intensity which none would have ever suspected to hear in any city surrounded by such terror.

"Those dreaded Assyrians shall not shoot an arrow...nor come before you with the shield!"

Jubilant, riotous, presumptuous laughter mixed freely with the even louder shouting.

"The Assyrians will not build a mound against the walls of this our city!"

Bold, undisciplined whooping and merrymaking engulfed

Tom Steinbach

the mountaintop capital!

"*By..the..way..that..the..Assyrian..king..came*—" he loudly screamed with all his might, "—*by...that...same...way...shall ...he...return...home! And!...he!...shall!...not!...enter!...into!... this!... city!*"

Completely unrestrained ear-ringing, boisterous, hand-clapping cheering and animate dancing filled the capital as the spontaneous praise and all became inextinguishable! The overpowering volume of the noise swept in waves over the walls, cascaded, and echoed down through the dry brook beds in the valleys below, and then careened up the encircling hills as a roaring, runaway fire: every mountain and valley surrounding Jerusalem launched their brazen, thunderous melodies heavenward.

"*I repeat! The!....Assyrian!....king!....shall!.....return!..... home!....and!....he!....shall!....not!.....enter!.....into!.....this!....... city!*"

With a grin nearly as large as the brilliant round glow he had seen in the clouds that other morning, certainly fully as bright, Hezekiah thought that the servant's shouts were so uninhibited the Assyrian soldiers who had to be awakening in their camps must have worried that King David was once again leading the holy ark of the covenant back into their famous city! Surely his shoutings and the overwhelming praise-giving by his unbridled citizens had to awaken the soldiers and filled them with some kind of fear.

Next, a sober thought dominated his being causing tears to wet his eyes and cheeks. He realized that another of David's lineage, *he himself,* was leading his own people back to their highly needed realization that the glorious Presence of the Lord God which dwelt between the cherubim which stood above the mercy seat in Solomon's Temple was still completely present.

It was an overpowering thought.

352

He could hardly breathe.

Nevertheless...on the heels of that wonderful, inspired moment came a terrifying doubting that harshly reminded him that the Lord indeed had not come to their assistance during the Assyrian's last visitation, and, that the brilliant yellow glow might still be the cloud's representation of Moloch's flaming midsection returning to devour him and his city. The surge of doubting began quenching his ever-growing confidence.

Think, mind, think!

It is different this time!

What is the difference?

This hope that has been expanding within me all evening cannot be a dream!

What is the difference?

Even my people and my elders realize it is different from the last time?

Our Lord God has come out to us!

That is the difference!

He is speaking directly to us this time

Isaiah has spoken this time! He has not stayed reclused in his closed house! Yesterday he stated that we would be defended by our Lord and tonight he has sent his messenger to proclaim it to all of my city!

Twice he has spoken of the Lord's coming protection! The Lord Himself even spoke directly to me while I was waiting in Solomon's Temple! And, since that first visitation, I myself have been given that most-glorious, miraculous personal healing and also an earth-shattering sign!

I have all those objective facts to hang my ever-growing faith upon. No, doubts, you do not have anywhere this time to dig your downward-dragging claws into me!

Begone with you.

You have no place to hang unto me.

Tom Steinbach

Begone.
BEGONE!

*

>>> * <<<

*

Hephzibah and Hannah arrived, and spotting Eliakim, Shebna and Joah, moved over to stand with them. Hephzibah smiled beautifully and confidently when Hezekiah looked over her way:causing whatever remnant of doubtings which might have still been hanging around to flee immediately from his being. Turning back toward his people he knew—*he knew!* what a feeling!—he knew that he was ready to offer to his caged-in people their inherited rightful gift to experience wholeheartedly in the thrilling, supernatural salvation brought to them solely by their invisible living Lord God.

Faith *had* come in its wondrous power!

Thank You, Lord.

Thank You for Hephzibah.

*

>>> * <<<

*

He stood up to speak.

Immediate silence fell across the city: as instantaneously, he thought, as its people's flaming faith is now expecting the terror of their awesome Lord to crush upon the ocean of men outside their capital's walls.

"My people!" he began, projecting his voice as far as he could make it travel. "On this clear, star-studded night I thank you for responding so favorably, and so generously, to our Lord God and to His promise to act on our beha—"

Never before had he been interrupted in an address. Never had he been interrupted by these his people, but with those words came from them an applause directed toward Heaven which was so overwhelming, that he simply stopped, looked up himself into the clear night sky, and joined in the clapping with all his might!

He gratefully knew that additional Assyrian soldiers rising in wonder at the unprecedented outpourings of joy within his besieged walls were also right in having some overt misgivings... not because the relatively few inside the walls were readying themselves for a major, all-out, fight-to-the-finish battle as soon as the light of day came...no, not that at all; but because his Lord God was finally receiving some very long-overdue, spontaneous response from His chosen people. And as their prophet had often said, their Lord God was a jealous, devouring fire.

"We read," he resumed when the applause began to die down, "in the second book of Moses that: 'at midnight the Lord smote all the firstborn in the land of Egypt.'

"You know the story.

"You have thrilled to the wonderful retelling of it many times within your homes. But tonight, you—we!—are going to personally experience the same! direct! Divine! intervention that was such an integral part of our spiritual heritage!

"Therefore I repeat: 'all the Egyptian firstborn were slain at midnight!' It is past midnight here in our besieged city but I can assure you!—I do assure you!—our salvation from the hands of the Lord Himself is going to be accomplished in this very night before the rising of the sun!"

Stamping, shouting, and clapping once again filled the primed, still silence of the night air!

And crying, *above all, came the crying*: the crying of joy, the crying of released tension, the crying of renewed hope, the crying of calmed fright.

Isaiah had begun the inspiration-building two weeks earlier after the two of them had announced that surrendering was not a possible choice this visit. Finishing his talk, he had looked up and prayed aloud, "O Lord, be gracious onto us; we have waited for You, be our salvation in the time of trouble."

Afterwhich, when he had spoken strongly for a time, he paused, looked wide-eyed above the hills off to the east, and, then loudly proclaimed these words against the Assyrian soldiers: "Woe to them that spoil and deal treacherously; they shall be spoiled and dealt with treacherously!"

Shutting his eyes...he then prayed again, "O Lord, be gracious unto us! We are waiting for You! Be our arm every morning! And our salvation also in the time of trouble."

Raising and spreading his arms out in front of him, he yelled: "At the noise of Your tumult the enemy fled! At the lifting up of Yourself the nations were scattered! Your spoil, O Lord, shall be gathered like the gathering of the grasshopper ...as the running to and fro of the locusts as they run!"

Looking down at his audience, he next shouted:

"The Lord our God is exalted for He dwells up on high! He has filled Zion with judgment and righteousness! Wisdom and knowledge shall be its stability and its strength of salvation! The fear of the Lord is its treasure! Its valiant ones shall cry outside its walls! The envoys of peace shall weep bitterly for there shall be no peace! Instead I have observed the trade routes lying waste and the wayfaring man gone. I have seen the enemy devouring the land and breaking his covenant and despising the cities and regarding no man!

"Now the earth is mourning and languishing, Lebanon is ashamed and hewn down. Sharon is like a wilderness, and Bashan and Carmel are shaking off their fruit. But do not fret! For I also see the Lord saying:

"'I will now rise!

"'I will now be exalted!

"'I will now lift myself up!'

"To the enemy He has said, 'You are conceiving chaff. You are bringing forth stubble. Your own breath shall devour you as fire. You shall be as the burnings of lime, as thorns cut up shall you be burned in the fire.'"

Turning toward the residential and toward the business section of the city, he added:

"When the sinners and the hypocrites of this city see the burnings, they shall be afraid and full of fear. They shall cry, 'Who among us shall dwell with the devouring fire? Who among us shall dwell with everlasting burnings?' I will tell you, even as I answer them:

"He that walks and speaks righteously. He that despises the gain of oppressions. He that shakes his hands from taking bribes. He that stops his ears from hearing of plotting blood. He that shuts his eyes from seeing evil. That man will dwell on high! His place of defense shall be the in the rocks! His bread shall be given him. And his water shall be sure!"

Isaiah certainly inspired the righteous among us back then, he laid the groundwork for this wonderful evening back then, Hezekiah thought, as he waited for another freeing release of tears to do their work among his people.

When he could, he began again:

"My people, my wondrously responding people, when our Lord God judges in His righteous wrath with judgment and justice, He misses not a single person! Moses told us that all the firstborn in Egypt were slain from the firstborn of the Pharoah who sat on his throne unto the firstborn of the lowly captives that sat down in the damp dungeon.

"And to make certain that we completely comprehended the great magnitude of our Lord God's wrath upon His enemy back then when He counted the Egyptians as our forefathers' ransom, Moses added this last final note: 'There was not a house in Egypt wherein there was not one dead.'

"'Surely as I have thought,' the Lord God told Isaiah, back in the year that my father died, 'so shall it come to pass! And as I have purposed, so shall it stand! I will break the Assyrian in My land and upon My mountains will I tread him under foot! Then shall his yoke depart from off My people and his burden shall depart off their shoulders!

"'My purpose, to protect My chosen people from the Assyrians, is settled!

"'By My protection of My people shall I show that My hand controls all the destinies of the nations of the full earth! I have purposed it! Who shall disannul it? My almighty hand is stretched out! Who shall turn it back?'"

At that hearing of the Lord's former words of deliverance, His people's fitting celebration of His approaching promised salvation broke forth again.

"My people!" Hezekiah shouted in conclusion as soon as he could be heard again, "I do not know when tonight!

"I do not know at what watch!

"I cannot tell you how He will do it!

"But I promise you that this evening our Lord God, the Creator and Ruler of the heavens and the earth, will strike terribly in our enemy's camp with a mighty, devastating, destructive blast!"

*

> > > * < < <

*

"Look!" Eliakim cried in awe to Shebna and Joah. "The Lord is accepting our love response to His promise of total protection and deliverance!"

"You are right!" Shebna agreed.

"He has sent a bright, yellow glow! A glorious brilliant yellow glow surrounding our city in the middle of this night!"

"It is His smile!"

"I like that!" Hannah shouted up to her mother. "This glow is the Lord's smile!"

"Me, too, Hannah."

"It really is a sign of His approval, right?"

"Hannah, I am certain of it. Your father would say, 'Yes, our Lord God has given to all of us a sign that He will indeed provide our miraculous deliverance tonight!'"

"Look at Solomon's Temple!" another in their immediate company exclaimed.

"Look at it, Mother!" Hannah shouted, pointing at it. "It has become the largest, the most magnificent, the most pretty golden gem I have ever seen!"

"I am looking!"

"It is awesome!" Joah said.

"I have never, ever, seen anything like it, Mother," Hannah said, trying to embellish her first statement. "The temple looks like a most precious polished jewel which has been beautifully seated in the walls of our glorious city."

"And with the brightest, yellowish-red rings surrounding it in lustrous brilliance!" Hephzibah added.

"Let us go over by Father."

"Yes, Hannah, let us do that."

"Possibly our God is moving mysteriously right now through the Assyrians' camps with His almighty blast," another person in their company said as a passing whim before they left the little circle of friends. It was a witless, passing whim, however, only until each one in the company looked simultaneously at each other in wonder. Even Hephzibah stopped and looked at Eliakim.

Tom Steinbach

*

> > > *THIRTY ONE* < < <

*

The shouting, clapping, jumping, singing, dancing, crying, and laughing again reached its highest zenith in King David's old city at the sight of the glorious halo which circumscribed the walls of the city.

The celebrating carried on throughout the rest of remainder of the night.

It lasted long past the fading away of the brilliant ring, and well beyond the coming of the first streams of the crimson and cadmium yellow dawning which lined the horizon, and which filtered faintly across the awakening sky.

When the dawning had fully come, there were no sounds from the other side of the wall.

None.

No dull, thudding sound.

No clear Hebrew filled with villainous threats.
No soldiers getting prepared sounds.
No sound whatever.

*

> > > * < < <

*

Those who were ordered to return to their posts upon the walls reported to their overseers that doubtlessly it was deathly silent beyond in the Assyrian camp.

Hezekiah, back in the midst of his people, was pleased that no rumors were being expressed that that silence might be an Assyrian trick to get them to open their gates. He had felt that none would dare—how could any man experience what they had just experienced, and then voice such a consideration?— but he was happy to see that none actually did. He was even more pleased to sense his citizens' bursting faith aching to spring forth out of the city at a moment's notice to see what the all-sweeping, inaudible blast from their God had actually accomplished. Completely justified in his peoples' eyes, he began striding purposely toward the gate as they followed densely behind as a single unit.

*

> > > * < < <

*

When the sun's orange sphere was fully visible, he ordered his men to commence with the unbarring of the secured main gates. The first sounds of the creaking of the 'locked' massive doors opening sent a thrill through the entire throng.

Standing on a wagon's seat in the view of everyone, but safely protected from the expected wild flow of humanity, Hezekiah cried: "Moses also wrote that our forefathers on the first passover night spoiled the Egyptians of their jewels of silver and gold! And, all of their raiment! As your leader on this another memorial morning, I also give to you full permission—"

Carried forward by their lunging faith and joyful expectation, his spirited inhabitants charged forward as a solid liberated wall bursting out in every direction!

                                                 *

\>\>\> * \<\<\<

                                                 *

A tall Assyrian groped through the early hours of the morning, at least he felt they were those hours...in his utter blindness he was not certain. Movement along the dusty road had been slow. It had been slower, but a few hours earlier he had heard a tumultuous shouting behind him which sounded like the peasant ruler's capital gleefully splitting at her seams. Certain that the whole city was spitefully determined to find and skin him alive—is not that what those 'eye for an eye and a tooth for a tooth' people did to those who were renown for flaying their victims alive?—he had quickened his pace. Highly quickened his pace!

The bushes and tree limbs into which he ran, the ravines along the sides of the roads into which he stumbled and fell, the thirst in his throat which had become all-consuming as that morning's sun moved upward toward its zenith: none of those things struck terror in his heart as deeply and as fearfully as the thought of the hot-in-pursuit Israelites: pursuing, that is, if indeed they even knew that he was still alive and had escaped.

Not knowing for sure what they knew, but firmly believing that many were indeed fast on his trail, he ran, and stumbled, and fell until finally one of the empire's post sentries heard his awkward, groping movements and came to his side.

He explained to the horrified soldier of the utter destruction of the empire's entire advanced forces by a mysterious, white-hot, brilliant blast of burning heat. He then demanded that the sentry speed him to King Sennacherib's headquarters near Libnah.

$$*$$
$$>>> * <<<$$
$$*$$

Manasseh and his three sisters had been forbidden to leave the capital on that victorious morning. They were allowed, however, to view the surging flow of human freedom as long as they stayed with their mother up on the wall.

In the course of observing the results of the vast destruction which had come upon the Assyrians' army and trusting that it would make the favorable impression on her son for which she had been in much praying and waiting, Hephzibah said to her children,"Now you have all seen the wisdom in waiting on the Lord for your salvation—instead of suffering so great a loss as we did the last time the Assyrians came, we are reaping a bountiful harvest simply by going out and spoiling their camp."

"Mother, I have always believed that you and Father were doing what was best for our nation," Hannah said. "Of course, not being your son, I have not had the opportunity to receive my instruction from the tutors in the court."

"Just because this appears to have worked out to our advantage in this visit," her brother said in defense of his training. "That does not necessarily mean that we should always behave against the empire so belligerently."

"Belligerently?" Hephzibah cut in, shocked by that incredulous accusation.

"Why did we have to act so—"

"We? It was those dreadful, terrifying Assyrians out there who were the belligerent ones!"

"They were not! The Assyrians were not to be dreaded and they were only coming over here to our land and up here to receive that which was rightfully theirs."

"How was it rightfully theirs when the Lord God gave all this land to us?" Hephzibah strongly argued, her hatred for his tutors having increased a thousandfold with the hearing of his words.

"It is rightfully the empire's because they came over here and with great military mastery claimed our land as being a portion of their empire. We should accept their claim and pay them their due. We could gain much if we would only accept our lesser place within their empire."

"Manasseh, are you not going to learn anything from this great experience?"

"Me? Are you not?"

"This nation is ours first because the Lord God gave it to us, and now He has proven that it is ours by completely destroying the empire's forces. Witnessing that overwhelming victory of the Lord without the help of any of our men...that should have made such an impression upon you. How could you see that, Son, and still accept seriously what those tutors have taught you?"

"The Assyrian Empire is too huge for this small defeat to have any real effect upon it."

Small defeat!

She was too angry to reply.

"I have been told of stories of an illness Father had before

I was born, Mother. A serious affliction which should have taken his life."

"He was that sick. If his life would have been taken, it would have ended King David's dynasty."

"So you believe he was spared so that I would be born?"

"At the time of your birth I did. I was so happy. You were our very first infant son."

"But you are not so happy now?"

"How can I be when at your young age you have already forsaken most of what King David, your father, and I, and all of the righteous Israelites believe in."

Manasseh did not respond.

"And yet, Son, of course I have to believe that one reason our Lord God spared his life was so that you could be born even if you are not accepting our ways."

"You do not believe I am going to follow Father to be the next king of Judah anyway, do you?"

"No, I do not, for I do not believe your father is ever going to die but that does not mean that I do not want you to be his crown prince forever. His faithful crown prince forever. Son, my hope and prayer is that you have been chosen for that glorious position. It is only that your beli—"

"—my beliefs do not coincide with yours and Father's."

"Son, how can you experience what we have just gone through and also know what our prophet Isaiah has promised about a soon coming righteous king whose kingdom is going to be an eternal one:how can you know and experience all that, and still reject our beliefs and way of life? Just this one huge victory should have been enough to change your entire concept of God and of life and of how you would desire to rule as the crown prince of the entire world. Son, this marvelous deliverance should have shown you that your father truly is that son of David who is going to reign forever even as Solomon would have if he did not allow his heathen wives to turn him away from faithfully following the Lord our God."

"You really believe all that?"

"Of course I do, Son."

"Well, I do not. My tutors use a lot of King Solomon's writings to convince me that an higher sophisticated outlook in life is the more correct one."

*

> > > *THIRTY TWO* < < <

*

King Sennacherib had been furious when he first heard that his Rabshakeh had left the besiegement of Jerusalem and had traveled to Libnah in the daytime.

His fury, however, had become a fearful apprehension when he was further advised that what was left of his Rabshakeh's face was parched black and that his eyes were entirely missing from their eyeholes.

His frightened apprehension turned to abject despondency the moment he heard all his nearly two hundred thousand marching army, including his entire elite forward unit, had been completely annihilated by some brilliant white-hot explosion.

By some mysterious silent blast which had instantly, silently, violently, torn through their camp during the night.

*

\> \> \> * \< \< \<

*

In the rejoicing capital up in the mountains, before a large thankful following by the eastern gate directly in front of their temple, Isaiah, filled anew with the Spirit of the Lord, shouted the latest word from the Lord triumphantly:

"'Comfort ye, comfort ye My people,' says our Lord God. 'Speak comfort to Jerusalem and cry unto her that her warfare is finished and over, that her iniquity is pardoned:for she has received of the Lord's hand double for all her sins.'

"The voice of him that cries in the wilderness said, 'Cry.'

"And I said, 'What shall I cry?'

"'All flesh is grass, and all the goodliness thereof is as the flower of the field. The grass withers, the flower fades: because the Spirit of the Lord blows on it. Surely the people are grass,' the voice continued. 'The grass withers, the flower fades: but the word of our God shall stand forever.'

"O Jerusalem, that brings good tidings. Lift up your voice with strength. Lift it up, be not afraid. Say unto the cities of Judah, 'Behold your God!'

"Behold, the Lord God will come with strong hands, and His arm shall govern for Him: behold, His reward is with Him, and His work before Him! Who has measured the waters in the hollow of His hand! He has meted out heaven with the span of his hand and comprehended the dust of the earth in a measure;he has weighed the mountains in scales, and the hills in a balance! Who has directed the Spirit of the Lord or being His counselor has taught Him? With whom took He counsel, and who instructed Him, and who taught Him in the path of judgment, and who taught Him knowledge, and, who showed to Him the way of understanding?

"Behold, the nations are as a drop of a bucket and are counted as the small dust of the balance! Behold, He takes up the isles as a very little thing! And Lebanon is not sufficient to burn, nor the beasts of it are sufficient for a burnt offering! All the nations before Him are as nothing and are counted to Him less than nothing and vanity!

"To whom then will you liken God? Or to what likeness will you compare unto Him? The workman melts a graven image, the goldsmith spreads it over with gold. He casts silver chains. He that is so impoverished that he has no oblation chooses a tree which will not rot. He seeks unto him a cunning workman to prepare a graven image from it that will not move.

"Have you not known?

"Have you not heard?

"Has it not been told you from the beginning?

"Have you not understood from the foundation of the earth? The Lord is He that sits upon the circle of the earth!

"The inhabitants thereof are as grasshoppers!

"The Lord God is He that stretches out the heavens as a mighty curtain, and spreads them out as a tent to dwell in!The Lord God is He that brings the princes to nothing!"

Moving up onto the steps of the outer courtyard to accommodate the ever-increasingly growing crowd, he shouted, "'To whom then will you liken Me, or to whom shall I be equal?' says the Holy One. 'Why do you say, O Jacob, and speak, O Israel, My way is hid from the Lord, and my judgment is passed over from my God?'

"Have you not known?

"Have you not heard that the everlasting God, our Lord God, the Creator of the ends of the earth, faints not, neither is weary? That there is no searching of His understanding? That He gives power to the fainting;and to them that have no might He increases strength. Even the youthful shall faint and be weary, and the young men shall utterly fall. But...*they that wait upon the Lord shall renew their strength; they shall mount up with wings as eagles, they shall run and not be weary and they shall walk and not faint!"*

Having stressed the last phrase, he looked over toward Hezekiah and smiled. Hezekiah nodded back a thank you—a thank you for the acknowledgment that his prophet had awarded him with that closing statement—and a thank you to him for being the one who helped him learn the lesson in the first place.

Isaiah smiled again and nodded an acknowledged: *You are welcome for you now deserve it.*

*

\>\>\> * <<<

*

When the charred Rabshakeh had been personally escorted before King Sennacherib's traveling throne, and as soon as the guards had seated him, he began with his report.

He told of his groping forward in his blackened blindness with the need to get out of their devastated camp before those peasants found him. He told of knocking over many standing figures of their soldiers whose flesh had been completely consumed away. He told of tripping over hundreds of skeletons as he sought for his escape.

Then, at one point in the retelling, he cried, "It began, King Sennacherib, O my king of kings, when I was awakened out of my sleep by an extremely loud shouting! It took me a moment to realize what it was! It was the Hebrews shouting and screaming for joy! Their great noise poured down upon us from within the walls of the their capital!

"Immediately after I realized what the abundant shouting was, I remember there was this brilliant flash as bright as lightning, but it did not instantly disappear as lightning vanishes! Instead, that intense brightness continued to flood our entire camp! I could see all our men as far as I looked in every direction!

"It was total daylight!

"It was extremely beautiful!

"It was exceedingly magnificent!

"It was glorious!

"It was resplendent!

"It was utterly awesome!

"It was a brightness I have never seen nor experienced before! At the same time it was scary!—weird!—very weird!—very eerie!—as if I knew something else had to come with it!

"When it came!

"It was a sudden wave of heat!

"It first felt especially good in the cool, brisk middle of the night!—except it grew hotter, and hotter, and hotter!—scorching!—burning!—scalding my flesh to the very bone!

"I knew there would be no escaping from it!

"The heat was too intense!—it was too all-compassing! My only hope was that I still had time to hide from its final blast; but I knew!—knew instinctively!—that I would have no such chance!—its intense fierceness hit almost immediately after that!—it was like no fire and heat that I have ever experienced!

"It burned!

"It blistered!

"It was all-consuming!

"It held no respect of position!

"Its rush broke as that of a dozen blast furnaces heated seven times hotter than those hottest flames that our furnaces have ever produced! Its searing, white-hot inflammation instantly incinerated all of my exposed flesh! Instantly! In a snap it dissolved my eyes in the most searing pain I have ever endured!

"I did not want to endure it!

"I cried out for death!

"I cried loud and hard for death!

"But death would not come!

"Death would not come!

"What came was just the excruciating, agonizing pain from every area of my body which was exposed to its incinerating heat!

"The flesh upon my face and hands was instantly charred to the bone! Our men who had risen earlier and were out of their bedrolls were simply burned as at a stake!

"But there were no stakes!

"There were no stakes!

"King Sennacherib!

"There were no stakes!

"My lord and king of kings!

"There were no stakes!

"There were no stakes!" he screamed, as he reached out for his king: groping forward, reaching out, groping forward, reaching out with arms flailing continuously forward:hoping to be able to grasp the protecting arms of his ruler, his monarch, who had tipped over to evade his faceless officer, who had begun crawling backwards as fast as he could toward what he prayed to his gods was the opening of the tent!

Hallucinating in his panic, the scrambling Rabshakeh, fumbling wildly, grabbed hold of King Sennacherib's robe

Tom Steinbach

with fingers which looked like charred sticks, and screamed:

"*Hide me!*"

"*Hide Me!*"

"*Hide Me! King Sennache—*"

Terrified, moving his feet as fast as he could in his backward crab-crawl, Sennacherib raced and crashed into a wooden table near the side of the tent but did not allow its presence to deter him for one second as he violently kicked the Rabshakeh's hand and arm off his body!

"*Where are you?*

"*DO NOT LEAVE ME!*"

Uncontrollably wild, utterly berserk, deliriously frenzied, he desperately swung his arms in a extensive sweep and caught hold of Sennacherib's robe again as his ruler tried to roll away from him, and he wheeled round in his twisting blindness, and pulled himself halfway upon his king, screaming, "*Hide me from that Lord God of the Hebrews!*"

Spasms shuddered through Sennacherib's body!

His muscles kicking every way in total abandonment as he tried to flip over so he could break free and move away on his all fours—he failed in the attempt for his berserk Rabshakeh, knowing that this was also his last chance, was desperately clinging and clawing his way up his thighs!

"*My master, keep me safe from that monstrous mountain God!*" he screamed as he continued to get a better grip on him.

"*Help me, King Sennacherib!*"

"*HELP ME, KING OF THE UNIVERSE!*"

Sennacherib responded with a massive wallop with his arm which surprised the officer, and caused him to momentarily forfeit his grip upon him. Sennacherib spun over, crawled as fast as he could toward the wall, and searched for any opening he could find!

The Rabshakeh stretched in an even greater hysteria, he groped awkwardly...but moved uncannily straight for his foreward crawling king...all the while pleading desperately in his high-pitched wail for him to immediately get him away from the crazy Hebrew Lord God Who had not stopped with 'an eye for an eye nor with a tooth for a tooth!'

In the midst of his Rabshakeh's begging, Sennacherib, far more shakened than he had ever been in life, finally broke free from the tent and scrambled foreward on all fours until he was certain that his Rabshakeh would not be able to lash forward and reach him ever again. He crawled far beyond any normal space of safety before he took a moment to catch his breath, and then, nearly in exhaustion, commanded his men to run his officer through with a dozen spears—though the first one could have easily done the task—he just kept ordering and ordering and ordering his men to thrust more and more and more spears through the dead lying figure of his Rabshakeh and threatened the same instant wretched treatment of even more spears to those who ever repeated even one word of his raving Rabshakeh's report!

He then collapsed upon the ground.

When he came to in the middle of the night, it took a moment or two before he realized where he was and why he was there—and immediately his first thought then was of his mad, clutching, screaming Rabshakeh!

Shaking fear immediately overtook him.

Petrified cause of what he had seen and heard, and desiring to waste no time in checking out the report's veracity, that is, only desiring to get out of this Hebrew God's beshrewed land as quickly as possible, he ordered a complete evacuation of all his remaining troops out of Judah and back to his capital.

When questioned about those former plans of sweeping next down into Egypt and becoming the very first Assyrian monarch to totally dominate all of that land also, he took off the asker's head with one swipe of his double-edge sword!

Dumbfounded...his troops hearing about the hostile action were greatly astonished, but not one of them asked him about the violent beheading nor why they were in a mad rush to get out of the land, nor why they were forsaking so many of their fellow soldiers up in the Hebrews' capital, nor did any of his troops ever ask him again what had happened to his grandiose schemings of taking over all of Egypt next.

*

> > *THIRTY THREE* < <

*

That night Hephzibah spoke softly to Hezekiah, "I was so proud of you last evening and through the night as you shared with our people concerning our forefather's deliverance from those Egyptians.

I was also very proud to be the one that was standing with you as Isaiah made that gracious statement to you and to all who are willing to wait upon our Lord God."

"Thank you, Hephzibah. It was wonderful to have you there next to me."

"It is good to hear you say that."

"I am saddened to think that at one time I really thought that I could have done just as well without either you or him. My love, I was wrong, definitely wrong."

"Thank you," she said softly.

They kissed.

"I am also truly proud and thankful that you and I have become one in the truest sense."

"Thank you for that statement, Hephzibah. Nothing means more to me here on this earth than that you and I have learned to share in our lives that oneness for which the Lord created us." Lifting her head up from his enough to stare at her, he added, "You are very beautiful, very lovely."

As she laughed happily, she said, "I will always remember you standing upon that wagon giving our people permission to plunder the Assyrian camp."

"I did not get too many words out, did I?"

"No, but you did not get trampled upon either."

"Would that not have been an extremely poor way to finish such a victorious day."

They both laughed.

They hugged each other.

After awhile...she whispered, "I am very thankful that you had the foresight to have the children and me go up on the wall. That fanatical rush of our people to get out there, and to see what had happened over in their Assyrians' camp, would have been disastrous to us if we would have been down on the pavement."

"I was glad you were up there also."

"Did anyone get trampled?"

"The report coming to me was that no injury came to any of our people."

"That is good."

"That is amazing."

After a moment's pause, he added, "I, too, am glad you and the children were up on the wall, Hephzibah. Even as I am glad that you are with me. Being safely here with me makes me doubly thankful that I am still alive."

"You talk really nice to me."

"That is because you are really, really, nice to talk to...and to talk about."

"Thank you."

"Today I got rid of some hatred," she said quietly. "I did not realize I was still carrying it."

"Hatred?"

"Toward Hannah."

"Toward our daughter?"

"No, toward the other Hannah."

He waited for her to explain.

"A realization came upon me really strong today that I still greatly resented you for having chosen to name our present daughter with her name."

"But that was over ten—"

"I understand, truly I do. It just...it just...came over me as a powerful wave of newly-found, latent jealousy. A rush of hatred toward the one you said was your favorite and would always be your favorite."

"Hephzibah, I said that long ago when you and I were—"

"I know, I—"

"Please, let me explain. Once you truly became a wife to me and began treating me like a husband and friend whom you really loved, and once you did not allow your cycle to control your emotions and your rationality,ever since then, Hephzibah, ever since then you alone have been my favorite. I have told you that many, many, many times."

"I know, and I have always tried to believe you, Hezekiah. It was just an extremely hard thing for me to set aside."

"My calling her my favorite?"

"That. And knowing that she was your favorite."

He hugged her closer to him and lightly rubbed her back as tenderly as he could.

"That is," she continued, "it was hard to set aside until this afternoon."

He waited silently.

"After the huge spear came hurtling over the wall, Hannah became really scared."

"That was the hardest part of the day for all of us."

"She ran over to me and cried out:

'These men will not be able to get inside our city again, will they? These men will not carry us away from here as they did my sisters, will they?'"

He shook his head, and said, "That must have been an extremely hard time for you, Hephzibah. I can see her crying it out. It must have been hard."

"It was very painful."

"At that same period of time I had an extremely difficult time myself lying on the floor before those veils of the temple...lying there and letting our Lord sort out a number of remaining prideful areas in my own life."

She lifted her head, and they looked at each other, smiling at their ability to talk to one another and at their willingness to simply, actually be one.

"I told our Hannah that the Assyrians would not carry her away as they had taken her sisters because our Lord was no longer angry at our family."

Not knowing exactly what she was going to say next, he waited.

"I feel ashamed now, my lord, extremely ashamed, I nearly told Hannah that you were the one our Lord was punishing when He so drastically—"

"But I was the one."

"No, no, my lord. The Holy Spirit of our Lord came right

into the room and strongly rebuked me within my being for ever thinking such a thought. His rebuke was so strong and clear: I began crying out of control. I have never cried so, so, cleansingly before. It was very wonderful, a very purifying experience. I am not glad of why it had to happen, but I am glad it did. It was certainly such an overwhelming time of getting washed out inwardly. When I ceased crying, I knew—*I knew*—it was not you and your having the house of women that was so displeasing to Him in our family. I knew then I was the problem beyond any doubt."

"No, Hephzibah," he cut in as his hands moved up her back to her head, to her face, to where he was able to lightly massage her eyes and lips and ears as lovingly as possible, quietly, he continued:

"It appears we both have cried more of ourselves out today. My experience of weeping in the temple was very close to yours. It is astounding that our Lord's Spirit chose the same time to deal with each of us on the exact same matter. During my time, the thought of the past visitation of the Assyrians also came fully into my mind.

"As with you, my mind was fast at work blaming you for only being a mother to me and not really attempting to simply fulfill your role of being my wife and friend. At that very moment, in the midst of my mind's presentation of why you were entirely the problem in our poor marriage, I too began to weep, an uncontrollable weeping overcame me, and I also cried as I have never wept before.

"Then and there, on the hard golden floor in front of the veils before the presence of our Lord, I accepted for the very first time in my life that it was I, and not you, who provoked the Lord to chasten our nation so drastically. Hephzibah, at that moment I realized that I was very wrong in having that house."

"But at that same moment I saw so clearly that it was me

who was wrong. That it was me who was driving you away from me toward those maidens."

"Possibly you were, Hephzibah. Life between us had grown very bad, but I was shown that it was my indifference toward you which was the major problem."

Hephzibah's composure broke.

When he acknowledged his former indifference toward her, hot tears streamed from her eyes, through his fingers, and down upon his face. Instantly, their tenderness toward each other turned into an overpowering hunger toward one another. Her mouth pressed upon his.

Her body lovely and desperate.

Her tears and mouth extremely sweet.

Her beautiful face, entirely wet with tears and free from his hands, was kissing him hard and wet and as passionately as she had ever kissed him in his life.

She had always been the one he claimed as his most passionate lover when and if they got together, this wonderful evening, after thirty years of being married, perchance their greatest time together was occurring as the result of their having come into an even greater understanding of what it was to be one, of discovering what being forgiving and patronizing in the right sense was all about. Naturally, passionately, uncontrollably, spectacularly, it spilled over into their physical oneness with each other.

Each accepting the total blame.

Each completely forgiving the other.

Each wanting nothing more than to be with the other.

To be with the other, to love the other, to give everything they could to the other.

The passions of young love could not even begin to meet, rival, touch, match, equal what they were experiencing. Total exhaustion would be the only thing which would ever stop their desire for one another.

Tom Steinbach

When it came.
It came to both of them at the same moment.